PRAISE FOR [illegible] DRAGON

"M Verant captures the voice of Elizabeth Bennet in a historical romance that encompasses the Napoleonic Wars, arcane marriage laws, and women with the power to command the fiercest, most dangerous, and wisest of beasts." – Vanessa MacLaren-Wray, author of *All That Was Asked*

"*Miss Bennet's Dragon* is a wholly fresh homage to Jane Austen, as well as a riveting novel in its own right that is thrilling, superbly paced, and moving. I highly recommend this novel to fans of Jane Austen, as well as to anyone who has ever pondered the mystery of dragons." – Katherine Sturtevant, author of *A True and Faithful Narrative* and *At the Sign of the Star*

"*Miss Bennet's Dragon* is a delicious story that blends *Pride and Prejudice* with a fully realized world of dragons and magic. I didn't want it to end." – Kate Pennington, author of *A Rose by Another Name*

"If you're looking for Austen-inspired adventure fantasy that's well told, this is it, and I recommend it to you." – The Review Curmudgeon

"All of the Austen and dragons that you want, as well as the sharp social commentary, droll humour, and discussions of sexual and gender politics that you forgot were what you loved about Austen in the first place TURNED UP TO 11. Five stars" – Goodreads

"This is a rewritten version of *Pride and Prejudice*; yet it is far more than that. It is a fantastically good version, and I loved it. If you've ever sighed over a historical romance novel; delighted over a fantasy full of dragons, then this is the novel for you." – Kylie's Reviews

"Step into the world of Jane Austen Fantasy and you will never want to leave. Dragons, legends, bonding, social injustices, intrigue and the power of good versus evil abound. It will leave you breathless and unable to put the book down!" – Carole in Canada

Miss Bennet's DRAGON

A PRIDE AND PREJUDICE RETELLING
JANE AUSTEN FANTASY - BOOK 1

M VERANT

Acerbic Press

Miss Bennet's Dragon

First edition: May 2021
Acerbic Press www.acerbicpress.com

Cover design by Streetlight Graphics

ISBNs: 978-1-7366629-1-5 (paperback), 978-1-7366629-0-8 (ebook), 978-1-7366629-2-2 (audiobook), 979-8507705849 (hardcover)

Publisher's Cataloging-in-Publication Data

Names: Verant, M., author.
Title: Miss Bennet's dragon : a pride and prejudice retelling / M. Verant.
Description: California: Acerbic Press, 2021. | Series: Jane Austen Fantasy, bk. 1.
Identifiers: ISBN 9781736662915 (paperback) | ISBN 9781736662908 (ebook) | ISBN 9781736662922 (audiobook) | ISBN 9798507705849 (hardcover)
Subjects: GSAFD: Fantasy fiction. | BISAC: FICTION / Fantasy / Historical. | FICTION / Fantasy / Romance. | FICTION / Adaptations & Pastiche.
Classification: LCC PS3622.E731 M57 2021 | DDC 813/.6–dc23

BOUND BREEDS OF DRACA

From greatest to least social prestige:

Wyvern: A winged, two-legged draca. Near the size of an English foxhound (60-75 lb).

Firedrake (drake): A winged, two-legged draca the size of a large goose or eagle (16-18 lb).

Lindworm: A draca with a heavy build like a bulldog or badger (20-25 lb).

Tykeworm (tyke): A draca the size of a Yorkshire terrier (5-7 lb). Does not throw fire. Unusually affectionate with their bound wyfe.

Roseworm: A draca the size of a rabbit. Distinguished by red or rose scales on its belly.

Broccworm: A tunneling draca with powerful front legs. Rather like a small badger.

Ferretworm: A tunneling draca, long and thin like a ferret.

Tunnelworm: A nocturnal, palm-sized draca that burrows and prefers to be underground.

1

It is a truth universally acknowledged that a hungry firedrake is an irritating beast.

I dangled a strip of raw steak between my outstretched fingers, then gave it a tempting wiggle. The entrance of our draca house, a three-foot-high stone kennel, remained stubbornly empty.

I hmphed. "If you wish to be fed, you shall have to endure my presence." Our firedrake's response was a ticking hiss like a heating and annoyed kettle.

I squatted down on my heels, and my skirt and petticoats piled onto the damp earth. It was a clear morning, but not cold enough for frost. In the garden behind me, drops of chilled dew sparkled on purple hollyhocks and crimson Portland roses.

Serene steps approached on the garden path, and Jane, my eldest sister, arrived. "Has he hid?"

"Of course." Our drake always hid when I was near.

Jane bent to peer into the kennel—but gathered a handful of her skirts so they did not brush the ground.

Our draca house was fireproof and placed well away from the manor for safety. An iron perch topped the waist-high slate roof. The walls were mortared puddingstone, a local Hertfordshire rock riddled with gravel and shells that gave the entrance a toothed look.

Inside, a glint of bronze shifted restlessly.

"I cannot imagine why he dislikes being fed by you," Jane said. She took the plate of raw meat, then held out a piece thick with enticing fat.

Jane was wearing a simple white dress and a bonnet tied with ivory ribbon. With a few escaped yellow curls shining in the early sun, she looked a portrait of country morning rendered slightly wild by her ungloved hand proffering bloody steak.

There was a stir in the shadows. When nothing more happened, Jane gave me an apologetic glance. I sighed and backed away.

Our firedrake emerged. He was sinuous and bronze, a winged male the size of a large goose. But a firedrake is scaly and muscular, much slimmer than a goose, with wings that unfold wider than any bird's and far more neck and tail. Two-legged, he was lithe as a cat, each step poised before his talons gripped the earth.

His chisel-shaped head stretched toward Jane's hand. Obsidian-dark teeth gleamed as he snatched the piece of meat.

"It is not being *fed* by me he dislikes," I said. "It is *me* he dislikes."

"Draca are not affectionate creatures," Jane said. Illustrating her point, our drake turned his glistening black eyes to me and hissed.

Annoyed, I mouthed, "Boo!" In a slither of bronze scales, the drake vanished into the stone kennel.

Jane's brow wrinkled. "Lizzy. Now how shall I feed him?"

"Perhaps I should try again. Mamma will be annoyed otherwise." I heaved another sigh. "Will it amuse the neighbors if I marry and fail to bind a draca? I expect that is worth several weeks of gossip."

"I am sure you will bind." Jane dangled another strip of meat. "I do worry, though. About Papa, I mean. I saw you help him this morning."

My father had come to breakfast late, his lips pressing thinner with each step until his hand froze on the back of a chair, arresting his progress to the head of the table. I saw the tremble of his fingers, so I took his other arm, pretending to tell some trifle of gossip. When we reached his chair, he squeezed my fingers in gratitude.

That silent admission of weakness had torn a deeper hole in my heart than any outward sign of his infirmity. I ate in silence for half of breakfast, afraid concern would choke my voice and embarrass him.

Remembering that touch, my fears slipped down an unwanted path.

If Papa died, we faced more than the pain of that loss. Our firedrake was bound to my parents, so if either died, our drake would leave. But our estate, Longbourn, was entailed—only bound gentry could hold the property. When our firedrake left, we would be cast out, a household of women with no livelihood and no home.

Our firedrake reemerged, crawling on the elbows of his folded wings. He cast a baleful glance at me. His talons—wicked things, two inches long—twitched, then sank their full length into the hard ground.

Our gazes fixed together, the drake's eyes impenetrable as two wet river stones. A shiver climbed my spine. Foreboding? Or standing too long in the chill.

My vision juddered.

A second vision overlaid mine, a flickering image of a woman with hair as dark and curly as mine. She shone with golden light, brilliant as the sun.

I blinked, and the image was gone.

"*What?*" I whispered. Sunlight glittered on the pebbly scales around the drake's eyes. Had it been a trick of the light?

The shiver returned, clicking my teeth. I wrapped my arms around my ribs and squeezed to still it.

Jane jiggled the meat, and our drake's head flicked toward her. She tossed the chunk, and his serpentine neck flashed to catch it midair. It made a visible lump passing down his long throat.

He cooed and stroked his cheek along Jane's hand. Jane drew a delighted breath.

I overcame my disquiet to produce an incredulous snort. "He is affectionate with *you*. It seems one Bennet sister will bind. I am now certain that you will marry a handsome husband, and he will love you so desperately that you bind a wyvern on your wedding night!"

"Lizzy!" Jane exclaimed, for such powerful bindings were said to require shocking passion.

2

To shake off that strange vision, I walked around the manor before going in. In the side garden, two of our hired men were digging onions. I had promised them a pail of onions for themselves, and they gave an enthusiastic wave when they saw me.

Inside, Mamma, Lydia, and Kitty had occupied the entryway to gossip about a wealthy new neighbor. I squeezed by and found Mary, my younger sister, waiting for me outside Papa's library. Her brow was furrowed over some dire Latin volume.

I tapped the library door and heard "Come, Lizzy," as Papa knows my knock. Mary trailed me as we entered, her nose still in her book.

Papa had the estate journals open. He waved us to wooden chairs by his desk, then lowered his glasses to inspect us.

"Mary," he said at last, "I am pleased you are accompanying your sister this morning. And, as I am devoted to fashion, allow me to compliment you on your black dress. It is a joy to see mournful respect from a daughter, although I admit surprise from learning that I have died."

Mary had opened her mouth to answer, but by the time he finished, she had closed it again. Mary was very literal, and Papa's humor often took her by surprise.

"Mary has worn black for a week, Papa," I pointed out.

"Ah. Then I was inattentive. A symptom of my grave state."

"I *am* in mourning," Mary said, having composed her reply. "But for the unjust death of our fellow sentient animals, not for you. You and I could not be speaking if you were dead." Papa nodded to this incontestable point, and Mary continued, "I have cast myself into the social movement for natural enlightenment, so I shun all animal food as it engenders disease and vice."

"What?" I said. Usually, I knew Mary's intellectual directions, but this time I had been as inattentive as my father, other than noticing her clothing.

"And did you eat no bacon this whole week?" asked Papa, astonished, although I thought that was for effect. Mary shook her head, her lips clamped. "Then I must take this seriously, for you were a great believer in bacon as a child. To what influence do we owe this new conviction?"

"I have been studying both Stewart and Hunt, in the *Examiner*."

Papa's white eyebrows shot skyward. This time his shock was sincere.

Seeing Papa's cheeks coloring, I said, "Papa, I should like to visit the tenants before the morning grows late."

We switched to discussing the tenants and business of Longbourn, with pauses for frosty and determined glances between my father and sister.

Mary's studious ways irk my parents because Mary is oblivious to both society and subtlety, which are the loves of my mother and father, respectively. I have some guilt also because Mary is a lure for irony, which is my bad habit, and one I sometimes regret the next morning.

But Mary is adventurous in her bookish way, and her disregard for convention is due to deep beliefs. She is like Papa, which is why they clash. I love them both, but once convinced of something, they are unmovable. Papa uses wit to belittle any disagreement, while Mary pulls like a determined mule wearing blinders.

However, disapproving of Mary for reading the *Examiner* was unfair. It was Papa who subscribed, not only to the *Examiner* but to many liberal opinions. And each week, after he was done reading, the pages had a habit of finding their way to me or to Mary, depending on who spotted them first.

After discussing the tenants, Papa eyed me, then said, "And will you join your sisters in moping and crying if I do not call on Mr. Bingley?"

"Who?" I asked innocently, although from overhearing Mamma I guessed this was our new neighbor.

Papa huffed, but a smile twitched as he dismissed us.

Mary and I added spencers and bonnets against the chill, then set out to visit the tenants.

Longbourn estate includes the Longbourn village, which is five scattered cottages for the tenants who work the farms. The Bennet sisters were well known to them, and I think we were all liked or even loved a little, as the tenants were families who had watched us grow from girls toddling behind our father.

My father had always managed his estate directly, believing that a gentleman should know his business but also for economy—Longbourn was too small to support a hired manager. And, as years passed and my parents accumulated five daughters and not a single son, it was I, the next-to-eldest after Jane, who became his companion for tours of the property.

I was always fascinated: the news and gossip, the unstuffy practicality of conversations about brooding sheep and dry wells. These topics would never be broached, even by Papa, at home. But on our walks, we would talk frankly of shillings, bushels, and livestock. He listened to my opinions, and I reveled in his radical encouragement of a favorite daughter.

For the last few months, though, Papa's health had made our companionable walks impossible, so I had toured Longbourn village without him, usually with Mary as a companion. We said I was "carrying Mr. Bennet's regards," but we all knew I was acting as my father's agent to manage our estate.

Our last stop today was the cottage of Mrs. Trew, who had been widowed a year but farmed her plot admirably with two almost-grown sons and some help for the harvest from our hired men, which I justified by claiming they were bored.

As Mary and I prepared to leave, I complimented Mrs. Trew on her plump pumpkins, planted by a sun-warmed wall.

"Thank'ee, Miss Lizzy," she said, an endearment that began when I was a four-year-old girl startled into tears by one of her chickens. "You've been a generous help, and we be managing, though it's hard being a woman on my own." Her wrinkled lips pursed. "Will you be giving our respects to Mr. Bennet?"

"I will pass them on until he is well enough to receive them in person."

"You are a brave lass." Her fingers, cracked by a lifetime of hard chores, rubbed my cheek before she turned into her doorway.

The scrape of her touch faded, but her affection lingered. Not only affection. Pity.

She did not expect my father to visit again.

Mary became impatient, tapping her fingers in memory of some music she had played, while I stood, my heart torn for the second time that morning.

We were a quarter mile from home when I heard a growl. We turned, and Mary drew a frightened breath.

A large, filthy dog stalked us. Its legs shook with every step. A snarl rumbled, pushing a rope of foamy slime from its jaws.

I caught Mary's hand. "Do not move. It is mad." A mad dog had bitten a child a few weeks before. Horrible stories of the child's slow death had circulated ever since.

My pulse pounding, Mary and I took a step back. The animal slunk closer. Hackles lifted its matted fur. Its reddened eyes fixed on Mary, and her hand tightened on mine.

I forced my fingers open. "Mary, go behind me. Run to the manor and tell Mr. Hill to bring the gun."

"I am too afraid," she said in a strained voice. "And you are the faster runner."

The animal crouched, its shoulders straining.

A blur of bronze flashed, the fleeting image impressed on my eyes like an etching in a book—our firedrake streaking through the air, wings furled to strike. He passed inches above the neck of the dog, seemingly without touching. There was only one sharp *thock*, like our cook cutting up oxtail with her cleaver.

The dog's head ducked, and its neck fell open, cut deep, the severed backbone protruding before the animal collapsed.

Mary screamed, a shattering cry unlike any of the pretty shrieks I remembered from teasing her as a child. Her running footsteps faded. I did not move, rooted to the spot by relief and horrified shock.

With a flurry of wings, the drake landed in front of me. He reared on his two legs, facing the obviously dead dog, his gleaming bronze head reaching my thigh. His wings unfurled. I had never been so near when they were open—wider than I could stretch my arms, ribbed like two huge fans, and spanned with skin so thin that I saw the glow of sunlight behind. It was a silhouette of violent protection, an animal's challenge to defend me and my sister.

The drake's chest swelled. With the howl of a rushing gale, a jet of flame shot from his mouth. It was unnatural fire, blue and transparent, almost invisible in the sunlight, but the heat was like facing a bed of coals. The dog's carcass burst into flames, filling the air with the reek of burnt hair.

I had never seen a drake throw fire. Or even met a person who saw it firsthand. But it was foolish to be so surprised. They are called firedrakes, after all.

The drake stepped toward the dog, as if he meant to attack again, or even to eat.

"Stop," I cried. "It is diseased! You must not touch it!"

His head swiveled on his long neck to observe me with black, unblinking eyes.

"You will die if you touch the dead animal," I said.

But the drake had touched it already, somehow. I saw that his hind talons, curved like small scythes, were glistening wet and red.

"You must wash your feet, or you will grow sick." I babbled. "Or… is only the bite dangerous? We could call for a physician's opinion."

The drake gave a screeching cry. I realized I was discussing medicine with a beast.

My shock broke, and my suppressed fear rose, cold as ice then hot and furious, my own belated challenge to danger. A shudder cranked through my shoulders and down my spine, leaving me trembling—fingertips, jaw, ankles—as though I raged with fever.

The world turned harshly exact and bright.

Again, another vision overlaid mine, but now vivid and vibrating with indescribable hues. This time, I recognized the woman I saw—myself as if seen in a mirror, but from below, a child's perspective. The delicate pattern of my muslin dress shimmered in woven violet, every detail phenomenally precise. My bare skin glowed with warmth. My dark eyes shone—blazed—with power more potent than heat.

The ground banged my knees. I caught myself, palms pressed on rough earth, and hauled in desperate breaths. I still saw myself, crouched, head tilted back to keep my gaze locked with our drake's.

The strange double vision cleared.

I must be fainting. Ladies are supposed to faint. This was good.

I counted wobbly breaths, waiting. Maybe I should lie down. But that seemed very dramatic.

Five breaths passed. I was giddy, my stomach roiling at the gore and fumes.

Ten breaths. I began to be disappointed. A lady in a novel would have swooned elegantly by now. And in the more salacious editions, she would then wake in the arms of an apparently roguish, but secretly landed, officer.

Mary thumped to a stop beside me, breathing hard and catching my hand while she helped me stand. Mr. Hill, no officer in his rough working clothes but carrying a long gun, advanced puffing while making *scat* noises at the firedrake.

Ribbed wings flexed and spread wide, causing all but me to jump back, and then the drake was gone, tracing a soaring curve on the sky like a pen stroke addressing an elaborate invitation.

3

Mary and I were escorted home by a shaken Mr. Hill, then met with loud consternation from Mamma, my sisters, and the servants. Even Papa asked serious questions before being satisfied.

"We are quite all right," I said. "Although Mary did scream prettily. Rather like an actress."

"An *actress?*" My mother was horrified.

"I only compliment her voice, Mamma. My ear still echoes." I tugged at the bonnet covering my ear. Mary studied me, considering whether to smile.

Lydia, my youngest sister and just sixteen, spoke up. "The dog is dead, then?"

"Quite dead," I replied. "Burned."

"I wish I had seen." She pouted. "It is unfair that it happened to *you!*"

"It was most dangerous, Lydia," Jane said.

Lydia set her shoulders and scowled.

"Has our drake returned?" I asked.

That question received blank expressions, so I led a curious parade out our front door and found the animal perched atop the draca house, wrapped in his wings with his head tucked out of sight.

"It is lucky he found you," Jane observed.

"Yes," I said. Very lucky, as we had been far from the house, and our drake had never before patrolled our fields.

I leaned close to look at his feet, hooked around the iron perch on the draca house roof. I had never examined our drake's talons before. They were lustrous and dark, like tarnished pewter, but the sheen was a blued-steel razor. There were gouges in the iron perch where he had tightened his grip.

They were clean of the gore I had seen after he killed the dog.

The drake stirred, unwinding like an unfolding scarf. His small face lifted inches from mine, black eyes watching. Then, as if my mental feet skidded loose beneath me, I fell forward into another awareness.

I saw a memory—water streaking by below, ripples the color of cold beneath a blurring sparkle of sunlit flashes. The shadow of outstretched wings extended on each side. Water hissed as my claws sliced the cold surface, causing a sudden drag and slowing I detested.

I blinked, and my mind was my own again. Although I was so close to the drake's chisel-shaped head that I was quite cross-eyed.

He had washed his claws. As I asked.

"Lizzy!" My mother's voice was sharp and worried. "Have mercy on my nerves and stand back from that creature!"

"Yes, Mamma." I stepped back, but after the others returned to the house, I stayed to watch our drake settle into his nap. Then I looked up and saw my father watching through the library window.

I went inside and knocked at the library door.

Papa greeted me from his desk, where he had, remarkably quickly, become absorbed in a book.

I tilted my head to read the title: *Fordyce's Sermons to Young Women*. "That is an unconvincing selection, Papa." Although he had at least managed to hold it right-way up.

Papa began to hem and haw about the distraction of daughters and dogs, and the merits of a good sermon. I occupied myself by very obviously studying the contents of the library. My father was a prodigious reader and collector, so this was a full six shelves of volumes, most of them custom bound in Longbourn bindings. Each row repeated the Longbourn crest in shining gilt: a wyvern, rearing with head high and wings spread behind, a pose called *segreant*, clutching a chest in its claws.

Papa had fallen silent.

"We have a prodigious absence of books about draca," I noted.

Papa's fingers rubbed pensively. "Sit, Lizzy."

I sat, wilting under my father's intense gaze, for once undiluted by humor or satire.

"You have had an eventful day," he said. "I was most concerned. Mrs. Bennet may be right that it is time we had an iron-barred carriage."

Iron-barred carriages were the new fashion, the iron purported to protect against attack by feral draca. That risk seemed farfetched to me. Certainly, it had never happened on the Longbourn estate.

"I think our ordinary carriage would dissuade a dog," I answered, "and our horses would much prefer pulling that to hauling a hulking pile of iron. Either way, I do not take the carriage because visiting the cottages by road would be very roundabout."

Papa seemed to be waiting. I found it hard to express why I had come. Finally, I said, "I am gentry of marriageable age. Destined to be a wyfe and bind. But today, I discovered I am woefully uneducated about draca."

"I am no expert on draca, Lizzy. I doubt there is such a man. Draca are mysterious and willful. I fear education is impossible, other than folklore and legend. One can find fanciful myths of dragons more easily." He cleared his throat. "I hope our limited fortune does not leave you worried that you will fail to bind when you marry. The wyves of our family have always bound draca, usually of exceptional breeds. Or, if you are apprehensive... That is to say, I recall from my own youth hearing much ill-informed speculation on the... the moment of binding..."

Papa was coloring with embarrassment, and my own cheeks were heating to match the fireplace, so I said, "Mamma has explained *that*." Actually, she had not, other than a few unspecific flutterings about her own wedding night, but at least binding was no more mysterious than other private behavior between husband and wife.

I did know that binding a draca required fresh gold never used in another binding. This was *marriage gold*, or as young ladies whispered when they wished to be shocking, *virgin gold*. It was the offering of marriage gold, together with the officiant's ceremony and the... I shall say... the marriage night that summoned and bound a draca.

But the process was uncertain. Usually, an eligible marriage would bind some kind of draca, but binding a potent breed, like our firedrake, was rare. Perhaps this was why fashionable society disparaged binding as old-fashioned. Laws and dusty documents reliably passed on wealth and influence, but ancient rituals were disconcertingly variable. Some aristocracy had even called for banning the binding of draca, either denouncing it as un-Christian or complaining that draca were impractical in modern cities like London.

Papa and I sat in silence. He seemed as preoccupied as I.

I remembered Mary's comment about fellow sentient animals.

"You called draca mysterious and willful," I said. "Are they intelligent?" I was thinking about my vision of our drake washing his claws, but I hesitated to relate something so strange. "Do they understand when a person speaks to them?"

"Understand *speech?*" Papa's eyes crinkled in amusement. "The higher breeds—firedrakes and wyverns—are certainly less stupid. They might feign understanding, like a dog who cowers when his master's tone is angry. But they are animals. Despite the current misguided attempts by our military, they are wild and untrainable. My personal observation is that our drake is most similar to a cat, content to eat our food but otherwise uncaring about people."

He looked away before continuing, "I was surprised our drake defended you. It is rare that draca notice even their bound wyfe. Others, they ignore completely."

I sat, tapping my fingers and unsatisfied. Our drake did not ignore me, but to explain that would be fantastic. What would I claim? That he cowered and hissed when I passed? That I stared into his eyes and saw visions?

Papa stood, pressing the desk to help himself rise. He felt in his waistcoat pocket then held out a key.

"Open that, Lizzy." He nodded to a polished mahogany lockbox. I turned the key, feeling the smooth working of a well-kept lock, and lifted the lid.

Inside was a journal. The cover was worn leather, faintly embossed with the Longbourn crest, although the markings seemed subtly different from our modern crest.

Papa moved carefully to stand beside me. His age-spotted fingers withdrew the book, weighing it in his hand while he spoke.

"It has been many generations since Longbourn was founded as an estate. The cornerstone of this manor was laid by my great-great-grandfather, and Bennet gentry have always held this house. Through that time, the master and wyfe of Longbourn have recorded private notes. My father passed this journal to me, and for many years, I hoped to pass it to my son before his marriage. Now, dear Elizabeth, I see more clearly, and with no reservation, I pass it to you. Like many tasks, I have ignored this too long. It is time I ordered such matters."

I was both moved and upset by his words, more when I saw him turn away to hide his feelings. I swallowed and said something unintelligible as I accepted the book. It felt ancient, with rough-cut sheets and primitive leather binding. The scent of stale vellum touched my nose.

Papa's usual humorous tone returned. "Make of it what you will, Lizzy. I found it obscure, a scattered record of household trivia and idle, amateur philosophy." He settled into his chair with a sigh, waving his hand in dismissal.

4

The next morning, I examined the journal.

The book was old and fragile, the vellum sheets punched with crude holes and bound to the leather cover by tied cords.

"The earliest date is more than a hundred years ago. 1709," I said to Jane, who was peering out our window. I squinted at ink faded to rusty orange. "But there are dozens of pages before that. I cannot make them out."

The script grew more old-fashioned on the early pages. I could decipher only a few words on the first, and those were ancient indeed, with spellings and letterforms older than Shakespeare's.

"That is interesting," Jane answered absently.

I turned a page. "Our ancestors bound three firedrakes in the last century alone. Mamma's family originates in Surrey..." My mouth fell open. "Her great-aunt bound a wyvern!" When Papa said our family bound exceptional breeds, he did not exaggerate.

A grim, fantastic idea caught me. What if our mother held our drake after our father's death?

But that was absurd. In all England, only a handful of widowed wyves held draca. All were formidable personages, and famous—or infamous. I loved Mamma, but an honest summary of her personage would be scatter-brained.

And even holding our drake was no guarantee of security. The world was not kind to a widowed wyfe who held draca. She was the target of jealous men deprived of their inheritance, and of prejudice from extreme factions of the Church. Many bound widows simply vanished.

Jane's nose grazed the window. "He appears nice."

"Who?" I said.

"Mr. Bingley. He was visiting Papa. He has just left."

I hmphed. "You should have called me. '*Nice*' is singularly unhelpful. You declare everyone nice."

Jane blushed, but I saw her hidden smile.

I would know soon enough. Mr. Bingley would attend the next ball.

THE PUBLIC ASSEMBLY hall in Meryton could host six dozen people beneath its plain shake roof and rough wooden beams. For balls, it was done up splendidly, with crisp linen covering the tables, trays of cold meats and winter fruits, punch for the ladies, and brandy for the men. Chairs were arranged for those who wished to rest from dancing, and for ladies tired of standing without being asked. Hundreds of candles illuminated a sea of silk and muslin gowns. The gentlemen's collars and cravats were white crests on the waves.

Every head turned when the Bingley party arrived. Mr. Bingley had a disordered mop of light-brown curls and blue eyes that matched his blue coat. Within a minute, we learned he had brought his two sisters and the husband of the elder sister. However, his final companion, a gentleman, remained mysterious.

"Bingley has *one hundred* guineas of marriage gold," Lady Lucas announced to my mother. "It is piled in a strongbox, ready for a wyfe."

"One hundred!" Mamma was astounded, as this exceeded her highest speculation at breakfast. "And to think Mr. Bennet and I bound a firedrake with only ten guineas of marriage gold. I have always said that, with another ten, we should have bound a wyvern."

Lady Lucas frowned. Sir William Lucas had earned his knighthood from a career in trade, and Lady Lucas took great pride in her freshly elevated title. But the Lucases had bound a tunnelworm, the lowliest form of draca, so the prestige of our drake was a sore topic between our families.

"Who is the tall man with Mr. Bingley?" I asked. I had noticed him immediately, and many ladies were following him with their gaze. He was dark-haired and serious. I had yet to see him speak a word.

"*That* is Mr. Darcy," reported Lady Lucas. "A fine figure of a man, with the largest estate in Derbyshire." This provoked gasps from the ladies gathered to listen. "But he was most disagreeable when introduced to Sir William. And, it is said he keeps no marriage gold at all!"

That caused great concern. While various explanations were suggested, I turned to watch him, my curiosity piqued.

No marriage gold. While not unheard of, that was very unusual, something I would associate with a social reformer or vagabond, like a poet or politician. But there was no mistaking the stance and dress of Mr. Darcy. He was a gentleman—one who had spent the evening towering behind his friend and projecting forbidding disapproval. Or was it contempt? It seemed worse than boredom. I cocked my head, trying to guess more exactly.

Mr. Darcy turned, and our gazes met. He had dark eyes to match his hair. I looked down, feeling a blush rise for being caught staring so boldly.

Mr. Bingley was introduced to my family. His eyes returned twice to Jane while he traversed our row of sisters. When he danced with Jane next, and then a second time, mother declared him a true gentleman.

As gentlemen of any sort were scarce, I had sat down for those two dances. That placed me close enough to hear Mr. Bingley when he finished his dances and spoke with Mr. Darcy.

"You must *dance*, Darcy," Mr. Bingley said.

"I detest meeting people." Mr. Darcy's voice was baritone and haughty. "I cannot suffer the endless banalities on weather and fashion."

Mr. Bingley was not at all put off. He said cheerfully, "Your sister would encourage you to dance."

"Georgiana is not here to persuade me."

"Why not? She was most mysterious about her other commitment."

"My sister is repairing the damage inflicted by our military foolishness."

I perked up my ears at that. The war with Napoleon was raging in Spain, but it rarely affected us. How could a sister be involved with the military?

"Then it is *my* responsibility to persuade you," Mr. Bingley announced. "I have made the most wonderful acquaintance in Miss Jane Bennet. She is a beautiful and charming woman. And look"—Mr. Bingley lowered his voice, which made me listen more closely—"one of her sisters is sitting behind you. She is very pretty, and quite alone. I believe she is a kindred spirit! Let me ask Miss Bennet to introduce you."

I was watching the dance while listening, but I could tell Mr. Darcy had turned to see me. The silence stretched. I became awkwardly conscious of my isolated status among the empty chairs, and my comfortably slumped pose. Then Mr. Darcy's voice pronounced, "She is tolerable, but not enough to tempt me. Return to your new friend and enjoy her smiles. You are wasting your time with me."

It was impossible not to feel hurt. Fuming and flushed, I stayed in my seat, not wanting to reveal I had overheard. But his entitled presumption gradually seemed ridiculous, and when I finally rose to visit Jane, I was relieved to discover my bruised vanity had healed into vast amusement.

Jane, glowing with a slight smile that only a sister would recognize as delight, described her dances with Mr. Bingley.

"He is just what a young man ought to be," she concluded, "sensible, good-humored, and lively!"

I studied Mr. Bingley as he spoke with one of his sisters. "He is also handsome, which a man ought to be if he possibly can."

"I was very much flattered by his asking me to dance a second time."

"I have thoroughly exceeded you. Let me tell you my own great compliment." I recounted Mr. Darcy declaring me tolerable but untempting, which became such a spirited recital that my good friend Charlotte Lucas came to ask what was amusing, and there was a second and even more animated retelling.

"That was most unpleasant," Charlotte said. "Everyone has agreed that Mr. Darcy is a horrid man. And poor Lizzy, to hear yourself called only tolerable. I should have been—"

Charlotte stopped, her eyes widening, and Jane blushed prettily. Biting my lip, I turned to see Mr. Bingley approaching with an eager smile, followed by most of his party, displaying various degrees of enthusiasm.

"Miss Bennet," he said to Jane, "may I present you to my sisters?" We met his elder sister, Mrs. Hurst, whose husband was absent in search of wine, and the younger Miss Bingley, who had hair as yellow as Jane's.

I curtsied through this with wicked anticipation because Mr. Darcy was standing with the apprehensive air of a man awaiting a dentist. I was not disappointed, for when Mr. Bingley ran out of sisters to spark conversation, he cast about for other opportunities.

"Darcy, stop lurking back there. Allow me to present my new friends!"

Mr. Darcy stepped forward, although he had retreated so far that, even with long legs, it required several paces. He met each introduction with a slight, silent bow. I found that an amusing affectation.

I had not anticipated that Mr. Bingley would then speak with Jane while his sisters engaged Charlotte, leaving me paired with Mr. Darcy.

We faced each other in silence. Mr. Darcy was very tall, rigid, and expressionless, and apparently engrossed by the wall behind me.

"Do you admire my hat, Mr. Darcy?" I asked.

After a delay, doubtless because I had no hat, he deigned to glance down. "Your party arrived before ours." His gaze rose again. "I had no opportunity to admire your hat."

"Oh. I thought I must have left it on. Something above my head fascinates you. I hope you do not see my thoughts? That would be impolitic indeed."

This provoked astonished silence, perfectly interrupted by the arrival of Sir William and Lady Lucas with my mother, whom they introduced to Mr. Darcy.

Mamma joined our conversation with exuberance.

"In all Hertfordshire," she exclaimed, aiming a frosty look at Mr. Darcy, "I am *quite* alone in having bound a firedrake. So, I was most disturbed to hear there are now gentry who do not even prepare marriage gold. Do you not agree, Lady Lucas?"

I suppressed a wince at Mamma's transparent boast, and at her unsubtle attack on Mr. Darcy—or at least, on his rumored lack of marriage gold. Of course, I had just assaulted him myself, but I flattered myself that I had been bold and clever.

"Yes," sniffed Lady Lucas. "A binding is most important for marriage. Although, the specifics of draca are perhaps given too much attention." She frowned at my mother, and there was a pause.

"I imagine the fashion on binding varies," I said. "The society in London, or other shires, may have different trends." Having tried to disarm my mother's insult, I could not resist undermining that by adding, "How do you find our country society, Mr. Darcy? *Tolerable?*"

He gave one of his short, sharp bows. "Indeed, I find it more than tolerable." I wondered if he had caught my meaning. He was watching me now, rather than staring above my head, and his gaze was steady. I remembered that I was sparring with a man of consequence.

Miss Bingley hastily excused herself from Charlotte and circled around Mr. Bingley and Jane, who were deeply engaged, to join our expanding group.

"Miss Elizabeth Bennet," she said, "you are insightful to recognize that high society is distinct. London would doubtless seem most foreign to you." That was not what I had said, and I enthusiastically prepared to argue. But she continued, "London society is excessively biased to refinement and accomplishment, and hardly values marriage gold at all. I fear wild beasts in draca houses will soon be relegated to the rustic lifestyle." Her laugh tinkled. "You must agree, Mr. Darcy, as you have such an accomplished sister."

Mr. Darcy had always shown precise posture, but now it became exact. Even his cheeks hollowed. "As I reside more often in the country than in London," he replied, each word distinct, "I defer to your opinion."

Miss Bingley's tinkling laugh choked. Hurriedly, she said, "Of course, Pemberley itself is a center for society." I gathered that Pemberley was Mr. Darcy's fabled Derbyshire estate.

"Do you advocate binding draca, sir?" Sir William said to Mr. Darcy. "I greatly support the keeping of draca by gentry. It is one of the grand refinements of polished society."

Mr. Darcy's pose stiffened further. "It is popular even with less polished societies. Every savage keeps animals." He strode away, leaving expressions that ranged from astonishment to offense.

I was simply mystified. He was disagreeable—rude, really—but I could not find a pattern in his comments. It seemed that draca, or marriage gold, caused a strong reaction.

Mr. Darcy's departure left a sizeable gap which was filled by Lydia and Kitty, who between them had captured Colonel Forster. The colonel commanded the militia regiment quartered in Meryton, and he was a favorite of society despite many ladies' despair over his recent engagement.

"What do you say, Colonel, to draca?" Sir William asked, unwilling to let the subject end.

"Draca are a great topic among our military planners. The regulars are eager to commission married, bound gentry as officers." The colonel then addressed the women, explaining, "The Spanish, and French for that matter, have no draca. So if the English can apply them in battle, and our opponents cannot, we should have an advantage."

I thought his explanation was superficial, but not all ladies purloin pages of the *Times* and *Examiner* from their father. My mother's brow was furrowed, as was Miss Bingley's.

"So they *are* being trained," I said. This must be the "misguided attempts by our military" that Papa had mentioned. That reminded me of Mr. Darcy's comment about "damage inflicted by our military foolishness." Could they be related?

"They are attempting to train them," the colonel said with a smile. "I cannot say if they succeeded."

Lydia's eyes had narrowed while I conversed with Colonel Forster. She cried, "Lizzy, you are *so* dull! The musicians are ready. Let us dance!" There was a brief contest for the colonel's attention between Kitty and Lydia, then Lydia set off with the colonel as prize.

Mr. Bingley excused himself from Jane and invited Miss Bingley to dance, casting forlorn glances at Jane as he departed. Kitty was claimed by another officer, and Jane and I settled in chairs to compare our impressions of the evening.

Mr. Darcy stood proudly, staring at a wall.

5

The days after the ball were eventful. Mr. Bingley visited three times in one week: twice with his sisters, and once with Mr. Darcy. By now, everyone in our household knew the story of Mr. Darcy's slight to me, and there were many outraged noises when he was spotted approaching. Mamma greeted him with exceptional rudeness. Fortunately, Mr. Bingley's attention was all on Jane, so he was oblivious to this mistreatment of his friend.

Mr. Darcy received mother's greeting in silence, then acknowledged Jane and me, as we had conversed at the ball. After his bow, he faced me for slightly too long as if he intended to speak, but he said nothing. Then he found the farthest chair and stared out the window for the duration of the visit. Afterward, I realized he never spoke a word.

"Why on earth did that disagreeable man come?" my mother scolded after they left.

"I imagine Mr. Bingley enjoys his company," I said, unfathomable as that seemed. "Or he required a new companion, as his sisters had visited enough for one week." A single gentleman could visit my father without harm, but Mr. Bingley calling alone on the Bennet sisters would launch gossip.

And if that excitement were not enough, I had a fresh refinement to enliven my days, although it would not impress Miss Bingley's London high society.

It was a little past dawn. I was standing in mud in front of our draca house, and most vexed with our firedrake.

"Will you not look at me *once* this morning?"

Our drake had emerged, but today he was sulky. He curled around himself and studied fallen leaves, the stone of his draca house, the points of his wings, and every available item other than me.

Each morning, I had tried to replicate the strange vision that occurred when the drake and I stared at each other after the mad dog's attack. Each morning, I had failed. I would have had more luck asking Mr. Darcy to sing.

With a huff, I crossed my arms and scowled. The drake twined restlessly, creeping closer then scuttling away, an endless cycle. Since the attack, he never returned to the kennel while I was present, but neither did he come close. Today, he would not even face me.

I had been rising early to avoid my family, but this was a washing day, and the household was waking. Frustrated, I pointed at the drake. "You are most ill-behaved." He crouched remorsefully, pressing his belly flat to the earth, then fled into his house.

There was an exclamation behind me. I turned to see a servant—a laundry maid, by the rough, red hands covering her shocked mouth. She was an older woman, gray-haired and wizened under her simple bonnet.

I knew our housekeeper, Mrs. Hill, brought in extra help for washing day, but I had not expected to meet a strange servant while I was apparently conversing with draca, not to mention having my petticoats inches deep in mud. But politeness serves in these situations, so I nodded and said good morning.

"Ma'am," she said, even that short utterance revealing a Scottish brogue. Eyes lowered, she continued toward the back entrance, tromping a wide path to avoid the muddy patch by our draca house. Or perhaps to avoid me, as I was equally filthy.

Inside, I changed for breakfast, and our housemaid added the muddied clothing to the laundry she had collected. I eyed the pile, feeling guilty. But I could hardly go outside in bare legs.

The journal from my father rested on my dressing table. Although the oldest pages were indecipherable, I had read several parts, sometimes with Jane beside me for another opinion. But I learned little, other than a disturbing mention of "corrupted wyfe" and mysterious references to "draca essence."

The day was warming when breakfast ended, so my sisters and I set out walking to Meryton. The town was a mile away, and the muddy patches can be avoided if you are not distracted by disobedient drakes. Lydia and Kitty were in high spirits and ran ahead, while Jane, Mary, and I followed at a brisk walk.

"Have you examined the cover of your journal?" Jane said, quite out of the blue. "For I believe it is *not* the Longbourn crest."

Mary asked what journal, and we explained. It was no secret, and I had meant to show it to her, despite a selfish concern that she would then borrow it for a week.

Mary's brow knitted. "You must keep it safe. An old document is valuable, even if it discusses only draca." She added, "If you wish references, you shall require comprehension of Chinese. Draca originate in the Far East. But I have heard it is a challenging language."

"I thought draca were exclusively English," I said.

"No, draca were appropriated from the East by the peerage, who used binding to enforce hereditary rule. Binding and hereditary title together established the aristocracy, the corrupt elite that today represses honest workers."

"Mary, what *have* you been reading?" I said, taken aback.

"Are they really from the Orient?" Jane said eagerly.

Mary blinked at us. Her scholarly comments seldom received such attention. "I was not much interested, so I recall only a little. Marco Polo described Eastern draca as most savage. Village headmen would sacrifice young virgins to their tremendous appetite."

Jane's eyes had gone round. "I will not believe that!"

"I find it quite plausible," Mary replied primly, hurt that her authority was questioned. "Our English patriarchy commoditizes unmarried ladies. Primitive societies, unless truly naturalistic, would be as culpable."

Jane was dubious. "But our drake would not eat a woman. He is quite tame. And small!"

"It is my impression that, in the distant past, the Eastern varietals were larger."

"How much larger?" I said. I had never seen a wyvern, but they were described as nearing the weight of a middle-sized dog.

But Mary's thoughts were proceeding on their own path. "I should be pleased to escape to a naturalistic society. The native tribes in America revere women and acknowledge them to be the wisest leaders. That would be most enjoyable."

I examined Mary's clothes, which, though she still wore black, were fastidious and impractical. "Are you *sure*? I should think practicing your music would be difficult."

"I would bring a smaller harpsichord. Or perhaps a clavichord. One of the braves could carry it for me. They are very strong from wrestling bison and bears."

This seemed an overly romantic view. "Are you *sure*?" I asked again.

We entered Meryton and found Lydia and Kitty, then strolled together until we reached a woman handing out abolitionist pamphlets. Parliament had outlawed the transport of slaves several years ago, but slavery was still rampant in the colonies. Full abolition was a prominent women's cause.

I donated a penny, which was generous. Mary dug a full shilling from her purse and pressed it into the woman's hand, then held tight with both hands and began listing horrors of the Caribbean sugar trade.

We walked on, leaving Mary with the increasingly wide-eyed woman.

Lydia flapped her pamphlet back and forth, then laughed.

"It is a serious issue," I said.

"You are joking. Nobody cares."

"You must not think that. Those poor people are as human as you or me. The color of their skin does not matter."

"It is not *that*." Her bright blue eyes studied me under her bonnet. She lowered her voice. "You are clever, Lizzy. You know. It is like worrying about people who are sick. We do it for show."

"What?" I said. But Lydia had spotted Lieutenant Denny and another young officer, and she ran off.

I looked at Kitty, who knew Lydia best. Her eyes, pinched with worry, caught mine before she ducked her head and followed her sister.

Jane was oblivious. She had taken to daydreaming when Mr. Bingley was not present.

Jane and I joined the group, and Denny introduced a third gentleman, Mr. Wickham. Again, the two youngest Bennet sisters raced ahead, this time on the arms of the officers. I was left to entertain Mr. Wickham, for Jane was absent behind a faraway smile.

I rather enjoyed this arrangement. Mr. Wickham spoke like an educated gentleman, and he was handsome, with strong cheekbones and a warm grin. He paid devoted attention as we examined the shops. It was nice to be flattered. I had spent much of the week idly wondering how long Mr. Bingley could gaze at Jane without blinking.

After pleasantries, I asked if Mr. Wickham had recently come to Meryton.

"Very recently," he replied. "I have accepted a commission in the militia stationed here."

Our local officers were all with the militia, the volunteer service stationed throughout England. The regular army was deployed to the war with France.

He offered his arm while we crossed a street, then asked, "Have you always resided in this neighborhood?"

I explained that Longbourn was nearby, and Mr. Wickham remarked he had passed through Longbourn village, which he found efficient and smartly organized, indicating a modern philosophy of management.

Should I tell him I traipsed the back paths to manage the tenants? Probably not.

After a few more steps, he added, "If I am not mistaken, Longbourn has bound a firedrake?"

I nodded.

"A remarkable binding," he continued. "Have you some tale of how it happened? A family recipe for attracting draca?"

I laughed. "I am unaware of any mystical lore. The Bennet wyves have always bound draca of exceptional breeds." I suppose that was boastful, but it was a boast for my sisters as well.

His eyes appraised me a long time before we resumed our stroll.

6

The next breakfast, I came down late and found Jane fastening her bonnet.

"I am invited to visit with Miss Bingley and her sister," she said. "The ladies are alone, with the gentlemen out until after dinner."

"Mind that you ride," Mamma called.

Lydia was buttering toast. "I rode yesterday. I wanted to make the ribbons on my hat flutter, but the horse was hopeless. She shied every two steps! I need a windy day instead."

"You may have your wish," I said, looking out the window. Black clouds squatted on the horizon.

"A horse relieves labor, but their sentience is problematic," Mary said. That drew curious looks, but Mary did not notice. She was staring wistfully at the plate of bacon.

After a bemused silence, I said, "Jane should take the carriage."

"Jane must ride," Mamma said firmly. "It is sure to rain, and then she must stay all night, and see Mr. Bingley after his dinner."

"That is a most obvious scheme!" I said.

"I do not want a sentient horse," Lydia said. "Can we get a white one instead? They are prettier."

"We are not buying a new horse!" I said, feeling the conversation was off track, if it had a track in the first place. I blew out an exasperated breath, reached for the bacon, and found the plate empty.

As Mamma planned, it rained ferociously. Jane certainly could not return. But the following morning, I received this note:

"My dearest Lizzy,

I find myself very unwell this morning from a sting, although I am sure it is no worse than a bee sting. My ankle is strangely swollen, which has caused a headache. My kind friends insist on my seeing Mr. Jones. I am sure he will set it right, so do not be alarmed."

Mamma was ecstatic. "A bee sting! Is not Jane clever to encounter a bee in such weather! But does she say nothing of Mr. Bingley?"

"She did not say it is a bee sting," I said, rereading with growing alarm. *Very unwell.* "I must go. I wish to be there when Mr. Jones visits." Mr. Jones was the Meryton apothecary and surgeon, and he had cared for our family since Jane and I were children.

"Go? Whatever for?"

"It is not a *bee* sting, Mamma!" I held the note in front of her. "Do you not know your own daughter? When has Jane called herself 'very unwell'?"

My father looked up from his book. "Shall I send for the horses?"

"They are loaned to Mrs. Trew," I said. "I shall be there faster if I walk."

"We can go as far as Meryton," offered Kitty, and Lydia nodded happily.

"Make haste, for I leave promptly."

We set out, Lydia chattering about visiting the officers' wives, but Kitty silent and concerned. We parted in Meryton, Kitty hugging me tight. I continued, jumping stiles and tromping puddles, and my stockings were dripping when I spotted Netherfield House.

The house had not been occupied for several seasons, and if I were not so worried about Jane, I would have admired the improvements. The park was trimmed and planted, the manor shutters repainted, and the chimneys smoking. It looked welcoming and grand, much larger than Longbourn.

But as I approached, I met a change I could not ignore. A draca charged to block my path. She was the length of our firedrake but wingless, a quadruped with a heavy build like a bulldog or badger—a lindworm, although there had been none in our neighborhood. She must be the bound draca of Mr. Bingley's elder sister, Mrs. Louisa Hurst, and her husband.

Unable to fly, a lindworm is considered inferior to our firedrake. But she was savage to confront, with long fangs and armored scales over a muscular frame.

I stopped, expecting intervention from the household, but nobody emerged.

"I must not be delayed," I told her, having picked up the questionable habit of arguing with draca from my dawn visits. Her response was bared teeth and a steaming hiss, and my worry for Jane flared. I snapped, "Move!" To my surprise, she slunk into the draca house.

I rang and was shown into the breakfast parlor. Mr. Darcy rose instantly, followed by a surprised Mr. Bingley. Mrs. Hurst and Miss Bingley greeted me from their chairs while eyeing my shoes, which were dripping muddy water on their polished floor.

"Have you been *walking*?" Miss Bingley asked faintly, a cup of chocolate half-raised in her hand.

"I wished to hurry," I said. "It is only three miles."

Mr. Bingley filled the astonished silence. "I am very pleased you came. Your sister is in no condition to receive visitors. The care of a beloved sister is most welcome."

I was shown to the guest room door, and my heart plunged when I saw Jane in bed. She was deathly pale, her eyes feverish, and her beautiful hair bedraggled and damp. I hugged her, shocked by the weakness of her grip and the extreme heat of her body.

"Oh, Lizzy, I longed for you to come. Although I am sorry. I should not have troubled you..." Even Jane did not dare pursue that direction when I gave her a glare. "All right, I admit I am only glad."

"What happened? You wrote... of a sting." It was hard to steady my voice. "Please show me."

She drew up the covers. There was a two-pointed puncture on her foot, fiercely scarlet, and bilious green-and-yellow swelling on her ankle. Even though I had guessed the truth, it was terrifying.

"Not a bee, then," I said. My fingers were trembling. I pushed my hands into my skirt to hide them.

"It was by the path, and the horse would not pass it. Oh, Lizzy, I was so foolish. It was beginning to rain, and Mamma would be angry if I returned, so I dismounted and found a stick to push it aside… The prick did not seem bad. I thought it nothing, truly. Only during the night did it grow worse. I was relieved when Mr. Bingley suggested sending for Mr. Jones."

"A foul crawler." It took all my control to pretend I was calm. Crawler stings were always described as deadly. Even horses shied from them. "Did you note anything we should tell the apothecary?"

A housemaid was in the room, a slip of a girl no more than twelve. At my mention of a foul crawler, I heard her gasp. Jane must have concealed the truth so she would not worry.

With a stifled sob, the girl fled, and I heard her crying in the hallway.

"It was about the length of my finger," Jane whispered, "greenish-black, with dozens of legs. The stings were in the tail, which it could curl over its head. I did not understand that until after."

I could think of nothing else to say, so I took Jane's hand, and we waited for Mr. Jones. After some minutes, the housekeeper escorted the young housemaid back and instructed her to see to our needs.

"Ma'am, can I get something for the miss or yourself?" the girl said in a timid voice. Her eyes were red.

I was about to decline but thought better and said to Jane, "They have hot chocolate. Would that not be a nice treat?" Jane nodded, her eyes closed, and the maid brought us two cups. But Jane could not touch hers, and mine grew cold beside it on the shelf.

The afternoon sun, emerged after yesterday's rain, dragged behind the closed drapes. I wiped Jane's wet forehead and cheeks, and the cloths came away rancid and bitter. We managed to change her soaked nightgown, then she fell into a fretful slumber, tossing and moaning. Still Mr. Jones did not arrive, and my fear grew and grew.

"When was Mr. Jones sent for?" I asked the maid.

"Miss Bingley sent a note at breakfast."

"What did she write?"

"I don't know, ma'am."

"Please tell the housekeeper to call for him again. Say it is desperately urgent."

The maid left with a stricken expression, and shortly the housekeeper herself returned. "I have sent two men on horses to find Mr. Jones. Ma'am, the master has been asking about Miss Bennet. What shall I say?"

They would be downstairs, playing cards or drinking chocolate, and wondering at my rudeness for not returning to remark amusingly on the trifling headaches of ladies.

I shook my head in reply. Mr. Bingley could not visit Jane in her room, and I did not wish to encourage a visit from his sisters.

At last, boots thumped up the stairs accompanied by the bellowing tones of Mr. Jones, who considered volume a crucial ingredient of any cure. I leaped up in relief.

"A lady has a bee sting and headache, is it?" he said jovially as the door opened. "Well, we shall see—"

His words ended on seeing Jane, and he bent over her, a hand on her forehead, his face grave.

"Her ankle, sir." I pointed, and he lifted the cover. The swelling had worsened, reaching her knee, and he cursed audibly. I explained, "She said it was small, greenish-black, with many pairs of legs—"

"*When?* The note said only she was stung by a bee. All afternoon I was with the midwife, for Mrs. Plowman is having a hard labor..."

"Jane was stung evening last."

He shook his head angrily even as his fingers touched the swelling, examining it or, I hoped, helping it heal. "Has your father come?"

"Only I." The question frightened me. "Should I send for him?"

"We cannot wait. You must trust my judgment, Miss Bennet."

"Of course."

"Your sister is gravely ill." I nodded. This was obvious. "I cannot overstate the seriousness of her condition. There is a chance if I treat her now. I cannot delay to send for a specialized physician. Further progression will remove all hope."

I had never seen him so serious. All I could do was nod again. He bowed and left the room, calling for the housekeeper.

I sat helplessly, almost unseeing, trapped in a strange house and terrified for Jane. The housekeeper entered, directing two maids with the brusque manner of housekeepers everywhere. They pulled the linens aside and pushed a heavy quilt under Jane's leg. Jane made no response as they moved her.

The room emptied. But the plain dress and shoes of a maid had stopped in front of me. I looked up and saw the wizened face and reddened hands of the Scottish laundry maid I had met outside the draca house at Longbourn.

"Ma'am," she said. I had to concentrate to comprehend her brogue. "Your sister, she is stung. 'Tis a cockatrice, or other foul crawler." I had said almost the same words, but hearing them cut away my hope. They tolled like a sentence of death. "Dragon wyves, your family be. I saw you. You commanded that drake, and you only a miss, not even bound."

"We are gentry, yes." Part of me laughed silently, mocking myself for once worrying about inconsequential vanities like marriage and binding.

"Your sister must be *dosed*, ma'am. She needs the essence. The poison will burn her away if you do nothing, and this doctor is no better."

"What are you speaking of? What essence?" This sounded like some folk tale.

"The draca hail from Scotland, lassie, afore the thieving English stole them. We keep the old ways and know the old cures. But do you have draca essence for a dose?"

"I have never heard of such a thing." But no, that was wrong. Those words were in the journal my father gave me.

Her thin lips hardened. "Raw draca blood, then. If she be half the wyfe as you, she will bear it. But the blood must be freely given, or it will not fight the venom."

"Draca blood is medicine, you mean?"

"Aye, against those foul creatures. Raw blood is dangerous but potent. A few drops only." Her eyebrows narrowed. "You are sitting like a lump, lassie. Go get it!"

Understanding dawned. I grabbed the sharpest thing I saw, a letter opener from the dresser, and the saucer from under my cold chocolate. I ran down the stairs. Mr. Bingley called as I passed a doorway, but I ignored him and ran out to the draca house.

It was empty.

I turned. The sun was falling below the horizon, casting long, darkening shadows.

"Where are you?" I called and heard a rustling growl under a bush. I ran and fell on my knees in front of the lindworm. She hissed, backing away, but I grabbed her muzzle and pulled until her glittering black gaze met mine. Her neck and jaws were corded with muscle—I could never have held her if she fought—but she just watched, her breath steaming around my fingers like a kettle ready to boil.

"You must let me take your blood," I said. But where could I prick her? The letter opener had a point but was not sharp, and even her muzzle had scales so hard they scraped like steel.

I let go of her muzzle and reached for a paw, the letter opener in my other hand.

Her jaws snapped a hairsbreadth from my cheek, fangs gleaming dark and burnished like our drake's claws. I froze, but her gaze caught on mine again, and the growling diminished. In the gloaming dark, blue flame flickered behind the jags of her teeth.

"Watch," I said. I held my hands up, took a breath, then drove the point into my palm. Desperation made me push deep, and the pain was sharp. I held the saucer beneath as drops fell. "You see? Now you must take a turn." I felt for a paw, and a strange certainty spread through me. I lifted her paw and spread her toes with my fingers, feeling soft skin between, and pushed the point in.

Her paw clenched, muscles bunching under her scaly skin. Claws I had not seen cut my fingers. But her eyes watched mine, and her fangs, so close that their heat warmed my lips as if we prepared a bizarre kiss, did not savage my face. One hard, hot exhalation crossed my cheeks, then another.

I had to look down to place the saucer. Drops fell—golden and clear, not like blood at all. One landed in the drops of my own blood and sizzled like hot oil.

I sat back, and the lindworm did the same on her haunches, suddenly doglike and docile. I grabbed the saucer, rose, and stopped.

Mr. Darcy faced me, no more than two steps away.

I did not know what he had seen, and I could not imagine what he thought.

"I…" he began. His voice failed, leaving his lips parted and his eyes wondering. Then, he was composed. "I hoped to inquire after your sister."

What answer could I make? I ran past him into the house, then to Jane's room.

The scene was frantic. Mr. Jones was pressing a brown flask of laudanum to Jane's lips while she fumbled to push it away. His method seemed reckless, as he usually prescribed ten drops.

Two burly men from the stables stood against the wall, which was unthinkable because the bed cover was pushed aside, exposing Jane's injured leg to the thigh. They stared at the floor, their faces pale with embarrassment.

No, they were frightened. What frightened them?

Then I saw the knives and butcher's saw on the bed beside Jane's leg.

"What are you doing?" I screamed. Mr. Jones fell back in surprise, and I beat him away from Jane with one hand, balancing the precious saucer in the other. Then the Scottish maid was between us, and the housekeeper was shouting, and it was a frenzy.

I reached Jane. The cups of cold chocolate were on the shelf by the bed, and I splashed a little into the saucer, having nothing else, and swished around the mess, trusting Jane would not be hurt by a few drops of her sister's blood in the mix.

"No… do not…" Jane was muttering, her eyes closed. She pushed blindly as I leaned over her.

"Jane darling. Drink this little bit. Please, for me." I tipped the saucer into her mouth, and she swallowed, coughing and grimacing.

Mr. Jones shouted orders, and a man's hands pulled me back. I twisted and saw one of the stablemen. "Remove your hands from me!" I said, shocked. He backed away, tugging his forelock, then ran from the room.

Other boots pounded up the stairs, and Mr. Bingley entered. "What on earth—" His eyes widened, recognizing that Jane's leg was exposed, and he fled, a hand shielding his eyes. Loud apologies echoed from the hallway.

There was a lull. Mr. Jones was panting, his collar askew and hair messed. My own hair hung loose around my face. I dared not examine my clothes.

"What is happening, Lizzy?" Jane said. She pulled the cover to her chin and stared at us as if we were mad.

7

The next morning, supplied with clean petticoats and stockings by the young housemaid, I went downstairs to find the breakfast parlor.

Breakfast was set, with candles warming the filigree silver pots, but the room was empty and the food untouched. The Bingley household had not yet risen.

I opened the pots, discovered chocolate, and poured myself a cup. We did not serve it at Longbourn because Kitty and Lydia would drink nothing else. I took a sip. It was silky smooth, swirling with cream, and had far more sugar than I was used to.

I topped up my cup. A reward seemed justified.

Yesterday, Mr. Jones had examined Jane, his bushy eyebrows furrowed in bewilderment. The swelling on her leg was retreating.

He spoke with me outside her room. "I am greatly relieved, Miss Bennet. Your sister's recovery is God-sent. I apologize for considering treatment that would have been excessively severe and dangerous."

"You acted on your professional understanding. Please do not apologize." There were vivid scratches across his cheek; those could be from my nails, or the Scottish woman's. "Feelings were high for all present."

He nodded. He had not seen what I gave Jane, being under assault by a Scottish maid. I knew I should explain, but I wished to answer my own questions first. And I was exhausted and wanted to return to my sister.

I slept beside Jane that night, unwilling to leave her unprotected. That was foolish, of course. Mr. Jones would not burst through the door brandishing a saw. But I was not the only guard. The little housemaid, who attended me now with such wide-eyed awe that I was quite self-conscious, had slept curled in a chair beside the bed, snoring.

Mrs. Hurst and Miss Bingley entered the breakfast parlor with a rustle of skirts.

"Miss Elizabeth, please tell me of dear Jane," Miss Bingley said, taking my hand. She was concerned and sincere, which made me feel better toward her.

"She is recovering well, but is tired, and has a headache and sore ankle. I should not expect her for breakfast, or that she will be about anytime today."

Miss Bingley expressed her great relief. I did not know what news had circulated, but it would be difficult not to be alarmed by shouting doctors and sprinting guests.

Whether the sisters were satisfied by my answer or not, I had left no polite avenue for further inquiry. They contented themselves with remarking on the weather and offering to lend me a dress while the servants ironed mine, for they had spotted wrinkles.

I repeated this exchange when Mr. Bingley arrived, absent the offer of a dress. He exclaimed happily and thanked me many times for attending to Jane. Mr. Darcy inquired and received his answer with distant formality. Mr. Hurst was last to arrive and thought only of his breakfast.

After breakfast, I returned to Jane. The sisters came up to visit, and Jane smiled and chatted a little and ate a bite of toast.

"You are receiving wonderful care," I said to Jane. "I should return home."

"We *will* miss you," Miss Bingley proclaimed cheerily. "I shall have the carriage brought around."

Jane grabbed my hand. "Must you go? I feel so much better having you here."

Privately, I was worried to leave. But I could not invite myself.

After a long silence, Mrs. Hurst said, "You *must* stay, Miss Elizabeth."

And so, a servant was dispatched to Longbourn to tell Papa and Mamma the events and to bring back a supply of clothes.

I left Jane with the sisters and asked directions until I found the housekeeper. I wished to speak with the Scottish maid and thank her again.

"That washerwoman has been dismissed," the housekeeper said.

"Dismissed? Whatever for?"

"She struck Mr. Jones, ma'am."

"After *I* struck him."

The housekeeper's expression conveyed that reprehensible behavior by gentry was no excuse for disorder amongst her staff.

I was disappointed, and concerned that the Scottish woman had lost her position. But as Mrs. Hill already retained the woman for Longbourn's wash days, I could address that at home where I had more influence.

I returned to Jane's room. The sisters had left, and Jane was sweetly asleep, watched with maternal care by the young housemaid. Reassured, I went exploring to find my hosts.

The breakfast parlor had been cleared, but there were voices behind a closed door. I approached and heard Miss Bingley speaking in scathing tones.

"You observed her, Mr. Darcy, I am *sure*."

I was reaching for the door handle, but I hesitated, wondering whom they discussed.

"To scrabble about in the bushes after draca!" Miss Bingley continued. "And to walk three miles, or five miles, or whatever it was, above her ankles in dirt! She seems obsessed with some country-girl display of roughness."

"I have seen only her affection and care for her ill sister," came Bingley's voice. "I find that very pleasing." His defense was mortifying proof of whom they mocked.

"I am afraid, Mr. Darcy," observed Miss Bingley in a wicked whisper, and I realized she was inches away, opposite the door I had almost touched, "that this endless grubbiness has rather affected your admiration of her fine eyes."

"Not at all," his haughty baritone replied, "they were brightened by—"

I fled to the hallway, then, afraid my steps had been heard, I ran out the front door.

The day shone, bright and pure, the air crisp from the rains. My arms locked over my chest and hammering heart. Humiliation and fury whirled in confused, painful alternation.

The foliage rustled, and the lindworm emerged to sit by my feet, tilting her head with concern. Had her hindquarters not been so lizard-like, I think she would have wagged her tail in sympathy.

"Go away," I whispered, and she slunk to her kennel.

Entering a room with those people was impossible. But I had accepted their invitation. Should I walk home, to abandon Jane and provide fresh fodder for their disdain?

I did have defenders. Mr. Bingley had been kind. And Mr. Darcy… well, Mr. Darcy's opinion was hard to make out.

But Miss Bingley was as clear as the daylight on my face. She was a hurtful, conceited woman. I suspected her sister was no better.

That convinced me, though. I would not abandon Jane to a nest of vipers. I wiped my eyes and marched back in. I passed the breakfast parlor and flung open the next pair of doors—apparently with vigor, for the lone butler within bowed hastily then eyed me with extreme trepidation. After my altercation with Mr. Jones, stories of the mad Bennet girl must be flying.

Informed that the Bingleys had moved to the drawing room, I made my way there, but I arrived resolved to be polite. Decorum is the armor of gentry, and I was a gentleman's daughter.

"Miss Eliza!" cried Miss Bingley with a wide smile. It seemed contempt had promoted our acquaintance to intimate friendship. I returned the smile, savoring my dislike, and she continued, "Jane is such a dear, even with a headache. I do so detest being ill myself. We were just settling for a game of loo. Will you join us?" She gestured to the seat beside her.

Armored or not, I was not prepared to sit beside Miss Bingley and gossip between hands. "Thank you, but I must return to my sister shortly. A book will serve for my amusement."

I went to examine the bookshelf, mostly to explain my refusal of cards, but stopped short when I saw the title *Upon the Mystyry of Draca*. I opened it, but it was all pictures, with flamboyant captions and not very accurate.

Behind me, conversation over cards resumed.

"How I long to see Miss Darcy again!" Miss Bingley said. "I never met anybody who delighted me so much as your sister. Such manners, and so extremely accomplished for her age! Her performance on the pianoforte is exquisite."

"It is almost savage the way she pounds the keyboard," Bingley said. "And she is so slight a creature! Oh, do not glower, Darcy. I am all admiration for your sister and her modern music."

"Does she play Beethoven?" I asked, and faces turned from the card table.

"She does," answered Mr. Darcy. "Do you, Miss Bennet?"

I laughed at that. "No, Beethoven is beyond my skill. But my sister Mary is an advocate of his work. I admire what I have heard."

"Indeed, Beethoven is my favorite," cried Miss Bingley. "How delightful that his music has reached you, even here. Although of course, you do not actually *play*. Are you too occupied pursuing draca?"

That was a petty attack by my standard, having grown up with my father's barbed wit. But I began to wonder why she disliked me. I had done nothing to provoke it.

"They say Napoleon is pursuing draca," Mr. Bingley said before I could jab back. "To buy them, or some such."

Mr. Darcy rose from the card table. His tall frame drew the eye, and there was an expectant hush.

He walked to me and indicated the book I held, open to an illustration of a firedrake. "Your choice is interesting."

"One that will not aid my pursuit of draca," I said smiling. "It is pictures only."

"Few serious books on the subject exist. It has been the work of generations to collect them at Pemberley."

Miss Bingley leaped to her feet. "What have you chanced upon, Eliza? I am all curiosity!"

"I thought you dismissive of draca," I said to Mr. Darcy, before remembering that was my private conclusion from the rumors of his lack of marriage gold and observing his extreme behavior at the ball.

An intense emotion played on Mr. Darcy's face, but it was unreadable beneath his well-mannered exterior. He bowed and returned to the card table. But the game did not proceed, for Miss Bingley had to effuse over my book, and then search the shelf for other volumes.

8

The day continued quietly for me. I spent most of it with Jane, and she slept through the afternoon. The swelling on her ankle subsided to bruises, and she took a few wincing steps to bathe. The young housemaid and I did up her hair—rather elaborately, for we were bored—and wrapped her in a borrowed dressing gown. Suddenly, beautiful Jane was smiling from the bed.

Miss Bingley and Mrs. Hurst came up and began a cheerful visit. I watched, wondering how Miss Bingley could be so nice to Jane and so vile to me. I suppose Jane's good nature brought out the goodness in others. Wisely, I ignored what that implied about myself.

The gentlemen had been out riding, and they returned with a clamor: the thump of boots pried off by servants and laughing exclamations about horses and fields. Mr. Bingley came upstairs and inquired from the hallway. After a few shouted questions, I intervened.

"Mr. Bingley," I called. "The sky will not fall if you enter. You have two sisters, myself, and a maid all here, and Jane is most presentable, sitting up in bed."

"Are you sure?" his voice came back.

"You are the master of this household. Who will object?" His sisters applauded as if this were a bold game, so he came in.

He beamed at Jane and told her a funny and modest story about their riding. Jane, in her restrained way, beamed back. His sisters and I were quite irrelevant. It was charming, and I was relieved my mother was not here. She would have announced their engagement to the room.

Miss Bingley smiled at first, but her pleasure faded. When the Bingleys left to prepare for dinner, her farewell to Jane was brittle, and her smile did not reach her eyes.

Jane was tired after the visit and slept again, and the little maid helped me dress for dinner. While she worked to fasten my dress, I became curious.

"You are very young to be a housemaid."

I moved a little to see her in the looking glass and saw her nod, her little face screwed up with concentration while she worked.

"Yes, ma'am. I'm lucky. I washed laundry before, and the lye in the water hurts." She flexed her fingers in remembered pain. It must have been some time ago. She had the hands of a lady's maid now, slender and smooth, a great contrast to the cracked, red skin of the Scottish woman.

"How did you become a housemaid?"

"A lady said I was pretty, ma'am."

"What did your mother think?"

"Don't have one. No father, neither."

"Are you…" What was I trying to discover? "Who teaches you? Do you read?"

"I don't have my letters, ma'am, but I'm taught how to wait, and curtsy, and speak properly to ladies and—" Her hands stopped, and her face became a picture of distress. "Am I doin' it wrong?"

"No, you do it wonderfully." She cheered up with the quick moods of a child, and I wondered if she was even younger than I had thought.

She began setting my hair, her tongue peeking out while her fingers pinned my curls. "Miss Jane is so pretty and nice," she said. "Like… a flower, with yellow petals, that always smiles."

"She is a wonderful sister, and so thoughtful that I do not begrudge her outshining the rest of us."

"And you are like a tree," she added decidedly. "One that is light and lively in the wind, but tough. Like an ash, but with dark leaves for your hair."

"I believe you are a young poet," I said, very seriously. "But I would make a short tree. A shrub, perhaps."

"I mean, she does not outshine you, ma'am." She took her hands away.

I had to move to see my reflection. She had set my hair higher than I would choose for dinner, more suited for a ball. But a few curls had been left down and loose, almost untouched. It had no recognizable style, but I would not have criticized her attempt even if I found a bird's nest on my head.

"Eliza! How nice that you..." Miss Bingley's voice stopped.

I had entered the dining room curious. I had never dined at Netherfield, even when it was kept by prior families. The room was twice the length of Longbourn's dining room. Under a horrid clutter of ornamental china, the furnishings were fashionable and in good taste—not always the case when an estate was freshly leased. I wondered who had chosen the furniture. Not the sisters, who preferred elaborate dresses and often wore both earrings and jeweled necklaces. And it was hard to imagine affable Mr. Bingley caring about décor.

Miss Bingley's silence made me look over. That seemed to restore her voice.

"How nice that you are able to be our guest for dinner, at last," she said tonelessly, her gaze locked on my hair.

So. It was to be insults at three paces. I examined her dress, choosing targets, but she simply indicated a chair, then sat herself as the others arrived.

Though we had breakfasted together casually, dinner began stiffly, which happens sometimes with the formality of servants and courses. I tried for a topic but without much goodwill, as Mr. Bingley was the only one I honestly liked. And every time I looked at one of his sisters—or at Mr. Darcy, who was seated opposite me—they seemed to be staring at me.

But Mr. Bingley was determined to thaw our party. "Darcy, for goodness sakes, *speak*, man! We have finished an entire course, and I think the only thing that has passed through your lips is soup."

Mr. Darcy gave a curt nod, accepting his friend's rebuke but oblivious to the irony of his silent response.

"I believe you scored a hit, Mr. Bingley," I said before I could stop myself, for Mr. Darcy looked like a fencer acknowledging a touch, although I had only seen fencing on stage in *Hamlet*.

"Indeed, you are right!" Mr. Bingley said in a wondering voice. "You must be my witness, for it will never happen again."

"Is he so hard to hit, then?"

"I fenced with him exactly once, and I have never been so humiliated."

This prodded Mr. Darcy to speak. "You are overly kind. There are many at my club who beat me soundly."

"His club filled with fencing masters, he means," Mr. Bingley said with a laugh.

"How remarkable that you have such skill and never mention it," Miss Bingley said. "I should adore to see you fence."

"It is a skill for exercise and discipline, not performance," Mr. Darcy replied.

"And for duels, surely. You have revealed yourself a hidden romantic." Miss Bingley thrust her fork through the air, stabbing an unseen opponent.

There was general laughter. Mr. Darcy remained grave and still, so I only smiled.

"Of course, only men duel with swords," Miss Bingley continued, and her eyes turned to me. "What was the inspiration for your hair, Miss Bennet?"

My sole surprise was that she had waited so long to attack. But as I opened my mouth to counter, I realized her scathing tone was missing. I changed direction mid-sentence but managed to say something about their young housemaid.

"She remembers from London, I suppose," mused Miss Bingley. "It is most *au courant*."

"Really?" I leaned to see around Mr. Darcy. There was a large mirror on the wall behind him, and my expression was dubious as I looked back at myself. The curls the maid had left loose almost touched my shoulders. "I thought it unfinished."

"No," Mr. Darcy said. I looked at him, expecting more, but that was all.

"I have a lady's maid, of course," Miss Bingley said. "Perhaps I should encourage this girl, too."

"She should learn to read," I said. Even for a housemaid, this was preferred, and a lady's maid must handle correspondence.

"She cannot read? Ah, well." Miss Bingley tossed her hand as if discarding a worthless card.

"I am sure she could learn." I thought of the maid's poetic description of Jane.

"Whatever for?"

"To become a lady's maid. Or to better her mind. Or for enjoyment. I often lend books to our housemaids."

"*Do* you?" Miss Bingley's eyebrows had soared.

"It is unfair that she has no way to learn. She has no mother or father —she is an orphan, I mean. So there is no path for her, is there?"

I was receiving incredulous stares. I suppose Mary feels this way when she quotes a reformist at dinner, and we stare at her.

"There is the Society for Promoting the Lancasterian System," Mr. Darcy said. "They are not active in Hertfordshire at this time. But they are sympathetic to education of the poor, and are establishing a program in the north."

"I shall have to inquire about them," I said. He nodded.

Mr. Darcy's clothes were elegant and finely tailored. As were the sisters' silk dresses. The large room around us shone with polished wood, damask-covered cushions, and gilded mirrors.

I was struck by a frustration I had never felt before. I was envious of wealth.

Not so I could lease an abandoned estate and fill it with expensive furniture. But imagine hearing someone's bold plan to educate poor girls, and then telling them to proceed.

Mr. Hurst shifted ponderously in his chair. "Educating the poor would be a colossal waste of money. We are at war, you know. Wellesley does not need his men reading while they charge Napoleon's guns."

"I spoke of a young girl," I said.

"She could sew uniforms," Mr. Hurst said. "I don't see why you are concerned. She has a roof over her head. Food every day. In London, there are hordes of girls worse off, filthy and swarming like rats for a crust of bread."

He was not wrong. But I found myself rigid with anger. Furious.

In another moment, I would have said something extremely impolite, but the butler entered with a letter on a silver tray, addressed to me in my mother's hand.

As I broke the Longbourn seal, I realized that, delivered at this hour, it might be grave news. My heart leaped to my father, and I wished I had left the room to open it. But when I unfolded it, I relaxed, then became mystified.

My mother wrote:

"Dear Lizzy,

I am sure this is no loss. Such a poor creature hardly merited the cost of upkeep. But Lady Lucas is violently distressed, and it has made my own nerves flare terribly.

Your mother."

She enclosed a letter from Charlotte, addressed to me at Longbourn. I broke the seal and read in growing shock, then looked up at the concerned expressions around me.

"The Lucases' tunnelworm—their bound draca—is dead."

9

I visited the Lucases the next morning, benefiting from the loan of the Bingleys' carriage and the gift of being unaccompanied by the Bingley sisters. They felt, correctly, that they did not know the Lucases well enough to visit so soon after misfortune.

Lady Lucas was red-eyed and fluttery. I had known her since I was a child, so I hugged her tight. I was not as close to her husband, but he was sadder to see. Sir William's jovial bluster had crumpled. He sat in silence, then abruptly started a strange boast of expecting condolences from a duke. That stopped mid-sentence, and his lips worked until his wyfe took his hand.

Had this been a family death, I would, unfortunately, have known what to say. But I struggled to express my condolences. There was no protocol or precedent to guide me.

Draca are hardy beasts. They never seem to die, at least not of old age. They are not invulnerable; a musket or heavy weapon can penetrate their scales. But they are dangerous and resilient, and they are considered outside of gentlemanly conflict—embargoed against violence, both as a symbol of gentry honor and because they cannot be trained to fight, so they are not a threat.

After I visited the family, Charlotte and I retired to talk in the garden.

Charlotte is a wonderful friend, sensible and practical, and she was completely calm.

"I was surprised," she explained, "but Lucas Lodge is not entailed like your estate, and our prestige is secured by my father's knighthood, which he will remember soon enough, and then cherish even more." She was smiling, and I laughed at that. "In truth, it was only a tunnelworm, no great badge of honor. I did not care for it. Indeed, I wonder sometimes whether I will be able to bind. Draca frighten me. They are ugly, vicious creatures."

My recent fascination disagreed, but this was not the time to praise draca, so I acknowledged her feelings.

Then I asked, "But how could your draca die?"

"We do not know. My mother found it dead when she went out in the morning. There was no mark or injury. Only a strange smell, like oranges and burned almonds, which faded. Perhaps that was a symptom of death. Nobody has experience with this." Her brow wrinkled. "Our neighbor suggested sickness. A draca plague."

"One death does not make a plague."

"No, but I thought of you. For if Longbourn…"

"You are a good friend to worry about us, but our drake is quite healthy."

"Oh! How is Jane?" Charlotte caught my hand. "I should have asked sooner."

"She is better now. But she was frighteningly ill. You cannot imagine my relief to see her cheerful and sitting up in bed."

"Is she well enough to enjoy her visit, then?" Charlotte said archly.

"You mean Mr. Bingley?"

"Of course. I saw them together at the ball." I smiled back, and she continued, "Lizzy, promise me you will advise Jane to secure him promptly. There is no benefit in delay. Happiness in marriage is entirely a matter of chance. It is best to know as little as possible of the defects of the person with whom you are to pass your life."

"Charlotte!" I laughed. "I shall do no such thing. That is excessively cynical."

THE LUCASES LIVED NEAR MERYTON, so I walked there afterward. The carriage had returned to Netherfield to collect the Bingley sisters, and we planned to meet in town.

I walked the few minutes with an increasingly foul attitude. I was not eager to be serenaded by the sisters' false concern for the Lucases.

The Bingley carriage had not yet arrived, but Lydia, Kitty, and Mary were outside the haberdashery with some officers, including Mr. Wickham. He offered his arm, and I latched on, amused at my behavior after scoffing at Charlotte's advice.

Lydia rewarded me with a grumpy expression. Mr. Wickham was now resplendent in his scarlet regimental uniform.

Fortunately, there were officers enough, including one for Mary. She tended to be stranded when competing with Lydia and Kitty, who were aggressive in securing gentlemen. Of course, I had snatched Mr. Wickham without even considering her. That was an uncomfortable thought, although it turned out all right in the end.

Pondering the dynamics of five unmarried sisters, I watched Mary converse with her companion. She was smiling, but to my eye, her pleasure seemed forced. I was not sure what was wrong, but I wished she were happier.

I returned my attention to Mr. Wickham, but he seemed distracted. I followed his gaze.

On the far side of the street, an iron-barred coach was being loaded with luggage. A steel mesh cage on top held a draca.

Wondering what fascinated him, I said, "Colonel Forster reports the regular army is recruiting married, bound officers."

Mr. Wickham turned to me with a smile. "Indeed, I have considered joining the regular army. Serving in the militia is an honor, but the regulars, even more. I have little patience for men who shout of patriotism while playing cards in drawing rooms." The corner of his smile dimpled. "Regretfully, I am unmarried."

I bit my lip to squash an impending blush. "I am sure you would be welcomed. They have a great shortage of officers for the war. They award commissions to those who demonstrate an officer's character."

"You are well informed," he said, abruptly defensive.

I kicked myself for overstepping. "I am sure I am *poorly* informed, compared to an officer of the militia." With a doting smile, I added, "Shall I call you Lieutenant Wickham now?"

The warm smile returned. "Truthfully, I enjoy hearing you say Mr. Wickham." He gave a bow. I felt we were set right again, although my method left me uncomfortable.

Then I had to ponder whether "Mr. Wickham" was a more intimate address than "Lieutenant," and I decided it was.

His attention returned to the cage on the carriage. The draca was agitated, jumping against the mesh so the cage shook. It was a smallish quadruped, about the size of a rabbit. A reddish underbelly pressed against the wire, and I recognized a roseworm, who take their name from their color.

Lydia and Lieutenant Denny crossed the street toward it.

Blue flame shot from the cage, shivering the blue sky, barely visible but heating my skin like an open furnace. A patch of mesh on the cage glowed red-hot, the center yellow-white and smoking. The roseworm clawed in a frenzy, and the metal tore like fabric. The creature scrambled over the carriage roof and fell into the street.

Even falling, it fell wrong. Draca of every variety are sinuous and exact in their motion, a graceful mix of stalking cat and hunting bird. But this was a flailing, painful plummet, and I heard a thump and an animal's shriek as it hit the ground.

People crowded close. Then a woman screamed, and they scattered pell-mell like children at a game. One man cried out with every step while a woman supported him, his trouser leg in bloody shreds.

I caught a flicker of rose among the running feet, then the roseworm darted free. It ran toward Lydia and tumbled to an awkward halt a few feet from her.

Lydia's hand extended in fright. The roseworm's chest swelled like our drake's had before it threw fire.

Ten paces away, my thought was an instinctive, silent scream: *Stop!*

The roseworm's threatening pose froze. Lydia's hand hung, outstretched like a command. Then Denny wrapped her in his arms and pulled her away.

The roseworm's head twisted toward me. My vision blurred. I felt... shame. Terror and confusion. And pain. Burning pain that had struck while trapped in the cage.

With a snap, the sensation vanished. The roseworm fell on his side, convulsing and screeching. It was horrid, a creature in ultimate agony. He bounced on the ground like a child's abused rattle, then lay still.

"She stopped the attack," Wickham said in a wondering voice. His gaze was on Lydia.

"Kill it!" someone shouted. Men ran for sticks. An officer drew his sword. But they hung back, afraid to approach.

"He is killed already," I whispered. I walked between the standing men and knelt by the poor creature. Dead, he was a little thing, with beautiful red scales that turned golden on his back and tail. The memory of his dying terror tightened my throat.

There was a strange odor. Sour orange and bitter almond.

Firm steps approached. "Miss Bennet, please come away—" a familiar baritone began.

"Elizabeth!" said Mr. Wickham's concerned voice.

On each side of me, a man's hand was extended. One was gloved beneath an elegant dark sleeve, the other bare beneath an arm clothed in scarlet regimentals.

As I rose, Mr. Darcy and Mr. Wickham turned from me to each other. Mr. Darcy's face became cold, then white with fury. Mr. Wickham was red-faced. He took a flustered step back before touching his hat in greeting.

With no word, not even the bare minimum of a nod, Mr. Darcy turned his back. His gray horse was a few steps away, untethered but waiting with perfect discipline. With a horseman's uninterrupted sweep, Mr. Darcy was into the saddle and trotting away. He kicked the animal and vanished down the street at a gallop.

Mystified, I turned the other way. Mr. Wickham's scarlet back vanished through the crowd in the opposite direction.

10

Why is a bound draca loyal?

I knew now that my strange episodes and visions were sensing a draca's thoughts. My memories of the dying roseworm were too vivid to deny. And even while that poor creature was overcome by animal confusion and pain, the strongest emotion was almost human: the shame of a failed loyalty.

Do draca love their wyves and masters?

I think dogs serve a master for love. A dog is raised from a puppy, and he dotes on his master, wagging and wriggling with adoration. But a bound draca arrives fully grown. They are found the morning after the wedding, often asleep as if binding were entirely mundane. The wyfe feeds them, and they wander off to amuse themselves until hungry again. This is not the behavior of a besotted creature.

It is like Charlotte's view of marriage. Do not learn too much about your companion. Attend your wedding, have breakfast together in the morning, then go about your life.

Why does Charlotte's practical philosophy make something ache under my breastbone?

I was staring through a tall six-pane window in the Netherfield sitting room. Outside the wavery glass, it was almost sunset.

Mr. Darcy was seated at a gilt-edged writing table, composing a letter.

Miss Bingley hovered at his elbow. She was astonishingly overdressed in gathered yellow silk, her hair piled in ringlets.

"Tell your sister I am quite in raptures over her performance of a new sonata," Miss Bingley said, "and that I think it infinitely superior to Herr Beethoven's last effort, or I will, once I hear it."

"Will you give me leave to defer your raptures until I write again?" Mr. Darcy said. "At present, I have not room to do them justice."

His dry reply reminded me of my father's wit. I watched his lips compress while he wrote. Perhaps I was beginning to decipher the hidden moods of the man.

The other mystery of the day returned—Mr. Darcy's rude cut to Mr. Wickham. It was all the more remarkable because Mr. Darcy was undemonstrative, to say the least.

Mr. Darcy's hints were lost on Miss Bingley. She rattled on until, at last, Mr. Darcy put down his pen and began a scathing response. Miss Bingley nodded along, wide-eyed, coquettish, and oblivious.

Oh. She was in *pursuit* of Mr. Darcy.

I laughed aloud. It was so obvious. How had I not noticed before? A minor mystery of Miss Bingley was solved. That left only the puzzle of her dislike for me.

At my laugh, Mr. Darcy shot up like an overwound spring had unfolded his long limbs. He strode over to me.

I looked up at his tense frame. Abandoned beside the writing table, Miss Bingley stared openmouthed at his back.

When nothing more happened, I said cautiously, "Yes?"

"In town today, you approached the dead draca," he said.

This was not a topic I wished to pursue. "I was affected by his death. It was very sad." That was honest, if unrevealing.

The tension in his frame cranked tighter. "Your companion was unaffected."

So, this was about Mr. Wickham. I folded my arms. "That is a remarkable insight, as you departed so hastily."

A muscle tensed along his jaw. "That was a matter of honor."

My lingering frustration from Mr. Wickham's unexplained departure returned. "How fortunate, then, that you left me in the company of an honorable officer."

"You attach high regard to the militia," Mr. Darcy said angrily.

I stepped closer. We were now face-to-face, abandoning any pretense of social conversation. "They serve our country in time of war."

"Honor is measured in the man, not the uniform."

Miss Bingley fluffed to an awkward stop beside Mr. Darcy. "What has the militia to do with anything?"

Mr. Hurst was tilting a glass of port back and forth. He spoke up. "The militia are a ragged group, but it is an economical method to train soldiers. Still, the way they parade about and bring their own guns is very amateur. It is sufficient for cannon fodder, but not for officers. No gentlemen could tolerate such company."

I remembered Mr. Wickham's comment about shouting patriotism while playing cards. "Many gentlemen have volunteered in the militia. And one does not need to be a gentleman, or an officer, to have honor."

Hastily, Mr. Bingley stepped in. "Miss Bennet, I was very pleased to visit with you and your sister today. It was a joy to see her so improved. I was disappointed that she could not join us for dinner."

Mr. Bingley disliked argument, and his effort to calm the conversation was so obvious that it was sincere, rather like Mr. Bingley himself. For Jane's sake, I owed civility to his friends.

"Jane has an appetite now," I said, forcing a polite tone. "We were able to walk several times around the room. But we will wait till morning before attempting the stairs."

"She will be down for breakfast then?" Mr. Bingley was so enthused that I expected him to begin toasting bread, even though we just left dinner.

"You have been most accommodating, but our stay is a great imposition. If Jane is well enough, we thought to depart directly in the morning." I did not mention that I had extracted this promise from Jane. I was eager to escape Netherfield.

Miss Bingley cried, "How wonderful!" even as Mr. Bingley said, "What a shame!" Miss Bingley gave him an angry look, and Mr. Bingley amended, "I mean… I am thrilled your sister is so much better."

"Miss Eliza Bennet," Miss Bingley said, but she watched her brother, not me, "I have discovered a pattern to your advocacy. You would educate servants and find honor in common soldiers. It seems you encourage people to rise above their station. Perhaps you are close to someone with such aspirations?"

Her tone was acid—an attack on Jane. But I must be mistaken. Even Miss Bingley would not dare such rudeness in front of her brother and Mr. Darcy. Jane was a gentlewoman, the social equal of Mr. Bingley.

"I cannot imagine to what you refer," I said coldly.

"Oh, I forgot. It was a conversation we had without you. Charles, do you remember? How an otherwise sweet girl could be ruined by her mother's scheming for marriage gold?"

Mr. Bingley's earlobes turned red, a color that spread to his cheeks. Mr. Darcy became as still as ice.

Now I understood her boldness. The too-quick silence of Mr. Bingley and Mr. Darcy was complicit. They had participated before. Raw embarrassment and sheer fury flushed my skin and left me voiceless.

"Mr. Darcy," she continued gleefully, "you had an observation about a girl who binds draca for prestige. Do you recall it?"

For all my anger with Mr. Darcy, I could not believe a man of good breeding would answer.

His face paled. When he spoke, his voice was a rough whisper. "A woman who binds draca for prestige is intolerable."

Miss Bingley turned to me, her smile vicious and triumphant.

Mr. Darcy continued, as if his words could not be restrained. "Even if she were… astonishing… she could never be my wyfe."

Miss Bingley's smile vanished. She spun and echoed, "*Your* wyfe?"

Into the silence, Mr. Hurst spoke, his port-addled mind stuck on our prior conversation. "Honor is not required in a common soldier. Wellesley tells them to charge, and they do as ordered. Or they are shot."

My anger at Mr. Darcy and Miss Bingley, which I could not express without profound embarrassment, now flew at a target—Mr. Hurst, whom I detested as much as any of them.

"Mr. Wellesley succeeds because of his regard for his troops," I said. "He is renowned for his defensive strategy."

Mr. Hurst blinked at me around a nose crisscrossed with port-colored veins. "Am I to be told military strategy by a *woman*?"

"I see no uniforms in this room." I turned to Mr. Darcy, seeking revenge. "But I forgot. Mr. Darcy had an observation on this. Do you recall it? I shall remind you: 'Honor is measured in the man, not the uniform.' I thank you for letting me measure the man."

"Be careful," Mr. Hurst said with a snort. "Darcy knows Wellesley."

"*You* know Arthur Wellesley?" I said, incredulous, for Mr. Wellesley was England's greatest field commander and no socialite.

"I have that honor," Mr. Darcy said. His gaze had been on the floor since he answered Miss Bingley, and he did not look up.

"And you compare military strategy over cards?" I said, so angry that I was having difficulty restraining myself.

"No." His gaze, at last, met mine. "Not over cards."

"Darcy, tell her," came Mr. Hurst's slurred voice. "Wellesley succeeds by whipping his soldiers to charge. Not through some pretty idea of '*regard for his troops.*'"

"I see no need to adjudicate a disagreement when one party obviously has the superior understanding," Mr. Darcy said. His dark brown eyes never left mine. Because it was unexpected, it took me a moment to understand that he supported me. That only left me frustrated, for I would have loved a fresh provocation.

Mr. Hurst mumbled something gratified, assuming himself vindicated. But Mrs. Hurst turned to me.

"Miss Bennet," Mrs. Hurst said, "the room has become very warm. I was about to step outside. Will you join me?"

I did not trust that she was well intentioned, but I was all too happy to have an excuse to leave.

A MAID FOLLOWED us out the front door into the early evening. Mrs. Hurst stopped a few paces from the stone draca house. The Hursts' lindworm emerged.

"Stay well back, Miss Eliza," she said. "It is a powerful beast, quite unlike your little drake with its fluttering wings. Even I hesitate to approach closer than this."

The maid passed her a bundle, a rabbit still in its fur and trussed with twine. It twitched, and I realized it was alive. And terrified.

Without a word, she tossed the poor animal to the lindworm, who killed it with a snap of her jaws and began to eat. It was quick enough, but an unnecessary and cruel ritual.

"The rabbit is quite overmatched, do you not think?" Mrs. Hurst said. "It should have remained in its little hole, rather than walking through miles of dirt to flaunt its courage."

It took a moment to believe this was intended to be clever and to intimidate me.

"Unoriginal wit becomes dull," I said. "I should vary the theme from dirt, to keep an edge. Perhaps… My lindworm is bored, for *she*—your lindworm is a female, not an '*it*'—for she is accustomed to London's society, and here she must amuse herself by rending some poor country mouse. Or… do not the scales on my lindworm shine? They remind me of Miss Bingley's golden hair. The rabbit's dark fur—what remains of it—is poor by comparison."

I sank down on my heels, allowing my skirts to settle to the ground. The lindworm abandoned her meal to come over, and Mrs. Hurst stepped back hurriedly. That could have fueled amusing comments, but I had lost interest in sparring.

If a bound draca does not love its wyfe and master, why stay? This lindworm will devote decades to the Hursts. Is she a servant? A slave? Is it like marriage, enforced, whether happy or miserable, by the conventions of some unfathomable draca society?

The lindworm was sitting on her haunches, pondering me while I pondered her. Wondering, perhaps, why I stayed in this house filled with people whom, for the most part, I disliked.

Draca are not creatures to pet or cuddle, but I touched her head, curious to feel her scales again. They are each as hard as a diamond but form a yielding, smooth surface. And warm to my fingers, though no warmer than a dog or cat.

Mrs. Hurst finally spoke. "Naturally, you would be experienced in caring for animals."

It was a brave attempt at sarcasm but, I decided, inferior to her sister's innate skill.

"My family has bound draca for more generations than I can count," I said, mostly to myself. I was thinking of my father's journal. My journal.

The Bingleys, of course, had become gentry when their father earned a fortune in trade.

I stood, and the lindworm returned to her meal. "Please convey my regrets. I must retire to care for my sister."

We departed in the morning, Mr. Darcy and the Bingleys gathering to see us off. I said farewell to our little maid, of whom I had become quite fond, and she bobbed a curtsy, looking forlorn herself. The Longbourn coach arrived, and Mr. Bingley attempted to bury Jane beneath four blankets and three pillows and a tray of warm toast until I laughingly dissuaded him.

While Mr. Bingley helped Jane into the coach, I noticed the Hursts' lindworm lying beneath a shady tree. Her legs were folded and her head alert, reminding me of engravings of the Egyptian Sphinx.

Even with her bound wyfe a few steps away, her attention was fixed on me.

Thank you, I thought, concentrating on the words.

She rose instantly, as if awaiting orders. My vision shivered. I clamped my eyes closed and held a gasped breath. Afterimages of brilliant gold flickered and faded.

The binding of draca is not universally admired. But it is a custom of the powerful aristocracy. So, it is respected.

Widowed wyves who hold draca are rare, and like all women, their rights are circumscribed. They become targets of rage. Populist preachers denounce them, claiming they hold draca through pagan rites or coarse passion—even witchcraft, absurd as that is in the dawn of the nineteenth century. Only women of exceptional standing and wealth survive with their reputations intact. Or survive at all.

The condemnation of an unmarried woman who saw visions and communicated with other wyves' bound draca would be far more fierce. Savage.

Mr. Darcy offered his hand to assist me into the coach, and I took it, only afterward finding that unexpected.

11

Jane stepped down from the coach. Mamma embraced her, then scolded her for not searching the Netherfield gardens for another bee to sting her.

Papa was outside the front door. I squeezed his outstretched hands. "Papa." Never had Longbourn felt like such a haven.

"This cannot be a *daughter* addressing me," he said with profound puzzlement, "for I heard no request for a new dress, nor any story of whose hat blew into the street to be fetched by an officer."

"Surely it has not been so bad!"

"Lizzy, you must not speak sense to me, for I have quite lost my capacity. If you continue, I shall reel about like a spinster after a glass of wine."

There was an obsequious cough. I turned to an unfamiliar man in a clergyman's black suit and white collar.

"This will steady me," my father added *sotto voce*, before raising his voice. "Mr. Collins, may I introduce my second daughter, Elizabeth. Mr. Collins is my cousin, whom I did not have the joy of meeting until today. He will visit with us this week."

"Mr. Collins," I said, curtsying. Then I recalled why the name was familiar. Due to the entailment, Mr. Collins would inherit Longbourn when our draca left and we lost our status as bound gentry.

It was strange to meet the person my mother had vilified so many times over dinner. Mr. Collins was a rounded man, with a rounded, perspiring pate even though the day was not warm. I thought his age mid-twenties, although his brown hair was already wispy. In his favor, he was at least a fair height.

Abruptly, he lurched forward, and I found my hand grasped in sweaty fingers. His height reduced precipitously, as he had been standing on the front step.

"Miss Elizabeth Bennet," he said with such pompous ceremony that I prepared a laugh before realizing he was quite serious.

Mamma escorted Jane past us without even introducing her, which was very improper, not to mention unfair. I stood, my fingers trapped, listening with growing bewilderment while Mr. Collins began chronicling the Bennet family's history of binding.

At last, Mr. Collins's eyes lifted rhapsodically to praise one Lady Catherine de Bourgh. When it was clear his gaze was locked skyward—perhaps her ladyship resided on a local cloud?—I mouthed "*Papa!*" to my father, requesting an escape.

My father had observed silently, stroking his chin. Now, he asked if Jane and I had broken our fast. We had not, so, with effusive apologies and much bowing, Mr. Collins ushered me into my own home.

MARY CAUGHT my eye while we sat down to breakfast, and she bent her head to whisper.

"Lizzy, be warned. Mr. Collins is—"

She was interrupted by Mamma calling from the end of the table. "Jane! Lizzy! Have you heard of the draca death?"

"I was there, Mamma," I said, recalling yesterday's frightening episode with the roseworm.

"No! Another, last night. And there were spies!"

Jane and I looked at each other in shock. After no draca deaths in my lifetime, there had been three in two days. Charlotte's mention of a plague seemed prescient and worrying.

"What do you mean, spies?" I asked.

Kitty answered with great excitement. "Napoleon has sent spies to steal draca! Two were killed last night, trying to take the Linfield family's draca."

Her face fell. "Oh, but the creature was killed also. It is very sad, and I feel so sorry for all of them."

I had met the Linfields once. They lived on the other side of Hertfordshire, ten miles from Longbourn.

There was no further news of draca, but Jane revealed that Mr. Bingley planned a ball at Netherfield, which delighted the ladies.

Then Mr. Collins spoke.

I learned that Lady Catherine de Bourgh was the patroness for his living and rectory, and that she lived not in the sky but in an astonishing manor that was extravagantly burnished with gold while being perfectly tasteful, and that she was the paragon of behavior for a person of exalted rank, showing gracious affability while demanding the utmost in decorum from her inferiors, of which there were many.

After breakfast, I suggested a walk to Meryton for news of the draca deaths. Kitty and Lydia agreed, but Jane was not yet fit for a long walk, and Mary had vanished to practice her music. I suspected she avoided Mr. Collins.

I had no such luck, and our departure required an elaborate leave-taking. Mr. Collins explained in intense detail that, although he walked extensively for his constitution, he did not walk so soon after breakfast.

In Meryton, the talk was all of the draca deaths. I learned that the apothecary, Mr. Jones, had attended the Linfield family after their tragedy. I left Kitty and Lydia, and hurried to his shop.

"A dreadful business, Miss Bennet," he said, after confirming that Jane's recovery was progressing well.

"Were they spies?" That seemed farfetched.

"Two men were found, dead. I examined them, as did the constable. Whether they were spies, I cannot say. Nobody knew them, although it was hard to judge in their condition. They had encountered the Linfields' worm, and one was burned savagely and killed outright, and the other seriously burned on his legs."

"But he was not killed?"

"The second man was shot. My professional opinion was a pistol to the head, and very close. The constable speculated there was a third conspirator, who killed his wounded friend because he would have slowed escape."

"How horrible. And the Linfield draca dead, as well. Was there..." This would sound strange, but I asked anyway. "Did you detect an odor? Like sour orange and bitter almond?"

"From the dead draca, you mean? No, nothing like that. It was shot. A good marksman, or lucky, for it was pierced through the eye."

I thanked him and wandered to find Kitty and Lydia. At least this draca death was not part of a plague. But Napoleon sending spies into Hertfordshire was incredible. We were north of London, far from any sensible port for a French spy.

I spotted the red-and-gold-piping of uniforms and went in pursuit, rewarded by finding Lydia and Kitty with Denny and several friends, one of whom was Mr. Wickham. Lydia surrendered him with a glare.

He winced as he reached for my offered arm. Instead, he stepped around me to take the other.

"I burned myself on a kettle," he explained with a rueful smile. "But injuries from tea are very respectable and English. Or so my fellow officers explained when they discovered the truth, to their loud amusement." I laughed, for he was wry, and handsome in his modesty.

The mysterious draca deaths soon became a topic.

"Do you think they were Napoleon's spies?" I asked.

"Bonaparte has offered tremendous sums to any man who delivers a living, bound draca. The French have none, and they fear the English will succeed in using them for war."

"But what use is a lone draca? Especially one that has been bound."

"You are right. Bonaparte is a fool. He seeks a bound animal because feral draca are no more than dangerous vermin. But a bound draca is also useless, as it will fight to return to its master."

"You are well informed on draca."

"As a child, I was a great friend to the Pemberley gamekeeper, who was as knowledgeable of draca as any man."

"Pemberley!" I exclaimed.

He crooked a half-smile. "I gather you recognize Mr. Darcy's estate. I grew up at Pemberley. My father was steward to Mr. Darcy's father. Darcy and I were like brothers." My shock must have been visible, for he added,

"You must be surprised after our cold meeting yesterday. Do you know Mr. Darcy well?"

"As well as I ever wish to," I said, a little heatedly. "I have spent four days in the same house with him, which was more than enough."

"I had thought Darcy a friend, but I discovered otherwise after the death of his father. The late Mr. Darcy bequeathed to me a generous living as administrator of the primitive Britons who scrape out an existence in the Pemberley hills. But when the affairs were settled, Darcy gave the position to another."

"Good heavens! He should be disgraced!"

"Wealth is powerful insulation against disgrace. I chose to make my own way in life. It was Darcy's betrayal that set me on my path to the militia, and so, to walk with you today. I should thank him." He bowed, and I tried not to color.

We strolled while I inserted this piece of despicable news into my mental puzzle of Mr. Darcy. For all that I disliked him, disregarding a father's bequest seemed out of character. But with some bending and prying, I shoved the defect into place.

Mr. Wickham was also pensive. "It is ironic that three draca are lost when Bonaparte would pay so handsomely for one. A superior breed, such as your firedrake, is very desirable. I hazard you have the most valuable creature in Hertfordshire. Rumor says Bonaparte would pay fifty thousand pounds for a drake."

"Goodness!" That sum would vault a family into wealth. But I was sure no gentry would part with their bound draca, and especially not to assist the French. "Perhaps the militia should set guards."

"I have proposed it, but the military is slow to act. So, we must all be on our guard. I have done a little on my own, when idle. Patrolling for miscreants." He gestured with self-mocking humor but winced when he flexed his burned arm.

And I had a ridiculous, but entertaining, thought—Lieutenant Wickham on secret patrol, thwarting a pair of French spies. Or three, or however many there were.

12

Jane traced her finger over the faint lines embossed on the journal's cover. "You see? On the journal, the chest is open, not closed."

We had borrowed one of my father's custom-bound books for reference. It showed the Longbourn crest: a wyvern rearing, clutching a chest in its claws.

On both the book and the journal, the chest was a strongbox with straps and a keyhole. But the Longbourn chest was closed and held tight to the wyvern's body, as if precious. On the journal, not only was the chest open, it was tipped upside down.

"It is as if the artist wished to show the chest is empty," I said. "Perhaps the ancient Bennets were poor."

"An impoverished family that chose penury for their symbol?" Even Jane, polite to a fault, sounded dubious.

"Well, said like that, it seems unlikely."

"I think it indicates discarding the contents. Charity?"

"Does it matter? If this is the only difference, I do not think it is a different crest. Just a variation, after many years and many copies."

"But look..." Jane touched the letters that spelled Longbourn. "There is a gap as if it is two words, 'Long bourn.' And I am unconvinced the first word is 'Long' at all."

The script was elaborate and almost illegible from age, with the 'g' in particular extending both high and low. I squinted, unsure. "It must be Longbourn. This is a journal of the Bennet family and the Longbourn estate."

"Yes..." Jane seemed unwilling to give up her argument. She placed a sheet of paper on the cover and rubbed it with a bit of charcoal. Rubbings of leaves and bark were in fashion, so we had supplies. She held it in the light but looked more puzzled.

THE DAY of the long-awaited Netherfield ball arrived. Really, we waited only three days, but every one was excruciating. Mr. Collins could stretch a minute into an hour. I had gone so far as to ask what times he recommended for exercise, then reversed that for my own walks.

But Mr. Bingley had asked Jane when she would be able to dance comfortably, then scheduled the ball for that date, so I had no complaint about his method.

The ball would be a grand affair. Even my father was attending, although he would sit most of the evening. This made a party of eight, for Mr. Collins would come also, and we had hired a second carriage to carry us all.

Evening fell, and the carriages pulled up. Wary eyes assessed Mr. Collins. When he walked to the first carriage, there was a scramble for the second. I was fast, so I should have won a seat, but Mamma barred the way with a stern expression. Despondent, Jane, Mary, and I turned to ride with Mr. Collins.

My mother patted my arm. "Do not be vexed, Lizzy. I have explained to Mr. Collins that Jane is soon to be engaged."

I did not see why Jane's engagement should matter to Mr. Collins, but that was the least of my concerns. "Mamma, promise me you will not speak like that at the ball. Discussion of Jane's engagement is premature and improper."

"Nonsense! It is common knowledge."

"What?" I said as she vanished into her carriage.

"Society's gossip is a wicked thing," Mary said. "The search for anonymous approval by the ill-informed is a great waste of the creative spirit."

"I agree," I said, then added, "You look nice, Mary." Her gown was dark velvet. Although that was an odd color for a ball, it was accented with bright blue, and her hair was done up with a ribbon embroidered in musical notes. The ribbon was beautiful; she must have saved to afford it. She held her music satchel, and I knew she was excited to perform. With luck, I could surrender my opportunity to her as well.

I had also dressed carefully, imagining dances with Mr. Wickham in his scarlet uniform. I wore ivory muslin with silk trim, and my hair up with ribbons and a pearled comb.

We arrived, and I circulated twice through the rooms without seeing Mr. Wickham. Finally, his friend Lieutenant Denny nodded to me.

"Wickham is on another of his mysterious woodland excursions," he said, and added with a significant smile, "Although he might have attended had he not wanted to avoid a certain gentleman."

Lydia swept Denny away to explore the food, and I was left irritated and alone. But Netherfield was a grand setting for a ball, so I resolved to admire it and enjoy the evening.

I heard an obsequious cough and turned, smiling, before recognizing the source.

"I hope to be honored, fair cousin," Mr. Collins said, heaving into an exaggerated bow, "when I take this opportunity to solicit your hand for the two first dances."

I had avoided other inquisitive glances already, thinking that clever while looking for Mr. Wickham, so I had no excuse to decline. Fuming at myself, I accepted. But two dances was a cruel commitment, so I found Charlotte and demanded sympathy.

"Ask me again," she said, "when I have been asked. Then I shall be more sympathetic."

"You will be asked, Charlotte!" But my encouragement embarrassed me. There were more ladies than gentlemen, and we chatted until the dance without anyone asking her.

Mr. Collins escorted me to the floor, and I wondered if I should hint that he ask Charlotte next. Then we danced, and I realized I should protect Charlotte from him at all costs. My feet were trampled upon and adjacent couples were collided with. I had to duck through the passes, for Mr. Collins was shorter even than me.

At last, Mr. Collins succeeded in knocking my pearled comb from my hair, and we had to scramble among frantic feet to catch it. I set it back in place with great care—so much care that we were too late to join the second dance. I expressed my disappointment profusely.

Rather frayed, I found Charlotte again.

"If only Mr. Wickham had come," I sighed.

"Are you so entranced with him?" Charlotte said.

"Entranced?" I considered. "I enjoy him. But I do not think I am entranced." Although I missed having a handsome officer to dance with, I could not summon any profound loss. That was concerning. It would be a pity to lose my moral superiority over Lydia.

"I do not like Wickham," Charlotte said. "He asked fawning questions about my mother and grandmother's bindings when he visited. He even admired our tunnelworm, the poor thing." Their draca must have died soon after that.

"Well, fawning is better than Mr. Darcy." I folded my arms. "He was most disagreeable when I was caring for Jane."

"You should not allow your fancy for Wickham to overcome your judgment. Mr. Darcy is ten times his consequence." I snorted at that, and Charlotte added, "Just consider your choice."

"It is not a *choice*. And the only advantage I can imagine for Mr. Darcy is that he is very tall, so he should not send my pearled comb flying."

"Lizzy…" she said in a warning tone.

"But tall or short, I may safely promise you *never* to dance with—"

"Lizzy!" hissed Charlotte desperately.

With a horrible premonition, I turned as Mr. Darcy arrived. I had to adjust my gaze upward, so I had a good view of his silver-and-pearl buttons and the black velvet edging of his jacket, then his high silk collars, before I reached his eyes.

"Miss Elizabeth Bennet," he said, unsmiling, "if you are not already engaged, would you honor me with the next dance."

I had been too surprised to curtsy at his arrival, so I curtsied, or perhaps I nodded, and he nodded gravely and left, and it seemed the matter was settled.

Charlotte's face was a study in suppressed mirth.

"I defy you to laugh at me," I warned.

Jane arrived breathlessly to ask, with sisterly consternation, if I had agreed to dance with Mr. Darcy. And then Charlotte could not help herself.

At last, wiping her eyes, she finished with, "I dare say you will find him agreeable."

"Heaven forbid!" I said. "To find a man agreeable whom one is determined to hate? Do not wish me such an evil."

To my delight, a gentleman asked Charlotte for the next dance. I gave myself some of the credit because Charlotte looked so charming while mocking me.

The musicians were ready, and Mr. Darcy accompanied me to the dance floor. We joined one of three squares for an extended cotillion. There were many glances from the room. In all his time in our society, Mr. Darcy had danced only twice: once with Miss Bingley, and once with Mrs. Hurst.

I tried to riddle his invitation. For better or worse, he had conversed more with me than anyone else in the neighborhood. Perhaps that merited a single dance of my own.

The music began. He danced well, which did not surprise me. Soon the patterns proceeded by rote.

Equally unsurprising, he was also silent. But that meant I had to debate which would annoy him more, outlasting his silence, or breaking it.

"Do you enjoy the cotillion?" I said at last, as we passed.

"Yes," he said, at the next pass, expressionless.

We passed twice more, and I began to smile. "It is your turn, Mr. Darcy. Shall I fetch a book of draca illustrations to spark your interest?"

There was a flicker of smile. "You declared me dismissive of draca."

I realized this topic led toward our argument at Netherfield—an argument whose passes included draca and Mr. Wickham.

By our next pass, Mr. Darcy's face was stern. Perhaps he remembered also.

We met, and he held my gloved hands. His grip was taut.

"I spoke improperly in our last conversation," he said. "Obsession with draca may be selfish and evil. But for others, it may be… inevitable. Preordained."

"Do you accuse me of obsession?" I asked, uneasy, as this brushed events I thought secret.

"I warn of those who pursue draca for self-importance. Or for darker purposes."

"I am afraid I do not understand."

"My sister—" he began, then missed a step and had to stretch to take my hand and correct the pattern. At once, his dancing became perfect again, and silent again, for several passes.

The cotillion is a refined dance, and it suited his posture, which was not stiff like a parading soldier, but exact and balanced. I thought of the stage fencing in *Hamlet*, and of our drake when he struck the mad dog.

The music ended with each couple holding hands. The other couples parted. Mr. Darcy did not release my fingers. This indicated he wished to continue our conversation.

"Your sister?" I prompted.

He dropped my hand. "I spoke out of turn. My apologies." He bowed deeply and strode away.

Jane approached with a mischievous smile. "Was Charlotte correct? Did you find him agreeable?"

"No."

"He danced well."

"Dancing, in itself, is insufficient to make one agreeable."

"Of course. But what is the cause of your dislike?"

"He is very *tall*," I said, and Jane laughed. Warming to my subject, I began a list. "Overly clever. Too well-mannered to expose his true thoughts. He intimidates with his dark eyes and sharp cheekbones, is impeccably dressed, and is fabulously wealthy."

"I begin to comprehend your intense dislike."

"In truth, my dislike is unchanged from my first meeting. He is self-satisfied and haughty. But now, he is also mysterious, which I further dislike because the subject is draca, so it makes me curious." Mr. Darcy's tall shoulders were heading toward Miss Bingley. He cut a broad wake through the crowd. "When we are home, I should like to share a confidence from Mr. Wickham. But how is your evening? I saw you take the first dance with Mr. Bingley. Will that be all?"

"He has requested the final dance also." Jane's eyes were lowered, but she smiled.

"Well, do not tell Mamma, or she will say something quite untoward." Dancing both the first and last dance was a serious statement.

"Oh, Lizzy, I fear she is already talking!" But before Jane could say more, Mr. Collins arrived.

"Cousin Elizabeth, may I commend you on your charming society. This room is a delightful, if inferior, likeness of Lady Catherine de Bourgh's smallest dance room. And I have made a great discovery! While you danced, I overheard that your partner is nephew to my patroness."

"Mr. Darcy is Lady Catherine's nephew?" Mr. Collins's endless praise had painted an amusing picture of her infamous ladyship, but I suppose it was possible. She had wealth enough.

"I shall introduce myself!" Mr. Collins announced. "I will justify my presumption and set him at ease through praise of her ladyship's extraordinary draca."

"At ease!" I could not invent a less likely phrase to describe Mr. Darcy, particularly if the topic was draca. But Mr. Collins was already marching to Mr. Darcy, who was conversing with Miss Bingley.

Openmouthed, Jane and I watched Mr. Collins hem and haw until Mr. Darcy turned. There was a great bowing and fluttering, observed with astonishment by both Mr. Darcy and Miss Bingley. Astonishment became shock as Mr. Collins began flapping his arms, apparently enacting the flight of a winged draca.

"We must intervene!" I said to Jane and began walking, desperately inventing a pretense to take Mr. Collins away.

So, I was close enough to hear when he turned to Miss Bingley and said, "And allow me to congratulate you on your brother's superior bounty of marriage gold. We anticipate a most prestigious binding when he is joined to my fair cousin Jane."

I stopped dead halfway across the dance floor.

Miss Bingley's face convulsed in anger.

Mr. Darcy's lips twisted in revulsion. With utter disdain, he turned his back. Even Mr. Collins's impaired social judgment registered the cut. He halted his soliloquy, jaw hanging.

Miss Bingley's furious laugh ripped the room as she swirled away.

Jane arrived beside me. "Poor Mr. Collins."

"Poor Mr. *Collins?*" I said, incredulous.

"It is not so bad, Lizzy. People will forget his peculiar flapping."

Jane had not been close enough to hear. But soon enough, she would know. At least a dozen people had been agog at the drama.

Mr. Collins rejoined us. "I am greatly pleased with my reception," he blurted, then wiped his beaded forehead with a handkerchief. "Recalling the conversation, I realize how highly he valued my report on Lady Catherine's—"

I could stand no more and walked away myself.

I ended up beside Mary, who was waiting her turn to perform on the pianoforte. Mary would be a relief from gossip, at least.

"I am quite relying on you for a wonderful report of the evening," I said. "Mine has been horrible."

"Do not practice your wit on me, Lizzy." Mary's voice was tight, her eyes bright with unshed tears.

"I did not intend wit." Had she already heard what had happened? "Jane—"

"Jane has danced every dance, and she and Bingley are in love. Should Bingley fall out of love with her, a parade of gentlemen awaits."

I reviewed the evening and realized what was wrong. "Has no one asked you to dance?" Mary's stiff silence was answer enough. "It is of no consequence. Perhaps next time, a light-colored frock—"

Mary turned on me. "Spare me the pity of a beauty!" I was speechless as she continued, "Witty Elizabeth Bennet, admired by men and dodging invitations with a laugh, then caught by the most elusive man at the ball. You do not comprehend what it is to *wish* you were wanted. Instead, you waste your intellect insulting suitors so they can marvel at your nerve."

"What is this, Mary?" I was hurt, and shocked, and frightened for Mary as well, as her voice was rising.

"*This*"—she swung her hand in an accusing arc, and heads turned toward us—"is a joke. And I am the object of the joke, for this chase is the greatest falseness of my life, and yet I envy your perfect success. And I am ashamed of my envy."

"Mary, I spoke thoughtlessly. I… there is some truth in how you accuse me. But do not accuse yourself of envy when it is only frustration. A public scene is no solution—"

"No? Shall I find the solution by standing, scorned for dull features and lank hair, at more dances? Shall I simper and flutter to attract a gentleman, when their attention repulses me? I hide my feelings and become an invisible fraud. What choice do I have? I am lonely, Lizzy, and I am not brave. The prospect of a life alone frightens me, as does surviving on fifty pounds a year if our estate is lost. And that is selfishness, for that sum would be wealth for the maids sharing our roof." She dashed tears from her eyes. "If

I were a man, I would go to London, or Paris, or New York, and I would… do *something* that mattered! Do you not see how unfair it is? Mamma bargains you off to secure our luxury, and I should rejoice because it frees me from this charade—even though I know you should refuse. I am a laughingstock for wearing a velvet dress, while around us, even in Hertfordshire, people die of hunger and cold…" She stopped, her spray of fury exhausted, a fire kicked into lifeless cinders. She finished, "Are you even *aware?*"

I had not known she felt any of this. I did not know what to say. What stumbled out was an answer to her last question. "You cannot think me so callous as to be unaware of the inequity of suffering."

"No. I think you only complacent."

The lady playing the pianoforte had stopped to stare, and she fled when Mary pulled a piece of music from her satchel and advanced to the instrument. Mary's satchel fell to the floor, and music scores flew. Mechanically, I knelt to gather them. I knew she treasured them.

Mary began to play.

I recognized the notes, something strange and new that she had practiced every day for weeks, like scales. But never like this. Not at speed, and angry. Defiant.

I rose, my arms full of music too challenging for me ever to attempt, while Mary's final accusation, *complacent*, burned deeper and deeper, and her music rolled over me like nothing I had ever heard. It was wonderful. Incredible. This was no Italian air, with the composer's words replaced by English doggerel in a pathetic nod to English patriotism. This was raw emotion, Mary's accusation pounded into the keys. There were tears on her cheeks as she played, and on mine.

Then, I saw the room around her.

People were smirking and laughing. And, cruelly, their grins made me hear the music through their ears—notes missed and tempo wavering, the passion that moved me overwhelming accuracy and control.

Our father was seated near me, as stunned as anyone. I ran to him.

"Papa, please, she is so upset. This will become a dreadful scene. Can you not do something?"

He nodded, and I helped him stand. He walked to the pianoforte and made a show of listening. But I did not understand his pose. It was almost… comic.

He removed the music in front of Mary and leafed through it with exaggerated confusion. The audience tittered. After a few bars, Mary's playing stuttered into silence. She sat, staring where the sheets had been.

"How very modern," he said and got a resounding laugh.

I was unable to move. Unable to believe the man I adored could be so inhuman.

Mary stood and cried out, "Enlightenment demands introspection into our shared humanity and emotion, regardless of class, or sex—"

"That will do extremely well, child," Papa interrupted. "We do not attend a ball to hear female philosophy. You have delighted us long enough. Let the other young ladies perform." This received a few amused claps, and Papa pretended a bow.

With a strangled wail, Mary fled. I ran after her.

Mamma found us outside Netherfield manor. Mary was sobbing in my arms. The valets and coachmen had turned away to provide a semblance of privacy. That was more consideration than we received from the gentry inside.

"What is happening, Lizzy? Everyone is gossiping a storm!"

"I am taking Mary home," I said.

"*Now?* The ball is not over. You cannot leave!"

"Mary is distraught. I have called for a coach. We are going, Mamma."

"Oh, very well. I shall have to go also. I will go and plead headache, and say you two are accompanying me. But Jane must stay for her final dance."

I was braced for a fight, so I was too surprised to answer. I watched our mother go in, then said, "Wait here, Mary. I shall return momentarily."

I climbed the front steps, and two footmen in Bingley livery swung the Netherfield doors wide for me.

Inside, I found my father chatting with two other gentlemen. He looked more animated than I had seen him in weeks.

The men fell silent when they saw my expression. I held out my hand for the music my father still held. He offered it slowly.

"How *dare* you," I said.

He called my name as I left.

As I reached the door, Mr. Darcy's voice came behind me, "Miss Bennet!" I was ready to curse then, but I stopped without turning.

He arrived beside me. I did not look at him.

"Please tell your sister that she played with great passion," he said.

That was too much.

"Have you discovered an interest in Mary? That is remarkable, for you ignored her for two hours while she hoped one gentleman would have the decency to take her hand and utter a few civilities on the dance floor." I turned to him. "Speak to me again when you have defended a heartbroken sister."

13

Jane remained at the ball even though gossip of Mr. Collins's humiliating claims circulated to her soon after we left. She braved the whispers but was not approached by Mr. Bingley until their final dance.

"It was so awkward," she told me, late that night in our room. "We said almost nothing, and at the end, he bowed over my hand and was gone. Oh, Lizzy, I think he is furious."

"I do not believe it," I said. "Not Mr. Bingley. Or if he is angry, it is not with you. He loves you too much."

At that, Jane finally began to cry, and I comforted her a long time before we slept.

But, when the morning sun lit our window, I was optimistic and told her so. Jane had done nothing wrong. And I was certain I knew Mr. Bingley's feelings. What harm could the ruffled pride of his sister achieve?

We went down to breakfast and found my sisters, my mother, and Mr. Collins. Only my father was missing, having requested a tray in his library. Hiding, in other words.

Mary was red-eyed but resolute. Mamma and Mr. Collins were fidgety and silent—a relief, but peculiar.

Mamma ate a single bite of toast, then stood. "Come girls! I want you upstairs." I rose, but she said, "No, Lizzy. I insist you stay." Mystified, I watched them troop out the doorway.

As Mary passed, she bent and whispered fiercely in my ear, "Do not surrender!"

Surrender what? If they were not back soon, I would have to eat breakfast alone with Mr. Collins. Surrender my sanity, most likely.

With a sigh, I prepared for a most dull morning.

To the empty room, Mr. Collins stridently announced, "Miss Elizabeth Bennet!"

I jumped a foot. "Yes?" I said, then tried, "I am… here?"

"You can hardly doubt the purport of my discourse," he said with great enthusiasm. "My attentions have been too marked to be mistaken!"

The only object of marked attention I saw was the piece of toast he was waving in one hand. The butter was already beside him, so I moved the marmalade within reach, achieving the last two inches by pushing with an extended finger, for he was not seated very close.

"My dear Miss Elizabeth, your modesty only adds to your other perfections!"

My mouth fell open in complete astonishment, and he continued:

"Almost as soon as I entered this house, I singled you out as the companion of my future life! But perhaps it would be advisable for me to state my reasons for marrying—and, moreover, for coming to Hertfordshire to select a wyfe."

A wyfe? Just in time, I realized I must not laugh, so I clapped a hand over my lips. But that prevented any attempt to stop him, and he was off again.

"My reasons for marrying are… *first,* it is a right thing for every clergyman…"

He continued in this vein, but I was now reviewing his visit in my mind. Had I given the slightest impression of interest in marriage? He paid more attention to me than my sisters, but I had attributed that to a clergyman's effort to reform the worst of the lot.

"…as I am to inherit this estate after the death of your honored father, I resolved to choose a wyfe from among his daughters, that the loss might be lessened when the melancholy event takes place…"

Oh.

If I said yes, and we bound a draca, Longbourn would be secured for my family.

The import sank in. My mother's behavior. And Mary's warnings. What an idiot I was not to anticipate this.

I rolled that back and forth for a few minutes. I was practiced at ignoring Mr. Collins, so his endless monologue was no distraction.

I could never marry Mr. Collins. I should rather be a maid to support my destitute family. But what if my parents insisted? Perhaps I could accompany Mary and drag her harpsichord across the American plains.

"… and *third*… although perhaps, I should have stated this first… so, *first!* Lady Catherine de Bourgh, as mistress of the most exalted draconian breed, a wyvern—"

"Lady Catherine has a *wyvern*?" I interrupted.

He came to a stumbling stop. I could not blame him for being surprised. I had said nothing thus far. I suppose, as a preacher, he could sermonize for an hour even if I were asleep.

"Her ladyship, indeed, has a wyvern," he answered.

"Is she not widowed?"

"Lady Catherine de Bourgh is blessed with such formidable strength of will and institutional grandeur that she has retained her bound draca, even after her husband's premature death."

Now I thought of it, I had heard her name in this context years ago. Perhaps Mr. Collins's effusive praise was merited. There were less than a half-dozen draca held by widowed wyves in all of England.

"Have you *seen* her wyvern?" I asked.

He was taken aback. "Do you… doubt my explanation?"

"Of course not. I am just curious. How large is it?"

He seemed unsettled by the direction of our conversation, but, gamely, he put down his toast and held his hands several feet apart. "The body would be… like this? Understand, I do not approach, for it is a most formid—"

"Would you describe it as *intelligent*? More than our firedrake, or less?"

"Intelligent? It is a beast."

"Quite," I said absently. Would it be possible to visit? Mr. Collins was watching me expectantly, so I waved him on. "You were saying?"

He took a breath. "*Third*… no, first… but we must be further…" His lips pursed in puzzlement.

I could see he had lost his place. Then I remembered the seriousness of this conversation, for him at least, if not for me, and I felt a stab of guilt.

"Mr. Collins—"

But he had found his stride again. "I shall now assure you in the *most* animated language of the violence of my affection—"

"Mr. Collins, sir!" I interrupted. "You forget that I have made no answer. Let me do so now. Accept my thanks for this honor, but it is impossible for me to do otherwise than to decline."

His lips opened and closed several times before his indefatigable self-assuredness, or maybe it was willful self-deception, returned. He waved my words aside.

"I understand it is usual for young ladies to reject the man whom they secretly mean to accept, when he first applies for their favor."

"Mr. Collins, I assure you—"

"And that sometimes the refusal is repeated a second or even a third time. I am therefore by no means discouraged, as I shall lead you to the altar before long!"

"*Three* times! I promise you that if such young ladies exist, I am not one of them. I am perfectly serious in refusing you. You could not make me happy, and I am the last woman in the world who could make you so."

"But Lady Catherine de Bourgh herself has blessed a union with your family. She wishes that I marry gentry and bind draca to maintain the prestige of her estate. She considers your familial history of binding most encouraging."

"How would she know *that?*"

"Her ladyship has condescended to advise my search for a wyfe. From her unique perspective, she values most highly the wyfe's lineage for a superior outcome."

That was intriguing, but I refused to lose sight of my objective. "I am certain she would not approve of me. Throughout your visit, I have many times demonstrated"—what would the stuffy Lady Catherine abhor?—"impertinence. No, wait… reformist sympathies!" That was much better.

I had succeeded in triggering a concerned expression, but at that moment, my mother burst through the door.

"Lizzy! I demand you attend me immediately. Outside!"

And thus, to battle. I listened to my mother in the hallway, but I was stony-faced, and cross that she had not even warned me.

But my heart sank when she said, "We shall see what your father thinks!"

The library door was open. That was unusual. Papa always required that we knock. He looked solemn, sitting at his desk and not even reading. I became nervous.

"Papa…" I began.

"Oh, Mr. Bennet!" Mamma broke in. "You must make Lizzy marry Mr. Collins, for she vows she will not have him, and she is our next prettiest and eldest after Jane, who of course is all but engaged already, and if you do not make haste, Mr. Collins will change his mind and not have her!"

"Mary has been to see me," he answered.

"Mary has nothing to do with it!" cried Mamma.

"Mary has offered to play only Italian airs, and wear white frocks, and make no more scenes that embarrass our family."

"Well, that would be a great relief, but I—"

"Please wait a little, Mrs. Bennet. It is to Lizzy that I speak."

I was angry at him now, remembering last night. "I am surprised that chastising Mary would achieve that result. I thought I knew my sister better."

"There was no chastisement. She arrived of her own accord to offer her promise to improve our social standing, in exchange for a promise from me. However, I declined the bargain, and instead, I apologized to her for last night. Her bargain shamed me, for I should not wish a beloved daughter to act so against her inclinations and beliefs. It is not Mary's responsibility to defend her sister"—he nodded to indicate me—"by bargaining with her inadequate father. I should defend my own children."

"Defend them from poverty and homelessness, I should hope!" cried my mother.

But I understood. Mary had been willing to sacrifice everything she treasured if Papa would not force me to marry Mr. Collins. As if the scraps of social standing she could offer were any recompense for the huge loss to our fortunes from my refusal.

"Come, Mrs. Bennet," Papa said gently, pushing to his feet and extending his arm to my mother, whose face was falling as she understood. "Let us have tea and commiserate with Mr. Collins. He shall not be sending any happy letter to Lady Catherine today, for I can spare you the trouble of suggesting Mary as an alternate, and if you can convince Kitty or Lydia to marry Mr. Collins, I shall be amazed."

14

It was a little past dawn. I was, once again, standing in mud in front of our draca house. Winter in Hertfordshire is a damp affair. But this time, I had a clearer conscience.

"I have been reviewing the circumstances when I felt draca thoughts," I said conversationally. Our firedrake tilted his bronze, narrow head. "They have been moments of extreme urgency, or at least high emotion. So—"

A contralto shriek rose behind me. "Miss Elizabeth! What have you *done?*"

"Mrs. Hill," I said reluctantly. Our housekeeper was staring, aghast, from the front doorway. "They are only boots."

"*Boots?*" Her lips continued to open and close as if reciting an endless row of silent B's.

I had borrowed my father's riding boots, which reached to my knees, and then pinned my innermost petticoat to the outside of my skirt to create a sort of basket, lifting my skirts… well, not *knee*-high of course, but I admit they were above my ankles.

Mrs. Hill's left hand landed on her hip, and her right stabbed at the doorway. "Get inside this instant!"

"I did not want to dirty more skirts…"

"Inside!" she snapped, and I clomped past her guiltily. "What if a neighbor had come?"

"It is so unfair, though, to dirty shoes and stockings and petticoats because—"

"No! No, ma'am, I am putting my foot down! I will button my lip while you chatter at drakes, but I will *not* stand for you traipsing about showing your ankles!" Feeling like a scolded child, I plunked down where the gentlemen removed their boots and reached for mine. She slapped my hand away. "Do not touch those filthy things!"

"Well, what am I supposed to do?" I asked while she pulled them off. "Drag my skirts in the mud every morning? The laundry maids cannot enjoy that."

"The joy of washerwomen is not your concern."

Mrs. Hill had been dumbfounded when I returned from Netherfield and asked to meet the Scottish laundry maid on our next wash day. She seemed offended that I had deduced the existence of wash day at all, even though an entire yard was hung with drying cloth each time.

But now, I frowned at her. It was so… *complacent* to ignore the effort I was causing.

Affection creased her stiff cheeks. "Miss Lizzy. If this must continue, perhaps you could ask your father to place boards by the draca house? Like the walks in Meryton?"

"*That* is a brilliant suggestion. Thank you, Mrs. Hill." Building anything, even a few boards, was so much a gentleman's purview that it had not occurred to me. Instigating the idea felt as bizarre as my father suggesting embroidery for my bonnet.

It was Friday, the day I visit the tenants in Longbourn village. Pondering Mrs. Hill's suggestion, I found Mary seated at our pianoforte but engrossed in a book, and I asked if she would like to come.

Changed to walking dress, we exited Longbourn. I took Mary's hand, and her light brown eyes questioned me from under her black bonnet.

"I am aware of your visit to Papa," I said. "You are too good a sister. And very brave."

She squeezed my hand. "Lizzy, I so regret my words to you at the ball…"

"Hush. We should not be proper sisters without making each other cross on occasion."

We set off arm-in-arm, and I broached the subject on which I wished her advice. We were in deep conversation when Mrs. Trew's cottage came into view. Even so, I noticed a large gray horse with gentleman's riding tack in the adjacent meadow.

"That is Mr. Darcy's horse," I said. Mary's elbow whacked me, and I looked in the direction of her thrust. "That is Mr. Darcy," I added, unnecessarily, as he strode toward us.

"Miss Elizabeth Bennet." His black hair was disheveled from riding and hung when he bowed. "Miss *Mary* Bennet," he said next, with a deep bow. That was an excessively generous greeting for a younger sister, and I heard a surprised breath under Mary's lowered bonnet while she curtsied.

"What brings you to Longbourn village, Mr. Darcy?" I asked warily, for my last words to him had been as I left the Netherfield ball, and they were exceptionally heated. I feared he would mention Mary's humiliating performance.

"Riding," he answered. "Pray do not let me keep you from your tour."

It would have been awkward if he accompanied us. For all practical purposes, we were two ladies on business, which would certainly shock him. Fortunately, he bowed again and went to his horse. I took Mary's arm, and we visited privately with Mrs. Trew.

We emerged and passed Mr. Darcy adjusting his riding tack in the meadow. He approached again, and we repeated our greetings. If he had not seemed so distracted, I would have suspected a satirical purpose.

This time, he asked, "What brings you to Longbourn village?"

Satirical or not, he was becoming inconvenient. If he would not leave us in peace, let him be shocked.

"A smithy," I answered. That jarred his distracted attitude, and I savored my victory. "Or perhaps, a wheelwright. Would you care to see?" I took Mary's arm, and we followed the path to the river that bordered Longbourn estate. Mr. Darcy accompanied us in silence.

"What do you say, Mr. Darcy? Is it a blacksmith or a wheelwright?" There was neither, of course, just a few boards where workers loaded harvests onto the barges that traversed this wide, sleepy stretch of water.

The wonderful thing about Mary is that, once she has begun a topic, she is relentless. As we had begun our discussion while walking, she resumed.

"*I* should say a smithy. Hertfordshire is predominantly rural, so has no concentrated market for a commodity such as wheels. Smiths, by contrast, fabricate custom products, so it is a skilled service."

"The Meryton blacksmith is quite overwhelmed," I explained to Mr. Darcy. "The fashion for iron-barred coaches, perhaps."

"You intend to open a blacksmith?" He seemed stunned.

"Not *myself.* That would not be proper. But it occurs to me that I am perfectly capable of having things built. Why not a smithy in Longbourn village?"

"Farming is hopeless for societal advancement," Mary added, having quite forgotten her audience. "But skilled trade improves wages for the working class, and apprenticeship spreads productive wealth, which is superior to the stagnant wealth of the corrupt aristocracy. It is a virtuous cycle that alleviates generational poverty." She frowned, then amended, "Absent government repression, of course."

"Of course," echoed Mr. Darcy, sounding a little dazed. I assumed he spoke from polite habit, as he was himself a paragon of the corrupt aristocracy. As was our own family, in Mary's eyes. She was cheerfully fair about such judgments.

"I am not sure *how* to proceed, though," I said, drawn into the puzzle. "I suppose we should encourage an apprentice to locate here."

I strolled to the grassy shoreline. Sun sparkled from ripples while the river murmured. A loan perhaps. It would be a form of investment, as Longbourn would receive tenant fees. Papa would have ideas. At least, after he recovered from his surprise.

A narrow, crested wave shot toward me across the width of the river, sinking into the surface a few feet away.

It left a wake of whitened, choppy waves. They spread in a frothy V with me at the point, then slid downstream, softening and bending around the occasional mossy rock.

A fish? I had no idea the local varieties were so vigorous. The bream we ate at dinner were not much longer than my hand.

I peered into the water. The dark murk swirled, impenetrable from the rains.

"Miss Elizabeth…" came Mr. Darcy's cautioning voice behind me.

Waves shot toward me from a half-dozen positions, upstream and down, each so fast that they traveled with a sizzling, slicing sound, like a linen-draper's knife cutting cloth. The water exploded in thrashing, frenzied spray.

I managed not much more than an "eep" before I was lifted and flying through the air. I came to earth yards away from the water, held by Mr. Darcy.

His hands were clamped on my torso below my arms, so we were face-to-face and closer than was customary, even when dancing.

In the daylight, his dark brown eyes had tiny green flecks. They were almost hazel.

Mary made a variety of excited sounds, whether due to the splashing or my position, I could not say.

"Are those fish?" I asked. I had never accompanied my father when he went fishing. Perhaps it was more exciting than I imagined.

"No," Mr. Darcy said. He appeared extremely concerned. "I have no concept of what that was."

The splashing had ended as quickly as it started.

I wiggled, which achieved nothing. My toes were barely touching the ground. Were all men this strong? That would be… disquieting.

"I shall not fall in from here, Mr. Darcy." He removed his hands, and my heels settled on the grass. "Thank you for steadying me."

"I will not see you again," he said. "I have been called urgently to London on business."

How abrupt.

He seemed to expect a response, so I tried, "What a pity."

"Draca have been deployed in war."

"*What?*"

"It was a disaster." His tone was bitter. "Draca and masters were injured and killed. No wyves were present, so the draca are distressed and violent. I go to meet resources I have dispatched from Pemberley."

"Your gamekeeper?"

He looked at me, surprised. "For one."

"Why is the absence of wyves significant?"

"A master's binding to draca is through his wyfe, so the wyfe's bond is stronger, always. This is why no man can hold draca after his wyfe's death." His lips thinned. "They were fools to think men could command draca in battle." He was speaking to himself as much as answering me.

"I have been told that draca cannot be commanded at all." I said that to test his reaction. He was already revealing knowledge I had never heard.

His eyes met mine, as intense as I had ever seen them. "They *should* not be commanded."

"*Should* not. It is possible, then."

"In extraordinary cases, their bound wyfe has some influence. But not their master. Even more reason why this military experiment was thoughtless and doomed."

Mary inserted herself. "The male bias of the establishment—" I discreetly raised a finger, requesting that she wait. To my surprise, she did.

How much could I ask without revealing myself? "Then, draca can never be influenced by… other parties?"

"That night, with the Hursts' lindworm. What did you *do?*" His eyes were wondering, but his tone was urgent and angry.

His intensity, and how he had discerned my true interest, frightened me. I fell back on social habit. "Please do not let us keep you from your urgent business." That was a meaningless deflection, how I would end an unwanted conversation at a ball. Immediately, I regretted it.

His expression became impenetrable. He bowed. "Miss Bennet. Miss Mary. If you will excuse me."

"Of course." I continued by formula. "We shall miss you at Netherfield."

He was already turning, but he stopped in his tracks. It was like I had slapped him.

He did not look at me as he said, "Mr. Bingley and his sisters also return to London."

"Why?" I asked, simple surprise breaking me from polite form. He did not answer. "For how *long?*"

Then he was gone, into his saddle and galloping away on his gray horse.

With growing foreboding, I rushed us home. I raced to our room and found Jane clutching a crumpled sheet of elegant paper covered with a lady's flowing hand. She would not speak but passed me the letter. I smoothed it, and tear-stained ink darkened my fingers.

Miss Bingley had written, curtly, that the Bingleys were departing this morning and would remain in London for the winter, if not longer. She continued:

"I am convinced that Charles will be in no hurry to leave, for Miss Georgiana Darcy is coming to London, and Charles is eager to meet her again. Georgiana

has no equal in beauty, elegance, and accomplishments, and Louisa and myself feel great affection for her ourselves.

To confess a secret hope, I dare imagine that Georgiana will soon become our sister. In friendship, I could not leave the countryside without confiding this, as it will assist you in denying any untoward rumors about your own sweetly innocent acquaintance to our family.

Yours fondly, Caroline Bingley."

"He is gone," Jane said, quiet but controlled, as I finished.

"This is false, Jane." My anger was growing with every breath. "His sister is a vile, manipulative woman. She seeks to separate you so her brother will marry Miss Darcy and she can further her own pursuit of Mr. Darcy. But I have just had reason to believe Mr. Darcy knows Mr. Bingley's true feelings."

"What does it matter?" The color had fled Jane's face. She looked lifeless as ivory. "He is still gone."

And, even while my heart was breaking for my sister, I remembered Mr. Darcy saying resources had been dispatched from Pemberley, and the letter saying Miss Georgiana Darcy was coming to London.

15

The next morning, Charlotte called to suggest a private stroll, as she had news.

"I wished to speak with you," she said once we were out of the house, "before Mr. Collins makes any announcement."

"Announcement?" I asked, puzzled.

Since Mr. Collins's unexpected and unsuccessful proposal to me, he had launched an extensive social tour of our neighbors, returning late each evening to pay brief regards to my father before retiring. I felt this was a superb outcome.

"Mr. Collins and I are engaged," Charlotte said matter-of-factly.

I laughed. "Impossible." We took several steps before Charlotte's silence made me stop. "You cannot be serious?"

"I suppose you think it incredible that Mr. Collins should win a woman's good opinion when he was unable to succeed with you."

I blinked, then I was mortified. "You have surprised me, that is all. It has been only—" I gulped back the rest, realizing it was wildly rude.

"Only two days since his proposal to you," she finished for me, but with a smile. "Yes, I am aware. I knew you would be surprised."

I learned that Mr. Collins's social efforts were visits to Lucas Lodge. He had expressed great sympathy for the loss of their tunnelworm, even suggesting that Lady Catherine de Bourgh would express her condolences if only she knew, and that he was certain this tragedy would encourage a wonderful binding when Charlotte wed.

"He is very eager to bind," Charlotte explained, now sounding uncomfortable. "It is all in deference to Lady Catherine's interest in draca, not any other goal, as we shall have a good house and living of our own. But this places me in a most uncomfortable position with you, dear Lizzy."

The entailment. Once Charlotte and Mr. Collins bound draca, they would, eventually, inherit Longbourn.

"ODIOUS, PONTIFICATING MR. COLLINS!" I cried. "How *can* she?"

I had run to Jane the instant Charlotte left.

"Charlotte has always been practical about marriage," Jane said. "Not everyone is romantic, you know. Mr. Collins has good connections and a secure position."

"I am hardly 'romantic' when I call Mr. Collins conceited, pompous, narrow-minded, and silly. You know he is. No woman who marries him is sensible, and you should not defend her!"

"I defend *you* from yourself, Lizzy. Charlotte is happy. It is you who are aggravated."

I harrumphed but could not think of a clever response. Finally, I settled for, "I am quite sick of men interfering in women's lives. Mr. Bingley will return, but I am vexed with him for being so influenced by his sister. And now, Mr. Collins has… has *proposed* again, and Charlotte's acceptance is troublesome."

"It seems you are complaining of women."

"Men are the root of it all." I flopped onto our bed, and the quilt puffed up around me. "And Mr. Darcy has run away."

"Surely you desired that?"

"Of course." I was not even sure why I had said that. "But I shall need a new partner for arguing."

"There is still Mr. Wickham. Or do you have other plans for him than arguing?"

I had told Mr. Wickham's story to Jane. That was a dilemma for her, who was so sweet-hearted that she could not believe Mr. Darcy would do something that dreadful, nor could she believe Mr. Wickham would say anything but the truth.

"I have no idea what my plans are for Mr. Wickham." I sighed at the ceiling.

Still, at least Mr. Wickham would not be missing any more balls. I should challenge Lydia to see who achieved more dances with dashing officers. That would be both vain and complacent. I may as well be efficient in my shallow pursuits.

And, I did enjoy him. I was impressed when we first met. Should I be entranced by now? Or in love?

If I put my mind to it, perhaps I could become in love. But a strategy of self-coercion, or worse, self-deception, scraped even more than Charlotte's philosophy of practicality.

There was a tentative knock at our door, and a Scottish brogue said, "Ma'am?"

I sat up. "Oh! Please come in." The Scottish laundry maid entered, curtsying. I stood, smiling in welcome. "Jane, do you remember…"

I realized I had never asked her name. Not even from Mrs. Hill. How idiotic. And complacent.

Jane rose and took her hand. "Of course, I remember. I have seen you at Longbourn often, and you helped when I was ill at Netherfield. I must have been a great inconvenience."

Only Jane could have such perfect grace while rescuing her foolish sister. Determined to make amends, I stepped in and gave the maid a hug, feeling her astonishment. "You have done more than help. I owe you my sister's health, or more likely, her life. You have my deepest and most heartfelt thanks."

"Your sweet sister Jane is up an' about. I am as happy for that as could be. What else is there?"

"Forgive me, but I have not had occasion to ask your name?"

"Bruichladdich, ma'am."

Good gracious. Perhaps I should not have asked. I took a breath and tried my best.

"Mrs. Brook-ladder," I said. "I was most concerned to discover you lost your position at Netherfield. I am fully responsible."

"'Tain't so serious, lassie," she replied, relaxing into a smile. "I go bout t' all the manors on wash days. That was just one of 'em, na' much.

And not my favorite. I been washing for Longbourn since you were wee 'uns."

I had struggled to follow her, but I thought I understood. "Would you *like* a position? Here, at Longbourn?"

"Are you needing laundry every day, then, ma'am? I see you dirtying even more petticoats than you used ta, and you were a terror as a girl." I felt myself coloring as she continued, "But laundry is na' a daily chore."

"But… some other position?"

"I wash laundry, ma'am. I wouldn't know what else to do."

We had reached my other reason to meet. "Perhaps I could engage your services to advise on draca?"

"Ma'am?" She seemed very taken aback.

"You are so knowledgeable. We have been attempting to interpret our family's journal…" I showed her the journal and the rubbing Jane had taken of the cover.

"I'm not for books, ma'am. I know only what any good Scot would know."

"But even that is so interesting. You say that draca are Scottish. I was told they were Chinese."

Her eyebrows rose. "They do na' look Chinese to me, ma'am. All Scots know draca hail from Scotland." She pointed, not to the journal but to the rubbing. "'Tis in front of your nose, as well."

I looked where she pointed. "Longbourn?"

She laughed. "It does not say *'Longbourn,'* lassie. Can you na' read?" She traced the first part, *Long*, before the space that Jane had noted. "That is *Loch*, not *Long*."

"*Loch* bourn?" I said in disbelief, trying to copy her Scottish pronunciation.

"Loch *bairn*, it says." She pointed to the *ou*, which, as if by magic, shifted in my eyes to an intertwined *ai*.

She was right. The elaborate, stylized *g* in *Long*, which rose both high and low, was an *h* preceded by a *c*.

"Is that Scottish?" I asked in a stunned tone.

"Aye, lassie. Loch bairn. It means, *Child of the lake*."

"It cannot be Scottish!" Scottish was… well, foreign.

"Bennet is a Scottish name, lassie. We're awash in Bennets in the north."

"You mean, both Bennets *and* draca are Scottish? Next, Mary will tell me Bennets are Chinese as well!"

She cackled with delight. "And what's wrong with being a Scot? I can show ye to dance proper, without all that silly clapping of the English dances."

"But we are *English!*"

My tone was sharp, and her gaze dropped—a servant disciplined by her better. "Yes, ma'am."

"No… I am sorry. You have been a tremendous help. It is just… unexpected." This had been a day for surprises.

"It is charming we have Scottish ancestors," Jane said. "What a delightful discovery."

"I must get back to washing, ma'am." The maid seemed eager to go. I hoped it was not because of my reaction.

"Of course, if you must. I would like to speak again. Wait, I have something…"

I went to my dressing table, where I had wrapped a little package in velvet and tied it with ribbon, as ladies wrap the gifts they exchange for amusement.

I pressed it into her hand. "I know you helped from your own goodness, but please accept my gift. I feel inadequate offering so little when what you provided was priceless."

"All right, ma'am," she said and left with a hasty curtsy.

I hoped I had made the right choice. Even though money would be unthinkably gauche within society, gentlemen did give farthings or pennies to servants on occasion. Money must be more helpful than an embroidered scarf or hand-painted saucer, which would be ridiculous. So, I had wrapped up four pounds, or more exactly, sixteen crown coins—four months' wages for a laundry maid, as I knew from assisting with my father's books. It was most of the money I had saved from my allowance, and all I could provide without asking Papa, which would have been difficult to explain.

"Loch bairn," Jane said. "Child of the lake. Could that be the original name of our estate? Or is it the ancestral name of an older estate? We have no lakes, after all."

PREOCCUPIED, I wandered, ending in our drawing room. The longcase clock, granite chimneypiece, and birch-framed mirror sketched an elegant triangle around me and the graceful furniture.

Charlotte and Mr. Collins would take all this. Presumably, they would remain at Mr. Collins's parish; the entailment was satisfied by a short stay at Longbourn. Would they lease the manor? It made no difference to my family's prospects. Without the income provided by the estate, we could never afford it.

I was not sure we could afford *anything*. For all that I scorned Mamma's pursuit of husbands for her daughters, she might be the most sensible of any of us. There was no other way for a gentlewoman to support herself. A governess was closest to a respectable position, and even that was little more than servantry.

I imagined applying with lowered eyes and great deference for the privilege of educating the Hursts' children. I could boast of my expertise in the exotic study of draca, explaining they were both Chinese and Scottish, and promise to keep my petticoats clean.

"You are being excessively morbid, Lizzy Bennet," I said out loud.

Outside the window, a horse with regimental markings was tethered by our entrance. An officer's horse.

Curious, I went out and walked around the manor. As I approached the rear, I heard Lydia's excited voice through the overgrown laurel hedge.

"The dog was utterly mad, barking and jumping and *very* terrifying. I was so frightened! You would not believe the way my chest pounded. And then, like a bolt from the blue, our drake swooped in! And... the dog was dead! Just like that! I thought I should scream!"

Lydia was telling the story of Mary's and my encounter with the mad dog, revised as if she were present. I was amused more than anything. Lydia was sixteen. Her exuberant personality turned heads, but she was still a child.

"And then... *fire!* It whooshed, and then I *did* scream! But from excitement. I was not afraid at all. He was protecting me!" Her excited tone became curious. "Is this what you mean, about power? I should like to tell draca what to do."

"I dare say you have a gift with drakes," a man's voice answered, sodden with flattery. "Perhaps I can encourage it."

My next step skidded on the gravel. I knew the voice.

Lydia and Mr. Wickham came into view. Together. Intimately close. Lydia was wearing short sleeves, a fashion fresh from London that I had not yet adopted. With astonishment—disbelief more than anything—I saw Wickham's hand cradling her bare elbow.

"Mr. Wickham." I heard the words. I must have said them.

"Miss Elizabeth," he said, turning with a charming smile. There was not even a hint of embarrassment, although his hand was now at his side. "We have been exploring Longbourn's park."

"Go inside, Lydia," I said. My voice tasted strange and stiff on my lips. "You should not explore alone with a gentleman."

"Oh, that is very nice," she said. "Are you a chaperone, now? You are not so old as *that*, Lizzy."

"Go inside."

"You are jealous!"

"Lydia! Go inside." I snapped it with all the authority I could summon from four years of seniority and my favored standing with Papa.

Lydia stomped off.

Wickham grinned as if this were a great joke. When the manor's rear door slammed behind Lydia, he came toward me—closer even than Mr. Darcy had been after carrying me away from the river.

"*Are* you jealous?" he asked in a teasing voice. His hands enclosed my arms.

"Mr. Wickham!" I tried to free my arms, but his grip was tight. "You forget yourself."

"Is forgetfulness so bad?" He pulled me closer. His leg brushed my skirts.

I slammed both hands hard against his chest, driving us apart. "That is *enough*. Leave now. You are not welcome at Longbourn."

"Who are you to say whether I am welcome?" He was annoyed now.

"I shall happily fetch Papa. I assure you he will agree. Or Mr. Hill can summon the footman to lead you to your horse."

He laughed and strolled away toward the front of the house.

I stood, rigid with fury and fear and dismay. An hour ago, I had lain on my bed and fancied whether I could love Mr. Wickham. The memory turned my stomach and climbed like bile in my throat. I was as angry with myself as with him. Almost.

A wide, sharp shadow flashed over the shrubs, and again. Our firedrake soared to an elegant, soundless landing in front of me.

"A little late," I said. I was shaking like a leaf. The drake spread his wings and gave a trilling cry. "But thank you for coming."

It was good he had not come sooner. I did not wish to raise dangerous questions in the mind of a man I could not trust. Questions I could not answer, even for myself.

16

I prodded my intact, finny bream through a slow circle on my plate. Ever since that unexplained splashing in the river, fish seemed much less innocent. Even when smoked.

It had been eight weeks since Mary and I suggested the blacksmith project to our father. After some daughterly cajoling, he was enthusiastic. I was rather proud of that. It was good to have a success, for I had made no progress in my draca research over the last two months.

I poked my fork into the fish and made the tail wiggle. One darkened, dried eye observed me, unamused.

Such huge splashes could not have been bream. Even Mr. Darcy agreed. I vividly remembered him saying so while he dangled me above the grass. Thinking of that, I experimentally grabbed my own sides. His hands were much broader than mine.

"Jane, darling," our mother said. "You must eat something. You are skin and bones."

"Yes, Mamma," Jane said and put a flake of fish in her mouth.

Jane's mood had darkened these two months, and it frightened me. She tossed at night, then rose so exhausted that her head nodded while our maid did her hair. Her face, now pensive and quiet, had thinned. Silence from Mr. Bingley had ground away whatever hopes she held—and mine for her as well, although I would never admit that. But even as one bright future faded, she seemed caught, unable to return to her prior happiness.

"I am *only* bones. I shall *die* of despair!" moaned Kitty.

Yesterday, we learned the Meryton militia regiment was moving to Brighton to be closer to the French threat. Many ladies, including Kitty, considered this a calamity. I would miss a few friends, but I was relieved that Mr. Wickham was leaving.

Lydia was eating with an almost smug expression. My eyebrows narrowed as she beheaded her bream.

The footman entered with a letter on his tray. "Miss Elizabeth Bennet. An express, from Mrs. Collins."

I recognized Charlotte's hand, although her married name was new. Their wedding had been two days ago at Mr. Collins's parish on the Rosings estate, south of London and almost fifty miles from Longbourn. That was far enough that I had not attended—or that was my excuse. Since the engagement, our letters had become reserved and stiff. The loss of intimacy hurt. I was not sure how to restore it.

"How rude!" said mother. "Crowing about her wedding by express. Lady Lucas has been eyeing my property ever since the engagement. They are a most vulgar, grasping family." In my mother's world, Charlotte and Lady Lucas had replaced Mr. Collins as chief villains.

But Charlotte would never crow about her wedding.

I said, "Excuse me," and went outside to our park.

It was January and cold, even on a sunny afternoon. I stood on the gravel walk behind our house, feeling the chill on my neck, and opened the letter, dated yesterday:

"Dear Lizzy, I wished to write privately with news. You will hear publicly soon enough.

Mr. Collins and I have failed to bind a draca.

That is so little to write but so confusing in practice. Mr. Collins hunted for draca outside our house this morning, even roaming through Rosings Park and searching the attic. He found nothing.

I was not surprised, for reasons I shall not write, and you know I was always ambivalent about binding. But I am most worried for the response of Lady Catherine, who has formidable opinions on all things marriage and domestic.

I am also relieved, for the guilt of my situation with respect to Longbourn has preyed greatly on my mind. Oh, but I am upset as well, for I fear it will be difficult here.

Very affectionately, Charlotte"

"Lizzy?" Jane asked, stopping beside me.

"Please do not tell Mamma," I said slowly, my mind racing, "but the Collins have failed to bind."

"Oh. Poor Charlotte!"

"Yes." Even though some dismissed binding as archaic, it was a pillar of standing among landed gentry. As gentry herself, Charlotte would retain the honorific *wyfe*, but it was a distressing loss of status, and Mr. Collins had been eager for that prestige. "Jane, I should visit her. I feel terrible that she is in unfamiliar company, and I did not bother to travel a few days to attend her wedding. That was selfish."

"I am certain she would welcome you. Although, perhaps you should not go immediately, or there will be gossip that it is you who are crowing."

"I shall write immediately, though." I turned to her. "What does it mean for the entailment?"

"It is unexpected." Jane's lips pursed, and I was relieved to see her attention caught. She seemed so adrift otherwise. "It has always been Mr. Collins who would inherit. But he cannot if he is not bound. It will be the next male heir, I suppose."

I led us into the house. Papa was still at dinner, his library open, so I retrieved a document with the Longbourn entailment.

Jane and I read silently, our heads side-by-side:

"The eldest male heire bound as gentry shall clame title to Longbourn, whole and indivisible, upon settling his draka in the empty draka house for a se'nnight; or if no eldest male presents, the consort of an heiress wyfe bound as gentry."

"Who is the next male heir?" I said. "*Is* there a male heir?"

"There must be. There are several branches of family."

"But he must present himself. What if he does not? Jane, you would be heiress."

"It says '*an* heiress wyfe.' I think that means any daughter."

The idea that Longbourn could be inherited by one of us sisters was astounding. "But… it could be you, Jane. Think of it. If you were married and bound."

"Or you," she said with her old, selfless smile.

Who else was likely to marry? Together, Jane and I said, "or *Lydia!*" then burst into laughter at the idea.

17

A farewell for the officers was planned for the last Friday of January. The officers' wives had, rain permitting, chosen a pretty meadow near Meryton bordered by elm forest and the river that meandered through Hertfordshire.

Although I had no desire to encounter Mr. Wickham, I was determined to go. I was fond of several officers and wives, and Mr. Wickham could not cause trouble at a public event. Let him hide. I would not.

Or, I had thought I would not. The day dawned clear, but windy and rimed with a white frost, so I arrived at the meadow wrapped in four petticoats, a wool skirt, a jacket, a muff, two scarves, and a woolen hat over my cap.

Lieutenant Denny somehow recognized me under my bundle, and when we spoke, I discovered that Mr. Wickham did, in fact, hide.

"Wickham is off in the woods again," Denny told me. "Shooting, perhaps. He is obsessive about his marksmanship. He said he might arrive late, but I do not expect him."

His tone was displeased, almost angry. Distrustful.

"You do not sound disappointed," I said.

"Pardon me." He gave an apologetic smile. "I am distracted. Would you excuse me?"

I watched him walk away, then be intercepted by Kitty. I was certain I had not misunderstood.

Fires and coal braziers had been lit to warm tea and chocolate, and they became the center of huddled groups. I chatted with officers and wives, ending with Colonel Forster and his new wife, Harriet, who was only seventeen.

She was enthusiastic about their move to Brighton. "Oh, I shall so enjoy the society. Brighton is an *event*. It is very exciting!"

"I am glad," I said, amused.

"And I know Lydia will adore it!"

"I beg your pardon?" I had no idea what she meant.

"She hasn't told you? How droll! I've invited her to visit. I should be quite lost without Lydia to explore the shops."

"How droll, indeed." That explained my sister's smug expression over dinner. She was clever not to mention it to me. Had she asked Papa already?

"Forgive my wife," the colonel said, glowing with the affection of a new husband, and, in the annoying manner of men, glowing with warmth although he wore only his regimental uniform. "She is determined that Brighton is a seaside adventure. I remind her that we are there because of the threat of French infiltration."

"Is it a risk?" I asked. The last event attributed to French spies was closer to home, in Hertfordshire two months ago—the deaths of the Linfields' draca and two mysterious men.

The colonel scratched the whiskers framing his chin. "Another spy was caught with incriminating materials. Yesterday, I ordered my men to be alert and to report anything unusual. Bonaparte remains determined to acquire draca."

"I thought our attempt to use draca in war had failed?"

"How did you hear that?" The colonel appeared surprised.

I could not mention Mr. Darcy, who had told me while frustrated and on official business. So I said vaguely, "In the papers?" and the colonel seemed satisfied.

I spotted Lydia with Denny, and excused myself to pursue my droll and clever sister.

I slowed when I saw she was in an argument. Denny was speaking sharply, and I knew Lydia too well to mistake her waving hands and jutted chin.

She stalked off, layers of wool flapping.

It would be hopeless to discuss Brighton when she was already vexed, so I resumed walking to Denny.

"Miss Elizabeth," he nodded.

"Lieutenant. Are you enjoying our sunshine?" That was unexpectedly witty as my teeth chattered.

He smiled, and we talked amiably. In fact, the day was warming, the frost melting in the sunny patches, and the wind had almost stilled.

Sour orange and bitter almond.

The scent was gone again as a gust flicked by.

"Did… Do you smell *oranges*?" I asked.

"I think there is flavored coffee. I have been smelling it all morning."

"Really." I looked around the meadow. For what, I was not sure. Draca, I suppose. But there was no reason to bring draca on a social outing, and the few married officers were not gentry, so they were not even bound.

But that was the wrong question—the odor had not been from live draca. It had been around the Lucases' dead tunnelworm and the dead roseworm in Meryton.

One mystery of draca was their origin. People accepted that bound draca appeared overnight, fully grown. But from where? I had asked and received shrugs and guesses. From the woods. Dropped from passing wyverns, as if they were delivered by some modern air post.

Could there be a dead, feral draca nearby? The elm forest was one of the few ancient, unlogged stands in Hertfordshire, overgrown with holly and dogwood.

The air stilled, and the scent reappeared, astringent and biting.

Denny, his nostrils pinched, interrupted his own story. "I cannot imagine who would *drink* something like that."

It was too pungent to be distant. I stepped back, and it diminished. "Forgive a question that seems improper, but might you have something on your person with that scent?"

He laughed and made a show of sniffing his sleeves, then twisted his neck to sniff at his shoulder. His face contorted. "*Phew!* Oof, yes!" He turned, trying to see his own back and looking like a dog chasing his own tail. "My sincere apologies. I must have brushed something…"

From the forest, a clattering sound was growing, like a military drummer banging sticks on a log at ferocious speed. Laughs and chatter faded as curious faces turned. Winter-bare branches jerked and swayed at the edge of the trees, perhaps thirty yards away.

A multi-legged, serpentine body, thick as a large man's chest, poured out of the dark underbrush. It kept coming—as long as a horse, then twice that—segmented in greenish-brown chunks a foot long, each with a pair of jointed, insectile legs that moved in lightning, clicking sequence.

The front swarmed onto the grass, coiling like a giant earthworm that had sprouted dozens of legs. Behind it, a loop of churning body climbed an elm trunk like a wave, surging higher while each pair of legs scrambled to push past, lopping branches and flaying bark, until the trunk splintered and fell.

Ladies screamed. A few people ran. The colonel shouted an order, lost as a dozen concerned voices rose.

The monster was into the open now, twisting as it explored the grass, more flexible than a snake. The body and legs had the glossy, armored appearance of shell.

"It is a foul crawler," I said.

The size had defied recognition at first. Crawlers, like the one that stung Jane, were inches long. Large ones—five inches—were called cockatrice, or sometimes draca bane, for they were said to fight draca. There was another name from myth…

"A basilisk!" Denny shouted.

That was it.

The monster's head reared up higher than mine. Pairs of jointed legs waved in the air. The head had four fleshy horns, like a slug. They hunted through the air as the creature twisted.

The head swung to face me. And stopped.

Oh no.

"Run!" I shouted, dropping my muff and grabbing Denny's arm. We pounded across the grass, Denny supporting me while layers of petticoats caught my legs. It was like running through a forest of laundry.

Too soon, I had to stop, panting.

The monster arrived where we had stood and nuzzled the ground.

"It is after me, Denny," I said.

"*What?* Why?"

Because I was intriguing to dangerous animals, draca or otherwise? I had no idea why.

"I just know," I said.

"All right," he said with the calm of a true officer. "Run to the coaches. I will distract it if it follows."

He gave me a little push, and I ran until, gasping freezing air, I reached the frightened people clustered by the coaches. The horses were tethered and whinnying, too spooked to be handled. Lydia and Kitty were in the crowd, the only others from my family who came today.

The monster's fleshy horns stroked and prodded the grass. Denny had run toward the river. He waved his arms and yelled, but the monster ignored him. I wondered if it could even hear.

The monster began to move, horns grazing the ground like a dog on a scent. The legs rose and fell in rhythmic waves. It followed the path Denny and I had run, then curved away from me, toward Denny.

I realized my mistake. It was not after me.

"Run!" I screamed.

Denny stopped waving so abruptly it was almost comic. I saw his courage become surprise, then concern. He sprinted away, but the monster's churning legs blurred. It charged over the ground, fast as a horse. Sod and mud flew from the spear-sharp tips of its feet.

Like a dog pouncing on a mouse, the monster's head reared high then pounded into the center of Denny's fleeing back. He vanished under a writhing pile of chopping legs and armored shell.

Ladies screamed. People ran every direction. A handful of officers, led by Colonel Forster, ran at the beast. The colonel had a sword drawn, but no one else had weapons, the standard for dress uniform at society events.

I ran after them, convinced I was not in danger and terrified for Denny. Clothing flopping, I lagged far behind. But draca were said to fight crawlers. Even though our firedrake was a mile away, I thought—I shouted in my mind—*help me!*

The officers surrounded the beast, trying to penetrate the thicket of flashing legs. A man kicked and fell back, cursing, his trouser leg bloody. The colonel thrust with his sword, but the end skittered across the armor.

Yelling, the colonel pushed with both hands, and the sword point caught between two segments and sank in.

The monster's head reared. A pair of olive-brown, serrated pincers two feet long opened and struck at the colonel. He backed away, but like lightning, the monster turned on another man. The pincers closed, catching the man's calf. The bloody tips emerged from opposite sides. And still they closed, scissoring as the man screamed.

My view was blocked. The colonel's strained face was inches from mine. He yelled, "Get away!" I nodded, and he turned back to the fight.

I was on the bank of the river, yards from the monster. I looked around, confused. Had I run all this way?

A sizzling wave was shooting across the water toward me, the wake tracing a path that vanished around the river's distant bend.

The wave slammed into the bank, shattering a fringe of ice. A translucent, fish-like shape flopped onto the shore at my feet. It twisted, grotesque and squirming, then the translucent body tore. A creature pulled free, discarding the casing like a butterfly leaving a chrysalis. It called out in the pure tones of a bird.

It was a small quadruped draca, dripping in the mud. Glistening, it staggered on wobbly legs like a newborn calf. Riverbank leaves and dirt had stuck, but I saw the distinctive color. A roseworm, full-grown.

The segmented monster swung to face it, and for the first time the creature made a sound other than the clattering of its legs—a whining, whistling challenge.

Another wave smashed up the bank beside me, flopping a shape onto the grass, and then another.

The roseworm, awkward and uncoordinated, rushed at the monster. My heart leaped, waiting for it to throw flame. Instead, one of the monster's gleaming legs flashed out, and a point speared through the roseworm and deep into the earth. The draca writhed, crying out, and became still.

Then the monster shrieked. Another dripping draca had caught one of the monster's legs in powerful jaws.

"We have Denny!" a man shouted. He and another man were carrying Denny toward the carriages. The man whose leg was savaged was also escaping, his arm over the shoulder of an officer.

The monster whistled and twisted in fury, trying to free its leg from the draca's jaws. The segmented body undulated like a whip, and the tail flashed over its head. A pair of spikes at the end squirted a vile, oily liquid over the attacking draca.

Sour orange and bitter almond. The scent burned, cloying, coating my throat.

The draca thrashed and shook in agony. The spray struck the other attacking draca, which fell as well.

Overhead came a descending call. There was a screeching clang, like an ax swung at an anvil.

The monster reared with a whistling scream. One armored segment of the body was scored and broken open, the clam-pale flesh exposed and twitching.

With a second cry, our firedrake flew between me and the beast, hovering in midair, his wide wings flashing in complex, curved beats that whirled stones and grass across the ground. Scorching heat exploded, and I threw my arm over my face.

The next whistling scream came amid swirling, roasting smoke. Stalks of burning grass floated in the air, sparking and glowing. The cloying odor became a sizzling, noxious reek.

Arms dressed in scarlet grabbed my waist. The colonel. I ran with him but tripped on my skirts. He pulled me to my feet, then half-carried me until he let me fall to the grass.

The officer with the injured leg was beside me, clutching his bloody calf and cursing. He had not noticed the arrival of a lady.

On my other side, Denny lay still on the ground.

"Denny!" I cried, frightened.

"Miss Elizabeth," he gasped. His head turned to me. "I… I believe I have its attention."

I laughed, dizzy from fear and running and relief.

Denny coughed, and blood sprayed, running down his chin and soaking his raised, white collar.

I scrambled to him on my knees. The side of his uniform was ripped, the proud, regimental scarlet soaked and dark as dirt. Blood was puddling on the ground beneath him.

"Help!" I cried. The colonel was with the officers across the meadow, chasing the smoking monster into the trees.

There were a dozen guests around us. I saw terror, and blank shock, and revulsion, but I could not distinguish features, as if people I had known my entire life had been erased to staring strangers.

"Denny…" I pulled off my scarf and pushed it against his side, but it was loose crochet, and the blood came through in seconds. I threw the scarf aside and pressed my hands. The blood steamed, stinging my cold skin. The side of his chest was pulp under my hands. Crushed. Splinters of broken bone scratched my palms.

He gasped a choking, wet cough like a man drowning, and hot blood and air sprayed between my fingers.

"Help is coming," I told him, hearing the panic in my voice. "I promise. It will be fine."

His arm reached across his body, and his hand caught my wrist then slid to take my hand. Even now, he was stronger than me, and his fingers threaded through mine, slippery with blood.

"Let go," I said, crying now. "I must hold the wound..." But his eyes stared at the sky. The pained tremors in his body stopped. His grip, so superior to mine, softened and became limp.

I crouched over him, wrenched by sobs, each convulsion tearing my throat. Our fingers were still interlaced, a grasp more intimate than I had ever shared with any man, even my father.

The colonel had to ask several times before I could let go.

18

"Read this, Lizzy." My father passed me the *Times*, his finger marking an article titled "The Monster of Meryton."

He had called me into his library. It was ten days after the horrible events in the meadow.

I read, afraid my name had been printed. An unmarried lady mentioned in a newspaper would be branded with scandal for life. Context was irrelevant.

No names appeared.

If I had not known better, I would have called the story lurid. In reality, it trivialized the horror. Draca were not mentioned. It ended by quoting an expert from the British Museum, who speculated the monster was a wild boar.

"It was nothing like this," I said softly. The events at the meadow were burned into my mind.

Of our return to Longbourn, though, I remembered only shards. Kitty crying in another room. Myself standing in the scullery while Mrs. Hill and a maid dropped layer after layer of bloody cloth in a sink. Washing my arms and hands over the butcher drains.

"I know the truth," Papa replied. "The colonel gave me his own account. He was astonished by your bravery."

"Bravery?" My voice cracked in disbelief.

"The *Times* has one fact correct." His finger tapped the story's title. "The monster escaped within a mile of Longbourn. I thought it prudent to correspond with Mr. Collins and speed your visit with Charlotte. An iron-barred carriage is hired for tomorrow. It was difficult to book. People are fleeing Hertfordshire in every direction. You can speak with Mrs. Hill to arrange a maid as companion for the ride."

"All right, Papa." Charlotte had already suggested a visit in early March, so this would be three weeks sooner.

"And I am sending Lydia to visit Colonel and Mrs. Forster in Brighton."

"What? Papa, you must not!"

A few days before, I had privately asked Papa to decline Mrs. Forster's invitation. I cited Lydia's immaturity, but I did not share my most serious fear.

I thought I had convinced him.

Papa rubbed his eyes. "Lydia is deeply affected by Denny's death. When I told her she could not go, she broke down. She begged to visit her friend."

Begged? I knew my sister well. She pouted, cajoled, and shouted. She did not beg.

I had seen no hint of the distress Papa described. In fact, I had seen no reaction at all, which worried me. Had Lydia suppressed her pain?

Regardless, Lydia unsupervised in Brighton could be disastrous.

"I am certain she should not go," I said. "She is young and—"

"I have decided, Lizzy," he said firmly.

I swallowed, caught by my own omission.

After Mr. Wickham had grabbed me—had assaulted me—I said nothing. One reason was fear of the result. Approaching Papa would be a tremendous escalation. Men dueled over less, although I doubted my father had ever held a pistol. And ladies' reputations were destroyed by such allegations.

Now I faced the result of my cowardice.

I breathed deep, hunting for words. My credibility had been damaged by waiting, but if any man would believe me, it was my father.

And again, I hesitated. The accusation could destroy me and taint my family with scandal. Shame my sisters, particularly Lydia, whom I sought to protect.

What if I stayed silent? That was horrible in its own way. Imagine if

Wickham did this over and over, and every woman kept his secret out of fear. But that was impossible. This was 1812. I had grown up in a century freed from outdated, authoritarian beliefs. Despite Mary's tirades at the corrupt patriarchy, I could not believe the modern world would permit a man to repeat vile acts and avoid the consequences.

"What is it, Lizzy?" asked Papa.

I trusted Colonel Forster. And I could not judge what pain Lydia concealed.

So, I shook my head and tried to believe that, for once, all would be well.

As Lydia and I would depart soon, all five sisters went for a walk. We were a quiet group. Jane said not a word, and my few comments about packing did not spark conversation.

Kitty began to cry.

"Oh, do stop snuffling over Brighton," snapped Lydia. "If you wished to go, you should have made friends with Harriet yourself."

"I would have, if I had known," Kitty said, wiping her cheeks. "But that is not why I am sad. I cannot stop thinking of poor Denny."

"Still? It has been more than a week."

"Lydia!" I said, shocked.

"What of it? Why are *you* all upset? He was my friend more than yours. We danced… oh, a dozen times at least."

I could not believe what I was hearing. "Denny is *dead*."

"Must you remind us endlessly?" Lydia grimaced. "It's a form of bragging, you know. The way you crouched there, pretending to nurse him."

I grabbed her arm, and we turned to each other. Disbelief and anger fought in my mind.

Lydia pulled herself free. She was inches taller than me, the tallest of all of us although the youngest, and she frowned down, petulant as a child. "Do not make superior faces at me! Denny was quite horrid that day. *And* a bad friend to Wickham. I cannot imagine why you miss him."

She stomped off. Kitty burst into tears again, and Mary said something that sounded dire but in Latin I did not recognize.

Jane had stopped to wait, but I was not even sure she had heard. For weeks now, walking with Jane was like walking with a ghost.

My disbelief and anger mixed and left a disturbed sensation. It took a moment to recognize it was fear. But I could not be afraid of Lydia.

Denny had been Lydia's favorite. A real friend among her many flirtations, and a sweet, honest man who brought out her best. I had even wondered if they would have a serious relationship when she was older.

Lydia reached the manor and entered without a backward glance.

It was like I had never known my sister.

"Papa," I said next morning while our footman carried my luggage to a coach crudely armored with strips of iron. "I am worried to leave. I feel as if our family is untethered. Our lives are teetering, each of us, in some way."

"That is what you get for *not* marrying Mr. Collins," Mamma inserted primly. But she straightened my bonnet and gave me a solid kiss on my cheek.

"Your trip will reduce my worry," Papa said. He looked tired, and he had spilled his tea at breakfast, twice. "Be safe. Enjoy your visit. Other than remembering I am abandoned here with Kitty and Lydia's silliness."

"Lydia left yesterday, Papa," I said, smiling.

"So she did. Mary will perform in her stead. She scolds me mercilessly over the health of my diet."

Mary, gaily clothed in her dullest black for my departure, stood beside him. Papa waited for her response with unabashed affection. Something had happened between them since that painful night at the ball. Perhaps when Mary defended me from Mr. Collins's proposal. There was a new closeness which I loved to see.

Mary said, "I shall do my best," which was raucous wit for her.

Papa's smile turned serious. "I will miss you, Lizzy. Greatly. What did Hamlet say? Neither a borrower..." He paused, pretending to forget the rest.

"It was Polonius, Papa," I said. This was an old joke. Nothing irritated my father more than self-important people attributing Polonius's words to the star of the play.

I waited for him to finish.

"Do not correct me," he said querulously. "It was Hamlet. Neither a borrower…" He licked his lips, blinking. Becoming distressed.

He did not remember.

"Neither a borrower nor a lender be," I said, as casually as I could. But my heart sank. Papa had recounted Polonius's full speech a hundred times. Still, anyone's memory could stick on a phrase.

I took Jane's hands last. If Papa looked tired, Jane was a wraith. Heavy shadows clung below her eyes.

"Promise me you will go out," I said. "And please take a trip of your own."

I had suggested that Jane visit our aunt and uncle in London. Papa would not object while the "Monster of Meryton" lurked, and that would put Jane close enough to call on Miss Bingley. But Jane had refused, saying if Miss Bingley had not answered two letters, calling in person would be improper. Even desperate.

Privately, I was becoming desperate on Jane's behalf. But I had not convinced her.

I hugged everyone and waved to our firedrake, mostly for humor although I would miss him. However, I would not miss his profound inattention while I stood on my new wooden platform in the freezing dawn.

The driver whistled, and the coach set out with groaning traces and rattling bolts. A four-horse team was harnessed to haul all that metal, and we would change teams twice.

I was on my way to visit Charlotte, observe Mr. Collins in his natural setting—which I expected to be amusing—and, perhaps, meet the formidable Lady Catherine de Bourgh, the only widowed wyfe to hold a wyvern.

19

The sun was low when, after swinging east to skirt the traffic of London, we clattered and clanked into Kent and crossed a stone bridge into Rosings Park, the estate of Lady Catherine.

The trees lining the road became uniformly spaced and trimmed. From Charlotte's letters, I imagined her ladyship lectured every crooked branch into submission.

The parsonage came into view—bits of it, at least. I had to bounce on my seat to catch glimpses through the narrow window. There was a garden, a small home of fieldstone, laurel hedges, and a pretty white gate.

Our horses stopped, blowing with relief. Charlotte and Mr. Collins emerged. I fumbled the locks open, and Charlotte and I hugged. The awkwardness that had struck with her engagement fell away, defeated by absence, or distance, or our mutual trials.

Mr. Collins, however, was profoundly unchanged. After minutes of roadside platitudes, I was grinding my toe in the gravel. Finally, he invited me to tread the stone path to their house.

We passed an uncovered rectangle of bare earth. Their empty draca house had been removed.

Mr. Collins demonstrated the door. The entryway was meticulously noted. Then we almost collided in the parlor due to another spate of bows.

"Would you like tea?" Charlotte asked, dodging with evident practice.

“Indeed, cousin,” chimed Mr. Collins, “after such extensive travel, passing near the noise and parching smoke of London, refreshment is most recommended. May we offer…” He stopped, flummoxed by the need for a concrete thought.

“Tea?” suggested Charlotte again.

“Tea would be nice,” I said.

Tea grew into a light supper. I learned such humble offerings could not properly be called supper in the shadow of the sumptuous feasts of Rosings.

My face was becoming sore from suppressing raised eyebrows and eye rolls.

Charlotte peered out the window. “How the shadows are lengthening.”

“Oh! My lettuce!” Mr. Collins excused himself, for he had a row of lettuce sprouts to weed, and, if that row was not weeded today, the task would cascade into tomorrow’s weeding, and thus onward until catastrophe.

After he vanished backward through the parlor doorway, Charlotte suggested a stroll.

I was determined to show no hint of amusement or disapproval, so we started stiffly, but in fifty yards we were chattering like any of our walks back home.

But not all the news was happy. Charlotte asked about the attack at the meadow. I had not written that I was present, so when I told her that—nothing more—we were silent for a time.

I decided to put the difficult topics behind us. “Charlotte, I am very sorry you did not bind.”

“I am honestly relieved. I am uncomfortable with draca. Everyone has been most considerate. Mr. Collins as well, after a few days of disappointment.”

Other than my sisters, there was no one else I would dare ask my next question. But Charlotte was my most intimate friend, and I was curious. “Had you no marriage gold?”

“Lady Catherine provided five guineas, which was extremely generous.” Charlotte had more to say, so I waited while leaves crunched under our steps. “Not all the Church approves of binding. But Lady Catherine does approve, and in Kent, she is a force. Our wedding was officiated by a neighboring rector. We touched the gold while the priest blessed us and said words to summon a draca. It seemed certain. But later…"

"Later?" I prompted.

"That night, we prayed for a successful binding."

Her tone was odd, but her expression was hard to make out in the dusk. I said cautiously, "Prayed?"

"Yes. Exclusively." There was no question. I heard her ironic smile.

"*Only* prayed?"

"I was prepared, you know. I am not a romantic, Lizzy, but I understood what happens on a marriage night."

That was extremely direct. I was not at all sure I understood what happens. "And what happened was… praying."

"Yes. I even mentioned tales my mother told me, of the great bindings and their passion." I was quite impressed she said that to me, let alone Mr. Collins. "But of course, those stories are not in the Bible."

"I see."

We walked a little way while my face cooled in the evening air.

"Do you wish to bind when you marry?" Charlotte asked.

"I think so."

I had hesitated, but not because of Charlotte's concerns. I neither sought nor condemned the status, although I thought it was silly to grant it for binding. And I was fascinated by draca themselves.

But, if binding was involuntary, it was cruel. The more I found draca mysterious and remarkable, the more disturbing it would be to entrap one for life.

"You are such a wonderful friend," Charlotte said, "that I am inevitably surprised when we differ on anything. I am very content with my life—no, I am very happy. But we *are* different, Lizzy. You overflow with passion. You should marry for love."

That was a remarkable thing to be told, and a little frightening.

LADY CATHERINE's invitation to Rosings arrived the next morning.

Mr. Collins was more than excited. "I should not have been surprised by her ladyship's inviting us to tea. But who"—his hands rose to invoke divine omniscience—"*who* could have foreseen an invitation to *dine* at Rosings so immediately after your arrival!"

The afternoon was clear, so we walked the half mile to Rosings. Mr. Collins alternated astonishment at her ladyship's affability with extensive notes about the park and manor—how many ash trees in that grove, how many pounds it cost for the lead glazing of her ladyship's windows.

The gardens were expansive, but stiff and formal. The manor, though, was remarkable. The building was large but modern, free of the rambling extensions that distorted many old homes. The famously expensive windows were wide and tall.

I had a particular interest, so I looked for the draca house. But there was nothing. Was it behind the manor? That would be strange.

We were led, with Mr. Collins rapturously commentating, through the entrance hall and antechamber, then into a sitting room.

Her ladyship rose with royal grandeur to receive us. On our walk, Charlotte had insisted that she introduce me. She did so with refreshing simplicity.

Lady Catherine was a tall, weighty old woman with strong features grooved by deep frown-lines. She wore full ball attire, a satin-and-silk golden gown with an ostrich feather in her hair. The effect was of aged majesty.

I learned why Charlotte wrote of her formidable opinions. They began to roll forth even before we sat, each pronouncement ending in dramatic tones followed by a huge indrawn breath, and then, an instant before anyone else dared to offer a topic, the start of the next.

Her daughter, Miss de Bourgh, was around my age but thin and scrunched, and so different from her mother I would have guessed she was a distant relation. She greeted us in a whisper, lifting her fan as if it would be rude to reveal moving lips.

"Miss Bennet," Lady Catherine said.

Guiltily, I looked up, for my mind was wandering. Thus far, the only audience participation had been enthusiastic nods by Mr. Collins. "Yes, madam?"

"Your trip was satisfactory."

That seemed a statement, not a question, so I replied, "Correct." She frowned, but I was reconsidering my answer. "Noisy, though. I rode in an iron-barred carriage, and the bolts kept coming loose."

"I beg your pardon?"

"We stopped several times, and the driver attempted to tighten them. He even tied some joints with leather straps. It seemed most inefficient to me."

"Upon my word. You give your opinion very decidedly."

"It is just that the purpose is unclear. People claim fear of feral draca, but the bars are..." I showed the gap with my hands. "Most draca could squeeze through. And the carriage itself is wood, so if a draca threw fire, a few bars will not stop it. In fact, I have seen a roseworm throw fire with the express intent of tearing open a metal cage, and it did so easily."

"My word." Her ladyship seemed stunned.

"It *was* remarkable," I agreed. Her frown deepened. Had I misunderstood? "Of course, bolts are the real issue. The debate over the standardization of screw threads." I had read essays while researching blacksmithing. Despite Mary's skepticism, I was still intrigued by the idea of commodities like wheels and bolts.

"What do you say, Darcy?" her ladyship asked.

My ears had played a trick. "What?"

"Miss Bennet has an interest in smithing," came a baritone voice behind me.

"My nephew is obsessed with such things," Lady Catherine said. "Come, Darcy, introduce yourself. I gather you know the Collins?"

I turned in my seat, astonished to see Mr. Darcy bowing over Charlotte's hand. "Mrs. Collins. I offer you my best wishes."

He turned to Mr. Collins, who appeared terrified. I remembered the disaster of Mr. Collins approaching Mr. Darcy at Netherfield.

"Mr. Collins," Mr. Darcy said, with a slight chill but a nod. Mr. Collins bowed back, vastly shorter and close-lipped for once.

I rose as Mr. Darcy approached.

"Miss Elizabeth Bennet," he said. There was a pause between each word. It gave the scene an odd sense of import, or perhaps unreality.

"Mr. Darcy," I answered as I curtsied. He was Lady Catherine's nephew, so it was hardly impossible to meet him here. But it was a surprise. My heart was racing.

"Do not stand and stare," Lady Catherine said, irritated. "What is this bolt nonsense, Darcy?"

"Bolts are difficult to fabricate," he said. He still had not looked away. I began to feel disconcerted. He turned to his aunt. "Imprecision in the threads loosens them."

"They should be precise, then," Lady Catherine said, lifting her nose.

Conversation proceeded. I half-listened, annoyed at myself for being surprised. No, annoyed at Mr. Darcy. It had not been necessary to lurk behind me like that.

True to form, Mr. Darcy had fallen silent. He was dressed for riding, and dusty. I was surprised he did not go to change. I had never seen him other than perfectly attired. I had guessed he was one of those well-dressed gentlemen who are more fastidious than ladies.

He might be with us the entire evening. Even for dinner. Here I thought I had escaped him when I left Netherfield. But at last, he said he had to greet a friend and departed solemnly.

20

Charlotte and I lingered after breakfast. The dining parlor of their little home was charming in the morning, sunlit and decorated with ornaments of crochet and ribbon. I recognized Charlotte's craft.

Outside, Mr. Collins was already at work in the garden.

"He has organized your garden beautifully," I said. Even this early in the season, there were rows of young plants.

"I agree. I think we shall feed ourselves, and more. Mr. Collins is insistent we help the poorer families. Lady Catherine aids those in Rosings Park, but outside our parish, they are not so lucky."

That was an aspect to Mr. Collins I had not known.

In a setting like this, I saw why Charlotte was happy. She was mistress of her own house and helping others. They might have a family. Perhaps fatherhood would reveal hidden depths in her husband.

Mr. Collins was attempting to move a large pile of leaves. It tumbled over, and a great number of insects flew out. I watched him run in circles.

"I encourage him to work in the garden whenever possible," Charlotte added with total unconcern. "The exercise is very healthful."

Charlotte would be a wonderfully calm mother.

She added, "I saw Mr. Darcy arrive yesterday. He stopped stock still when he saw you."

"Well, he quite surprised *me*. I had thought myself free of him."

"Is he so persistent?" Charlotte sounded intrigued.

"Not persistent. We simply encounter each other too often."

Mr. Collins was waving a tree branch at the insects. I doubted that would succeed.

"He was very attentive to you," Charlotte said.

"Mr. Darcy? I thought him strikingly silent."

"Silently attentive."

Thinking of Rosings reminded me. "Have you seen the Rosings wyvern?"

"A few times when it flies overhead. I have no wish to approach closer." I hmphed, for I had been about to suggest we visit. Charlotte smiled. "You could go, Lizzy. I am sure the gamekeeper would assist you. Perhaps you would encounter Mr. Darcy."

I groaned. "I should have asked how long he was staying. Well, he is easy to spot. If I stay alert, I shall avoid him."

"He is destined to marry Miss de Bourgh." Charlotte pronounced that hesitantly, as if it were a delicate subject.

"Really?" I did not recall them even speaking.

"Her ladyship is quite open with her plans. She and his mother, Lady Anne Darcy, were sisters. The alliance of Pemberley and Rosings is greatly desired by Lady Catherine."

Mr. Collins had now draped muslin over his head and was crawling while patting the ground, trying to find his shovel by touch. "Well, they shall make an excellent pair. Miss de Bourgh will whisper behind her fan, while Mr. Darcy says nothing."

I APPROACHED ROSINGS OBLIQUELY, keeping a wary eye out for tall gentlemen, then strolled around the back of the manor. Then farther, to see the remaining side.

No draca house.

Where would they hide a wyvern?

An older man was leaning on a fence and watching my circuit. He wore good but worn leathers with a battered hat and had various pouches slung on his person. That was almost a uniform for gamekeepers, so I walked over.

"Ma'am," he nodded.

He was about my father's age, but wiry and vigorous with a weathered complexion. He seemed amused to meet a lady walking.

"Good morning. Are you familiar with the local animals?"

"A bit," he said with a smile. "What would you be looking for?"

"A wyvern."

"Well, that'd be a handful for a lady."

I folded my arms. "I wish to see it, not carry it." He snorted, and I decided to try flattery. "The Rosings wyvern is most famous."

"Aye."

His intonation was familiar. "Are you Scottish?"

"That I am. Been in England a long time. I thought my tongue had lost its brogue."

"I understand there are Bennets in Scotland."

"Are you a Bennet, then?"

"I am. Our family has Scottish ancestors."

"Lang may yer lum reek."

What on earth? I chose "Quite" as a reply, which works in most circumstances. One grizzled eyebrow rose.

Perhaps I should ask directly. "Where is the Rosings wyvern kept?"

"Well, you don't so much *keep* a wyvern."

"No draca house?"

"No ma'am. They do not require a house. They fly."

"Our family's drake flies, and he has a house."

"You have a drake?" Both eyebrows rose. "What have you named him?"

"Named him? I would not name a draca." This felt like a test. Draca were not pets.

"You think draca don't have names?"

"If they do, they are not chosen by people."

He thought about that. "Well, let's see if she'll come. It's a rare day when…" His voice trailed off.

I heard rushing wind and turned as a powerful bronze shape winged to a graceful landing, scattering leaves and sand, and billowing my skirts.

"Good gracious," I said.

Her body alone was twice the size of any draca I had ever seen, heavy and muscular like the Hursts' lindworm, but two-legged like our drake. The size of a hunting dog, fifty pounds or more. Her wingspan was only a few feet more than our drake's, but her wings were much deeper and heavier, with prominent bones and bands of sinew that flexed under the skin as she tucked them away.

I crouched to be level with her head, and we examined each other. Her neck was stout, not sinuous like our drake's, and her head larger. Almost like a spaniel, if spaniels had no ears and were clothed in shining bronze scales. She was curious and alert, studying me while I studied her.

And her eyes…

Her eyes were remarkable. Stunning. Every draca I had seen had black eyes, but hers shifted color in the sunlight like a spinning crystal, flickering through purest green and blue and red.

"Incredible," I breathed.

"Aye. That she is." The man crouched beside me and clicked his tongue. Loosening her wings for balance, the wyvern took two waddling steps forward. Close enough to touch. "She likes you."

"She is beautiful." I touched my fingertips to her neck. The scales were smooth and warm. That was the same as other draca I had touched.

There was a surprised laugh beside me. "You're a bold one."

"Me?" I was not sure which of us he meant.

"You, lassie. 'Twas years before I touched a wyvern. Only seen two other women do it, ever."

I touched the leading edge of her wing. It was a thick as my thumb, and it felt… powerful. Our drake had the same sense of toughness but was built on a finer scale. Almost delicate by comparison.

"She is both like our drake, and different." I looked at her feet. "Her talons are large."

"Not talons. Claws." He held his hand in the air, mimicking a claw with three fingers and his thumb. "Hunting birds—raptors, like an owl or an eagle—*they* have talons. Talons are spears, sharp at the tip, so"—he pinched his fingers and thumb together—"birds drive them into their prey, then carry it to their nest. But flying draca, wyverns and drakes both, they hunt large game, and they don't nest. They eat where they kill. So they have claws, edged like a razor their whole length. No good for carrying game. They'd cut through and drop it. But if you want to kill something… aye, that's a sight. They can twist their foot for the strike, to cut with either the big rear claw or the three front claws. A weapon to behold either way."

"I have seen our drake fight."

"Have you now? You're ruining all my perceptions of fine English ladies. I thought they embroidered all day."

I touched the burnished arch of a claw where it rested beside my skirt. Like our drake, the wyvern stood with her claws spread, and each foot spanned wider than my stretched hand. Most of that was claw. "I embroider also."

"Well, I drink also. We both have our bad habits."

I laughed and turned to him. "Are Scottish ladies different?"

"The great dragon wyves were Scottish."

"What made them great?"

"War, ma'am."

I turned back to the wyvern. "War does not appeal to me." The shifting eyes were running through oranges and blues and yellows. It was mesmerizing. "Have you been the Rosings gamekeeper long?"

"Not Rosings, ma'am. Just visiting. I'm gamekeeper for Pemberley."

I shot to my feet, and the wyvern backed in surprise.

I was sure I would discover Mr. Darcy lurking, but no one was near. I turned a full circle to be sure he was not sneaking about on those long legs.

"You all right, ma'am?" The gamekeeper had stood also.

"I… I have remembered a commitment. I must depart." I thought through what I had heard. "You mentioned two other women who touched a wyvern. Who were they?" I had assumed he meant Lady Catherine and her daughter. Now, I was not sure.

"Lady Anne Darcy was one, my master's late mother. Lady Anne was sister to Lady Catherine de Bourgh. Two sisters, and two bound wyverns. That tells you the strength of the bloodline. I was Pemberley gamekeeper for Lady Anne, and I miss her greatly. 'Course, her wyvern is gone with her."

"And the other?"

"Miss Georgiana Darcy. Never been a draca she couldn't touch."

I said goodbye and began walking back to the parsonage, rather distracted.

The stretched shadow of the wyvern's wings flashed across the ground at my feet. A minute later, it passed again.

child

I stopped among the trees. I was sure I had heard someone speak. But there was nobody.

21

At Longbourn, I had memorized and inverted Mr. Collins's exercise schedule. Now I dusted off that knowledge and took long walks in Rosings Park, sometimes with Charlotte but more often alone as she was often busy with the household.

The Rosings formal gardens were like the wrapping of a lady's gift, layers of meticulous hedges concealing flower beds as exact as embroidery and lawns scythed and clipped to velvet. I visited them once to admire the tulips and daffodils, but that was sufficient.

But Rosings Park was an immense estate, and even the opinions of her ladyship could not stamp it all into submission. An open grove edged one side of the gardens, and there was a path that wound under ash and oak, with rough patches and fallen logs to deter more sedate walkers.

I sank into a pleasant routine. There is an inescapable bustle living with four sisters. Here, the weather was warming, the woods were greening, and even Mr. Collins's silly behavior—if rationed, like a sweet—became amusing.

Charlotte and Mr. Collins called on Rosings several mornings each week. I walked with them the first time, then wished them well and followed my own path through the trees.

We met on their return.

"Lady Catherine asked after you," Charlotte said.

"Really? I thought she had enough of bolts."

"She was quite insistent that you return. As was a gentleman." I looked at her questioningly and saw a smile. "Mr. Darcy. Were you expecting another gentleman?"

"I was not expecting *any* gentleman." Had his gamekeeper spoken to him? I hoped not. I preferred to keep my interest in draca private.

Two days later, this repeated, but we were invited to dine the next day. That was inescapable.

"At least the food is good," I said grudgingly. "But I shall have to prepare facts on screws to offer over soup."

"I detected disappointment that you would not be present until tomorrow." Charlotte had an arch expression, but I could not imagine why her ladyship was impatient.

That afternoon, Charlotte read her correspondence, and I started a letter to Jane. Then the doorbell jingled. Mr. Collins dashed into the small drawing room as the maid announced Mr. Darcy and Colonel Fitzwilliam.

Charlotte had mentioned Colonel Fitzwilliam, another nephew of Lady Catherine. I looked him over while Mr. Collins bent and flounced. He was about thirty, rather tanned, and had a frizz of sandy brown hair. He was not handsome exactly, but he had the confident bearing of an officer and the manners and speech of a gentleman. When Mr. Collins released him, he bowed to my curtsy with a relaxed smile. I immediately liked him.

Mr. Darcy wore gray afternoon calling dress as impeccable as anything he had worn in Hertfordshire. He paid his compliments to Charlotte with his usual reserve, and Mr. Collins's ludicrous bowing and scraping did not affect his composure.

I was a little perturbed to encounter him again. I curtsied without speaking, and he gave one of his sharp bows in equal silence.

Colonel Fitzwilliam began conversation and soon mentioned their visit.

"Darcy and I are cousins, but good friends nonetheless." He laughed disarmingly, and Mr. Darcy concurred with a barely perceptible nod. "While walking, Darcy mentioned his acquaintance with Mr. Collins. Naturally, we had to call."

Charlotte and I traded a glance. Calling Mr. Collins an acquaintance of Mr. Darcy was unfathomably generous—doubly so from what I knew of Mr. Darcy's taste.

I spoke with the colonel, who had interesting observations on Rosings, including a few polite but amusing allusions to her ladyship's opinions. Then it was news of the war. He was well informed, and interested in my view, and the whole thing was vastly more entertaining than dull topics like the weather. We conversed rather too long until he remembered his manners and shifted his attention to Charlotte.

That left Mr. Darcy, who was rigid and serious. He had ignored Mr. Collins, which I found oddly reassuring. But he was capable of conversation. At Netherfield, he had thawed enough for several long exchanges. They were even, if one listened closely, witty.

Noticing my attention, he inquired about the health of my family.

"They are well," I said, the usual response. Then I added, "I wonder if you remember my eldest sister, Jane?" He had to nod, so I continued, "I am afraid her days are rather lonely with me away."

That was a provocative and strange thing to say in company. But I was certain Miss Bingley had forced her brother away from my sister. Mr. Darcy's reaction when he told me of Mr. Bingley's departure made me suspect he knew the truth.

Conflicted emotions crossed Mr. Darcy's face, too fleeting and well concealed to be deciphered. "I am sure your sister's charm will ensure society even in your absence. I fear more that, in her absence, you will find your own visit dull."

That was polite, but a laugh escaped before I could stop myself. The dullest society I knew was sitting in front of me in a gray jacket. He stiffened, so I asked if he thought the days were growing warmer.

WHILE WALKING THE NEXT MORNING, I met the Pemberley gamekeeper again, hiking in his leathers and battered hat.

"Ma'am," he said politely, turning to head back.

"Please, do not leave. I was about to return myself."

But I hesitated. On hunts, gamekeepers are respected, or even deferred to, by gentlemen. That fostered a relaxed attitude toward mingling. And this man had remarkable knowledge of draca.

"Are you visiting the wyvern?" I asked.

His weathered lips smiled. "If she deigns to visit me."

"I am Miss Elizabeth Bennet."

"Tom Rabb, ma'am." He touched his ragged hat.

Thank goodness there were pronounceable Scottish names. "I am sure she will come down."

"Down, ma'am?"

I pointed to the tree where the wyvern watched, perhaps a hundred yards away. I had become adept at spotting her.

Mr. Rabb folded his arms, apparently vexed I had seen her first.

I could not resist. I concentrated. *Please come down.*

Then, thinking better of what I was revealing, I waved and added some clucking noises. It sounded like I was inexpertly calling a flock of chickens.

The performance was too late anyway. The wyvern was winging toward us.

She landed on a fallen trunk a few feet away, the wood snapping and popping as she tightened her claws for balance.

"Hello," I said, delighted she had come so quickly. She hissed and stretched out her neck. I had discovered she liked to be scratched under her chin, which was a surprise. Although other draca did not object to being touched, they never seemed to enjoy it.

One did have to scratch hard, though, and in a single direction. The scales were knives if you went the wrong way.

"Are all wyverns so affectionate?" I asked, leaning in to get leverage. She was panting in pleasure, her nose by my cheek. Her fangs were impressive, lustrous ebony and much longer than a dog's. And thin, like blades. I peered closer. They were serrated on the back edge.

When there was no reply, I gave her a pat and turned back, afraid I was being rude.

Mr. Rabb was slack-jawed. "Crivens!" he exclaimed, then added several unintelligible words. He seemed to have reverted to Scottish.

"These are her woods," I said, a little self-conscious. "I meet her most days."

"Do you, now." He seemed flabbergasted.

I tried to think of a topic that would set him at ease. "I suppose wyverns are aquatic while growing?"

"*Aquatic?*"

"Or… is amphibian the correct word? I have no books on the subject, but I recall an article." He stared. "An article on frogs." Surely a gamekeeper would know about frogs and tadpoles.

He pushed his hands into his pockets. "Well, now I'm dead certain."

"Certain of what?"

"Why we're still here. Suspected it was you."

"I beg your pardon?" I was confused.

He laughed and touched his hat with a half-bow, then turned and walked back the way he had come, whistling.

WE WALKED to Rosings for dinner that evening.

As we threaded the hedges, Charlotte said, "I should thank you, Lizzy, for yesterday's visit. Mr. Darcy would never have come so soon to wait upon me."

"I enjoyed meeting Colonel Fitzwilliam. Let us hope he attends dinner. That will liven things." I had thought about the visit a few times. "Is it not peculiar that Mr. Darcy has friends?"

"What?" said Charlotte, laughing in shock.

"I do not mean that he has *any* friends." My cheeks were heating. That had come out ruder than I intended. "But Mr. Bingley and Colonel Fitzwilliam are charming. They seem very fond of him. Is that not unexpected?"

"I imagine they see another side of him. Mr. Darcy is different when you are not present."

"Different? How?"

Charlotte did not answer until we were climbing the stairs. "He speaks more."

"He could hardly speak less."

THE COLONEL WAS AT DINNER, with Mr. Darcy, Lady Catherine, and her daughter. With us, that was seven, and conversation flowed, although occasionally it splashed to a halt when her ladyship became jealous of another group's topic and demanded a report for her benefit.

Cheesecake was offered. I declined because I found Rosings's sweets overly sugared. Mr. Darcy declined also.

Lady Catherine's potent voice rose.

"Miss Bennet. Your father's estate is entailed on Mr. Collins. Or would have been, had he bound." That was thoughtless to say, but I answered yes. She continued, "I think it ridiculous to entail estates from the female line. In any event, I held my draca after Sir Lewis's death. Will your mother do the same?"

"I prefer not to speculate," I said, a little testily. The question was prying and morbid.

"It is a matter of will," her ladyship continued. "When Lewis passed, I was greatly affected. I feel all events, whether in life or in art, most profoundly. But a woman requires stature. I refused to accept the loss of a wyvern."

That was intriguing, so I bit down my annoyance. "Were you not concerned about condemnation? A lady alone may gain stature from draca, but society does not always approve."

She snorted. "*Men* do not approve. Binding is a force of women. There will always be men who challenge a woman of intelligence or stature. Both I and my sister, Lady Anne Darcy, bound wyverns. That is the force of our maternal bloodline. But my sister was a fussy, fastidious thing. She lost her wyvern on her husband's death. She had not my will."

Mr. Darcy's hand landed on the table with a bang. "My mother released her wyvern."

"Impossible. There is no such action as release. And even if she did, what did it get her? Wasting away from binding sickness…" Lady Catherine's voice stopped.

I had never heard any of this. When the silence stretched, I asked, "What is binding sickness?"

Lady Catherine's eyes, strong blue behind her wrinkled lids, had teared. The unexpectedness of that moved me. It was like discovering a wall of flint could cry.

Colonel Fitzwilliam answered. "Binding sickness is a strange malady. It can affect bound wyves if their draca is killed. It is, however, rare even then. And because draca are so seldom killed, it is almost unheard of." He paused. "It is thought to be more likely with a strong binding. I knew Lady Anne, a little. She had remarkable affinity with her wyvern."

"I attended the only recent case," Mr. Darcy said. His tone was rough, concealing emotion of his own. "Draca were killed in the idiocy of attempted application to war, and I feared those deaths would cause the sickness. But the French used some more foul weapon. Some draca died, but others were… driven mad, perhaps. It was as if their bonds were broken. One young wyfe of such a draca did not survive. We even attempted to restore her binding."

"It was a wretched thing," Colonel Fitzwilliam said softly.

No one spoke for a minute. But my curiosity got the better of me.

"But how could you restore a binding?" I asked. "I thought there was only one opportunity to bind. On the…" I stopped, realizing where the topic was headed.

"The marriage night," Lady Catherine said. Her impenetrable exterior had returned. "Restoring a binding is nonsense. Marriage gold and passion create the binding. And not blind passion. Love. Sir Lewis and I had love. Although he performed well. The maternal bloodline is key, but men do contribute. It is a matter of technique."

"*Technique?*" I had not intended to speak. The word just popped out, rather squeakily.

"Of course, technique. Your generation is hopelessly inferior at educating gentlemen for their marriage night duty." She cast her formidable gaze at her nephew. "Are *you* educated, Darcy?"

"I prefer not to speculate," he replied, so instantly and dryly that I almost laughed.

Her ladyship scowled at him while the next dessert, lemon tarts drowned in crystallized sugar, was served. Again, both I and Mr. Darcy declined.

Her blue eyes fixed on me. "Do you perform, Miss Bennet?"

I decided to match her boldness. "Given the subject, I am unsure how to answer."

A man chuckled. The sound was from Mr. Darcy's direction, but that was impossible.

Lady Catherine was unamused. "I refer to music. There are few people in England who enjoy music more than myself. Or have more innate talent. Do you play? Sing?"

"A little."

"You will perform for us."

"I am quite woefully out of practice. You will not enjoy it."

Lady Catherine frowned, again.

"Elizabeth sings beautifully," said Charlotte, my so-called friend. I tried to kick her, but the table was too wide.

"Music and romance both require passion and technique." Her ladyship's rolling tones were reminiscing. "Anyone may develop technique with practice, but brilliance requires talent. If I had ever learnt, I should have been a great proficient."

"At which, madam?" I asked innocently. This time, two men laughed. One must be Mr. Darcy.

Lady Catherine's frown twitched. "Music, of course. Go, Miss Bennet. Perform with something other than your wit."

22

The next morning, while Mr. Collins visited his parishioners, I explored his garden. There were neat rows of sprouted peas, lettuce, and onions, a scatter of tiny white butterflies, and bright-green shoots too young to reveal a personality.

I was sniffing a fragrant bush with white-rimmed leaves—thyme?—when the maid arrived with Mr. Darcy and Colonel Fitzwilliam in tow.

After greetings, Mr. Darcy said, "If you are at leisure, we would appreciate your assistance on a professional matter." His clipped tone suggested he did not approve.

"A military matter," the colonel added, with a mysterious smile.

"Military?" I said.

"We plan an experiment with the Rosings wyvern," the colonel replied. "It will be brief, but it is important to the war effort."

"My gamekeeper, Mr. Rabb, suggested you attend," Mr. Darcy said deliberately. "He feels you have an affinity with the wyvern that may help us judge her reactions."

That left me a little nervous. I had hoped Mr. Rabb would keep our meetings to himself. But the colonel seemed unconcerned, and I could hardly refuse, so we set off toward Rosings.

Lady Catherine, the Pemberley gamekeeper, and a servant waited on one of the large lawns.

"Mr. Rabb," I said with a severely cool nod. I was not sure about being proffered for wyvern experiments.

"Ma'am." He touched his worn hat with an unrepentant grin. Apparently, a nod was insufficient to chasten a gamekeeper.

The colonel was casting bemused looks at the sky. "And now we require our wyvern! Should we place bait?"

The gamekeeper cocked an eyebrow at me. "I'm sure she'll come down."

So, Mr. Rabb knew the wyvern would come to me. But his manner suggested he had kept that to himself. That was reassuring, and I forgave him a little.

I let my mind drift outward. Feeling for her. I was not sure how I did this, or even if it was me doing it or the wyvern, but it had become easier each day.

South. I shaded my eyes, but she was too far to be in sight.

I concentrated. *Will you come, please?*

I felt her begin to move. I turned and squinted at a different stand of trees so I would appear uninvolved.

Her glide was silent, but I heard exclamations as she was spotted. Then she flapped powerfully, whipping my skirts and knocking my hair from its pins as she landed exactly at my feet.

She peered up at me, eyes glistening through a rainbow while she preened in delight. Everyone was staring at us.

"Yes, you are most clever," I said. She gave an ecstatic coo.

"My word." Lady Catherine stomped over to glare at her wyvern, who ignored her.

"Quite," I agreed, trying to pin my hair back in place. It had gotten rather long.

Colonel Fitzwilliam nodded in an officious manner. "I will now disclose information of a military nature, but that I may share for the purpose of scientific research. Indeed, the crown is indebted to Mr. Darcy for his considerable effort in this area."

Mr. Darcy gave a ghost of a nod in acknowledgment. Lady Catherine made an impatient, unimpressed noise. The colonel hurriedly resumed.

"We know Bonaparte seeks to recruit draca for military advantage. Whether or not we approve, his actions require a response. Unfortunately, the first attack by an English regiment with bound draca failed terribly. Mr.

Darcy warned of the risks, and I trust his advice will be weighed closely in the future.

"However, many factors contributed to the disaster. The French clearly knew our plans before the attack. They had defenses prepared against draca. They even attempted to steal our draca, using a vile and unknown chemical that attacks the bond between draca and master."

"Draca and wyfe," Mr. Darcy said.

The colonel acknowledged the correction and continued, "This matter has become more urgent. Several weeks ago, while I was assisting with militia training in Brighton, the bound draca of a gentleman in town died mysteriously. Two days ago, a second died. But this time, evidence suggests these deaths are the work of French spies. We believe the draca was killed with the same weapon used against us in battle.

"The evidence from Brighton has been sent to me. We wish to determine if it is the chemical in question." The colonel gestured and the servant handed him a large jar sealed with a wide cork and wax.

"You cannot be serious!" I cried. "You will test a *weapon* on the Rosings wyvern?"

"We are not testing the weapon," the colonel said reassuringly. "In battle, the French weapon sprayed a liquid on the affected draca. Here, we will not touch the wyvern, or even approach. We merely wish to determine if this is, in fact, the chemical used in the attack. The cloth in this jar has a pungent odor, and reports suggest that even the odor of the weapon distressed our draca."

This seemed poorly thought through to me. "Surely this is an argument *not* to proceed."

"I agree with Miss Bennet," Mr. Darcy said. "As I have already expressed."

"You are all ridiculous," Lady Catherine said. "Whoever heard of a dangerous smell? My wyvern is exceptionally robust. Proceed, colonel. I wish to join my luncheon."

"We will proceed with the utmost caution," the colonel said. "If everyone would step away from the wyvern?"

We backed up several steps, forming a sparse circle. Mr. Darcy stood beside me, his arms folded in disapproval. Lady Catherine stood across from us, scowling back. The wyvern twisted her neck to observe us.

The colonel drew out a pocketknife and scraped the wax from around the cork. "First, I shall release the cork to judge if the odor is still present." He pried at it with his fingers, then with his knife.

The cork popped free and fell to the ground. He bent to retrieve it.

A scent grew. Sour orange and bitter almond. The same astringent odor I had smelled when the monstrous foul crawler sprayed vile liquid to attack draca.

"Stop!" I cried. "I know what it is."

The wyvern screeched a rending, rising cry.

Terror and fury swarmed up my spine. My vision blurred with a second scene, peculiar and brightly colored as if drawn in pastel.

The colonel was fumbling to find the cork in the grass. I saw Mr. Darcy run to help him, but I saw it twice—once through my eyes, his motion lithe and quick, but a second time with the lightning perception of a predator who saw a plodding, slow enemy attempting to flee.

The wyvern's powerful body crouched to strike. "No!" I shouted and threw myself to catch her. One hand skidded uselessly off a spreading wing, but my other caught her muzzle. Her leaping body slammed into me like a charging horse. I was thrown hard onto the ground, and we tumbled into a pile with me on the bottom.

Her muzzle was above my face, prismatic eyes fixed on mine. Like a shared dream, our minds sank into each other.

I felt her terror, her body trembling with panic and fury, her wings spread to strike, her breath hissing past my fingers clamped around her muzzle.

She felt the prickle of grass against my neck, her weight pressing me down, my lungs struggling to fill after the impact. My ribs hurt. One hand stung where her scales had scraped my palm. My other hand held her muzzle, the scales like warm steel under my fingers.

Below that, around my wrist, was the thinnest hairline of pressure.

Her foot was raised, and her burnished, razor claws encircled my arm. The heavy rear claw, an obsidian scythe at least four inches long, meshed with the three front claws. It was like being held in a pair of shears.

I had seen her sever a two-inch oak branch by tightening those claws. It had been effortless, an idle amusement while she stretched in the sun.

My vision still flickered and blurred, a blend of her vision and mine. Panic and fear grated and buzzed.

"You are safe," I said. I concentrated. *You know me.* The fear diminished.

The strange odor was fading. The colonel or Mr. Darcy must have closed the jar.

Slowly, I raised my other hand to touch her neck. Her scales had lost their suppleness, locking together like a sheet of metal. It was like stroking a bronze sculpture, if bronze could breathe in frenzied pants.

Mr. Darcy and his gamekeeper were speaking tensely. That stopped, and through my confused vision, or perhaps through the wyvern's, I sensed Mr. Darcy approaching.

The line of pressure encircling my wrist became more exact. That was all—there was not even pain—but a drop of warm wetness ran down my forearm inside my sleeve.

"Do not approach," I said, not loudly but, I hoped, audibly. Mr. Darcy stopped, then retreated.

The strange smell was gone. I felt the wyvern calming. I concentrated. *There is no enemy here. There is no threat. I will let go. Then you may release me.*

I opened my fingers. Her jaws spread, not far, but I felt the heat behind them.

Her claws around my wrist opened, stretching wide before she moved her foot away. Her weight on my body lessened as she found the ground.

"Thank you," I said out loud.

She made a strange huffing sound, her nose twitching.

Oh no. "Do not—"

There was a peculiar, coughing snort. It would have been comical if not for the flash of heat. I clamped my eyes closed, but it was gone in an instant, like slipping a finger through a candle flame.

There was a buffeting of wind, then her weight was gone. Half my mind ripped away.

I opened my eyes to see the sky, now drawn in simplistic shades of blue. Hands helped me stand. Mr. Darcy was facing me, his hands grasping my shoulders.

"Are you all right?" he said.

There was a burned smell. Hair. I lifted a bedraggled lock. Yes, the ends were crisped. Mrs. Hill would be vexed. No, that was wrong. She had not done my hair for years. But my sleeve was bloody. Had I fallen?

The gamekeeper and Colonel Fitzwilliam were also facing each other. The colonel held a pistol, but the gamekeeper had grasped his arm, forcing the weapon to point at the ground.

The gamekeeper let go with a scornful laugh. "You brought a *pistol* to fight a wyvern?"

"I was prepared to protect Miss Bennet," the colonel said stiffly.

"If you pulled that trigger, they'd be picking pieces of you out of those damn hedges for a week. All of us, most likely."

"Are you able to stand?" Mr. Darcy asked me.

"I…" It was difficult to organize a thought. My mind felt lost. Abandoned. His hands tightened on my shoulders. That helped. "I am, as yet, a little unsteady."

"She is standing perfectly well," snapped Lady Catherine. She was beside us, glowering.

I looked up at Mr. Darcy. "I know what the French weapon is."

23

The next day, hobbling with a sore ankle and stiff ribs, I told Mr. Darcy and the colonel about the monstrous foul crawler in Meryton and the venom it sprayed.

"The French collected the venom of crawlers," the colonel mused. "A dangerous task."

"Worse than dangerous," Mr. Darcy said. "Crawler venom is evil."

"It is certainly poison," I said. "But evil?" That seemed flamboyant.

"Old writings claim that crawler venom has power," he said. "But they are superstitious scrawls. And revolting. I thought them repugnant fantasy. I should have paid more attention."

Mr. Darcy and the colonel sent a report to the army. Then my routine resumed, albeit slowed. But I had wonderful news to cheer me while I healed. Jane was recovering.

Her first letter was encouraging. A week later, her second made me smile. She described a ball—the sparkling light from candles, the tunes that were played, and even her dance with a handsome man with tousled fair hair.

It was charming, although unusually rambling and fanciful. Jane has a warm soul, but she is concise.

I was a little disconcerted by her interest in a new gentleman, and by his resemblance to Mr. Bingley. But until I visited London to stuff Mr. Bingley in a crate and ship him to Netherfield, I would be grateful for any improvement over the wasting, silent sister I had left.

The second week passed, and my bruises faded. Spring burst forth. Charlotte and I became so casual it was like visiting a sister. Mr. Collins was unchanged, but his garden grew.

My walks resumed, but solitude was evasive. Gentlemen were constantly underfoot.

I met Mr. Darcy often. The first time was on my favorite path, in the exact spot where I had encountered his gamekeeper. It was like that patch was magnetic to men.

We exchanged somber greetings, and he offered to accompany me. I bit my lip and tried to think of an excuse. Calling the wyvern would not frighten him off; he grew up with one, after all.

While I considered that, we began walking in what could be mistaken for companionable silence. Mr. Darcy was, naturally, at the correct distance for a gentleman accompanying a lady.

But it did feel companionable. He was clearly a walker, comfortable with the rough trail and more relaxed than sitting at dinner.

"Rabb told me his view of the wyvern attack," he said.

"And what is his opinion?" I said cautiously. I feared Mr. Rabb guessed more than I liked about my connection to the wyvern.

"That she intended to attack me, not you."

I concealed a relieved sigh. That was harmless, the insight of a man experienced in observing animals. "The scent confused and frightened her. When you ran to help the colonel, she thought you a threat."

"How could you know that?"

"Uh…" I should pay attention to my own words instead of worrying about Mr. Rabb. I invented an explanation. "She spread her wings, rather like our drake does before he… when he is angry."

"And you threw yourself in front of an attacking wyvern?"

"I would have done it for anyone," I said, quite truthfully.

"I was… I referred to your courage."

"Oh. Quite."

He fell silent in that way he often did, and we walked for a while.

"You must enjoy visiting Lady Catherine," I said, for a topic.

"I observe that you do not." His tone was amused, not accusing.

"*That* is a problematic response. I must either agree and offend you, or profess my enjoyment and risk more invitations."

He did not smile, but perhaps his lips twitched. One needed a lens to analyze Darcy expressions.

I picked up a stick and tapped a few passing trunks. Since the experiment, the wyvern had been as affectionate as ever. Yesterday, I even tried throwing a stick for her. Her reaction had been far easier to read than Mr. Darcy's. I would describe it as disappointed disdain.

It seemed I was required to do the talking, so I resumed. "Visiting your aunt would be unpleasant if one were intimidated. But I find her interesting. She is utterly certain of herself. In most people that would be tiresome vanity. But at Rosings, she is a queen. I have never observed royalty before."

"Can a queen not be tiresome and vain?"

"So far, the queen is entertaining. I shall change my mind when my head is lopped off."

He said nothing. I suppose it was an odd conversation.

"You have not said why you visit your aunt," I said, feeling rather adventurous.

I had wondered. He arrived the day after me and showed no sign of leaving. That seemed devoted for a nephew, at least one who did not need to flatter for an inheritance.

Twenty steps farther, he replied. "The bold answer would be that I enjoy the company."

I would call enjoying her ladyship peculiar, not bold. But he had no living parents, and his sister was much younger. It must be strange to have so few family. "I suppose Lady Catherine reminds you of your mother."

He stopped dead in his tracks.

"No," he said, very definitely.

Colonel Fitzwilliam was also often walking, and I met him every day or two. Conversation ranged widely. I discovered, after some friendly prying, that he was the younger son of an earl.

"Of course, younger sons are little more than household pests," he laughed good-naturedly. "I have neither title, nor property, nor funds. Just an obligation to advance our family by bargaining my ephemeral hint of rank to marry a woman of large fortune."

"I think it rather pleasant that gentlemen can face the same challenge as ladies. What is the price to marry an earl's younger son? I suppose you would not ask above fifty thousand pounds. But I fear I cannot bid. I should be hard-pressed to purchase a fashionable hat."

I expected a laugh, but he was quiet before replying, "I am glad I accepted an officer's commission in the regulars. It has reduced my dependence."

"You seem at leisure. I thought the regulars to be consuming."

"For a country at war, all of us seem extraordinarily at leisure. However, I am on leave after six weeks in Spain with Wellesley. That was a different experience. Battle swiftly removes the shine from glory. And Wellesley is a man who cannot abide leisure in himself or others. In that, he is like Darcy."

I did not reply, but perhaps the colonel saw my expression because he continued, "You have not seen Darcy up all night, corresponding on matters of policy and government. I am relieved to see him finally take a breath and enjoy life. Since his father and mother died, he has been a driven man."

FOUR WEEKS INTO MY VISIT, I received a letter from my father. It finished:

> *"The greatest news, or absence thereof, is that the Monster of Meryton has made no further appearance. The constables twice drove dogs through the woods but found neither scent nor sign. I admit that your iron-barred flight, which I advocated, appears foolhardy.*
>
> *Indeed, Lizzy, many neighbors more timid than yourself have returned to march about in self-satisfied triumph. Perhaps you should return. The estate suffers without your efficient interference, and I feel your sister Jane would benefit. Also, I miss you greatly.*
>
> *Your loving father, James Bennet."*

I pondered his letter while the maid braided white ranunculus blooms into my hair. This evening would be my seventh dinner at Rosings, an outing I did not enjoy. I had heard more than enough of Lady Catherine's proclamations and Mr. Collins's pandering.

Charlotte was beside me, fastening a ribbon I had offered for her bonnet. She enjoyed my company—she told me so every few days—but my visit had exceeded our original plan.

Even so, I was resistant to my father's suggestion. Surprisingly so.

"How long will Mr. Darcy visit?" I asked.

"You would know better than I," Charlotte replied.

"He is much more tolerable here than in Hertfordshire." I was trying to put my finger on what bothered me about leaving.

"Be careful, Lizzy. He began by calling you tolerable."

"What is that supposed to mean?"

"You walk together a great deal."

"That is unavoidable. There are only so many paths."

Although, the park was enormous. I just kept to my routine, even though it interfered with his.

Was I enjoying Mr. Darcy?

At dinner, I watched him while I stabbed my defenseless, and quite defeated, piece of trout.

Mr. Darcy wore his customary exquisitely tailored dinner dress, this evening black and gray with bone buttons and simple silk collars.

He was handsome in a tall, stiff sort of way. But that was nothing new. Everyone had noticed him when he arrived at the ball in Meryton. And why would it matter? We walked together. It was not like we attended balls.

He did speak more now. A few days ago, we debated East India trade policy. That had been fascinating, if occasionally intense. Was he a friend? That would be unexpected. I distinctly remembered deciding to hate him.

A footman, perfectly presented in knee breeches and a powdered wig, offered a plate of custard tarts topped with browned sugar. I declined.

Dinners at Rosings were infused with sweets. Sugary courses were offered between savory, and there were two or three desserts at the end of every meal. They were all cloying, and I had taken only a few bites in all my visits.

Mr. Darcy declined the tarts with one shake of his head. I had never seen him accept a sweet course.

"Miss Bennet," Lady Catherine announced, ending all other conversation at the table. "I insist you try a tart."

"They are rather sweet for my taste, madam."

Her ladyship's frown stirred. "You have not tried them."

"I have tried others." Lady Catherine scowled, far more vexed than I expected, so I tried to soften it. "I am not a large enough person to eat so many courses and then a tart." I looked dramatically around the table and made a discovery. "Mr. Darcy is much more imposing. He may have mine."

Immediately, I knew my joke had failed.

Mr. Darcy's face hollowed, and the shoulders of his black dinner jacket moved to rigid alignment.

Lady Catherine, in elaborate layers of peach silk, assessed her nephew through narrowed eyes. "Offer Mr. Darcy a tart."

The footman returned to Mr. Darcy and offered the silver plate. Mr. Darcy shook his head.

The guests watched this strange contest in silence. Charlotte was expressionless. Mr. Collins was squirming.

But Colonel Fitzwilliam was serious. He became apprehensive the moment I made my joke. There was some prior conflict here.

Had Mr. Darcy and his aunt argued over the sugar boycott?

The cheapest sugar came from the Caribbean colonies, but those plantations were reviled for their appalling use of slaves. For a decade, abolitionist ladies had led a movement to boycott colony sugar. I discovered the boycott when Mary, then twelve years old, tipped our prized sugar bowl onto the floor and smashed it to bits. She replaced it from her own allowance with one prominently labeled "East India Sugar, Not Made by Slaves."

But Lady Catherine did not need to economize on the price of sugar.

Her ladyship's face was granite. "Your manners do no credit to your breeding."

"I think they do." Mr. Darcy's dark eyes were unmoving.

Mr. Collins, who had been wriggling more and more, grabbed a tart in each hand. He stuffed in a huge bite and began chewing with rapturous sounds.

Lady Catherine ignored him and addressed Mr. Darcy. "You sit in my home. Rosings flourishes on the prosperity of my plantations. Your refusal is both rude and hypocritical. Pemberley does not lack for colony profits."

The truth sank in, bone-deep. This was not an argument over the boycott. Lady Catherine herself owned sugar plantations.

I was, for all moral purposes, dining with a slave owner.

"Excuse me," I said. Voices were rising, but they faded as I passed through three double doors, each opened by liveried servants, and exited into the night air.

It was cold, the moon a narrow, setting crescent barely bright enough to light the ground. The lack of light had not been a concern when we arrived. Her ladyship always called a lit carriage for us after dinner. One of her many carriages, as Mr. Collins never failed to note.

Despite my exit, I still stood in Rosings Park. I could walk for miles before I escaped. Around me, the moon silvered elaborate hedges and flower beds. The same ones I smugly judged as ostentatious while hiking to and fro, building a good appetite for dinner.

I felt polluted and sick. And stupid. Angry at myself. Sometimes, I had even admired her ladyship's fierce independence.

Did Charlotte know the source of her patron's wealth? She could not live in Rosings Park without discovering the truth. It would be prize gossip for anyone who disliked Lady Catherine, and there must be many.

But Charlotte might have been told after her marriage. Imagine learning you are committed to a life funded by brutal slavery.

Mr. Darcy stopped beside me, his familiar stride grinding sand and grit on the flagstones.

It was gratifying to have a target for anger other than myself. "How could you not tell me? How can you *stay?* It is abhorrent."

"My aunt and I disagree on this. Often, and strongly."

"*Disagree?*" I remembered the pamphlet I took in Meryton. The cover was a cartoon—a plantation owner stirring a vast pot of boiling syrup while a slave's limbs flailed in the liquid. "How strange I did not guess the strength of your condemnation. After all, you refrained from eating custard."

"She is my aunt."

"And therefore, she is beyond your censure? I assure you, I do not treat my relations with that deference."

"I would not want you to." He said that with strange passion.

"You are in no position to *want* anything of me."

"This is… I have endeavored to—"

"*What?*" I was furious now, and I knew why. All those perfected manners had made me forget his abominable entitlement. I had started to imagine a person lived beneath those layers of exquisite etiquette. But it was an act. A ploy to exploit my complacence. "Was it a struggle to spend four weeks strolling Rosings Park to amuse your aunt? You are your own man. Surely you can find a better use for your time."

His face worked. He looked lost, hunting for words.

I was more angry than I could explain. "Speak, for once!" I shoved one of his solid shoulders. He retreated a step. "She said Pemberley also profits from slavery. Is it true?"

"Pemberley is an old estate. There was a time when—"

"Oh, do not plead that to me." I turned and began walking. "I am done."

"Miss Bennet." He followed. "It is late and dark. Allow me to accompany you."

"No!" I turned, lifting a sharp finger between us. "Goodnight."

I stalked off. There was not a single footfall behind me. He must have stood where I left him.

The path was visible where the moonlight struck, but pitch dark in every shadow. Common sense fought with anger until I slowed my pace enough to be safe.

Returning to Longbourn would be easy. I could order a coach tomorrow and leave the following day. That was soon enough that I would not embarrass Charlotte by declining an invitation to Rosings. Although I was unlikely to be invited back after storming out.

My cheeks were wet. I stopped in the dark, frustrated by flickering, conflicted feelings. I wiped my eyes, then wiped my hands on my skirt. "What is *wrong* with me?"

I felt, more than heard, the wyvern glide above me. She settled beside the path a few steps away.

I had not met her at night before. Her eyes were black voids, but when her head moved, they caught flashes of moonlight, sparking red or gold.

child

I heard her. In the dark, in the moonlight, it seemed natural. My anger was lost in wonder.

"You spoke to me before," I said. Her head cocked, scales like frost in the moonlight. "How can you speak?"

i do not speak

That was true. She was making no sound.

When I first studied French, I had laboriously translated each word. But then, after being peppered mercilessly by my father, foreign phrases had become meaning without thought.

This felt the same, but silent.

"This is... astounding. Fantastic." Her eyes watched me without response. "Why do you call me child?"

you are young

"I am twenty years old. How old are you?"

old. i have lived many lives

"Many lives? I do not understand. Do you mean many bindings? I cannot imagine you refer to the Hindu ideas of reincarnation." The wyvern's eyes flickered cool sapphire as her head turned. "Or do you?"

Her jaws opened, panting like she did when I scratched her. Laughter, or joy.

Powerful wings spread. Wind buffeted me, and she was gone.

24

One part of that night was spent reviewing the hundreds of important questions I should have asked a talking wyvern. Even the most idiotic was profoundly more intelligent than asking if she was Hindu.

The other part of the night was confused. My argument with Mr. Darcy had left my emotions splintered and rutted, like a boat flung against an unseen rock.

Bleary-eyed, but bored with staring at the ceiling, I went down when the household woke. Charlotte was friendly but subdued. Mr. Collins was oblivious. When the post delivered two letters for me, I retreated to my room.

The first letter was from Jane, but it was old. She had misaddressed it, and an unknown hand had written a correction.

The other letter was in Mary's distinctive hand. Mary wrote rarely, at least for pleasure, so that was unusual.

I decided to read in order of posting and unsealed Jane's. Her last letter had described another ball, so this might be light-hearted. Mary's letter would likely require that I wade through Latin.

Jane began with no salutation as if continuing a prior page:

"The river is slick and beautiful with rain. Denny just slipped in and floated,

instead of that terrible violence, and was never seen again, happy when he stopped, caught in reeds or sunk at last.

So I danced again. Charles held my hand, and we spun and spun. Cold, though. The snow on my slippers, my hair soaked. He carried me to warm me, and my feelings replenished until the moon drew them. But now I am alone. Mamma is irksome, rattling about Charles leaving when he is underneath—"

That was all. I turned the page over and back, then said out loud, "What?" Charles seemed like a reference to Mr. Bingley, but my mother would have written by express had he returned. And anyway, it was... fantasy. Incoherent.

I opened Mary's letter. The page was dense with her angular writing, marked by sharpened hooks even on the corners of her a's and e's:

"Dear Lizzy,

I write with extreme concern for our sister Jane. She has not left our house since you departed and hardly leaves her room. Her words, whether spoken or written on the peculiar notes she leaves in the hall, have become bizarre.

Papa and I have argued on this. He declares Jane upset over Bingley, or star-crossed, or invokes Ophelia. That is an offensive categorization of female fragility, as if a missing man will fracture our sanity. I told him he was incorrect, but I influence his opinion less than you.

Sadness over Bingley I would believe. But Jane is too sound and sensible for what I see. Therefore I have, for the last eight days, pressed to determine the cause.

After much wasteful investigation, I chanced upon our Scottish laundry maid visiting Jane. Through forceful insistence, I discovered you treated Jane's venomous poisoning by administering draca blood.

I will note that it would have simplified my task had you told me this directly. But do not mistake me; I do not question your decision to treat Jane, for you had no choice.

Through examination of the Loch bairn journal, I suspect Jane has an illness variously named "torn bynding" or "binding sickness." An old passage describes a woman who "drinkes golden ichor most potente" while in love. The man she loves dies before they bind, and she contracts the disease.

I think Jane loved Bingley when she was treated. Because she has not married and bound, the disease has begun.

Lizzy, I am frightened for her. Your return would be welcome. Jane's physical illness seems minor, but her mental symptoms progress.

Mary Bennet.

P.S. Today I consulted with Mr. Jones. He suggested leeching. I doubted the efficacy of this treatment for a mental disturbance, so I requested he demonstrate on myself. Leeching had no discernable effect upon my mind other than disgust. As he could provide no logical reason for leeching when women naturally lose blood every month, I have rejected this treatment for Jane. From this, I have also decided that establishing female physicians would be beneficial. Homo sum: humani nihil a me alienum puto."

I fumbled back through Jane's letters. There were three, all describing balls and dancing and dresses. But Mary said Jane had not left the house, and Mary was exact in her statements.

Read again, the letters were eerily vague. Unfamiliar names mentioned like intimate friends. No places. No dates. Because I had believed them, they were even more frightening.

Mary thought the illness was *torn bynding* or *binding sickness*. That was the same illness Mr. Darcy had attempted to treat in an afflicted wyfe. Although I did not wish to speak with him, I appeared to have little choice. But Colonel Fitzwilliam might know as much. I would see whom I found first.

The colonel was wandering in one of the clearings I haunted. He hailed me when I approached.

"Miss Bennet," he said with an unusually serious bow.

I curtsied with equal formality. "Colonel Fitzwilliam. I have been thinking of our discussion of binding sickness. Can you tell me what treatment you attempted?"

This topic was unexpected. The colonel tugged at his collars before replying. "I hesitate to call it treatment. Darcy was convinced restoring a binding would help, but we found no means to achieve this. He may know more…" His voice trailed off before resuming awkwardly. "I saw him go after you last night."

Last evening's argument returned with all its violent emotion. "Do not speak to me of Mr. Darcy," I said heatedly.

The colonel seemed to approve. He relaxed and gestured to our usual path. We began walking.

"I understand your dismay," he said. "I partake of Rosings's hospitality with unease myself. It was Darcy that convinced me to attend. You must not be too hard on him. He did not assume control of Pemberley until his father died. Father and son loved each other dearly, but they disagreed over policy. I imagine Darcy has divested Pemberley of investments benefiting from slavery. At least, as much as is practical. He is astute in business."

"This sounds greatly like speaking of Mr. Darcy," I said tightly.

"Then I shall apologize for myself. I saw your shock at dinner. I should have exposed Rosings's reprehensible underpinning to you. It would have saved you embarrassment."

"That was not your responsibility." It was Mr. Darcy's. I stopped walking. "Why did Mr. Darcy ask you to Rosings?"

"So, we *are* speaking of Darcy?"

I hmphed but nodded.

"You know I am involved with the military's effort to utilize draca," the colonel said. "Darcy advises that. Or criticizes it. When he called on his aunt for a business matter, I came up from Brighton to discuss the project. Then Darcy lingered, and… I chose to stay. My visit has been unexpectedly enjoyable." The colonel gave me a gallant half-bow, and I smiled to acknowledge the compliment. He held the bow, serious. I looked down, a little flustered, and we resumed walking.

The colonel did not speak for a time. When he did, it was with a chuckle to indicate a lighter subject. "Darcy did convince a friend to divest his investments from the colonies. I met him. A friendly, good-natured fellow."

I matched his humorous tone. "Was he rescued by the Darcy talent for business?"

"In more ways than one. Darcy also saved the fellow—Bingley was his name—from an unfortunate marriage."

Propriety required I speak. All I had to say was that I knew Mr. Bingley. But my heart had stopped. Words would not come. Part of me leaped to a horrid conclusion, while another part could not believe it.

Into my silence, the colonel continued, "The astounding thing was Darcy had to overcome both Bingley's feelings and those of his sisters. Bingley's married sister liked the girl, and Bingley was so passionate that his other sister was wavering. But for Darcy, the challenge was spice. He recruited Caroline, and together they convinced Bingley."

That was so ironic a reversal of my blame for Mr. Bingley's departure that it cut home as the absolute truth.

I no longer cared for propriety. "Why did Mr. Darcy oppose the marriage?" The words emerged thin and uninflected.

"Apparently the girl was pleasant enough, but a puppet of her mother's scheme to acquire Bingley's marriage gold. And the father was a scoundrel. Darcy described a cruel scene at a ball. Darcy is devoted to his sister. He was repulsed to see a father mock his own daughter."

"I must go." Every ounce of my will was consumed to keep my voice from shaking.

"Already? I had hoped… but, of course. May I accompany your return?"

"Thank you, but I received serious family news. I prefer to walk alone. I must plan my travel."

"Travel? Are you leaving?"

"Yes. Tomorrow."

"Tomorrow! But… May I see you before you depart?"

I said something about next morning and turned away. I fixed my eyes where the path vanished behind trees. I had to reach that.

Somehow, I arrived. The moment I was concealed, I bent, racked by tears. Each sob tore like red-hot thorns.

My sister's happiness had been ruined, utterly and casually—almost as sport—by Mr. Darcy. And, because my own hand had poured draca blood into her mouth, that lost love was driving her into madness.

25

Charlotte and Mr. Collins were out when I returned. I brushed past the maid and ended in Charlotte's drawing room, surrounded by embroidery hoops, neat skeins of thread, and a few woven ornaments hung on the walls.

I had cried myself out among the trees. Now I was calm but brittle, as if sealed with cracking varnish. My emotions had parched.

But my purpose was clear. I must cure Jane. Nothing else mattered.

I wrote a note ordering a carriage for tomorrow, traveling first to London then continuing to Longbourn. I sealed it and handed it to the maid, who gave a nervous curtsy and left to deliver it.

Then I stood, thinking.

Discard supposition and fancy. What did I know? Mary had found knowledge of this illness in our journal. The Scottish maid might have wisdom. Those, I would trust. But there was no reason to approach Mr. Darcy. Even if the idea were not abhorrent, the wyfe he treated had died.

The doorbell jingled, unanswered because the maid was out. It rang again. I did not move.

The sunlight shifted across Charlotte's embroidery threads, their hues ordered to follow a rainbow.

The front door rattled as the maid returned. I heard her speak to someone outside. She entered the drawing room.

"Mr. Darcy, ma'am."

He strode in on her heels without waiting to be acknowledged, and she left hurriedly.

His hair was disheveled, his hands clenched. He crossed the room twice, anxious or upset, his riding boots heavy on the floor.

My eyes followed him. This was the man who had harmed my sister. It was bizarre that he was present. Surely, he would recognize his mistake and leave.

He turned to me. "In vain I have struggled. It will not do. My feelings will not be repressed. You must allow me to tell you how ardently I admire and love you."

"What?" I spoke simply because his words were incongruous. Preposterous.

"I cannot bear to continue my silence. I hoped that the danger of our union could dissuade me, but…" He gave a despairing laugh. "Oh, I have tried! I see how draca worship you. Every dark memory cries that you must not be exposed to Pemberley. But the infatuated regard of those draca mirrors my own. I have tested myself by submerging in petty disgrace. I imagine your heartless, disporting father. Your mother scheming for marriage gold. But the degradation of my relations, the censure of society —even the mockery—is nothing to me. I love you. The sensation overwhelms anything I have experienced before. It is a glorious agony. Desperately, passionately, I ask that you end my torment, and consent to be my wyfe."

My disbelief had become… blankness. Not surprise. Not anger. After all the emotion that had ravaged me, this was a farce, a pathetic play that failed to engage an iota of my belief. A tasteless display by a strutting actor with poor lines.

He was waiting, looking down at me from all that height.

"It is expected," I said, "that an offer of marriage is met with civil appreciation, however unequally the avowed sentiments may be returned. If I could feel gratitude, I would thank you. But I cannot. You speak of torment. I had thought I would regret inflicting pain on anyone, but today, I am singularly uncaring. At least your suffering was unintended. I suppose that is my defense."

Surprise or disbelief crossed his features, then he whitened with anger.

"Is this Wickham?" he said. "Has he drawn you into his evil?"

"*Wickham?*" I had not thought of him for weeks, other than worrying about his proximity to Lydia while she visited Brighton.

"You take an eager interest in that gentleman's concerns!"

"I have not the slightest interest in Mr. Wickham. Or his concerns."

Mr. Darcy's lips sneered, the next moment he was puzzled, then he was angry again. His hand grabbed the mantelpiece, and ornaments rattled. "Then what? Why, with so little regret, am I rejected?"

There it was. His privilege, bare and obvious. To think that, once, I had almost been fooled. Hot anger climbed in my chest.

"Shall I remind you of the language of your declaration? We stand in your aunt's estate financed by the misery of slaves, and you dare to disdain my relations? Pemberley itself has benefited from this moral corruption, and you declare me a disgrace? A degradation?"

"So you wish I flattered you? Concealed my struggles? But disguise of every sort is my abhorrence."

"How strange, when you are so skilled at concealment. Have you not egregiously misled and betrayed me all these weeks?" He had the temerity to appear confused, and my anger erupted. "Do you think *any* consideration would tempt me to accept the man who has ruined, perhaps forever, the happiness—indeed, the very life—of a most beloved sister?"

Realization dawned over his face, but he said nothing.

"Can you deny you have done it?" I repeated.

At last, he answered, "I have no wish to deny that I did everything in my power to separate my friend from your sister."

"Your vanity astounds me. Did you think I would not discover the truth? Did you imagine the Darcy name would overwhelm my senses, or purge my love for my family? But I can guess the answer. The wealthy believe their money buys anything. You satisfy every selfish whim with your purse. Why not a wyfe?"

"And this is your criticism! With no knowledge of my family, or of my work—indeed, in ignorance of every aspect of my life—you condemn me as self-indulgent and decadent. But perhaps, if I had hidden the vile history of my fortune, you would have been comforted. Even though I have worked tirelessly to level that moral balance." He stepped closer, rigid with anger. "To think I admired—" He recoiled as if struck, although I stood unmoving, then his posture became entreating and his voice desperate. "I *admire* your insistence on truth. *You* gave me the courage to challenge the dark pall of Pemberley."

His intensity penetrated my anger. "What dark pall?"

He fell utterly still, his lips a fraction apart.

A breath passed, and another, and my fury broke free. "Silence, again. Your scruple for truth is most one-sided. Scrutinize yourself, for your disdain is illuminating." My voice rang out. "What deficiencies condemn my sister and me? Lack of wealth? Insufficient influence? Those are superficial, egotistical concerns. They are beneath consideration for a gentleman, and they are inconsequential to me. As are *you*. Indeed, immediately upon our acquaintance, your arrogance, your conceit, and your selfish entitlement proved you were the last man in the world whom I would ever marry!"

There were inches between us. I stepped back, my shoulders rising and falling as if I had run a mile.

Mr. Darcy paled like death. My heart pounded my ribs.

When he spoke, his voice was cracked and pitted—brittle iron hammered flat. "You have said quite enough, madam. I perfectly comprehend your feelings. Forgive me for having taken up your time, and accept my best wishes for your health and happiness."

He snapped a bow and left.

26

Charlotte returned, and I stammered an explanation of my sudden decision to leave. Then I retired to rest, pleading exhaustion. That was true—I had not slept the night before. I collapsed on the bed and woke to a brightening window.

The Collins's narrow guest bed was cozy with layers of wool and cotton. Birds chirped outside. Yesterday's disconnected scraps of ideas returned, but coherent. What had felt desperate, now seemed possible. Maybe it was the birdsong and a rising sun.

I organized my things to depart, ate a bite of breakfast, then stepped outside for one last walk to fit the final pieces, hopping familiar logs and dodging rough spots while I thought.

When I saw Mr. Darcy approaching, I stopped to see what he would do. That part of yesterday seemed remote and fanciful.

He held out a letter. My fingers took it.

Precisely, he said, "I have been walking for some time in the hope of meeting you. Will you do me the honor of reading this letter?" With a slight bow, he strode off and was soon out of sight.

Apprehensive but curious, I examined the envelope. The Darcy seal, pressed into burgundy wax, was elaborate. I pressed my thumbs to shatter it thoroughly, then opened the envelope.

There were two sheets of paper written in a close hand. I forded a few yards of wilderness to reach a groomed lane where I could read while my feet wandered.

The letter was dated from Rosings, at eight o'clock in the morning:

"Madam, be not alarmed that this letter contains any repetition of those sentiments or renewal of those offers which were yesterday so disgusting to you. This letter would be unnecessary had not my character required it to be written. I trust your sense of justice will require you to read it.

First, on the matter of Mr. Wickham—"

I stopped reading with a snort. "What is his obsession with Wickham?" I skipped forward until I saw this:

"Next, at dinner, I observed your dismay and revulsion at Rosings's investment in colonial plantations. Your—"

The remainder of that sentence was crossed out. Curious, I held the page to the sun. I made out *"Your eyes"* but the ink had been wet when covered, and the rest was obscured.

After that hidden passage, it continued:

"It was only when I came into my inheritance that I had authority to act as my conscience dictated. Pemberley was then purged of all investment that benefitted, directly or indirectly, from slavery. This was accomplished at great financial risk and cost due to the speed with which I acted. My only delay was first to separate and protect my sister's inheritance in case disaster resulted. I will write no further on the specifics, other than I have striven since to restore Pemberley and my family's fortune.

As our lives are not to intersect, I see no necessity to rebut your accusations of selfishness in pursuit of wealth and influence, other than to say my conscience is clear."

I hmphed. Doubtless he prided himself on creating jobs for tailors.

"Lastly, and for you, most importantly: I had not been long in Hertfordshire before I saw that Bingley preferred your sister to any other woman in the country. But it was not till the dance at Netherfield, when I had the honor of dancing with you, that he told me his feelings were a serious attachment.

My initial concern stemmed from observing your sister. Although she received Bingley's attentions with pleasure, I was convinced she did not return them in any serious manner. Your superior knowledge of your sister requires that I accept your judgment. If by my error I inflicted pain on her, your resentment is not unreasonable.

However, my concerns sharpened when I saw your mother's obsession with binding and her public and unconscionable pursuit of Bingley's marriage gold. And then I was repulsed by your father's cruel public shaming of your sister Mary. From the history I have recounted, you understand the irony and potency of your final words to me that evening—'Speak to me again when you have defended a heartbroken sister.'"

What had he recounted? I must have missed something when I skipped his passage on Wickham. The letter finished:

"This, madam, is a faithful narrative that I provide, trusting to your honor and discretion.

Fitzwilliam Darcy."

I had stopped walking as I became engrossed. Now, for the first time, the incredible nature of his proposal sank in. Mr. Darcy, a man of extraordinary consequence and wealth, had asked me to marry him. He had been in love with me for some time. All those long walks and sudden silences, in hindsight, seemed charged with significance.

It was, of course, unbelievable. But Charlotte had noticed. She even warned me that he was promised to Lady Catherine's daughter. What had happened to that? Presumably, this would annoy her ladyship more than refusing a tart.

In fact, Charlotte had prodded me several times about Mr. Darcy's attention. Was I so oblivious?

"Miss Bennet?"

Colonel Fitzwilliam was a dozen yards down the lane, hesitant to break my reverie.

I put away the letter, remembering I had promised to meet the colonel before I left. "Good morning, Colonel. I am sorry I did not find you sooner."

"I am happy we have met. Do you have some time before you depart?"

"Of course. Shall we walk?" Lighter conversation would be a relief.

"I am honored." He bowed, and we set off toward our favorite path.

I walked in silence, considering Mr. Darcy's letter. His excuse for interfering between Jane and Mr. Bingley was offensive and cruel. But Jane's restrained manner did conceal her feelings. So perhaps that part was credible. With a shock, I realized Mr. Darcy did not know his interference had hurt Jane's health.

Colonel Fitzwilliam cleared his throat. "I wished to speak with you before your travel separated us."

"Yes?" I stopped. We were in a pleasant treed area, dappled with sunlight.

The colonel turned decisively to me, his posture exact. A gentleman officer, and extremely serious.

"Miss Elizabeth Bennet." He took a breath. "I have, for some time, wished to speak with you on a topic that is most personal and significant."

He waited, as attentive and considerate as always. When I looked puzzled, he said hesitantly, "I shall, of course, desist if you do not welcome this conversation. I am fully aware of my limited prospects. For myself, I am decided. I care not for my father's wrath. But the admiration that prompts me to speak also makes me hesitate, for you deserve a match of greater consequence. Say a word, and it will be as if I had never spoken. My respect for you will be unchanged."

Oh.

How different this was from my conversation yesterday. The colonel was a man I respected and genuinely liked. A man I would never wish to hurt.

And yet, I knew my answer was no. Why, though?

"I... Your regard honors me. Truly. And I care nothing for prospects. But I... This is a difficult time when I am unable..." I struggled to find words. Part of me wondered if I might, in time, say yes. Another part knew I never would.

"I understand. Shall we finish our walk?"

He offered his arm, and we proceeded in silence, my bottom lip crushed between my teeth to hide my feelings until I was alone.

27

I packed slowly in my room, or, more honestly, I unpacked and repacked, rearranging skirts and gloves and ribbons.

Colonel Fitzwilliam's proposal, with his selfless decorum, left me feeling sad and cruel. And confused, for I was unsure why I refused. He was not odious like Mr. Collins. And for all his claims of penury, compared to my prospects once Longbourn was lost, the colonel offered a comfortable life.

In fact, if Jane and I were correct that a bound Bennet daughter might inherit Longbourn, I should jump at the first marriage proposal I got. Instead, I had declined three.

And why was I constantly being surprised by proposals of marriage? That seemed a poor way to move through life. I must be horribly inattentive.

"It is because I wish to be in love," I said to the mirror. I had never said that before. The words sounded silly and selfish. Then, irritatingly, the image that popped into my head was walking through the trees with Mr. Darcy.

"I will cure Jane," I announced. That was better.

The coach would arrive soon, and I had farewells to make. I closed a hatbox, stretched tense shoulders, then went lightly down the stairs. After checking that Mr. Collins was engrossed in his book room, I exited into the sunlit garden behind the house.

I found an area free of fragile young sprouts. A few breaths later, the wyvern glided to earth several steps away. This time, she came no closer.

you are leaving

"My sister is ill." Did sister mean anything to a wyvern? Did illness?

I concentrated on Jane as I had seen her last, wasted and silent.

The wyvern stamped one bronze foot, distressed, her wings half-unfurling. Like memory, I saw an unknown woman, gaunt and staring from a crude bed of reeds. A victim of binding sickness?

The wyvern's wings settled, her eyes leaf-green like the foliage around us.

you are leaving him

"Who?"

Images flickered through my mind. Postures and strides, not features or dress as I would describe a person. But it was Mr. Darcy.

"Yes, I am leaving him." My throat tightened. Anger? Emotions blurred and chased back and forth.

go to the lake

Deep water the color of cold. The lowered path of the sun in the north. People's faces striped in brilliant patterns of glowing indigo.

"I do not understand. What lake?"

for your sister

Her wings fanned, leaves and twigs whirled, and she was gone.

"Lizzy?" Charlotte's voice was hesitant behind me. "The carriage is here." My turmoil must have shown because she took my hand. "You have hardly spoken since we were at Rosings. Are you so angry?"

I had told her that Jane was unwell. But nothing of... everything else.

"Not angry with you. You have been a generous and wonderful friend."

Her smile was relieved. "I greatly enjoyed your visit. I feared you would be bored with so little society."

I laughed at that, which cheered me up. "I assure you I was not bored."

"Will Mr. Darcy come to see you off?"

I kept my smile, determined to be amused. "I fear not."

We walked to the front. The driver was loading my bags while Mr. Collins squawked inane advice.

Charlotte looked down the road. "Perhaps you were mistaken?" One of her ladyship's carriages was approaching.

Although I knew it would not be Mr. Darcy, I was surprised when the footman unlatched the door and Lady Catherine descended. She frowned at my iron-barred carriage and clanged it with her cane before approaching.

"Lady Catherine." I curtsied.

"So, you depart," Lady Catherine observed.

"Yes, madam."

"Whatever for? Mrs. Bennet could certainly spare you for another fortnight."

"But my father cannot. He wrote to hurry my return."

"Your *father?* What use has a father for daughters? If you will stay another month, it will be in my power to take you as far as London. There should be room for you, as you are not large."

"You are all kindness. But I believe I must abide by my original plan."

"Hmph. And where is my vexatious nephew?"

"Which one, madam?" I asked innocently.

"Darcy, of course. I was certain he would be here."

Charlotte raised her eyebrows. I wished I had told her a little more so she could stop reminding me of how idiotic I was.

Her ladyship prodded open the door of my carriage with her cane. She peered inside, perhaps to ensure that Mr. Darcy was not hiding. "Did your father not send a servant?"

"I hired the coach myself."

"You are traveling *alone?* Not through London, I hope!"

"I will not pass through London." Because I was stopping in London. That was a false distinction, but it was none of her business.

"Very well. You will return in the autumn. Mrs. Collins will be glad of your company. I shall expect you at Rosings."

I did not answer. Her ladyship drove off without noticing.

"Will you come back, Lizzy?" asked Charlotte softly.

"To you. Not to Rosings. We shall need a plot for that."

I finished my farewells. Then I paused at the door to the carriage. The interior was stifling and dark, with narrow beams of light through the barred window slots.

"Do you need a hand up, ma'am?" the driver called from his perch.

His seat looked wide enough for two. "May I ride up there?"

"*Here*, ma'am?" He laughed.

"I have seen passengers ride atop."

"Yes, ma'am. Them as can't pay for the coach. Even had a woman sit up here, once. Not a lady, though."

"A woman and a lady sit the same way."

"Not sure I agree, ma'am." I folded my arms and waited. "All right, then. Best I pull you up." He reached down a hand.

It was a high step, and Mr. Collins turned red, then turned his back. But I reached the seat. The driver hopped down and locked the carriage so my luggage would survive if a pack of draca ate us.

We set off with a whistle and the clop of hooves. Loose bolts jingled festively. The view was wonderful, much higher than a usual carriage seat.

With a rustle of parted air, the wyvern flashed over us.

"Devil take me!" The driver cried. "It's a dragon!"

That was, by far, the most vulgar language ever uttered in my presence. I tensed, waiting for an apology.

The driver twisted to watch the wyvern, his mouth hanging. He exclaimed again. Clearly, no apology was forthcoming.

I could sit with my mouth pruned like Lady Catherine. Or not.

"She is a wyvern," I said. "A breed of draca. Dragons are only myth."

"Is that so?" Our heads turned as she arced and swept over again. "What's she doing?"

"Saying goodbye."

"Blind me. She's beautiful. A clever girl, too. See how she comes from behind and turns? Not spooking the horses."

"I had not realized. I suppose she learned that from hunting."

The driver explained how horses see the world, and the good and bad of blinders, and I chatted about draca, and we clattered along the road to London.

WHAT CURES an unwed woman who must bind? Mary would search the journal for answers. Our Scottish maid could quote lore and legend. The wyvern advised an unnamed lake.

Common sense offered a simpler path. Jane should marry Mr. Bingley. But if wishing produced weddings, my mother would have five married daughters by now. So, I would do more than wish.

I was willing to call alone on Mr. Bingley. But that was brazen, and a scandal would destroy any hope of reconnection. Also, I had no idea where he lived.

But Jane had corresponded with Miss Bingley, and I remembered the street name from the envelope, and that her sister, Mrs. Hurst, lived on the same street.

Mrs. Hurst approved of Jane, according to Colonel Fitzwilliam. And nothing prevented me from calling on Mrs. Hurst. Other than our mutual hatred.

When the driver stopped for directions, I climbed down to sit in the carriage. This was a time for decorum. We rolled on, questions were shouted, then we stopped. The carriage door opened.

"Ma'am. The Hurst residence." The driver was all formality now, but he winked as I stepped down.

The Hursts lived in a narrow four-story terrace home on an elegant block. The entrance had huge white columns framing a wide, black door. The effect was modern and severe, but, judging from the rest of the street, in fashion.

I was nervous. Who has made a social call where the life of their sister depended on the outcome?

I rang. The door was opened by a white-haired man with a slight stoop. He was soberly dressed and subtly proud. A butler.

"Good afternoon, madam."

"Good afternoon. I am calling without appointment for Mrs. Hurst." I placed my card on his silver tray. "Please tell her it is an urgent matter."

He nodded and left at a snail's pace. A clock ticked ponderously. I scuffed at the marble floor, then checked my hat for dust in the mirror.

The clock had advanced eight minutes when he returned. "Madam." He gestured to a doorway. I puffed a sigh of relief. I had not been sure I would be received.

I was shown into an elegant drawing room, long and thin by the standards of a country home, but good-sized in town. Mrs. Hurst stood at the far end, hands crossed against her elaborate floral dress.

She made no motion of greeting. She said nothing.

"Thank you for receiving me," I said.

"You are visiting London," she observed, which seemed rather obvious. Then she added, "Alone."

On the drive up, I had considered behavior so much more egregious than traveling alone that I forgot how scandalous my mere presence was. A lady did not travel unaccompanied. Perhaps Mrs. Hurst had received me solely to gather gossip.

But social fencing would end this interview in moments. We had to reach the real topic before I was cast out.

I took a deep breath and began.

"Mrs. Hurst. Unintentionally, and through private communication, I have learned the cause of Mr. Bingley's sudden return to London and his separation from my sister Jane. I should add that my sister knows nothing of this, and she is unaware of my presence here."

There. I was committed now.

Mrs. Hurst was silent.

"Part of my information," I continued, "is that certain parties"—Mr. Darcy—"believed the separation of your brother and my sister was of little consequence, for my sister held no great affection for your brother." My voice caught. I swallowed. "I can assure you that is untrue."

There was dead silence. I could feel my opportunity to reach this woman closing. I rushed on.

"I am aware that my visit and request are extraordinary—"

"I have heard no request," she interrupted sharply.

It was a relief to hear a response, even that.

"I… I will presume to suggest that the separation of Mr. Bingley and my sister, however well intentioned, may not be in their mutual best interest. Not… conducive to their happiness. I have reason to think you are sympathetic to my view. Therefore…"

"Therefore, what?"

"Perhaps we could… have them thrown into each other's way somehow? I am sure it would take no more than that. If only they met again—" I stopped. I sounded like a meddling fool in a terrible romantic novel.

Mrs. Hurst was staring like she had admitted a lunatic to her drawing room. Perhaps she had.

"How does your brother feel?" I asked, clutching at any straw.

She stiffened and turned, staring at a vase of daisies as if her brother's innermost secrets hid in the petals. Seconds passed. "My brother was devastated."

"Then why did he *leave?*" Pathetically, my voice quavered on the last word.

"Charles is very influenced by the 'certain parties' you mentioned. Will you name them?"

That was a brilliant, vicious request. Now I was forced to utter a specific accusation. If I was wrong, or if she wanted to use my words against me, all was lost.

But her escalation broke my restraint. Fear of society's rules—those vacuous moats that hold everyone in their allotted place—fell away. The rules still existed. Their practical power was unchanged. But if they blocked me from helping Jane, they were unjust. Unworthy of consideration.

"Mr. Darcy," I answered, in a tone of moral condemnation that would have impressed even Mary.

Mrs. Hurst laughed bitterly.

"Your sister Jane is a gentle, kind-hearted girl. I thought she loved my brother, and I know my brother loves her. But I do not like you, Eliza Bennet. You are a clever, pretty flirt. The sort who drifts through life pursued by doting men whom you treat thoughtlessly, as if it is an accomplishment to bend hearts. The sort who never learns that life is a battle. Have children, and you will learn what it means to care, and to fight for something, and to defend those whom you love from those who would take everything you cherish."

I had never been called a flirt before. I thought it a poor attack. Compared to her sister's unblushing pursuit of Mr. Darcy—or to my two youngest sisters—I was a cloistered nun. But her words stirred unpleasant echoes of Mary's criticism at the ball.

A lot had changed since then.

I said, "I think, madam, that you do not know me. I certainly do not know you. I will say only that I love, and defend, and am fighting for my sister."

She shook her head, derisive or disbelieving. "For my brother's sake, I would not oppose your plan. If I could call it that. But Charles is traveling."

My relief at securing so crucial an ally made me light-headed. Now, there was hope of success. More than success. A happy ending. A fairytale ending.

Then I realized what else she had said.

"Traveling? May I ask when he will return?" Perhaps I could have Jane in London by then.

"He is in America. He is not expected back for a year. Longer, most likely."

My relief—my vision of hugging Jane and Mr. Bingley at their wedding—fell to dust.

28

The rattle of iron bolts and bars ceased as the coach stopped on Gracechurch Street, a respectable but more economical neighborhood.

This destination was a haven, the home of Mr. and Mrs. Gardiner, my uncle and aunt. They were sensible and efficient people. That was desperately appealing right now.

I rang. A housemaid not yet eighteen, with brilliant yellow hair escaping her cap, peered through the opening door, then swung it wide and broke into smiles. "Miss Elizabeth!"

"Hello, Dorothy," I said, smiling back. From private talks with my despairing aunt, I knew Dorothy was a marginal maid, but she was full of infectious good spirit and wonderful with the children. My aunt had two girls and two boys, all younger than nine, so this was a gift.

"Oh, my goodness! Let me tell the missus!" Dorothy ran off, forgetting to invite me in. But I had visited many times, so I invaded their entryway, closed the door, and shook out my shawl.

"Lizzy! What a wonderful surprise!" My aunt gave me a hug. Her grip tightened when she realized I needed a good squeeze.

"I am sorry I did not write before coming," I said when we separated. "It has been a confused and worrying few days."

"What is wrong?" Her face was drawn up in concern.

At that moment we were assaulted by squealing children. Mrs. Gardiner shooed them away with promises of a visit later, and she and I retired to the parlor.

She straightened her dress as we sat, choosing her words. "Mr. Gardiner will be in the office for several more hours. Unless... Lizzy, should I send for him?"

"Please do not. I must continue to Longbourn. I am here in part to see a friendly face"—at this, my aunt reached over to hold my fingers—"but also to ask a large favor."

I explained that Jane was seriously ill, although I hoped not in immediate danger. I continued, "It is a rare and exotic illness that relates to draca and binding. I have it on good advice that a cure exists in the northern lakes."

"That is very strange." My aunt looked dubious. "What authority gave you this advice?"

"You will think I am mad, but you must believe me." My aunt's eyebrows rose. I took a deep breath. I had not shared this with anyone. "I was told by a draca."

"You cannot be serious."

"I am quite sincere. A wyvern told me. I have discovered they are capable of speech. Well, not *speech.* Her mouth could not make the sounds of human speech. But we communicate. Her words rather pop into my head. If she is in the mood."

My aunt's eyebrows vanished behind her tasteful curls of hair. "How extraordinary," she said in a tiny voice.

"I have not heard of anyone else who can communicate this way. And I am hesitant to share the knowledge broadly. There would be disapproval." In America, I would probably be burned at the stake. Even here, the Church would condemn me.

"Of course, Lizzy. I will keep it secret. I shall not even tell Mr. Gardiner unless you wish it. But... how is this possible?"

"I do not know." A tired laugh escaped. "I always thought draca disliked me. Now I suspect I have some kind of affinity with them."

"Are you certain? If you are upset over Jane, might it be nerves? A... wishful fancy?"

I cast my mind outward, remembering their bound draca. I found a presence and concentrated. Then, like a disreputable street performer, I waved dramatically at the doorway as their little draca scurried into the room. He barreled over, cooing, and I scooped him onto my lap.

"My word." My aunt's eyes were round. "You can *speak* with him?"

The Gardiners had bound a tykeworm, a quadruped no bigger than a tiny Yorkshire terrier. Tykes were energetic little beasts and considered good in town because they enjoyed indoor living and did not throw fire, so a stone draca house was not required. This one was nutmeg brown with ripe-pumpkin toes and lighter orange patches on his sides.

I lifted him, and we stared into each other's eyes. His head tilted like an inquisitive puppy. It was hard to be cute without fur or floppy ears, but he had big, black eyes and panted cheerfully, showing a row of blade-like black teeth.

"I sense his mood, and I can call him," I answered. "But I have only heard words from a wyvern. Perhaps the other breeds do not have that ability."

"I have never seen him act this way. Even when you visited before."

"My affinity began recently. It started with our firedrake, a few months ago." Had the fright of the mad dog's attack affected me somehow?

We exchanged observations on how unusual this was. Hopefully, my aunt was coming to terms with her niece having a peculiar ability.

Then she asked, "What has this to do with the lakes?"

"When I told the wyvern that Jane was ill, she showed me an image of a large, cold lake. Somewhere in the north and surrounded by… strange people. She said it would help." My aunt's brows had returned to their invisible perch behind her hair. "I will continue to Longbourn to see if I am needed there. But my mother and father are home, and Mary is most competent. If there is nothing more to do, I wish to visit the lake country."

"You expect to find this lake? There are hundreds of lakes. Thousands."

"I have more guidance than I can put into words. I know… how north it is. I know the feel of the land." My aunt's lips compacted into skeptical lines. I said hastily, "This is where I hoped for your help. We had planned a northern tour this spring."

"A tour for *pleasure*. This is extraordinary. What would you do if we found this lake?"

"I hope to know when the time comes."

"You are placing a great deal of trust in an animal. In your… impressions of an animal's thoughts."

"A wyvern is an extraordinary and mystical creature. And this wyvern is old. I feel the years in her. She is wise."

My aunt shook her head. "All this 'feeling' and mysticism is most unlike you, Lizzy." My face fell, and she smiled. "You mistake me. Of course, we can do the tour. What is different from our plan, in any case? Except that we must visit Longbourn first to see Jane. I am worried by your news."

"Of course."

"And I shall insist you enjoy our tour. I grew up in the north, and it is beautiful. I will be hurt if we dash about, casting a glance at each lake and then departing, for it is the wrong one."

I bit my lip. I had been imagining exactly that. Was she indulging me without believing?

However, we did not have the resources to race about the country like a military brigade. And I could not travel alone. While my one-day dash from Rosings to Longbourn would shock some people, I had the excuse of an ill sister. But an unmarried lady staying alone at inns would be inexcusable.

We agreed that she would ask Mr. Gardiner about departing next week. Then, if all worked as planned, we would set out to the north, hunting a mysterious lake and a miraculous cure.

29

The next week, on a bench in the Longbourn garden, I took out Mr. Darcy's letter. The paper unfolded like velvet, creased and uncreased many times by now.

I began by rereading his insulting excuse for interfering between Jane and Mr. Bingley. That always left me vexed, so it was a firm footing from which to proceed.

What came next depended on my mood. Because I was in our garden, I reread the account of Mr. Wickham. I had not read this the first day, and it was remarkable.

When Mr. Darcy inherited, he granted the old Briton villages within Pemberley's borders autonomy over their affairs. That eliminated the administrative position Mr. Wickham had filled for a year. In compensation, Mr. Darcy gave Mr. Wickham a generous bequest.

Those funds were squandered. Mr. Wickham then demanded more and more money until Mr. Darcy discovered disturbing abuses during Mr. Wickham's period of authority and cut him off.

But the conclusion was more shocking, and it rang of truth given my own confrontation when I caught Mr. Wickham with Lydia, a few paces from where I now sat:

"Wickham, angry and desperate, then exploited my sister Georgiana's lifelong affection by persuading her to believe herself in love, and to consent to an elopement. She was then but fifteen, which must be her excuse. I am happy that I owe my knowledge of this to herself. Georgiana was unwilling to grieve a brother whom she looked up to as a father. She acknowledged the whole to me before it was too late.

My confrontation with Wickham was intense, and more than once threatened violence. Wickham unquestionably sought both my sister's fortune and revenge on me. But in the heat of argument, Wickham revealed a worse goal.

Wickham was obsessed with old myths of mystical power drawn from draca. He pursued marriage with Georgiana to achieve this. My father's estate granted Georgiana a formidable stake of marriage gold—a provision that she and I have since chosen to dissolve. But with that, and because our mother and aunt both bound wyverns, it was assumed Georgiana would have a remarkable binding. And, as Wickham grew up intimately connected to our family, he was aware that Georgiana had other extraordinary abilities."

At this point, I stopped reading in frustration. *What* extraordinary abilities? Mr. Rabb, the Pemberley gamekeeper, had said Miss Darcy could touch any draca. Was she like me? But my acquaintance with Mr. Darcy was irrevocably ended. I had no way to discover the truth.

And then there was their renunciation of marriage gold. I had no legitimate reason to wonder about this, but I was strongly curious.

I sighed and looked at Jane, who was seated beside me on the bench. "How shall I solve these riddles?"

After much coaxing, I had convinced Jane to come out into the sun. She was sallow-skinned, her eyes sunken and too bright. Her brow and cheekbones cast shadows on her wasted face.

Her eyes rose to meet mine, and she smiled. My breath caught.

"The moon will pull it." She looked at the empty blue sky. "Oh. Gray. Charles, lost like a silver charm…" The rest was wisps of words. Her long fingers lifted to tangle in her yellow hair. She twisted, winding a strained ball, and began to keen in distress.

"Jane, darling. You must not." I eased her hand into her lap, and she became quiet again.

"Lizzy?" Mary, holding the journal, had come from the back door. "I wish to speak before you go."

I touched the bench beside me, and she sat, fiddling with the journal in which she had inserted many dark ribbons.

She opened a page marked with black satin. "This part: '*Her wæs eac eorðstyrung on lak manegum stowum.*' I have determined it speaks of an earthquake at a lake. Later, it mentions the third lake. So, there is more than one..."

"Mary, you have told me this already."

"I have?" Mary looked as tired as Jane, although for Mary it was too much worry and too little sleep.

"Yes. I am certain you have found every clue hidden in these pages. All you must do now is care for Jane until I return." Mary nodded, and I hugged her close. "It will be fine. Wait and see."

Mary hugged back hard, then grasped my shoulders so we faced each other. She had changed her hair while I was gone, wearing it down so it hung straight from her black bonnet to her shoulders. Once I had gotten over my surprise, I thought it pretty. It surrounded the warm brown of her eyes. But I had not said that to Mary, who likely wished to be shocking.

"Loch bairn," she said intensely. "I wonder if we have overcomplicated the problem. That could be the name of a lake. Perhaps that is what you seek?"

"A Scottish lake? I fear my aunt and uncle do not intend to go all the way to Scotland."

"Then go without them."

"Mary!" I reproached. She raised an eyebrow, unflinching, and I sighed. "If Jane's situation becomes so dire, I will, although I fear we will end this as social outcasts. But I would need more direction than 'look in Scotland.'" I paused. "There is another resource. If things become so dire. Pemberley has a collection of writing on draca."

"Pemberley? Mr. Darcy's estate?"

"Yes. He told me of it himself."

"Derbyshire is north. Could you not visit on this tour?"

I gave a weak smile. "I cannot visit Pemberley."

"Oh, Lizzy." Mary had the temerity to laugh. "I am certain Mr. Darcy would receive *you*."

Had even Mary noticed what I had not? "I think not. While I was at Charlotte's, Mr. Darcy and I… argued."

"Over what?"

I discovered I was extremely impatient to tell someone. In normal circumstances, I would have shared this with Jane the first night. "You must keep it secret. Mr. Darcy proposed to me." Mary's mouth fell open, and I recounted the scene between us and parts of his letter, though nothing concerning his interference with Jane and Mr. Bingley.

"That is most remarkable," Mary said. "What a pity he was so arrogant. I thought him more considerate than that. But arrogance is a symptom of wealth. I applaud that you condemned him vehemently and irreparably."

"Thank you, Mary," I said dryly.

Rereading the account of Mr. Wickham had convinced me to attempt another task, so I went inside to tap on my father's library door.

"Come, Lizzy," he called, holding out a hand as I entered, which I took with a smile. "And so, you depart again. We have barely subdued the chaos from your last absence."

"Mary has done very well."

"Indeed, she has. I fan a spark of hope that I have three sensible daughters, not two." His smile fell away. "I was most happy to see Jane outside with you. Is she better today?"

"The same, I am afraid." He nodded, wrinkles worn deep around his eyes. "Papa, we have another daughter absent. I worry about Lydia alone for so long. Is it time for her to return?"

"Lydia writes—when she writes at all—of her ecstasies in Brighton. She is a foolish girl. But why do you keep asking? Has her behavior frightened away some gentleman you fancy?"

Unwanted, a phrase from Mr. Darcy's letter returned: "*And then I was repulsed by your father's cruel public shaming of your sister Mary.*" How would Papa feel if he knew his own behavior, which he regretted horribly, had helped ruin Jane's chance for happiness?

"Lizzy?"

I started, my fingers touching the letter in my pocket. Again, I considered telling my experience with Mr. Wickham. Again, I remained silent.

"I AM ENDEAVORING FRANK CONVERSATION TODAY," I said, "with mixed success. Now, it is your turn."

Our firedrake was curled and brooding on his iron perch. His narrow, bronze head emerged from under a wing.

"I have spoken with a wyvern. She told me… advice, or knowledge. If you have that ability, I require it now. For I am desperately in need of help."

Two gleaming black eyes watched. I relaxed, letting my awareness flow outward.

There was a wild squawk. The drake backwinged off his perch, half-falling to the ground. He hissed, twisting through agitated curves on the dirt.

"What is wrong?" I cried. "Other draca approach me, but you retreat. Do you hate me? I do not understand."

Images flashed in my mind's eye, sharp as night lit by lightning—sketches charged with meaning, like a dream where vision and insight are impossibly entangled. A heavy iron cage, closed by an immense force. A crushing boulder, its weight an inescapable trap.

The drake's wings spread, and with two massive beats, he soared high above. I watched him vanish into the distance.

30

"What's your business, sir?" asked the militia soldier outside our carriage window.

I recognized a Derby accent. After seven days traveling with my aunt and uncle, I could distinguish northern dialects.

The soldier's tone was brusque, but Mr. Gardiner was polite. "Touring, for pleasure. We will stay in Taddington."

The soldier, a skinny, sandy-haired man in his late twenties, leaned through the open window. The top button of his jacket was undone, and he had a slovenly attitude I disliked.

His gaze lingered on me. I hardened my expression, imagining Lady Catherine sternly counting uneaten tarts, and he looked away.

"I am surprised to encounter a militia officer in the Peaks," my aunt said. "Is there some threat?"

I knew enough insignia to see the man was no officer, but he did not correct her. "French spies, ma'am. Bonaparte's men were spotted not far from here."

"Here? We are in the center of England." My aunt was offended, perhaps because she had grown up nearby.

"Probably lost their way," my uncle said jovially.

"You'll have to change your way," the soldier said. His tongue protruded, working at a tooth. "We closed the west road. You got to go east."

My uncle frowned. "That is inconvenient."

"No!" I broke in. "East is good." I squeezed past to leave the carriage, brushing by the surprised soldier. The Gardiners' tykeworm, which traveled with us inside the coach, gamboled across the leaf-covered dirt at my feet.

It was almost noon, the sun at its peak for late March. The angle looked… right. I closed my eyes, summoning the impressions from the wyvern, and turned in place. The warmth of the sun spun, and the shape of the land turned around me. Not the land itself—the things living in the land. Draca.

For the first time, we were high enough. The horses had been toiling upward for hours.

I stopped and extended my arm so I would not lose my bearings, then opened my eyes. "Yes. We should go east."

The soldier's jaw hung, exposing crooked, brown teeth.

"Very good," my uncle said, as if young ladies spun like compasses every day. "May we proceed, officer?" I climbed back in, impatient and ignoring their discussion of landmarks and distances.

The driver backed and turned the coach, then we set off, bouncing over a road rough with forest roots. The entire morning's travel had been exceedingly bumpy.

My aunt and uncle exchanged a glance of the sort acquired by married couples after many years. I thought I knew the topic. Me.

"This is the closest we have been," I said, a little defensively.

"How encouraging," my aunt said. That was polite, considering I had sent us coursing wildly in the last three days.

We were north and west of Longbourn, farther from home than I had ever traveled. My uncle journaled our trip each evening. He estimated we had driven over two hundred miles. Some of that was wasted—side trips when I heard of large bodies of water.

This morning, I felt every one of those two hundred miles in my seat. The roads had been bad since yesterday.

When we departed Longbourn, I guessed my goal was the Lake District, simply because it was famously wet. That was far north, almost in Scotland. But at half that distance, we climbed into a mountainous area called the Peaks. And something changed. The hills and trees felt familiar.

"Traveling east will please Mrs. Gardiner," my uncle said with a smile.

"Are we near your old home?" I asked her.

"We will pass close to where I grew up." She was peering out the window. The view was good, as the Gardiners were too sensible to insist on iron-barred coaches. "Perhaps we can overnight in Lambton. I would love to see how it has changed." She gave me a teasing smile. "If our guide permits a slight delay?"

"That would be wonderful, Aunt," I replied, and swatted down my twinge of frustration. They had been extraordinarily patient.

The roads improved. My aunt began to name peaks and streams. When we stopped by a tiny church to rest the horses, she led us into the woods beside.

A mossy stone shape rose taller than me in the cool shade. It was a cross overlaid with a circle, a single massive rock carved with unfamiliar, weathered patterns. One arm was broken off.

My aunt ran a finger over the stone. "I used to walk here from Lambton. The church is old, but this cross is ancient. The Irish druids were first in these woods and built a shrine here. Then came the Scots. The Church was last."

"The Bennets originated in Scotland," I said.

"I had a Scottish grandmother. She brought us here for the old festivals. Samhain. Imbolc. And *Là Bealltainn*, as the Scots say. Beltane." My aunt arched an eyebrow rakishly, and her husband chuckled. "May Day, if you do not wish to offend the local parson. It is a shame we are too early. It is a month away."

We resumed our travel, and my aunt reminisced. Her words hummed without requiring much attention. Between the warming afternoon and the smoother roads, it was very restful.

I stifled a huge yawn.

My aunt laughed. "Have my stories disturbed your nap?"

"No! I am enjoying them. But I am recovering after being shaken to pieces this morning."

"It should be smooth to Lambton. The roads are good near Pemberley."

I almost flew off the seat. "*Pemberley?*"

"The Darcys maintain the roads for miles around their estate," my aunt said. "And Lambton is within the estate. Did you not know?"

I shook my head. My mouth opened, but nothing intelligible emerged.

"How near is Pemberley to Lambton?" asked my uncle.

"No more than five miles," my aunt said. "It is a beautiful house."

"I should like to see it," my uncle replied. "What do you think, Lizzy? I recall you met the gentleman but did not like him. Still, you must have heard tales of Pemberley. Shall we go?"

I realized my aunt and uncle were waiting for an answer. I forced a breath. "You may go. I think I shall rest. After touring so many great houses, my eyes are full of fine carpets and satin curtains." There. That was a sensible answer.

"Are you sure, Lizzy?" my aunt said. "If it were merely a grand house, I should not care myself. But the grounds are delightful. They have some of the finest woods in the country. And"—her smile grew teasing—"they have a *lake!*"

"A lake?" I echoed weakly.

My aunt found an inn and began an animated conversation with the owner. I stood outside, watching the tiny town square while the inn's footman carried bags to our rooms.

Pemberley. I knew traveling in Derbyshire brought us closer. But nearness is a relative thing. Derbyshire is large. I had not expected to stumble into an inn so close I could walk there.

My heart was tripping in my chest. "Stop it," I whispered.

Any meeting with Mr. Darcy was unthinkable. If the mutual mortification of a spurned proposal was not enough, I had utterly severed our association with my insults.

So, I would stay while the Gardiners visited. But what if the lake was the one I sought? That would be irritating. And strange, also.

My aunt arrived beside me. "You cannot imagine the memories I have! I was younger than you when I was last here. Let us take a stroll. My legs are sore after sitting so long." We started down the street at a pace my aunt could manage.

Mrs. Gardiner exclaimed over everything, changed and unchanged: a door that was now painted red, a shop sign that had only faded. I smiled at her enthusiasm.

"This is new," she said as we reached the corner.

There was a good-sized building with large, modern windows and a sign that read, Lancasterian System for Children. The door stood open, and I heard young voices singing.

We exchanged a look, then peeked inside.

A dozen children were seated at rows of desks. A neatly dressed young lady, the teacher or governess, stood in front, directing them through a song. It seemed to be a funny recitation of types of trees.

The teacher caught our eye and gestured to wait, then told the children to continue without her. They did so with giggles, then ardent volume.

"Is it a school?" my aunt asked as the teacher joined us.

"Yes. This is our third year since opening. As you see, the class has grown large."

The students were dressed in simple farm clothes, some even homespun, though all looked freshly scrubbed.

A memory from months ago returned. A comment Mr. Darcy made during dinner at Netherfield.

"The Lancasterian System," I said. "Is that not a program for educating"—I paused, not wishing to call them poor—"children of limited means?"

"Yes." The woman laughed, not self-conscious at all. "We would take them all, poor or rich. But in practice, it is those who cannot afford other schooling who attend."

"Do they succeed?" My aunt was fascinated.

"Wonderfully. Our education is most thorough. There was skepticism from the parents at first, either over the benefit of schooling, or because it took the children away from helping at home. But that has been overcome. We teach four days a week now, which seems a good balance."

"You must have a generous benefactor," I said and found I was tense, anticipating the answer.

"It is Mr. Darcy's program. Young Mr. Darcy, of course. After he became master of Pemberley, he purchased this building and began seeking instructors. He visits often to assess our progress. I think he is a most remarkable man." She colored prettily. "I had the honor to be chosen for this position by Mr. Darcy himself."

I snorted, and my aunt looked at me in surprise. But surely this woman should not be unashamedly admiring her employer? Especially when she was so… pleasantly dressed. And taller than me.

My aunt and I thanked her, and we headed back to the inn.

I remembered the dinner at Netherfield. I had said the little housemaid should learn to read, and Mr. Darcy mentioned educating the poor in the north. He gave no hint that he supported it himself, or that he had already opened a school.

"You are pensive," observed my aunt.

I nodded. I was reviewing the astounding attacks I had thrown at Mr. Darcy over his selfish wealth.

On the way, we passed a skinny, sandy-haired man in slovenly working clothes. He ducked his head as we passed, but I felt I had seen him before.

As I CLIMBED THE STAIRS, I realized I might be worrying over nothing. I asked the chambermaid if the Darcys were at home.

She shook her head. "Afraid not, ma'am. Mr. Darcy has been away for some time, and his sister, too. We'd hear if they was back. There's always a great fuss from the staff when they arrive, and orders for the kitchens."

I bit my lip to hide my relief. I could visit the mysterious lake in safety. And, with guilty satisfaction, I discovered I had tremendous suppressed curiosity about Pemberley itself.

Over dinner, and with a proper air of indifference, I mentioned that I did not object to visiting Pemberley after all.

31

"When will we reach the park?" I asked as the carriage wheels hummed over the road.

The early morning sun shone on fresh vistas at every curve. Each perspective was more magnificent than the last—great old oaks, stands of silver birch, rowan snowing white blooms.

But this was forest. I had expected expansive grounds. There was no sign of the formality that had marked Rosings Park.

"Pemberley does not have a park in the common sense," my aunt said. "There are gardens on the mansion grounds, but the transition is subtle. The Darcys have always shepherded the woods, not conquered them."

Before we departed, I had closed my eyes and spun, then marked the direction against the distant peaks.

Now, I leaned out the open carriage window. The breeze swirled loose hairs while I studied the horizon. There was no question. We were heading exactly where I had pointed.

I fell back into my seat with confused emotions. Excitement, because a cure for Jane might be ahead. Worry, because I had no idea what that meant.

And my stomach was fluttering. Since we arrived in Lambton, people kept mentioning Mr. Darcy, usually in tones of admiration and affection. It was exceedingly disconcerting.

The coach climbed. Around us, spectacular sweeps of meadow and forest emerged, shining with spring green.

"Is it not beautiful!" My aunt and uncle were in raptures. I was too distracted to answer.

We crested the hill, and Pemberley House became visible across a valley.

I managed two words at last. "My goodness."

The house crowned a rise before the final peak of the hill. Silvery stone walls soared, free of ostentatious columns and ornaments, the granite hues warmed by copper and sunlit quartz. The central manse was three lofty stories, each a row of shining windows, the highest arched. To each side, the building extended shallower wings shaded by towering trees.

The grounds were the opposite of Rosings's felt-cropped lawns and squared hedges. The house nestled in a meadow dotted with flowers. The front gardens began gradually, sculpting the hillside below into riotous color. Craggy boulders and ridges stood untouched, silver bedrock kin to the majestic walls.

Behind and above, wild woods climbed the far ridge, each ancient tree seizing the hillside with a giant's fist of root. The forest's crest and the slate roofs matched each other's curves and rises.

The house was rather large.

No, that was wrong. I was thinking the trees were the size of those near Longbourn.

The house was very large.

The coach wound into the valley. At each reversal, we crowded across the seats to look through the other windows.

"It is beautiful," I said, mostly to myself. My aunt and uncle's praise did not need encouragement.

As if whispered in my ear, I realized I could have been mistress of Pemberley.

A sensation rose at the idea. Panic, mostly. A walk in the morning would hardly be sufficient to assess the estate. It might not be sufficient for the house.

I laughed wildly, and my aunt looked at me curiously.

A stream coursed beside the house, swelling into pools through the gardens. My eye followed dashing falls until the water reached the shaded valley floor.

And the lake.

"Stop!" I shouted, banging my hand behind the driver's seat. "Stop here!"

"What on earth—" my aunt began, but I had opened the door and jumped down.

My breath shrank. I knew this place.

The images from the wyvern swirled and settled. Deep water the color of cold. The lowered path of the sun in the north. Strange people striped in glowing indigo.

"We have found it!" I shouted.

My uncle, his shoes removed and his trousers rolled up, touched a toe to the lake.

"Ah! That is *very* cold."

My aunt laughed. "I warned you!" She was seated on a large fallen log.

My uncle turned and looked in my direction, and then my aunt as well. Even though I was fifty yards from the shore, I could see their bemused expressions. I waved self-consciously. My uncle went back to exclaiming over the chill.

I should approach. But standing beside water had dramatic results in the past, so caution seemed wise.

Then again, I had skills now I did not possess before.

I closed my eyes and let my awareness flow out. Feeling for draca in the water.

The Gardiners' tykeworm was a spark of happy energy digging in the turf a few feet from me. There was nothing else. Good.

But… no, that was odd.

I relaxed further. Forgetting my mission. Forgetting where I was. Sound drifted away.

Nothing. Absolutely nothing. Even the forest around us was empty of draca. The sensation was eerie, a void of moonless night.

Uncomfortable, I opened my eyes.

The tyke seemed happy. He was tugging at a root with great abandon, although he had to shift his grip for each pull. His little teeth sheared through the tough wood with ease.

I walked to the water. My aunt and uncle fell silent. The tyke stopped his game but, unusually, did not follow me.

I stopped at the shore. Ripples licked the gravel by my toes. No strange crests raced across the surface. No draca popped out at my feet.

I crouched and touched the water. Ice cold. I scooped a little and tasted it. Clean and pure. But just water.

"What am I supposed to *do?*" I said aloud. I swirled my fingers through the surface, hoping for inspiration.

"Did you have an expectation, Lizzy?" my uncle asked.

I had shared almost every detail of my encounter with the Rosings wyvern. My aunt and uncle had listened, expressed their concern for Jane, and supported my desire to help. They had also been delicately skeptical.

"I had no idea what would happen," I replied.

"Could the water be medicinal?" asked my aunt.

Curing waters were fashionable. The resorts at Bath were famous for them.

But, why *here?* It was too strange that the lake should be at Pemberley.

I considered the one statement by the wyvern I had not shared: "*you are leaving him*," with images of Mr. Darcy.

Could I have misunderstood? But the wyvern said, "*for your sister.*"

Frustrated, I stood up and shouted, "What should I *do?*" The words echoed back across the lake. I felt slightly better.

I turned to my aunt and uncle, who were taken aback.

"Did either of you, by chance, bring a jar or bottle?" I asked.

They shook their heads.

"Perhaps the housekeeper is out?" I suggested. "I am sure we can purchase a jar in Lambton."

My uncle had rung the bell a few seconds ago.

"Give them a chance, Lizzy." He leaned back to gaze upward. Far upward. "They have only begun walking. Or they may be summoning a carriage. It is a large house."

It was, indeed, a large house. The door alone was intimidating.

The latch clicked, and the door swung wide to reveal a respectable-looking older woman, dressed simply for such a grand setting. She gave a friendly smile and introduced herself as Mrs. Reynolds, the housekeeper. When my uncle expressed his admiration for the building, she invited us to tour the open rooms.

I trailed as she guided us. At first, the perspective at each window halted me—a stand of trees or a still pool of water. Then, I saw the intimate interior. Exquisite, minimal furniture and open, uncluttered surfaces. Serious works of painting and sculpture, never more than one in a room—classical Grecian busts, modern portraits in bold oils, red silk frames displaying paper brushed with strange symbols of the Far East.

I had seen this style before, in a way. A few rooms at Netherfield emulated this in aspiration, if not in perfection. At least until Mr. Bingley's sisters had hung excessive gilded frames on the mirrors and splashed garishly painted china over every tabletop.

I heard my uncle ask, "Is your master away?" and I perked up to hear the answer.

Mrs. Reynolds replied that Mr. Darcy was traveling, adding, "But we expect him tomorrow, with Miss Darcy."

Tomorrow! One day from disaster. That meant we needed to finish our errand today. I began inventing a pretense to borrow a jug.

We entered a long hallway hung with paintings. Five marble statues, larger than life, were spaced far apart. Two were heroic men. Two, wise older women. The last was a young wyfe, her arm raised in defiance, a wyvern rearing at her feet.

I was arrested. This made the extravagance of Rosings seem gaudy and useless.

The wyvern was superb—the set of the scales, the razor claws. Sculpted from life. The woman was beautiful and powerful. The hand at her side dangled a doubled red cord, perhaps two feet long, the only part not carved from stone.

"Who is this?" I asked.

Mrs. Reynolds's fingertips traced the base. "It is titled, *The Wyfe of Pemberley*. The woman is my master's mother, Lady Anne Darcy. She stood for the artist after she married and bound."

The hall was crossed with sunbeams that illuminated the statues. The paintings were on the south wall, well lit but protected from fading. Everywhere I looked, subtle details emerged. Perfectly fit granite. Burnished birch in the arms of a simple chair.

Mrs. Reynolds was showing a collection of miniatures, each a carefully drawn portrait on a hand-sized oval.

"And that," Mrs. Reynolds said, pointing to one, "is my master—and very like him."

"It is a handsome face," my aunt said, examining the picture. "But, Lizzy, you can tell us whether it is like him or not."

Mrs. Reynolds looked at me with increased respect. "Does the young lady know Mr. Darcy?"

I felt my face warming. "A little."

"And do you not think him a very handsome gentleman, ma'am?"

"Yes, very handsome." I prepared to burst into flame.

"And who is this girl?" asked my aunt, raising another portrait.

"Ah. That is Miss Darcy, when she was eight years old. She lost her father and mother three years after that was painted. It makes my heart break even now to think of it." Mrs. Reynolds paused, her eyes glistening. "She is sixteen now and has grown into a wonderful lady."

"I have heard she plays the pianoforte," I said.

Mrs. Reynolds laughed a strange, unguarded laugh as if I had spoken both a painful truth and the most naïve idiocy in one breath.

Wordlessly, she walked down the hall. We filed behind her in silence.

We reached a pair of wide mahogany doors carved with a motif of musical clefs. For the first time, I saw another servant. A little housemaid was bent, polishing the door handles.

The housekeeper said, "The music parlor." She gestured to the maid, who opened the doors wide. We gasped.

The room was on the back of the house, so we faced up the hill, peering into old forest.

The entire north wall was windows.

I had toured an orangery in London that boasted a wall half-filled with windows. That was a token compared to this. Here, the narrowest frames separated endless panes of perfect, polished glass. Gnarled, towering oaks rose in majesty beyond.

My eyes followed the branches upward, unobstructed. The windows continued for half the roof. The entire hill enveloped us in ageless woods until the sky broke in brilliant blue.

"It is a new method," Mrs. Reynolds said, who had walked to the far wall. She tapped the glass with her knuckle. "Two layers, with a gap between. My master hired artisans from Scotland. They said there is no installation like this in the world. There may not be another for decades."

I walked over. I could discern a faint, second reflection of myself. "Why two layers?"

"There was a requirement for the instruments." Mrs. Reynolds's lips crinkled. "An issue with temperature."

"It is like layers of clothing," I said, realizing. "To keep out cold and heat."

"Yes. Very good, ma'am. That is precisely as Mr. Darcy described it." Mrs. Reynolds gave me an appraising look as if I might hold further secrets. Little did she know.

But I had ignored the purpose of the room. I turned. And counted. "*Seven* pianofortes?" Two large instruments were in the center of the room, surrounded by comfortable chairs, settees, and end tables. The other instruments were arrayed along the side walls.

"Eight," our guide corrected, indicating a large crate in the corner, by which the little maid was standing, her head lowered. "This one is newly arrived for Miss Darcy—a present from my master."

"Eight seems extravagant," I said. For the first time, my dislike for the privilege of wealth stirred. It had been happily silent until now.

"Your pardon, ma'am. Miss Darcy would not stand for anything wasteful. She keeps two instruments here, and another in her room. These others are sent by the great pianoforte builders, and they will be returned when she has provided her opinion of their work."

My aunt was surprised. "They ask the opinion of a lady of sixteen?"

The housekeeper smiled proudly.

"Why two here?" I asked. Perhaps she enjoyed duets.

"They break, ma'am."

"Break?" Our pianoforte had never broken, although it was often out of tune.

But Mrs. Reynolds had returned to her prior topic. "Mr. Darcy would not stand for extravagance either, although whatever gives his sister pleasure is done in a moment. Miss Darcy has become quite firm in telling him no. But the master takes after his father. Old Mr. Darcy was a generous man and affable to the poor. Young Mr. Darcy exceeds even his standard."

"Does he?" I asked, trying for a tone of casual interest.

"I dare say I do not know the half of it, for he is a modest gentleman. But the schools are one project all his own, and a great effort."

"We saw the school in Lambton," my aunt said. "The children were most eager."

Mrs. Reynolds turned her attention to the little housemaid. "Lucy would know, for she takes lessons there." She gave an encouraging smile. "What do you say, girl? Are the children eager?"

The silence lengthened. Perhaps the maid was too shy to speak before visitors.

The white cap lifted, and a familiar set of eyes found mine.

In an apologetic voice, the little housemaid who had done my hair at Netherfield said, "Hello, ma'am."

"Oh, my goodness!" I ran over and caught her hands. "How did you come here?"

"I don't rightly know, ma'am." She was grinning now. "It just happened. Mr. Bingley went traveling, and Miss Bingley was going to dismiss me, with not enough housekeeping to do. But then a coach came to London, and I was offered a position." Her smile widened. "I greatly enjoy it, ma'am."

"I cannot believe it!" I said.

Mrs. Reynolds stepped beside us, for the first time a stern housekeeper. Lucy dropped my hands and gave a silent curtsy.

"It is quite all right," I said to Mrs. Reynolds. "We have an old acquaintance from when she served at Netherfield."

Mrs. Reynolds considered that, then nodded regally. She patted Lucy on the shoulder and led the way from the room.

I lingered, catching Lucy's hand for a squeeze. I had not realized how fond of her I had become.

"Will you visit again?" she whispered.

The answer was no, but I was reluctant to say it. I mouthed, *I do not know.* Then I had to run to catch up with our guide.

32

Mrs. Reynolds saw us to the front door and introduced the gardener, a solid fellow of middle years with a deep tan and a big smile.

"The young lady knows the master," finished Mrs. Reynolds.

He laughed deep in his belly. "A rare treat, then."

Mrs. Reynolds harrumphed and received a cheeky grin in response, but she smiled as she turned away.

The gardener led us outside to a path beside the stream. He and my uncle began discussing the construction of the pools, the date of the original building, and other details that fascinated a man in trade.

I slowed, realizing I had forgotten to ask for a jug. Then I stopped, trying to understand my feelings. This visit had been different than I expected.

The stream chimed beside me. The valley shone with life. Below, the lake lay still, dark, and cold.

With a tremendous splashing, the Gardiners' tykeworm bounded across the stream, arriving at my feet soaking wet and happy.

I smiled down at him. "You have escaped the carriage." He cocked his head proudly, the scales on his nutmeg-brown muzzle sparkling with drops of water. He gave an enthusiastic, whistling coo and looked behind me.

I turned to see what caught his interest.

Mr. Darcy stood, frozen, no more than ten yards away.

Impossible. He was not to arrive until tomorrow.

Mr. Darcy was white with shock. His brow creased. His lips grimaced as he said in a curdled voice, "You have *married*."

That jolted me into awareness. "What?" I looked around as if I had forgotten a husband. The dripping tykeworm peered up from my feet.

Oh.

"He is the bound draca of my aunt and uncle," I stammered. "He… tends to follow me." I looked back at Mr. Darcy, whose expression had contorted. I swallowed past a hard lump in my throat. "I have not married."

Mr. Darcy visibly mastered himself, his posture straightening in jerks. That left a sense of wonder in his eyes.

He gave a self-conscious bow. "Miss Bennet."

"Mr. Darcy." I curtsied.

Then I realized how this must look. He would think I had thrown myself in his way. I babbled, "We were informed you were not at home. I had an urgent errand in… in the neighborhood…" I stopped. I could hardly explain that.

"I am back a day early," he said. "To prepare the house for my sister."

I heard a polite cough behind me. The gardener had stopped a discreet distance away with my aunt and uncle.

I turned back to Mr. Darcy. "May I introduce my aunt and uncle?"

"I would be honored," he replied, staring into my eyes.

"Mr. and Mrs. Gardiner," I said. I could not tear my own gaze away. "This is Mr. Darcy."

Mr. Darcy bowed, never looking away from me.

It was a strange introduction, but it seemed sufficient. My uncle came forward and added a few words. Mr. Darcy replied, and they began to discuss our tour. My uncle mentioned trout.

My aunt stepped beside me. Softly, she said, "You are more acquainted with Mr. Darcy than I had known."

"We have spoken on several occasions." I was having trouble keeping my voice steady.

"He is taller than I imagined."

"He is quite tall."

When my aunt did not reply, I braved a look at her. She had a most amused expression.

I looked quickly away.

"Mrs. Gardiner," Mr. Darcy said. He was now standing beside us. He smiled—smiled!—at my aunt, and she complimented Pemberley House.

I gathered Mr. Darcy had released the gardener. He would show the grounds to us himself.

How was this happening? I only came here because the wyvern said it would help!

My aunt and uncle paired up, my aunt linking an arm with Mr. Gardiner. Naturally, I would be expected to walk with Mr. Darcy.

I eyed him warily and was gratified to see him look uncertain.

"If you… I understand if you prefer not to accompany us," he said. "We shall return promptly."

A ridiculous, desperate idea occurred to me.

"I would enjoy a tour," I said. I rotated, considering the many exquisite options. Down through the gardens. Up toward the woods. "Which way?" He nodded to the gardens, and, without a glance back, I shot past him at a pace my aunt could not hope to match.

After a surprised pause, there was a flurry of steps. He caught up beside me.

We whooshed up a charming stone bridge that crossed the stream.

"In 1765, my grandfather visited a unique bridge…" began Mr. Darcy. And ended, as I raced down the far side without breaking stride.

Next, the path followed an elegant S through fractured black rock that sparkled with silver crystals. Stony edges sketched skeletal ridges sunken in ivy and moss. They seemed scattered at first, then hinted at musculature and limbs lost beneath waves. Morning glory trumpets spread like foam.

I realized the rocks sculpted a breathtaking, submerged draca, the twining neck completed by charcoal gravel on the S of the path, as we virtually ran from the far side.

"That was a garden," noted Mr. Darcy in a dry tone.

There was a grassy clearing ahead. I made for it at full speed then stopped in the center.

Mr. Darcy arrived, puffing. My aunt and uncle were nowhere in sight.

"I am here on an urgent errand," I said before I lost my nerve. The wondering look returned to his eyes. "You showed great trust in your communication to me. I must return that by sharing a most private topic, some of which is unknown even to my aunt and uncle." I filled my lungs. "You may recall that my sister Jane was gravely ill at Netherfield."

"Of course. I was most concerned for her."

"She had been stung by a foul crawler." Horror crossed his features, then puzzlement. Because she had not died. "Jane survived because I treated her with raw draca blood, taken willingly from the Hursts' bound draca." His eyes widened. "But I was unaware of a risk from treatment. An unbound wyfe, in love, must bind once she is treated with draca blood. My sister was in love, you see." My eyes were beginning to tear, but I forced myself forward. "Because she has not bound, she has fallen ill. It is a form of binding sickness. Due to my intervention."

Mr. Darcy was bent forward with shock. I saw his expression change as he understood all this implied.

I dashed a hand over my eyes, angry to appear weak. "Will you *say* something?"

"Even before you told me this," he said, "I have thought constantly of your feelings on my intervention between your sister and Bingley. I have dwelled endlessly upon my actions."

"I do not admonish, sir," I said tightly. "I have spoken from urgent necessity, not for any personal reason."

He straightened. There was a nod. "Of course."

"I am in no position to require your help, but, from your sense of decency, I hoped you would share your knowledge of this ailment, and how to treat it."

"May I ask her symptoms?"

"She is… at first, she was increasingly reserved, then… then she…" A barrier broke, and words flooded out. "She eats only under duress. She is wasting away. Her awareness of reality is sundered. She lives in fantasy, other than speaking of the man she lost. She barely knows even me." My voice broke at the end.

Mr. Darcy took several harsh strides over the grass, then back, as if desperate to move.

"I have never heard of this cause for the illness," he said, "or even that draca blood can treat crawler poisoning. However, the symptoms you describe are binding sickness. From my reckoning of the date, the progression is slower for your sister than is usual. I can only speculate why. Perhaps because she needs to bind, rather than having had her binding broken, it is less severe."

Hope grew in my heart. "You mentioned Pemberley has a collection of writing on draca."

"You are, of course, welcome to use the library. I caution you that I have studied the contents, and there is no mention of this form of the malady."

"Still, I will try."

He nodded.

I braced myself for my next request. This, I feared, would be rejected. "I have wondered if Mr. Bingley would wish to be notified of Jane's condition."

There was no hesitation. "I am sure he would. With your permission, I shall write to him."

"Oh. Thank you." I was astonished that was so simple. "How long will it take a letter to reach him?"

There was silence before he answered. "Mr. Bingley is in America. To my current knowledge, the post is ten weeks. A return trip, at least as long."

"*Twenty weeks?*" My heart sank even as I realized he had guessed my desperate hope that Mr. Bingley might return. But perhaps we had that much time. "In your experience, how far have Jane's symptoms progressed?"

The answer came slowly. "The symptoms you describe are advanced illness."

"And what is the outcome of binding sickness? How long…" I knew my question, but I could not speak it aloud. "Perhaps your library would inform me of the usual duration?"

The silence stretched longer. When he spoke, his voice was quiet and exact. "After more consideration, I feel you would not be well served by the literature in Pemberley's library. I will, of course, put it at your disposal if you wish. You need but say a word. However, I suggest I review it on your behalf and forward any practical advice."

"Oh no." I had to stop to regain my voice. "Is it so dire as that?"

"I assure you there is hope." He stepped forward. We stood close now. "I give you my word." His voice was intense, deep, and resonant with sincerity.

I nodded. My fear retreated at his certainty.

"I have a last request," I said. "A small one. But you must indulge me by not asking why." For all I had admitted, I dared not reveal that I had conversed with a wyvern.

He waited, as if agreement was undeniable.

"May I borrow a jug?" I said. "Or a jar? Something that can be tightly sealed?"

His formality relaxed. An eyebrow arched. "Without asking why, if you explain further, I could choose a suitable container."

"I wish to take a sample of water from the lake. *Your* lake. Pemberley's lake, that is."

"I will have a sample of the water delivered to you tomorrow." He betrayed no surprise at my odd request. "May I ask where you are staying?"

I told him the name of the inn. And then, I had nothing else to say.

We stood in silence. Even as I realized we were inches apart, he retreated a step, then looked around.

"We have lost Mr. and Mrs. Gardiner," he observed.

"I cannot imagine where they have gone," I said. We had spoken long enough for them to catch up.

Mr. Darcy indicated the path back, and we proceeded at a sedate pace.

The Gardiners were by the pool where we had begun, sitting on a bench.

"I am sorry," my aunt said. "I found I was more tired than I knew. We decided to rest here."

"Then you must visit again to finish your tour," Mr. Darcy said. He addressed Mr. Gardiner. "The trout you spotted prefer the eastern pools. There is also excellent coarse fishing in the lake. I would be pleased to provide you with tackle."

"That is exceedingly generous, sir." My uncle gave a bow.

Mr. Darcy continued, "Regrettably, I must leave you now for pressing business. You are welcome to enjoy the gardens in my absence."

My uncle thanked him but said we should depart, and began goodbyes, but could not resist a question about the trout. The two men turned and began pointing to areas of the stream.

My aunt took my arm. "Are you all right, Lizzy?" she said softly.

"Yes. I am quite relieved, in fact."

33

I waited the next day, not willing to stir until the sample of lake water was delivered. Not that I was certain it had any value. But I would pursue every chance.

My aunt and uncle raved about Pemberley, then puzzled over Mr. Darcy, then raved about Pemberley again. I paced, trying not to listen.

"Lizzy," called my uncle. "Should I accept his offer to fish? Mrs. Gardiner and I have difficulty making him out. I found him charming, but from your description, I expected a very different man. If he is so changeable in his moods, perhaps I will be chased off if I return?"

"I think he is not changeable," I said. My uncle appeared unconvinced, so I added, "My original description may have been in error."

"Oh. Well, I should like to give it a try, then." To his wyfe, he said, "What do you say?"

My aunt was studying me with a disconcertingly perceptive expression. "I am not yet sure."

I heard a carriage outside and ran to the window. A curricle with a gentleman and lady was driving up the street, followed by a large coach with a four-horse team.

"Oh." I turned to my aunt and uncle. "It is Mr. Darcy."

They exchanged a look, and my aunt folded her arms triumphantly.

I plunked down in the nearest seat. An excessive number of feet began stamping up the stairs. There was a knock, and my uncle invited them in.

The chambermaid opened the door and curtsied, announcing, "Mr. Darcy." Even as we rose, Mr. Darcy strode in. He greeted my aunt and uncle cordially, then turned to me and stalled. Finally, he bowed. "Miss Bennet."

I nodded, distracted by the stream of footmen placing large wicker boxes beside the wall. This continued until there were twelve, which filled half the floor.

A footman opened the lids, revealing a variety of glass containers packed in straw, from the size of saltshakers to huge jars, all filled with clear liquid and corked and waxed.

We had fallen silent at the display, including Mr. Darcy, who appeared abashed. As the last lid opened, he said, "I hoped this would assist your project. But this may be excessive for transportation by carriage."

"Perhaps we could take just one?" I suggested. He nodded, and I chose a box with a collection of manageable jars.

While the footmen packed up the remaining eleven boxes, Mr. Darcy stepped closer to speak privately. "I have reviewed my notes from other cases. Only one treatment for binding sickness has proven benefit, an extract of rowan flowers. It is not a cure, but it slows progression. My apothecary has begun preparing the medicine and will finish tomorrow. I can have it sent to Longbourn, or to here if you will still be in Lambton."

"Thank you. That is wonderful. Please send it here. I would prefer to carry it with me." My aunt and uncle were too settled to leave today anyway.

Once all but one wicker box had vanished out the door, a young lady, reed-thin and slightly taller than me, entered. She wore a dark blue muslin dress and bonnet, impeccably fitted but simply cut.

"Miss Elizabeth Bennet," Mr. Darcy said. His tone had become serious. "It would be my honor to introduce my sister, Miss Georgiana Darcy."

We exchanged hellos while I recovered from my surprise at such a significant introduction. Under her bonnet, her eyes were as dark blue as her dress. I knew she was sixteen, but I could have guessed her younger or older. She was a wisp of a creature, like a child who has shot up in height, but her voice was melodious and mature.

Beautiful voice aside, each time she spoke, her words were brief. She was well-spoken and polite, but I wondered if she was shy.

"Your brother speaks of you often," I told her, smiling and trying to put her at ease.

"And of you, very often," she said with her own smile, and I was the one who felt shy.

Unsure what to say next, I introduced her to my aunt and uncle.

After greeting them, Miss Darcy said to my uncle, "I understand you will visit Pemberley again. Will you attend this afternoon?"

When my uncle agreed, having little choice when invited so directly, she continued, "If you are not engaged, would you dine with us after?"

My uncle accepted, but I saw his stunned surprise.

Then Miss Darcy gave her own gasp of surprise and bent to peer under the table. She had spotted the Gardiners' tykeworm, who was observing the bustle from a safe location.

Miss Darcy dropped to her knees, her reticence forgotten. "Oh! You are a handsome creature!"

I waited for the tyke's reaction. Ever since the Pemberley gamekeeper spoke of Miss Darcy, I had wondered if she had the same strange ability as me.

However, the tyke showed none of the friendliness he showed me. He crouched, his head lowered and little shoulders stiff. I had almost forgotten that was a draca's response to inquisitive people. They are not friendly animals like dogs.

I prepared to ask him silently to behave.

Then Miss Darcy began to sing.

Her voice was wordless and soft, scarcely more than humming. The tone rose and fell in strange intervals, like a Chinese song that Mary had played years ago. There was no melody. The rhythms did not repeat. The notes wandered, calming and natural, like the music of wind rustling a branch, or rain falling on a puddle.

She held out her hand, and the little tykeworm crawled forward and nuzzled her adoringly.

When we arrived at Pemberley House after rushed preparations, we were greeted outside the mansion by Miss Darcy, who was strolling in the gardens.

"My brother remained in Lambton for business, but he will join us for a late dinner. May I be your host in his absence?"

My aunt and uncle accepted her offer, and my shoulders released enough tension to tie a horse. At least Mr. Darcy would not jump out of some corner for several hours.

I watched Miss Darcy converse with my aunt and uncle. Her manner was changed, surrounded by the dazzling blooms and foliage of her estate. Although she was a quiet hostess, preferring to prompt my uncle into long answers than speak herself, she was poised, and relaxed enough that girlish hints of youth escaped. Even so, it was hard to believe she was no older than Lydia.

She wore an unusual long-sleeved red silk dress that wrapped in front, almost a morning robe. It fastened with gold cloth buttons and had a high collar like a gentleman's shirt. A thread-thin chain around her neck dangled a delicate musical note in gold.

The silk of her dress was patterned in flowing gold shapes.

"Are those draca?" I asked. The sinuous outlines reminded me of our firedrake.

Until now the conversation had been polite niceties. She was caught by my more personal question, then smiled. "They are Chinese renderings of their dragon folklore."

"Is it a Chinese dress?"

"It is a Chinese style they call a *qípáo*. But not this." She touched her cap, which was a traditional at-home cap for a lady, although in red silk. Underneath, her hair was as dark as her brother's. "The Chinese ladies wear strange things on their heads. But I like their dresses if I have the sleeves fitted closely. I wear them at home sometimes. I thought I would be brave and wear it for you. I should not be brave enough to wear it out."

"It is beautiful."

She had skin light enough to freckle, and her blush was evident. In whole, she was a charming young lady, and blossoming into a beautiful woman. And a wealthy one. Her brother would be fighting off suitors.

I remembered Mr. Darcy's letter describing Mr. Wickham's attempted elopement when she was fifteen. No wonder Mr. Darcy had been furious when they met in Meryton.

The Pemberley gamekeeper, Mr. Rabb, was approaching with fishing rods over his shoulder.

Miss Darcy turned to my uncle. "My brother mentioned that you fish. I am no fisherman, but I have found you a guide."

Mr. Rabb caught my eye with a grin then began discussing tying flies with Mr. Gardiner.

Mrs. Gardiner and I joined Miss Darcy to tour the gardens. We set off at a gentle pace, but after a few minutes, my aunt's legs tired. She settled on one of the benches while Miss Darcy and I continued.

Our pace sped up, but we fell quiet. The gardens were stunning, but admiring flowers seemed old-fashioned for two young ladies alone.

I decided to try a more intimate topic. "Pemberley is a remarkable estate. But large, for a brother and sister."

"You are right. We entertain at times, but I do not travel as much as my brother. I am often here alone. Fitz tried retaining a lady companion last year, but I did not like her."

Fitz? I tried to imagine anyone addressing Mr. Darcy as "Fitz" and failed spectacularly.

"Mrs. Reynolds is dear," continued Miss Darcy, "but very old. Most of the staff have lived here longer than I." She gave me a conspiratorial glance. "You must not tell, but our new housemaid is great fun. She has taught me games from her school."

"Lucy. Yes, she is sweet. I met her at Netherfield."

"She told me."

I sighed in dismay. "Does *everyone* at Pemberley speak of me?"

"Of course not." We walked a few steps. "When I found Mr. Rabb this morning, can you imagine whom he knew?"

I stopped, and she looked at me innocently.

"This is most unfair!" I said, and she broke into laughter. A layer of reserve broke as well, and we linked arms to walk as friends.

As sunset colored the sky, our group reassembled, including the Gardiners' tykeworm, who had been freed from our coach for fear he would claw his way out.

Mr. Gardiner displayed the two trout he had caught, while his fishing companion, Mr. Rabb, ruefully showed his one. I suspected that being outfished by gentlemen was a talent of gamekeepers.

The fish were admired and taken to the kitchen. Then Miss Darcy's face lit. "My brother!"

In the distance, Mr. Darcy, hatless and dressed in practical riding gear, trotted his gray horse into the stables and vanished.

Miss Darcy invited us into the drawing room, then excused herself to meet her brother.

I sat down, but sitting made me more nervous, so I began pacing the room. On my fourth pass, my aunt got up and invited me to admire the view. We went to the window, glowing gold with sunset, and I blew out a big breath.

My aunt took my hand. "It is evident, Lizzy, that this invitation was not offered because of Mr. Gardiner and myself."

"Oh, Aunt. You do not know how difficult this is."

"I am sure I do not. But I am also sure that Mr. Gardiner and I should excuse ourselves before dinner. We shall not be missed."

"You shall be missed by me!" I said, but she only raised an eyebrow. "Do not leave me alone."

"We will stay if you wish. But silent stares at Mr. Darcy will not make things less difficult. You must talk it through. To whatever outcome."

"Do not be wise, Aunt. I am beyond wisdom."

"You are my most sensible niece and a very competent lady."

"But I do not even know what I *want*."

"That is when talking is most helpful. You have made Miss Darcy's acquaintance. Nothing prevents you from dining at Pemberley with her and her brother." When I said nothing, she added, "You can always depart after dinner and regale us with tales of finery. Besides, you will not be alone."

She pointed to the floor, where the tykeworm sat loyally at my feet.

"What do you think?" I asked him and received a bored yawn in response.

34

Lucy, the little housemaid, stepped back from dusting my petticoats, her hands on her non-existent hips and her feather brush dangling. Her bottom lip poked one way, then the other. "I can fix your hair, too."

After the Gardiners expressed their regret to Miss Darcy, Lucy had shown me to a guest room to tidy for dinner.

"What sort of fix?" I said suspiciously.

"Just fix it," she said, eyes round with innocence.

Grudgingly, I sat, adjusting the looking glass. While Lucy pulled out pins and began brushing, I said, "What do they teach you at school?"

"Everything," she answered with unabashed confidence. "Reading, mostly. I didn't know none of it. But there's a girl my age with no teaching"—she stopped, then continued in a refined tone—"who had not yet been educated. So, we study as a pair."

"Goodness. You sound like an elegant lady's companion."

"D'you think?" She grinned in the glass, then added, "The boys are learning to blacksmith."

"That is wonderful." Mary would be pleased that skilled trades were taught. It would further her plan to undermine the corrupt aristocracy.

"Mr. Darcy told his sister you suggested it. He said you like making bolts."

"I am intrigued by the production of bolts. But what are you doing to my hair?" I had spotted omens of an elaborate crown braid.

"Nothing," she said, as convincingly as a child caught with a large lump of sugar in their cheek.

"It is only dinner. It should be simple, please."

"Yes, ma'am," she said softly and switched course to a tucked braid. She finished, then pulled one dark curl free to dangle past each ear.

I tilted my head, and the curls swung. "Are you sure?"

"Mr. Darcy will admire it."

"You are very young to speak of what gentlemen admire."

"I'm sure I'm thirteen. Maybe fourteen!"

"Even so." I suppose my hair hardly mattered. "Thank you."

The reminder of meeting Mr. Darcy had set nerves tingling in my belly. I puffed out my cheeks, then repeated my aunt's encouragement to my reflection. "You are a very competent lady."

"You are, ma'am," Lucy said and gave one of my dangling locks a twist around her little finger. "I knew you'd be back."

Mr. Darcy greeted me in the dining room with a graceful bow very different from his customary curt dips. He had dressed casually, his cravat simply knotted around muslin collars above a smokey-gray tailcoat and pearl waistcoat. Perhaps he tailored his choice to me, as I had not brought a gown for dinner.

He offered his hand. I placed my fingers in his, and my tingling nerves climbed my spine.

"I am so pleased you were able to stay," Miss Darcy said, beaming beside us.

"I, also," Mr. Darcy said. "I am sorry to have missed Mr. and Mrs. Gardiner. I wished to further our acquaintance. But my business was urgent."

"He left last *evening*," Miss Darcy said in an aggrieved tone.

Mr. Darcy's fingers were still intertwined with mine. I let go belatedly and felt his hand open at the same moment. To distract my nerves, I asked the first thing that came to mind. "Last evening? Where did you go?"

"My principal task was in Liverpool."

"Liverpool!" That was the largest port in western England, and we were far from the coast. "You traveled all *night?*"

Mr. Darcy held my gaze, his eyes serious. "I was posting a letter."

He had written to Mr. Bingley. My heart skipped a beat.

"Why go to Liverpool to post a letter?" asked Miss Darcy, folding her arms with a sibling's skepticism.

Mr. Darcy chose not to answer that. "Our cook has an excellent dinner prepared. But I hoped to have an activity first." He sounded unusually tentative.

Anything would be better than staring at each other over a huge table. "That sounds lovely!" I enthused.

"I thought music," Mr. Darcy said, watching his sister.

Oh no.

"How fun!" exclaimed Miss Darcy. She made further delighted noises, but they were drowned by the tolling bells of doom inside my head.

Perhaps all was not lost. I summoned my most charming smile for Miss Darcy. "I have heard you are most accomplished. I should very much enjoy hearing you play."

"I will play also," Miss Darcy said, taking my arm. "But you first! My brother says you sing delightfully."

"I do not!" I protested.

"Mr. Darcy has good taste," she said as if that settled it.

She led us through the house with distressing efficiency. Outside, the warmth of sunset had cooled to violet dusk. A housemaid walked ahead lighting wall-mounted sconces. Another trailed, cranking chains to lower the wide chandeliers for lighting.

The Gardiners' tyke padded beside me but drifted to examine each marble statue we passed. For an animal I imagined as puppy-like, he behaved differently than a dog—peering at the shapes, not sniffing for scents.

Miss Darcy swung open the doors to the music parlor. She smiled enthusiastically while the maid lit the fire and candles. "I feel we have become friends, Miss Bennet. Please allow me to hear you sing."

I was trapped now. Accepting the inevitable, I leafed through the thick, if untidy, stack of music she plucked off an instrument and found an Italian air I knew tolerably well.

I played and sang, trying not to wince when my fingers struck the wrong note. The instrument was superb, flawlessly tuned, and much larger —and louder—than I was accustomed to.

Miss Darcy wandered while I played, listening attentively. Mr. Darcy watched us both, but he was tense when his eyes followed his sister. He was nervous about her opinion. Strangely, that relaxed me. Miss Darcy had been so sweet that I could not be concerned over her.

When I finished, Miss Darcy clapped with delight. "That was lovely! Fitz is right. You have a charming voice. Very natural."

I laughed. "If by natural, you mean untutored, I will agree."

"I do," she said. "But that is perfect for an air. Most are from folk music, after all." Her gaze shifted to my fingers resting on the keys. There was a pause. "Perhaps a duet next time? I could play while you sing."

"That would be most welcome," I said with heartfelt sincerity. "Will you play now?"

"All right," she said and took my place at the instrument.

I was curious to hear her perform after so many comments on her skill. But even more, I was intrigued by her manner in the presence of her instruments. It was like a flower had opened. Her reserve had lessened throughout our visit, but here she was confident. Almost exuberant. Yet there was no hint of the pretension or self-promotion that marred many accomplished ladies.

Without thinking, I stood next to Mr. Darcy.

"This is everything to Georgiana," he said softly. "I very much wished you to see." That left me flustered, and I did not look at him.

Miss Darcy's head was cocked, considering. I noticed she did not consult the stack of music.

"Perhaps another air?" she said.

"No," Mr. Darcy said. "Beethoven. Play the Appassionata. The last movement."

Her smile faded, and her gaze flicked to me before returning to her brother. "Are you sure?"

"I am," was all he said.

She rose and went to the side of the instrument, which was at least six feet long, and with astounding casualness heaved the heavy lid open, then propped it up with a stick. I had never seen such a thing.

She returned to her seat, her hands in her lap and her face lost in thought. In her red dress, closely fitted even through her sleeves, she looked like a waif beside the huge instrument.

Her hands rose, then pounded into the keys. Chords rang out, strident and dissonant, a desperate cry. The room reverberated as if a natural force was unleashed. Thunder and gale.

I knew the music.

I had heard it practiced on our simple instrument at Longbourn. I had heard it performed once, desperately, when Mary threw it in the face of our society at Netherfield before she was mocked by my own father. A performance Mr. Darcy had also heard.

But for all that the emotion and pain were the same, it had been nothing like this. This was knives of sound that cut, agony and ecstasy in turns, triumphant and terrible, brooding and breathtaking, accelerating endlessly as if the world had no limits on speed, or power, or freedom.

The music turned lyric, and Miss Darcy's lithe form swayed, her eyes closed while her hands danced over the keys. The volume grew, and she threw herself at the instrument. Her scarlet and gold robe twisted like a roaring flame against the mahogany frame and the white and black of the keys.

The final chords soared. The room fell silent.

Miss Darcy sat, her hands on the keyboard, motionless except her shoulders heaving with each shaking breath.

When I could move, I walked to her. "That was extraordinary." There were tears on my cheeks.

She reached out blindly, and I took her hand. Her fingers were slim but strong, her tendons like steel wire.

Facing the keys, she said, "I require a moment to… to come back." After several more breaths, her posture relaxed. She tipped her head and peered under the instrument. "We have a little lover of music."

The tykeworm was watching her from beneath the pianoforte. It was odd to see a draca interested in someone other than myself.

Miss Darcy straightened, then played a single note, the high E. The tone buzzed unpleasantly. "I have broken a string," she observed.

"I am unsurprised," said Mr. Darcy's baritone behind me. I had forgotten he was present. For once, I did not jump out of my skin.

To my astonishment, Miss Darcy proceeded, with no assistance from her brother, to haul the heavy cover of the pianoforte to one side. She rustled through a cabinet at the side of the room, returned with a complex tool, and began loudly cranking something inside the case. The tyke rose with an irritated shake and padded over to lie by the fire, his nose tucked under his belly.

After several savage yanks, and annoyed noises from both the instrument and Miss Darcy, two halves of a wire string came free. She examined them with a disgusted expression, then opened another drawer of the cabinet. This drawer was wide and flat, and displayed fragments of strings and pieces of mechanisms, each with a small paper card. She found a blank card, wrote a note, and added the broken string to the collection.

"Your sister is most remarkable," I said to Mr. Darcy. She was now fishing through another drawer, searching for a replacement string.

"After the death of our parents, she played endlessly. Her emotion manifested in music. But it was not a grieving child's obsession or retreat. It was… an awakening. When your sister Mary played, it moved me the same way. It was revelation. Honesty." His words touched deep feelings for my own family, of trials and of love. I drew a breath to dare a real reply, but before the words came, he raised his voice to address his sister. "I wrote to Herr Beethoven, asking his advice on strings."

Miss Darcy spun to him, her mouth open in shock. "You must not! He should not be disturbed for frivolous questions."

"It is not frivolous to ask his advice for a virtuoso and advocate of his work. For so I described you. He has replied already, suggesting the German who supplies his wire."

She crossed her arms, her eyebrows notched. "Did you *pay* him?" Mr. Darcy did not answer immediately, and she looked at me and added, "My brother believes he can purchase anything."

With mortified horror, I realized that was the same accusation I had hurled at Mr. Darcy after his proposal.

He was very still. Finally, he said, "I know that is not true."

"Oh, you are so serious," his sister said, coming over, a coiled wire in one hand. "I will forgive you if you do not write to him again."

"That will be difficult," Mr. Darcy admitted. "I have been his patron for some years."

"You *do* pay him!"

"I believe he appreciates the frivolous distraction of patronage." Mr. Darcy was smiling now. It lit the hint of hazel in his eyes.

"Hold this." She slapped the coil into his palm then turned to me. "Miss Bennet, will you walk with me? I require a tool from my room."

"Of course," I said. I had watched their exchange with amusement, but below that, my wildly swinging feelings had settled into a wistful flutter under my breastbone. A rather heated flutter that threatened to warm the back of my neck. I clasped my hands together and blew out a breath to cool myself.

Miss Darcy left the room. I hurried to follow, exchanging a silent nod with Mr. Darcy. But I had made my decision. I would follow my aunt's advice and find an opportunity to talk.

35

The hallway was bright from the chandeliers, each a web of wrought iron that held twelve ivory candles.

Miss Darcy led me toward sweeping stairs. The top vanished into gloom, and her brow furrowed while she lit a candle from a sconce. "Mrs. Reynolds has the house lit for guests, but they have neglected the next floor." After being so open with her brother, her glance was abashed. "We do not light the full house for ourselves. Do you think that strange?"

"I think it dramatic," I answered lightly as we climbed.

Actually, the sprawling darkness on the next floor was disconcerting for a stranger. Large, many-paned windows stared like faceted eyes. As we passed each, a ghost twin to Miss Darcy's candle followed outside.

There were no servants. Our steps echoed. This was very different from Longbourn, which overflowed with bustle and chattering ladies.

"Fitz worries that I am lonely here," Miss Darcy said. Her tentative smile glowed in the candlelight, and the gold note on her necklace gleamed. "I worry that he is too serious. So, I tease him."

"It is good he has a sister, then."

"He is changed since returning from Rosings. He wrote so often of you while he was there. I felt I almost had a sister." That was a suggestive choice of words, and I wondered what he had written. "You should tease him, also," she added decisively, now sounding more like a girl of sixteen. "He is far less formidable than he acts."

"I shall have little chance. I depart tomorrow." The flutter in my breast went still.

She stopped, her face falling. "So soon?"

"I must see my sister. She is ill."

"Oh. I am sorry. I hope she is better when you return." I nodded, the rote response sticking in my throat. After a silence, Miss Darcy held the candle forward. "There! They are lighting the library. It has a special chandelier. Let me show you."

Ahead, light spilled from an open door.

When Mr. Darcy and I discussed the library, we assumed I would not visit. But Miss Darcy walked through the door with the candle, so I had little choice.

The room opened around us, sprawling and shadowed, lit by our candle and three lamps carried by men. Each man stood by a different bookshelf. The ovals of light from their lamps swung when we entered, revealing the room.

The collection was huge, which by now was no surprise. Shelves filled every wall. An oak table had neat stacks of books beside pens, paper, and blotters. Another was swamped with haphazard volumes spilled everywhere.

As the three lamps converged on us, they shone through a chandelier lowered for lighting. It rested crookedly on the floor, a confection of Venetian blown glass that reached my waist, swirling with violet and gold and crimson. Even in the poor light, it was a masterpiece.

"Who are you?" Miss Darcy said in a frightened voice. And I realized this was wrong.

The chandelier's unlit candles were askew and broken. The crooked angle was from smashing into the floor. The base lay in a heap of glinting shards. Loops of iron chain had spooled down from the ceiling, snapping delicate flowers and birds of glass.

There was a flurry of steps and moving lamps. Heavy hands threw me against a wall of shelves. Books bounced off my shoulders and slapped the floor.

A man's hand covered my mouth, shoving the back of my head against a wooden shelf. His eyes stared into mine, inches away.

"See this?" he said, and a knife blade rose between our faces, bright in the light. "You make a sound, and I cut your throat. Understand?"

I nodded against his hand, so shocked I was not yet frightened. His hand left, but the blade waited. After I made no sound but gasps for air, he stepped back.

A lamp glared into my eyes. Beyond it, the man joined two other dark figures and conversed in hushed, angry tones.

They spoke French.

"What is this?" whispered Miss Darcy, backed against the shelves beside me. I reached and met fingers seeking mine. We clasped hands.

"Thieves," I whispered back. But in a library?

Some decision was reached, and a man began lighting the crooked candles in the fallen chandelier. They spat and flickered, burning fast from their angle. Their long, smoky flames drew beautiful glows from the broken glass.

The room brightened. We were against a bookshelf beside the doorway. A maid lay on the floor next to us, tied hand-and-foot with rope and gagged with white cloth. Frightened eyes met mine, and she made a muffled sound.

"Quiet!" a man said harshly. He had a pistol in his belt and a sword at his side. He drew the sword, a long, wicked piece of steel, and pointed it at the maid. She nodded.

The man was skinny and sandy-haired, with crooked, brown teeth. I had seen him before. The militia soldier who stopped our carriage.

He looked toward me. I turned my face away, instinct warning me not to be recognized.

The men's French resumed, fluent and fast with a rough accent different than I had learned. I caught snatches. *La Tarasque* several times, which I did not know.

Then, urgently, *l'enfant du lac*.

Child of the lake.

I stole a glance at Miss Darcy. Her lips moved, silently echoing a word.

"What is *la Tarasque*?" I whispered.

"A French myth, very old. A fearsome dragon that lived in the water and was tamed by Saint Martha." She listened. Presumably, she had excellent tutors for her French. "They are searching for it. No… searching for *books* on it. And the 'child of the lake.' I do not know what that is."

"Stay still," I whispered. "They will take their books and go."

I was frightened, but not terrified. If they tied up a maid instead of harming her, they would not dare harm ladies.

And my mind was buzzing with the strangeness of their search. Child of the lake. The same name as my family's journal, Loch bairn.

With the added light, two men swiftly searched the shelves while the sandy-haired man guarded us. One searcher cried out in triumph. He smashed a locked, glass-covered shelf. They began pulling out books and placing them in a large canvas bag.

Were those the prized draca books?

Abruptly, I realized I might be able to do something. Raise the alarm, if nothing else.

I closed my eyes and reached for the little tykeworm.

The void that surrounded Pemberley came first, like blindness. But where was the tyke? I concentrated, searching but finding nothing. I forced a calm breath. Forget the whispered French and the book spines pressing my shoulders. Open yourself.

The little gleam of the tyke appeared. A faint star, nothing like his usual rambunctious spirit. I nudged. Nothing. It was like prodding a lump of unresponsive clay.

He was sleeping. I remembered him lying down by the fire in the music parlor.

I prodded, hard. Nothing. "Forgive me," I whispered, then threw myself into the little glimmer, screaming in my head, *Wake up!*

There was an alarmed scramble of awareness. And I could see.

One aspect of my mind was muddled with sleep, the other bedazzled. A fire was a roaring conflagration a few feet away, a thousand indescribable shades. The music room loomed, sized for giants and filled with hulking instruments. Every color was wrong, replaced by vibrant hues distinct and different from the warm woods and fabrics I remembered.

The view swung, hunting for the wyfe who had screamed. She was not in the room. The view centered on a tall opening and began loping toward it. The doorway.

No! I thought. *Do not come to me.* Instead, I imagined Mr. Darcy, remembering how he appeared in the wyvern's mind, all postures and angles.

The loping motion spun, bounced, then settled, looking upward. A giant sat, his clothes shining warm, his hands and face even brighter. He shifted the ponderous way giants do, looking down. He spoke, but the sound was muddled and deep. Unintelligible. His features were indistinct in the tyke's perspective, but I sensed the shoulders and straight back of Mr. Darcy.

Now what?

Nudge him, I thought. *Make a sound—*

The tyke's vision vanished as fingers grabbed my jaw and jammed my temple against the books. I opened my eyes to see the face of the sandy-haired man.

"I know you," he growled.

I shook my head.

"*Allons-y!*" hissed a man by the door. "*Tout de suite!*" They were leaving. Only these two remained. The one with the bag of books was already gone.

The man let go of my face. Then he struck me—slapped me so hard that my head banged the shelf and my vision turned white. Hot pain flared on my cheek and lip.

"How do I know you?" he hissed.

There was rapid French. I blinked, head hanging, trying to clear my thoughts.

The tyke padded through the doorway. He trotted to my feet then sat and looked up, like five pounds of scaly, proud puppy.

If only the Gardiners had bound a firedrake.

The men had fallen silent, stepping to either side of the doorway. I heard familiar footsteps approaching. Mr. Darcy. The sandy-haired man pointed his sword at us, demanding silence, and the other man drew his sword.

Mr. Darcy's steps halted outside.

Please have men with you. Please be armed.

Mr. Darcy entered as nonchalantly as the tyke, alone and unarmed. "Miss Bennet?" he inquired and then froze as the man on the far side of the door placed his sword against Mr. Darcy's collar.

The sandy-haired man was looking from the tyke to me. "You was the lady in the carriage." He spoke to the other man in French. They argued, loud now, abandoning silence. I heard the word for uniform.

Miss Darcy drew a horrified breath.

The sandy-haired man took a step back. His sword rose, the tip of the blade pointing at my chest. His expression was fierce, but the sword hung, as if caught in the air.

Part of my brain parsed the French I had heard. *Tue-la.* Kill her.

The other man shouted, goading, and gestured in a flamboyant, Gallic style. His sword left Mr. Darcy's throat.

Mr. Darcy reached out, as casually as if he wished to shake hands, and savagely bent the man's wrist. There was a crack, and the sword fell into Mr. Darcy's grasp. He turned and lunged, a long fencing thrust that extended his sword arm above a well-balanced forward foot, his other arm straight back. He looked gentlemanly and poised, exactly like the stage actors I had seen in *Hamlet.*

My gaze followed his outstretched arm, then the shining steel exposed before the blade vanished into the sandy-haired man's side. The sword's tip protruded high on the far side, tenting the man's upper sleeve like an embroidery needle pushed through fabric.

It seemed a strange fencing hit—sideways, both chest and arm. Something that might be disallowed as unsportsmanlike.

Mr. Darcy recovered from his lunge, and the blade withdrew. When he struck, I had heard a gasp—his, or the man's, or mine. When he pulled back, there was a scrape of metal on bone. The sandy-haired man fell like a cloth doll into a pile of unmoving limbs. I stared down at him. It was so fast. Less than a breath.

The other man staggered back, shouting what were likely French obscenities because the words were utterly unfamiliar. Awkwardly, he drew his pistol with his left hand. He pawed at it with his injured right, then abandoned that and pressed the back of the pistol against his thigh. Trying to cock it with one hand.

Mr. Darcy was staring in disbelief at the man he had killed.

"Mr. Darcy!" I said. He did not move. Georgiana was making distraught sounds beside me. "Mr. Darcy!" I shouted. He just stood.

The pistol's hammer clicked into place, a sound I knew from my father cleaning and checking his hunting guns.

I reached for the tyke's awareness even as I screamed, "*Stop him!*" both in my mind and aloud, envisioning the French man.

The familiar, confusing double perspective returned as the tyke ran and sank his teeth into the man's ankle with a stomach-turning crunch.

The man screamed, pointed his pistol at the tyke, and fired.

The pistol shot was deafening and bright, a flash of flame I saw twice, once a shaft of light brighter than the candles, and again as a huge spray of multi-colored heat and sparks.

And pain.

A door of red-hot fury slammed, throwing me out of the tyke's awareness. The shock was incredible. I collapsed to my knees, head ringing, retching at the wooden floorboards a foot from my nose.

The man's scream ended with gurgling. Then there were only the snarls of the tyke.

"Miss Bennet!" Mr. Darcy's strong hands held my shoulders. He helped me sit. "Are you hurt?"

The French man lay on the floor. The tyke was tearing at his throat and face. Grotesque, wet shreds flew from his muzzle.

"Enough!" I called dizzily to the tyke, trying to crawl past Mr. Darcy. The tyke turned and charged at me, stopping just short of attacking, his bloody teeth bared. I recoiled in disbelief. I reached for his mind but struck that impenetrable wall of pain and fury.

Miss Darcy fell to her knees beside me. She sang a shaky note, becoming melodic, descending through strange tones. She crouched lower, easing past myself and Mr. Darcy, singing. The tyke quieted, his knife-edged teeth still bared in a soft hiss. Unafraid, she reached out and touched his head. Stroked his back. The hiss dissolved into a desperate, pained whimper.

"You are shot." She sang the words into her song, soft and sad.

Dreadful thoughts burst into my mind. Fear for the tyke. Realization that I sent the Gardiners' bound draca into danger, which I had no right to do. What if he died? What if my aunt was struck by binding sickness?

"How bad is it?" I crawled past Mr. Darcy to see.

She lifted the tyke onto her lap. "Grazed," she sang gently, then hummed while she turned him. His flanks rose and fell in rapid pants. "Here." Without touching, her finger followed a long, straight mark on one side of his torso. The scales were bent in a shallow groove, and shining, as if scraped to a high polish.

Her song faded to quiet. When the tyke remained calm, she spoke. "When they are angry, their scales lock. A shot must be square to penetrate. He is hurting, but not grievously injured." Her blue eyes were serious. "They are much tougher than we are." I let out a relieved breath.

Mr. Darcy had risen. He cut the ropes that bound the maid, who thanked him and sat up, rubbing her wrists. She seemed far calmer than I would have been. He threw his jacket over the ruin of the Frenchman's face and throat.

He returned to look down at the man he had killed. After several seconds, he turned to his sister.

"Are you well, Georgiana?" he asked.

"Yes," she answered distractedly and began humming to the tyke again.

I closed my eyes, still kneeling, and felt for the tyke's awareness. The wall of red fury was gone. His pain folded into my own body, a burning line on my ribs. *You are very brave*, I thought, and felt his head turn to me.

"How do you do that?" asked Miss Darcy. My eyes snapped open and met her curious gaze. "Command him, when you are not bound?"

At his sister's question, Mr. Darcy turned. Waiting for the answer.

Wonderful. Trying to choose a reply, I licked my lips and felt the sting of broken skin.

There were distant shouts. A bell began to clang. The alarm was raised at last.

Mr. Darcy headed toward the doorway.

"Wait," I called to him. My secret was revealed anyway. "There was another man. Let me check first."

I closed my eyes and encouraged the tyke to go into the hall. I heard him plop from Miss Darcy's lap, then his paws padded past me, limping, even as I saw myself through his eyes, my dress shimmering in peculiar shades. I could have counted the individual threads.

The hallway would have been dark to my eyes, but the tyke saw differently. Violet light streamed through the windows.

"The hall is empty..." I said, even as something warm appeared at the end. "Wait. A man approaches."

The man was walking stealthily by the interior wall, although he was obvious to the tyke's eyes. But the tyke felt curious, not concerned. The man's gait was familiar to me as well, and he wore a misshapen hat. "It is Mr. Rabb."

"Rabb!" Mr. Darcy shouted, startling me to open my eyes.

Mr. Rabb ran into the room, a pistol in his hand and another jammed into his belt. "Sir, there are intruders—" He broke off, seeing the bodies on the floor.

"We have encountered them," Mr. Darcy said dryly.

"And killed them," Mr. Rabb said. He appraised Mr. Darcy. "You?"

"I took one of them," Mr. Darcy said. "Then I froze like a fool. Wellesley will be scathing when I tell him. He always accuses me of having a gentleman's delicacy when we fence."

"Mr. Wellesley is a soldier," Mr. Rabb said. "He knows what it means to kill a man. I was horrified my first time."

"I will not freeze again," Mr. Darcy said firmly. "Not when those I love are threatened."

I had fixated on the beginning of that exchange. "You *fence* with Arthur Wellesley?" Mr. Wellesley was the commander of England's forces in the Peninsular War against Napoleon.

A memory returned: me, mocking Mr. Darcy at Netherfield by suggesting they played cards.

Mr. Darcy looked at me. "Yes, Miss Bennet. And you commanded a draca, bound to another husband and wyfe, to fetch me from the music parlor, and then to save my life. Which is more remarkable?" His forehead wrinkled. "Your lip is bleeding."

He fell to his knees in front of me and lifted my chin with his fingers. His thumb grazed my bruised cheek, almost too light to feel.

My breath had stopped. My eyes were wide.

He felt in his pocket for a handkerchief and dabbed my lip. "Am I hurting you?"

A little, but it was comforting. I nodded, then realized that was the wrong answer and shook my head. "No. It only stings." Although my cheek throbbed where the man's palm had struck.

"Another man took books on draca," Miss Darcy said. "They sought writing on la Tarasque. And something else. The child of the lake."

Mr. Darcy stood. "I should like my books returned. He may still be on the grounds. Rabb, assist the ladies while I assemble a party to search."

"Respectfully, sir, hunting is my skill."

"I trust you to keep them safe. That matters more than books." Mr. Rabb nodded reluctantly.

Mr. Darcy touched his sister's shoulder, and she smiled at him. Her fear had vanished the moment the tyke was injured.

Mr. Darcy gave me a stiff, short bow, then his running steps faded down the hall. It seemed we were back to bows.

"The household staff are gathered in the kitchens," Mr. Rabb said. He collected an abandoned lantern from the floor and led us out the doorway.

The tyke was in the hallway. I scooped him up as we passed so he would not have to walk with his sore side.

Watching me, Mr. Rabb said, "If I heard the master right, you were 'commanding draca,' Miss Bennet."

"It was remarkable," Miss Darcy said. "I have seen nothing like it."

"You would have if you had not been so young when your mother died," Mr. Rabb replied.

Miss Darcy stopped stock still. "Mamma could do that?"

Mr. Rabb aimed the lantern down so light pooled around us in the dark hallway. "Lady Anne was a miracle with draca. All draca, not just her wyvern. Made me think of the legend of the Scottish wyves. But the missus was not quick to explain, and old Mr. Darcy did not wish it widely known." His eyes, glinting under grizzled eyebrows, met mine. "You are not quick to explain, yourself."

"I also do not wish it widely known," I said. "Nor can I explain much. I would like to understand better."

"I won't tell a soul, ma'am. But I know some things you should hear. Maybe we can have a chat when the evening's business is settled. I might need a dram for that, if you fancy whiskey."

I had never tasted anything stronger than port. "Perhaps a sip."

"How were you able to see Mr. Rabb in the hallway?" Miss Darcy asked me.

I found I was tired of keeping secrets. "At times, I can see through the tyke's eyes."

"How wonderful," she breathed.

That was a pleasant change from skeptical disbelief. Of course, Miss Darcy had her own unusual draca ability.

"They see differently from us," I said. "And extremely well in the dark. Let me try…" I closed my eyes and felt for the tyke's awareness. The void that surrounded Pemberley opened first. "Why is the forest around Pemberley so empty? It is like nowhere else. It is blackness."

"The darkness of Pemberley," Mr. Rabb said in a disturbed tone. "Lady Anne spoke of this before her death, but I do not know the cause."

I found the tyke's awareness and fell into it. He squirmed in my arms to look at me.

I saw my own face. My cheek and lip were shining hot. Ouch. I would have a bruise.

"I wish I could show you how they see," I said. "It is all shades of heat and cool, and astonishingly exact, but faces are hard to recognize." We were by a window, and I encouraged the tyke to look outside. "But outside is bright, even at night with no moon."

There was a brilliant spot of heat. "There is a man in the woods. With horses."

"Alone?" asked Mr. Rabb urgently.

"Yes."

"Not a Pemberley man, then. I taught them to search in pairs. Where?"

I opened my eyes and pointed. It was black forest, the same as anywhere else.

"Downstairs, quickly," Mr. Rabb said. We ran down the curved staircase to the lit hallway below.

He stopped by a window. "Can your tyke see here, even with the candles?"

I closed my eyes. We were closer now. The man was leaning against a tree. The horses' breaths were warm puffs that dissipated like steam in the night.

"Yes. He is just waiting. With three horses."

"Waiting for his two companions," Mr. Rabb said with some relish. "I think I shall reclaim my master's books." I opened my eyes to see him squinting into the dark.

"Should we not call for your footmen?" I said.

"A man with a horse can be gone in a moment."

"I think you are foolish."

"I survived fighting the American rebels in '79. I wasn't much older than you. That taught me a few things." His weathered cheeks creased in a grin. "A man hearing alarms is frightened, and frightened men shoot poorly in the dark. Mind that you ladies stay here. The master will run me through if you get a scratch on you."

He touched his hat gallantly, then ran down the hall and eased out the door, a silent shadow that vanished into the woods.

I closed my eyes and saw him again, a warm silhouette advancing toward the waiting man.

Miss Darcy's hand squeezed my arm, and I put my fingers on hers. "Can you see?" she asked.

"Yes, but it frightens me," I said. "He is mad. He is walking straight to him."

The waiting man's arm stretched, waving a pistol toward Mr. Rabb. The gamekeeper walked faster, turning sideways and weaving, his feet crossing as smoothly as a dance.

Twenty steps apart, the pistol fired, brilliant and hot. I heard the shot, muted through the glass. A horse reared, and the man turned to control it. Mr. Rabb advanced within a few steps and fired. The man fell.

"He has done it," I gasped. "He is safe."

The tyke twisted violently in my arms. Hissed. I pressed him to look where Mr. Rabb knelt by the fallen man.

Mr. Rabb lifted a hanging shape. The canvas bag of books.

A writhing, cool mass with dozens of legs poured down the tree above him, burying him in coiling frenzy.

"No!" I screamed. The vision vanished as the tyke forced himself from my arms and scrambled away.

In the darkness, a pistol flashed in the woods.

"What has happened?" asked Miss Darcy.

I ran to the door and threw it open, but I stood, frightened by the blackness beyond the trees. Hiding in that dark was a monstrous foul crawler like the one that killed Denny.

Shouting men were running across the lawn carrying lanterns and torches, pointing where the shots had flashed. Mr. Darcy was with them. I should show them where to look, but my feet were rooted to the step. The memories of that awful day by Meryton were vivid as life. I smelled bitter almond. I saw Denny's bloodied face. I felt his body go still under my hands.

Like a coward, I closed my eyes and sought the tyke's vision instead.

Two figures stood with two horses, deep in the trees. Different horses. A different place. I was not sure where the tyke had gone.

One figure was a man. The other was… shrouded in dark. Rank with corruption. Some strange sense detected it—the dark was not truly visible. The tyke's fear prickled my skin.

The man helped the dark figure mount a horse. No, helped the *woman* mount. I saw skirts. The man lifted her from her waist, the way a lover might steal a touch. She settled in the saddle, tall for a woman, and adjusted her hat. That gesture was oddly familiar.

The man mounted the other horse and swung a dangling shape over his shoulder. The bag of books.

They rode away together. The tyke turned, picking through brush and trunks illuminated by violet light, seeking me, his side aching.

36

"Elizabeth, dear." Aunt Gardiner touched my shoulder. "Can you wake?"

I blinked at the covers of the inn's bed. Bright sunlight streamed through the window.

I had been delivered back to the inn after midnight by coach, the tyke-worm curled on my lap and a shaken Mrs. Reynolds seated across from me. Four armed footmen rode outside.

Mrs. Reynolds's explanation to the Gardiners was muddled in my memory.

"How is Mr. Rabb?" I asked. My head ached.

My aunt bit her lip. "Mr. Darcy is here. He hopes to speak with you. He will wait while you dress, if you are well enough."

I sat up, hair hanging in a confused mess. "Yes. I will be down shortly."

My aunt touched my chin, turning my face toward her. The memory of Mr. Darcy touching my cheek returned.

"Oh dear," she said, lips pursed in concern.

"Is it bad?"

"You look like you fell off a horse."

"How delightful." I sighed. "Well, I do not like to ride, so this spares me the trouble of falling off a real horse."

I expected a smile, but my aunt only kissed my forehead and left.

I found my looking glass. Impressive. My cheek was a remarkable purple, and my lip cracked and swollen.

But I was alive. A bruise was nothing. How was Mr. Rabb?

I threw on a petticoat and traveling dress, and twisted my hair into a scrambled tangle that could be pinned. Then I joined my aunt, uncle, and Mr. Darcy in the inn's small parlor.

Mr. Darcy rose when I entered, his eyes widening.

"I am well," I said, anticipating his question. "It is only a bruise. How is Mr. Rabb?"

Stillness spread before he spoke. "Mr. Rabb died last night. I told you then. You were very affected."

I sank into a chair, the morning sunbeams swimming behind tears. A murky memory of crying before returned, and of Mr. Darcy's pained, grieving face. "I remember. I am sorry to ask you again." I sat until I could speak again. "Did you kill the monster?"

"Whoever shot him escaped." Mr. Darcy had chosen a chair a respectable distance from me. My aunt and uncle were in the farthest two seats.

"*Shot* him?" I said. "He was attacked by a foul crawler."

Mr. Darcy straightened in his chair. "He died from a gunshot. But there were other injuries. You did not say this last night."

I wet my lips, and my cracked lip twinged. "I was not myself last night."

Mr. Darcy nodded. "We saw no sign of such a creature, so it must have fled. I will not keep you from your recovery. I wished to be sure you were well, and to deliver this." He held out a small brown-glass bottle. A folded paper was tied to the neck. "This is the medicine, the extract of rowan flowers. It should slow the progression of disease in your sister. My apothecary wrote instructions. Each dose is small, so this will last six weeks."

"This is miraculous. I cannot sufficiently express our gratitude." I turned the bottle in my hand, watching the white surface tip. I drew a breath to ask how to get more, then let it out. He had been so generous that I feared I knew the answer. That six weeks was more than enough.

"We must leave immediately," I said.

"Of course," Mr. Darcy said. "My sister sends her best wishes for you and your sister."

"Thank her for me."

He nodded. The room was silent.

My aunt cleared her throat. "Lizzy, you received an express letter from Longbourn. I did not wish to press you to read it, but if your business with Mr. Darcy involves Jane's care, perhaps you should look before he departs?"

I had not seen the letter on the table, addressed in Mary's angular hand to the inn we had planned to visit in Taddington, then forwarded. That had added days.

I picked it up, frightened it was terrible news. But it could not be the worst news of Jane. Papa would write then.

I broke the seal and read, first with puzzlement, then shock. "What..."

My aunt was beside me. "What has happened?"

"Lydia has... escaped from Brighton. Has *eloped* with Mr. Wickham! Oh, she cannot be such a fool." I read on. "She left a note saying they are running to Scotland to marry." A girl of sixteen could not marry in England without her parents' consent, but Scottish law was notoriously free about such things.

I checked the date. If they had traveled north from Brighton, they would be past London by now. Perhaps even in Derbyshire. Lydia could be within a few miles of me, though I would never know.

My aunt seemed more confused than horrified. "Was not Mr. Wickham the officer you admired?"

I forgot I had mentioned him in my letters. "No! Well, yes. But then I did not. Wickham is despicable. Aunt, you do not understand. An elopement would be terrible enough, but I doubt even that. I do not believe he will marry her."

"Lydia would not be so foolish as that," my aunt said.

"Not by design. But she is quite foolish enough in practice."

"But she would be ruined."

"Not just her," I said. Our entire family—all Lydia's sisters—would be shunned by society. Stained by one sister's transgression.

"Lizzy." My aunt hugged me. Comforting *me*.

"It is not *me!* It is Jane. I had hoped—" I stopped, not wanting to admit my pathetic fantasy that Mr. Bingley would sweep back and marry Jane so all would be well. But if Lydia was ruined, no gentleman would marry a Bennet sister. Particularly not a wealthy man of social standing like Mr. Bingley.

"You are assuming the worst—" began my aunt bracingly.

Mr. Darcy interrupted. "Wickham will not marry your sister." He was standing, taut with fury.

Mr. Darcy's terrible history with Wickham rushed into my mind. The attempted elopement with Miss Darcy. The confrontation with Mr. Darcy.

Mr. Darcy took an angry step, his boot thumping the floor. "Wickham will marry only to bind draca. He has ruined women before. If they are traveling together, in secret, it is impossible that she will be… it is impossible she would bind on their wedding night."

Lydia had no marriage gold. That alone crushed any hope of binding. And if their nights were already intimate, even a proper marriage would fail to bind.

My aunt was looking between Mr. Darcy and myself, a new concern dawning as she saw Mr. Darcy's furious reaction.

"I am sure you desire my absence," Mr. Darcy said bitterly. "Or that I was gone before you opened your letter. And I have my own business to attend. I will not torment you with vain hopes in this grave affair. But I offer my sincerest wishes to your sister Jane." He was already reaching for his hat.

"Wait," I said. "I wish to speak with you."

My words came out unthinking, a remnant of the resolve I had built at Pemberley before the interruption by thieves.

Mr. Darcy stopped, his hat, a topper of black silk, clenched in his hand. He did not look at me.

"Come," my aunt said softly to her husband and pulled his arm. They left, my uncle looking back in confusion before his wyfe closed the door.

I was alone with Mr. Darcy.

But I had nothing to say. The fumbling words I had pieced together while wandering the halls of Pemberley could no longer be uttered. Not after the news of Lydia.

Into the silence, Mr. Darcy spoke, almost whispering. "You will be a great wyfe."

"What?" I said uncertainly.

He looked at me, startled, and a flush heated the angry pallor on his rigid cheekbones. He stammered, "You will be a great dragon wyfe. Your skills mark you as a great wyfe."

This was not why I had asked him to stay, but it was too interesting to ignore. "Mr. Rabb spoke of the great dragon wyves, but they are unknown to me." Mr. Rabb's name caught my throat, so the rest was hoarse.

Mr. Darcy's throat worked also before he replied. "Rabb was the first to tell me the story. The great wyves were three Scottish noblewomen who fought the English many centuries ago. So long ago, it was not even England they truly opposed. But English rule outlawed their story. The great wyves are a forbidden legend now, but still told in secret in the north."

"But you know of them. Can you help me comprehend my ability?"

He shook his head. "I only recognize it. I understand the other wyves better."

"*Other* wyves?"

"The three great wyves had different skills. Since their death, those skills have never been seen again. Not until our lifetime, when the three skills returned in three new wyves."

"Who?" I said. Already I thought of Miss Darcy.

"My mother was the wyfe of healing. Her abilities woke when she bound, and when I was of age, she confided in me. My sister is the wyfe of song. You have seen her skills… *some* of her skills. And the third…" he nodded to me.

"You think I am the third wyfe?" I said. "This sounds like mysticism. Prophecy."

"I am no mystic, and there is no prophecy. But for whatever cause, the three wyves appeared together once, so it is reasonable that they would appear together again. Their skills are named in their legend." He recited:

> *"To sound our claim,*
> *the three wyves came:*
> *Of healing, wise.*
> *Of song, who cries.*
> *Of war. Arise."*

My eyebrows squished dubiously. "If your mother was the wyfe of healing, and your sister is the wyfe of song, this seems more unlikely." His dark eyes watched me. "You claim I am the wyfe of *war?*"

"You command unbound draca. You are fearless."

"I assure you I am quite fearful. And small and timid." Mr. Darcy gave an incredulous laugh. How rude. "Is this why you proposed? To complete your set of wyves?"

"Of course not! I knew only that you were brave and—"

I held up my hand. "Stop." My feelings were confused enough without hearing a recitation of imaginary virtues.

What I had planned to say last night could no longer be said. I took a deep breath. "I understand this alters our situation."

"*What* alters it?" His voice had become dangerously soft.

"Wickham. With Lydia. The worst outcome is that she is ruined. Even the best is that they marry." To call that "best" made my stomach curdle.

"Why should that matter?"

"Because you hate him. Because your sister could not bear to be near him."

He flinched like my words burned, then pushed a hand through his tousled hair. "You said 'this alters our situation.' Had we a situation to alter?" My answer would not form, trapped between my heart and my head, and he rushed on. "Every night, I recall each word we spoke. I—"

"Stop!" I turned my back, gasping into my hands over my face. "What am I to say? Jane is dying. Lydia is lost, and with her, all prospects for my sisters. I have one duty. Rush home and comfort my family through disaster."

His voice came behind me, much closer. "There could be a miracle."

I laughed bitterly at the wall I faced. "You promised not to torment me with vain hopes."

"You perform miracles. Why not deserve one?"

I turned to him. "You are not helping!"

His right hand still held his hat, but his left was outstretched, a few inches from my face. He started and stepped back, then a step farther. "Of course. You are correct."

"If you understand what is happening to me—what these abilities are—have I any ability to help Jane?"

"To my knowledge, no." He hesitated. "My mother could have cured her."

"Can you not *think* before you speak? Why say that!"

There was a tearing sound. His expensive hat collapsed in his hand.

"Forgive me," he said. "I cannot think while seeing you hurt."

"Hurt? Who cares if I am hurt? I came here to cure Jane." I held up the bottle he had given me. "You have helped, even if it is no more than a few gracious days of delirium. But I have achieved nothing." I searched the mysteries piled in my mind. "What is special about Pemberley lake?"

"The lake? Nothing."

"There must be something."

"Some call it Pemberley lake, but it has a Gaelic name. *An treas piuthar*. The third sister." His eyes were distant. "There are two sister lakes. Larger lakes. Pemberley has the smallest sister."

The smallest sister. Like me. I laughed at myself for grasping at coincidence. "What is the 'darkness of Pemberley'? Mr. Rabb was disturbed when I mentioned it."

Mr. Darcy backed a step. "You have seen this?"

"Yes. There is nothing around Pemberley. When I search, it is a void. Dark. Empty."

His eyes were wide. His complexion became ash.

"You must go." His voice was rocks falling on glass.

"*What?*"

"Leave. Never return to Pemberley."

"That is insane." The rational part of me was saying this did not matter. Deeper, my heart was screaming.

"Go. Leave now."

He spun and was gone, running, the door yawning behind him. I heard an exclamation from my uncle in the hall, then boots on the stairs. The inn door slammed.

His hat was left, twisted to shreds on the floor.

37

Outside Longbourn, I stopped as I passed the draca house.

The coach horses were blowing and stamping, cooling in the night air. My uncle had accepted my plea and hired four-horse teams. That made for a grueling but fast two-day trip home—days that passed in fear for Jane and Lydia, and in my own confused, lonely haze.

In the sparse light of the coach lanterns, our firedrake glistened, motionless on his perch, his eyes glinting like black jewels.

I cast my awareness to him.

This time, there was no wild squawk or retreat. Just sullen resistance. A crystal wall, gentler than the red fury when the tyke threw me out, but still a wall.

The drake began to hiss.

"Why do you fight me?" I whispered. I remembered the images he had shown before. Cages and traps.

"Lizzy?" asked my aunt, stopping beside me. I resumed walking to our door.

We had arrived as my family prepared for bed, and it was a reunion in nightclothes, happy and relieved and tearful and fraught. I hugged everyone and deferred questions about my hurt face while my uncle greeted my father in serious tones.

Mary hugged me tight, then murmured, "Mamma is retired with

nerves." I heard my mother call from upstairs, demanding I attend her. "But you must see Jane first." Jane had not come down to greet me.

"Let us go." I already held the bottle of medicine. I had dug it out a mile from home, clutching it like a talisman.

In our room, Jane lay curled under the bed covers. I stroked her hair. "Jane, darling. I am back."

Her face turned to me, and I stifled a gasp. Her bones stretched her skin like paper, gaunt and fragile as a bird. The sunken skin under her eyes was as dark as soot.

Like feathers, her wasted fingers traced my bruised cheek, which had turned a mottled purple and ugly yellowish-green. "You are changing," she whispered. "You will be a dark fairy, with black wings."

I held her. It was like embracing a bundle of sticks.

Mary had read the paper tied to the medicine, and she sat down beside us. "Lizzy has brought medicine for you." She held out a teaspoon full of white liquid. Jane dutifully swallowed, then made a child's disgusted face. I laughed, and then Mary laughed, and then we were all laughing in one desperate embrace.

My aunt and I visited Mamma. I tried to be patient while she rattled on about the agonies of her nerves. Then I went down to my father, who was in his library with my uncle.

"Papa," I said from the doorway, and he beckoned me in. He had aged twenty years, his eyes red-veined, his white hair unkempt.

"Your uncle and I are discussing the recovery of Lydia," he said. "Or whatever remote chance of that remains."

"Do you know where she is?" I asked.

"Colonel Forster is ashamed to have failed in his protection of my daughter and has expended great effort to track them. First to London, where we feared they had remained. But they proceeded farther."

"To Scotland?" I asked with a spark of hope. Maybe they had married.

"He has reason to suspect Derbyshire. Wickham had gambling debts in London, and so fled. But he grew up in Derbyshire and has nefarious acquaintances to shelter him." He added dryly, "Doubtless my freshly nefarious daughter will be welcome."

"Then they have been together, unmarried, for more than a week." My hope was gone.

"Yes. Rumor already spreads amongst our neighbors." My father steepled his fingers. "Lizzy, you warned me of the dangers of permitting Lydia such freedom, and you have proved most wise. The blame is mine."

"I think the blame is Lydia's. Or Wickham's."

"Lydia is a child who should have been protected. For once, let me feel the blame I deserve. I am not afraid of being overpowered by the impression. It will pass soon enough." I reached out, and we held each other's fingers. He exhaled a long, uneven breath. "I am thankful you have returned. It frees me to go after her."

"You are not well enough," I protested.

"I must be well enough. This is a father's responsibility. I will not shirk it."

"Let me go with you," my uncle said. That made me wince. I had just dragged my uncle through a strenuous sprint from Derbyshire, and he offered to reverse that.

"I will meet Colonel Forster there," my father told him. "That is sufficient. You have children of your own to love and care for."

My father shifted his hand to hold mine firmly, as if we were two gentlemen. As if we were equals. "Lizzy, your mother is distraught. Jane is ill. I rely on your courage and good sense. You must be the rock of Longbourn until I return."

I swallowed against a lump in my throat and nodded.

THE MORNING DAWNED WITH A MIRACLE.

"Lizzy!" Jane's voice was concerned. "What has happened to your face?"

I blinked groggily. Exhaustion and my own bed had provided my first proper sleep in days. "That is a long story. I am most happy to be home."

"Your hair is frightful." A brush pulled. But the stroke trembled.

Remembering, I sat up in bed, astonished.

Jane was frowning at my tangles. "Had you no maid?"

Her face was more shocking by daylight. Her cheeks clung under her cheekbones. Only her lips remained full, suspended too prominently by her teeth.

But her eyes were focused and loving, and she held a brush, just as we sometimes brushed each other's hair when we were younger.

"It is good to see you more yourself," I said. After Mr. Darcy's warnings, I was intoxicated by relief.

"I feel much better," Jane said. "It was gray while you were gone. There was mist even in the house." She brightened. "Shall we see if breakfast is out?"

Our cook, who scowled until noon, cooed and fussed over my bruised cheek. When Jane suggested—with no mention of fairies—that I must be hungry from my trip, she vanished toward the kitchen, crying, "It's grand to have our two eldest down for breakfast again!"

"I believe we shall be served more than toast today," I said. A tremendous pounding of pots and scolding of scullery maids had risen.

"Good. I am hungry," Jane said.

After crumpets, soft boiled eggs, sausage, and strong tea, Papa departed north by hired coach to meet Colonel Forster in Taddington, the town that the Gardiners and I had planned to visit before we were turned aside by the sandy-haired man wearing a slovenly militia uniform.

That was another mystery—French spies in the center of England seeking books on *l'enfant du lac*, the child of the lake. But I had enough puzzles without speculating about the war between England and France.

I touched a finger to my cheek. Seconds after he struck me, the sandy-haired man was dead, killed by Mr. Darcy. The last mark of a man's life was a fading bruise on my cheek. That seemed sad.

At luncheon, I opened a jar of water from Pemberley lake, poured some in a teacup, and gave it to Jane. She drank it.

"How does it feel?" I asked breathlessly.

"Like water?" she offered, eyeing me like I was mad.

Days ticked by in the settled routine of home. I played my role by rote, unconvinced any of this was real. Layers of worry cocooned me—for Jane, for Lydia, for Papa—and beneath that, buried as deep as I could force it, there was a canker of selfish loss.

Mamma kept to her bed, raving of her nerves and ranting of Mr. Wickham "who was so handsome in his red coat." Kitty, chagrined and sad, sat with her often. Kitty had been profoundly reprimanded by my father after she confessed knowledge of Lydia's plan from their private letters.

On the third day, Jane became frightened by the shadows under the laurel hedge and ran inside to hide. On the fourth, she cried that fairies were spitting foulness on her food. On the sixth, she refused to come down for meals, and ate a slice of toast in our room, crushing it into a mass she hid in her hands while her eyes darted.

Mary and I cajoled and begged for a quarter hour to have her take her spoonful of medicine. I convinced her by saying Mr. Bingley had sent it as a gift. A minute after she swallowed, she collapsed into a moaning slumber.

Mary left and returned, settling herself in our room and stacking three books beside her chair.

"Lizzy," she whispered. "Go and rest. I shall watch her."

I had been staring blankly.

As I went down the stairs, a letter arrived from my father.

38

In Mamma's room, I read aloud from my father's letter:

"I have, in remarkably expedited fashion, completed my business in Derbyshire. Your sister Lydia is found, and with her Mr. Wickham, who admirably fulfills all my recollections of his superficiality and arrogance, and whom I will be obligated henceforth to refer to as my son."

"Oh! Oh! They will marry!" cried Mamma, bouncing in her bed while Kitty stared at me with a stunned expression.

Mary listened also but had already read the letter. I gave it to her after I read it, and we had both rejoiced. But on this second hearing, Mary was impassive, her brown eyes, framed by her long, straight hair, narrowing with each sentence.

My mother clapped her hands. "Married at sixteen! What a clever girl! Have my clothes set out at once! I will go to town and share the news. And I shall certainly call on the Lucases. Oh, your father must raise marriage gold! He foolishly insists we can afford only ten guineas for the lot of you, but with Lydia marrying such a handsome officer we *must* do more. I am sure he can raise five guineas for her while the banns are called."

"Mamma," I interrupted. "They are already wed."

"Already?" Her face puckered. "But she was not at home. Without her marriage gold..."

"You should be thankful they are married at all," I said. "Listen." I resumed reading, trying not to worry at the shakiness of Papa's hand:

"Prior even to my or Colonel Forster's arrival, Lydia and Wickham were discovered, and through reliable authority I know that Wickham had no intent to marry. We have been beneficiaries of a most galling negotiation, which has left me with an unpayable debt and no merit. If it were not for some sacrifice of health, I would call the entire trip a deplorable bargain, for it has cost no more than an outing to London."

"How can it be deplorable when I have a daughter married!" exclaimed Mamma.

"I dislike his mention of health," Mary said. "And what is an unpayable debt?" I shook my head, although I had a wild suspicion. I read on:

"As they have bound a ferretworm—"

"Bound!" my mother shrieked. She jumped from her bed in her crumpled nightgown. "*Bound!* Oh, my darling Lydia!"

She subsided into excited peeping noises, so I resumed:

"As they have bound a ferretworm, Wickham has secured a married officer's commission in Newcastle, where they will travel directly. They will not be received at Longbourn. Although further affairs remain to be settled, I am forced to return. Expect me a day after this letter.

"Your loving father, James Bennet."

My mother's expression had collapsed like a fallen loaf. "Not received here? Why ever not?"

"Papa is angry with Lydia, Mamma," I said.

"Angry? Whatever for?"

I exchanged incredulous expressions with Mary while mother enlisted Kitty and a maid to prepare her clothes.

Papa's coach arrived the next morning, but he was not alone. A doctor traveled with him.

"Doctor Culpepper," he introduced himself as I helped Papa from the coach. "I hoped to speak with Mrs. Bennet?"

"She is away until luncheon," I said. Mamma was making an extensive series of social calls.

My father's weight fell on my arm. In a windy voice, he said to the doctor, "You should speak to Lizzy." Then he nodded toward his library, and we settled him in his chair with a blanket and a cup of tea.

In the hall outside the library, the doctor addressed me. I listened with my arms wound around myself, as if our house had chilled.

"Your father's health took a sudden and severe turn," the doctor said. "His circulation remains poor, which will shorten his breath and greatly limit his activity."

"For how long? What is the cause?"

"The cause is disease of the heart, which is prone to sudden attacks. Your father has had a long and productive life. The best care is quiet rest and love from his family."

My chill was growing. I had been steeling myself since reading the letter, but not this much. "You are considerate, but our circumstances require forthright advice. You said nothing of recovery."

"Improvement is always to be hoped for." He chose his next words slowly, and every hesitation drove my chill deeper into my chest like a knife of ice. "However, it would be prudent to prepare for a worsening, which may be abrupt. Have you a local physician?"

"Mr. Jones. A surgeon and apothecary." Meryton was too small for a physician.

He nodded. "I should like to consult with him before I depart."

I asked Mrs. Hill to send for Mr. Jones. Then I stared at my father's open library door for a minute, straightened my shoulders, and went in.

Papa was shrunken in his chair. A sheet of written paper rested on his desk.

He nodded for me to sit. "Has the illustrious doctor befuddled you with his niceties?"

"No." I was proud my voice was steady.

"Good. I knew I could rely on your sense." He drew a labored breath. "It is a dark day when a rogue like Wickham joins our family. I would have refused their marriage and condemned Lydia to her fate were it not for the damage to you and your sisters."

"You would not do that." For all I was furious with Lydia, she was family.

He smiled through gray lips. "No. I admit you are right. But I did give Wickham a firm account of my mind. I bested him well in our argument, but I paid the price after. How pathetic that passion and moral outrage—emotions that spiced my life and drove my work in my youth—are now a poison."

He placed his forefinger on the sheet of paper on his desk. "I have written a power of attorney that authorizes you to administer Longbourn. Legally it is little protection, as the entailment declares a bound male is heir, and the law gives women no right to conduct business. However, our estate has longstanding and mutually profitable relationships, so you will find our partners eager to proceed as usual. Has Mr. Jones been summoned?" I nodded. "When he arrives, he and Doctor Culpepper will witness it. Then you may continue. Until someone chooses to challenge you."

"Continue?" I said, and finally my voice was uneven.

"Until Longbourn is claimed, I consider it yours. It is an unfair burden, Lizzy, as you assume responsibility without reaping reward, but I know you will shine. You must care for our family, household, and tenants as long as you can. You are mistress of Longbourn."

DOCTOR CULPEPPER FOUND me in our garden, embedded in incongruous calm. The scent of hyacinths and lilac. The hum of bees.

"Miss Bennet. I have consulted with Mr. Jones, and we have assisted your father with his legal preparations. I regret that I must depart to return to my own practice."

"Thank you for attending him," I said. "Has my father arranged payment of your fees?"

"I am physician to the Pemberley estate, present at Mr. Darcy's request." He gave a slight bow.

That name was no surprise. Since reading Papa's letter, my wild suspicion had become certainty. Who else had the resources to find Wickham in the vastness of Derbyshire, and the power to bribe and threaten him to marry?

I suppose the physician to Pemberley did not bother with trivialities like fees.

"Was there any message?" I asked.

"Message?"

"For me. From Mr. Darcy."

"No, Miss Bennet."

After the doctor left, my mother bubbled through the front door, chattering and happy, then ecstatic that Papa was home. Mr. Jones took her upstairs to visit my father.

Mr. Jones came down after ten minutes, upset beneath his professional manner. We took a wordless cup of tea together. I watched the tea tremble in my shell-thin cup until he departed, telling me to send for him if there was any change.

It was an hour before my mother emerged, her face wretched.

I held her, and she moaned. "I am so frightened, Lizzy."

"Hush," I said, stroking her hair like a child.

I went outside and walked circuits around the manor, reviewing what business required attention. April was rather a lull with the main crop of peas sown, but there were potatoes to plant and lambs to protect.

My feet stopped at our draca house. Our firedrake watched me, silent and waiting, an icon of our gentry status and our sole inviolable claim to Longbourn.

"I understand now," I whispered. "You know the end approaches."

The sky turned fiery with sunset and faded to silver dusk. I went up to my parents' room.

Papa rubbed the bed beside him with a shaky hand, and I sat close to him.

"I wish to understand what happened in Derbyshire," I said.

"Perhaps we can explain it to each other," he said, his dry humor sharp even with a weak voice. "I shall tell my side first. Colonel Forster arrived the day before me and made inquiries about certain friends of Wickham. Gambling acquaintances, to be blunt. Within an hour, he received a remarkable visit from a gentleman."

"Mr. Darcy," I said. This much I had guessed.

"Yes. Mr. Darcy spent some time ascertaining the colonel's purpose and credentials, then revealed he knew the whereabouts of Wickham and Lydia. He had, in fact, already confronted Wickham in very strong terms."

"Why?" I asked. This was my real question.

My father pondered me for a good half minute, as if the answer hung in my eyes, then continued, "I arrived the next morning and met both Wickham and Mr. Darcy. Mr. Darcy and I spent a day and a half together, including a late night where we spoke at length between bouts of negotiation with Wickham. And between my arguments with Lydia, whom I found greatly changed, and not for the better."

Papa took my hand. "Mr. Darcy, to my surprise, is a man who draws confidences. We spoke earnestly, and I found him principled and of remarkable consequence. Wickham, of course, is his opposite. Wickham had thought up a variety of selfish demands before he would marry Lydia, mostly escaping debts which added to a formidable sum. But the great challenge was his obsession with binding. This, even though it was grotesquely evident that he and Lydia traveled with unfettered intimacy."

"Then how could they have bound?" Everything I knew said it was impossible.

"You may, because of your proximity, not appreciate how exceptional it was that your mother and I bound a firedrake with so little marriage gold. The Bennet wyves have an extraordinary history of binding, as does your mother's maternal line. I shared this with Wickham, although I suspect he knew, and that was what drove his interest in our family. But that alone would have been insufficient, had not Mr. Darcy provided his own extraordinary incentive in the form of marriage gold." Papa licked chapped lips and shook his head in slow disbelief. "I lifted the chest myself, and it was the weight of a good-sized goose. I would hazard there were more than five hundred guineas."

"Of *marriage gold?*" Five hundred guineas in any form was a large sum. In marriage gold, it was worth twenty times that, and all the value lost after the wedding. And this from a man who, for reasons I did not understand, had renounced marriage gold for himself and his sister. "Why would he do that?"

"I think you know. You have a part in this, Elizabeth. Will you confide in your father?"

There was so much to say. What spilled out was simple. "I care for Mr. Darcy. He told me to leave and never return." Tears splashed down my cheeks. "We did not quarrel. He… something frightens him."

My father stroked his thumb once over each cheek, wiping my tears away. "The only thing to frighten a man like Mr. Darcy is fear for those he loves."

Papa wore a ring to commemorate his wedding, what was called a posy ring, plain gold with verse inscribed inside. He pulled it off and pressed it into my palm.

"Mr. Darcy loves you, Lizzy. It is plain on his face every time he speaks your name, which he did at every excuse he could invent. But he is captive to some past torment. We spoke frankly in our long night—" His voice cut off as his fingers clenched, driving the heavy, warm circle of his ring into my skin. He drew a hoarse breath. "My dear Lizzy. Of all my daughters, I have worried most for your happiness. I could not imagine what man could earn your respect as a husband. I have met such a man, if you resolve to have him. I could not part with you to anyone less worthy. Carry this ring as my blessing, if I cannot deliver it otherwise. Now, fetch Jane for me if you can, and my wyfe, and your sisters. And it would be best to call for Mr. Jones, also."

I ran to find Mary and asked her to help Jane. I found Mamma and Kitty and sent them up. Last, I dashed through the laundry and scullery before I found Mrs. Hill with the gardener and asked her to summon Mr. Jones.

I ran back up the stairs, puffing, and into my parents' room.

My mother was collapsed on my father's chest, shaking with silent sobs. Mary and Kitty were curled around her, and Jane standing with grieved, distant calm.

"Papa?" I said uncertainly. His head had fallen back on the pillow, eyes staring sightlessly. I walked a step, and another, and touched my mother's shoulder. Surrounded by the weeping of my sisters, I felt grief rack my mother's body.

Outside the manor, a keening cry climbed, ascendant and strange—the inhuman mourning of our drake. And even as the finality of loss ripped my heart, I knew. This was the moment when we would keep or lose Longbourn.

"Mamma," I said, "you must hold our drake. If he leaves, Longbourn will be taken from us. You must do it now. Or all will be lost." I hugged her close. I whispered. I cried. She shook and wailed in my arms.

I staggered downstairs, the walls and steps swimming behind tears, and out the front door.

Our firedrake was stretched high on his perch, head lifted to call his mourning song to the darkening sky. His wings spread as I approached, ribbed and huge.

"You must stay," I begged. "Please."

His wings arched, gathering air for flight.

I cast my mind to him and struck a crystal wall of resistance. He screeched savagely. Metal shrieked and sparked as the iron perch bent in his claws like a blade of grass in a fist.

"Stay," I said and pressed my will. The crystal wall was unyielding, cold and defiant, a castle erected to block me.

The drake's chest swelled, and blue flame roared past inches from my side, scouring the ground and crisping stray hairs beside my face into fleeting curls of flame that fell as ash.

Into the raging gale, I whispered, "You will not hurt me." I summoned every trick of focus I had learned. I tore away the conventions and doubts that tangled my mind. My grief and loss and loneliness sank through me like molten iron pouring into a mold—a mold that spits flame, then cools to birth a new form, harder than bone and colder than flesh.

I threw out my hand and screamed, "I command you to stay!"

The drake's blue fire roared closer. The edge of my sleeve burst into flame. Then the weight of my mind struck, a thrown anvil, and the crystal wall shattered like thinning ice on a spring pool.

The drake's roaring defiance broke into wails and whimpering. He slithered down from the perch, awkward and groveling, pressing his bronze belly and neck flat on the earth, wings outstretched but shoved into the dirt, helpless and fragile and subservient.

I heard my gasping breaths. The smoking earth snapped and sizzled. I wiped the tears from my face, then beat at my sleeve until it only smoldered.

I turned to go inside. Mary stood by our door, watching, and Mrs. Hill was beside her, open-mouthed.

39

I blew over the paper, drying the glistening ink to dull black. The loops in my signature, *Elizabeth Bennet*, looked like the lace on my ebony sleeve.

This last note ordered a bolt of cloth for mourning dress. We all had dark outfits for calling on bereaved friends and had worn those for the funeral, but mourning required more than one gown. The traditional fabric was bombazine, a twill of dark silk. It was expensive, so I hoped one bolt would stretch to fashion dresses for six ladies.

No, it was dresses for five. Lydia was gone to Newcastle and would not return.

I sealed the note and dropped it on a stack of correspondence, a mix of social notes required after Papa's funeral and business affairs too urgent to defer.

I stretched to unwind my shoulders, then laid my fingers on the old walnut of Papa's desk. I was using his library. The business journals were here, and Papa would have told me to make it my own, doubtless adding some dark joke. He had little patience for what he called the "social pretense of mourning."

But I had never sat in his chair before. That thought caught me off guard, and I dabbed some tears into my handkerchief before I finished cleaning the pen.

I left the library, met Mary in the hall, and stared in disbelief.

Mary was wearing a vibrant canary-yellow dress printed with little flowers, brighter than anything she had worn since she was a child.

"What are you *wearing?*" I burst out, even as part of my mind recalled that Mary had a dresser full of black clothes, so it was dresses for four, not five.

"I am mourning Papa," Mary said. "He was cross when I began wearing black, so it seems wrong to wear it now. He would like this more." She held out the skirt, considering. "He was angry with Lydia, so I stole this from her clothes. I took in the bosom myself."

An unexpected laugh reached my lips. "You are right. Papa would applaud."

Mrs. Hill joined our hallway assembly. "Ma'am, the parson is here with other gentlemen, calling on Mrs. Bennet. But she does not wish to see them."

"Very well." I blew out an unenthusiastic breath, but with some sympathy for my mother. Our parson was a petty gossip and dismissive of the women in his congregation. He had been priggishly disapproving when we provided a single male mourner for the funeral—my mother's brother—and had added a five-shilling charge for "another man to attend the committal."

I asked Mrs. Hill to accompany me. Our uncle had departed yesterday, and I did not wish to face unfamiliar gentlemen alone. Mary could not come as her dress would raise eyebrows, while Kitty would be little help, and Jane was impossible.

The men rose as we entered our drawing room. I curtsied and sat, while Mrs. Hill stood to one side, looking nicely formidable.

"Good morning, Miss Bennet," the parson said. "We had hoped to speak with Mrs. Bennet?"

"My mother is resting. May I help you?"

A notch appeared in the parson's narrow brow. Apparently, my mother's absence was an issue.

I knew his two companions by sight, gentlemen who held estates in Hertfordshire. Both were stiff, and one was frowning at me.

The frowning gentleman spoke in a contemptuous tone. "There are concerns for the Longbourn firedrake. We thought it best to see for ourselves the keeping of the animal."

"I have not the honor of our introduction, sir," I said tightly.

"This is Mr. Sallow," the parson said hurriedly.

Mr. Sallow was in his fifties, with grumpy eyes and dirty pockmarks. I recalled his estate now, larger than Longbourn but poorly managed and drowning in debt.

"Our drake seems content to me," I said. That was not strictly true. I had fought down a challenge this very morning. But if our drake was vexed with me, that was a private matter.

Mr. Sallow's frown puckered his chin. "I have disturbing reports about Longbourn, confirmed by members of the Church." He pointed at our parson.

The parson stutteringly said, "I merely mentioned a letter which drew unusual events to my attention." His eyes were apologetic. "In which your name was mentioned."

"*My* name? Who would send such a letter?"

"I had corresponded on the terrible business of your sister Lydia—"

"Lydia is properly married," I corrected, angry now. After Papa's sacrifice to protect our family, any other suggestion was painful.

"Of course. We all rejoice in that happy outcome." The parson cleared his throat. "In his reply, the rector for Rosings remarked—"

"Mr. *Collins?*" My anger soared as I imagined him pontificating from his little desk.

"Yes. He emphasized the extreme benefit to your family from his inexplicable failure to bind, which deprived him of the inheritance of Longbourn. And then your mother's extraordinary retention of your firedrake after your father's death."

Inexplicable. Extraordinary. Those were dangerous words. "We have been fortunate," I said slowly. "I cannot understand how my name would be mentioned."

Mr. Sallow spat his accusation. "It was unnatural forces that spoiled Mr. Collins's binding. The same sinful evil that bound a firedrake to this estate. Evil rising from forbidden female rituals."

I laughed. He sounded like a crazed street preacher in London. "You cannot be serious." He stared aggressively. "Do not be coy. You accuse my family of witchcraft."

"Another word for the same thing."

"That is insanity. We are not in the Middle Ages or America. This is enlightened England. There is no such thing as witchcraft."

"Explain how you bound a firedrake! How it remains!"

"I owe you no explanation. But if you troubled to inform yourself, you would know Bennet wyves have a history of strong binding." I turned to the parson, who was watching wide-eyed. "I trust you do not mistake affinity with draca—a principle of gentry rank—for something unnatural?"

My direct appeal sparked a reply. "Certainly not. The Archbishop himself has reiterated that binding is a pillar of—"

Mr. Sallow broke in. "There are many opinions in the Church. And the Longbourn firedrake *is* unnatural. It was always strange that it bound to a minor estate. And now it lingers after its master's death, uncontrolled."

"You forget yourself," I said coldly. "Our drake is bound to my mother. That is not uncontrolled."

The man snorted. "No proper widow holds a draca. And your mother could no more control a firedrake than she could manage an estate."

I stood, taking the opportunity to stare down at this offensive man. "Mrs. Hill, please see our guests out. The gentleman is distraught over my father's death. I fear he will say something unseemly."

Mr. Sallow shot to his feet. "I will not leave without satisfaction."

I was turning to go, but that stopped me. "What satisfaction would that be?"

"The firedrake must be moved. Taken to an estate where it can be properly kept."

"I believe you bound a tunnelworm?" I said, knowing it was true. He flushed. A tunnelworm was the least prestigious of draca, a palm-sized creature that preferred to burrow in a bucket of sand during daylight. "You have neither the right nor the means to demand our drake, for I discern that is the satisfactory outcome you desire."

"That animal is a menace. Do not mistake me, girl. If he threatens my livestock, I will take him."

This time, I did laugh. "Have you seen our drake fight, Mr. Sallow? I have. I should like to see you try."

I left, letting Mrs. Hill escort them to the door. She joined me at the window. We watched Mr. Sallow argue with the parson before they mounted their horses.

"Ooh, my blood is boiling," Mrs. Hill muttered. "You should sic the drake on them. Have him burn off their hats!"

I wanted to smile, but accusations of witchcraft were no joke. "My *mother* will do no such thing."

"Yes, ma'am. Of course, it would be Mrs. Bennet." She drew a long breath. "Don't you worry. I won't make that mistake again."

Of everything unpleasant in that visit, the presence of our parson disturbed me the most. I went to see Mamma, who was sitting up in bed, a sleeping bonnet pulled down past her eyebrows as if to help her hide.

"Have they left?" she asked timorously.

"Yes, Mamma."

"All my friends stared when I went into town," she said. "I thought I had worn the wrong hat. I had no wish to be a widowed wyfe, and they glare at me as if I chose it. Can we not be rid of the beast?"

"Mamma, you must not say that. To anyone. Our drake is all that keeps us in our home."

"But that dreadful Mr. Collins did not bind. Who would take Longbourn from us?"

"Other men," I said softly.

Four days passed. Lydia did not answer my letter about Papa's death. I signed a draft on the estate to purchase barrels and two scythe blades, and breathed a sigh of relief when the bank honored it. Mary stole another of Lydia's dresses, scarlet this time, but could not resist sewing a fringe of black ribbon around the skirt.

I found Kitty weeping in her room, which she had shared with Lydia.

"Poor Kitty." I gave her a hug. "Are you missing Lydia?"

"No. But I wish I could go outside."

"That is a strange wish. Why can you not go out?"

"When Papa was angry, he said I was not to leave the house for ten years. I wondered if he joked, but I was afraid to ask, and now…" She dissolved into sobs.

I bit my lip to hide a smile. "I am sure he did not intend ten years. You should take Mary to the shops. I feel she is bored with colors and will wish to examine all their black ribbon."

"Do you think so?" asked Kitty with wide, watery eyes, and I sent her to find Mary.

That left me beside Lydia's abandoned dresser. I ran my fingers through the froth of lace, and I missed how simple things had been. Then I imagined what Papa would have said to Kitty dutifully staying home for ten years. I smiled. "Papa, you are missing the most diverting behavior."

On the twelfth day, Jane did not know me in the morning. I woke to her screams while her feeble fists pummeled and clawed my face.

I settled her, and she twisted into a knot on the bed, thin as rope, fingers splayed like dry twigs.

I got a bite of bread from the kitchen, soaked it in her dose of medicine, and brought it up on a saucer, crooning with shamelessly false enthusiasm, "Mr. Bingley has sent a treat!" This ruse worked, but once per day, the only food she took.

Jane slipped it into her mouth, then chewed, methodical and without tasting, no longer even noticing the medicine. Her cramped muscles relaxed as the medicine worked, and she fell into a limp mass on the bed.

I sat beside her. Her eyes were roving, as if she dreamed with her eyes open. I whispered, "Dearest Jane. I do not know what to do. Our family is perched on a knife edge. To slip one way or another is to be cut. To teeter back and forth is to fall."

Her eyes—sapphire jewels, the last vestige of my beautiful sister unravaged by disease—met mine. With a child's trust, she said, "You will keep us safe." I stroked her hair and tried to forget the bloody scratch she had opened over my eyebrow.

Our housemaid tapped on the doorframe. In a wavering voice, she announced, "Ma'am, Miss Lydia asks—I mean, Mr. and Mrs. Wickham request that you join them in the parlor."

40

"It is good to be home!" exclaimed Lydia, roaming the room in a fluffy white dress. "To think I have not been back since Brighton. You are all the same as ever, but I am married. What a laugh!"

She stroked everything she passed—the clock, a table, a vase—as if anointing them with proprietary longing. She arrived back at Wickham, who lounged on the settee, and stroked him as well. "Is this not nice, Wickie?"

"*Wickie?*" I said, distaste curling my lip. Wickham gave an indulgent smile.

"You are so cross!" Lydia flounced to me and poked my chest with her finger.

There was talc on her face, and rouge on her cheeks to offset the pallor. That was odd. Lydia was proud of her natural complexion. Powder was an antiquated cosmetic of elderly ladies.

Under the chalk, spidery lines covered her forehead as though her veins had darkened.

Lydia's fingertip still pressed me. I stepped out of reach. "How are you here? Mr. Wickham has a commission in Newcastle."

Wickham rose, feline-deft, and slipped his arm around Lydia's waist. She rested her head on his shoulder adoringly.

"I have found better opportunities," he said. "The advantage of a paid commission is that it may be declined. There was even some return of funds."

I had wondered if Mr. Darcy purchased Wickham's commission. Men who did not prove their merit in the militia had to pay for the security of an army officer's rank. It would seem that Wickham's merit remained obscure.

Thousands of pounds would have been paid to secure a respectable living for him and my sister. Without doubt, most of it was lost already.

"You kept the uniform," I noted.

"My wyfe enjoys it," he said with a roguish grin.

"It is very handsome," Mamma added sincerely. I bit back a groan.

"*Why* are you here?" Mary asked.

For all that Lydia accused me of being cross, Mary was openly hostile, her arms folded and her face like stone.

"Oh, Mary," Lydia said in a pitying tone. "What *has* happened to your hair? And that dress is—" She stopped, her eyes narrowing, then her mouth opened in a furious O as she recognized the clothing under Mary's stitched layers of black lace.

"Lydia," I said to head off a shouting match. "Please tell us why you have come."

With a spiteful glare at Mary, Lydia turned to me. "Well, Papa died…" she said vaguely, as if discussing the weather.

I waited. When nothing more came, I said dryly, "I am aware."

"I wished to visit my new family," Wickham inserted smoothly.

"For how long?" Mary shot in from across the room.

And then I knew why he had come. I even knew his answer before his lips moved.

"Oh, a week or so," he said with a smile.

"Let us see the garden!" Lydia interrupted. She grabbed Wickham's hand and dragged him toward the rear of the house. My mother hurried after them, leaving Mary and me alone.

I flexed tense fingers. "I do not like this."

Mary's reply was bitter. "Why dislike receiving the sister who killed Papa?"

"Mary! She did not intend such an outcome." Mary stared, unbudging. "I admit Lydia's lack of grief is shameful. But Wickham…"

"I never trusted Wickham, and Papa's dislike was more adamant than mine. As for our ungrieving sister, in the last year, Lydia has become opaque to me. She was a selfish child, but this behavior is more than shameful. It is vile. Her indifference to Denny's death was equally evil. As a woman, she has perfected self-absorption."

That was a savage critique. I had always thought of Mary's condemnations as abstract and scholarly. Then I remembered her criticism of me at the ball. Perhaps I had learned to listen more closely.

"When did you last read the entailment?" I asked.

"Never," Mary said. "The male heir inherits. What is there to read?"

"To claim Longbourn, the heir must settle his draca in the *empty* draca house for a se'nnight."

Mary's folded arms relaxed enough that her fingers could tap thoughtfully. "This is why you forced our drake to stay."

"Mary, be cautious what you say aloud."

"I am cautious. I have not spoken of what happened." Her eyes were assessing me. "Your feat left me curious but puzzled. Now, I am impressed."

"There is more. The consort of a bound heiress may claim Longbourn. And our freshly bound brother has asked to stay a week."

Mary gave a most un-Mary-like snort of disgust.

I made my decision. "I shall speak with Mr. Wickham. Alone. Can you take Lydia and Mamma to visit Jane?"

We found them in the garden. Lydia, flapping with frivolous lace, was chattering at Mamma and Kitty about her wedding. Kitty, clad in sober black, had the good sense to appear uncomfortable.

Lydia was mid-story. "It is so annoying when people do not know I have married! We overtook William Goulding in his fancy curricle, and I was determined *he* notice, so I let down the side-glass and had our ferretworm climb up and hiss. The man jumped a foot and lost his hat! I had a good laugh before—"

Mary barged in. "Jane is too ill to come down. Shall we go up to greet her?"

Lydia frowned, but she grudgingly followed Mary into the house. Kitty and Mamma trailed behind.

Wickham, of course, could not visit Jane in her room. He lounged by the laurel hedge with a half-smile.

We were steps away from where he had accosted me. That was before he was married, but even so, it was an unpleasant sensation.

I gave my own half-smile and said, "Shall we speak inside?"

I chose our sitting room, unused this early. The fireplace was unlit, and the windows faced away from the morning sun. The lingering chill cooled the back of my neck as I claimed the center of the room.

Wickham stopped in the doorway, leaning against the frame. He swung the door back and forth a few inches. "What shall we speak of, dear sister?"

"Regrettably, you will not be able to stay at Longbourn."

"No? I wonder if you have thought that through." He stepped into the room and closed the door, shutting us in together, alone.

That was improper—even threatening—but it only made the remaining fragments of my discomfort fall away.

"My thoughts are straightforward," I answered. "Our draca house is occupied, and Longbourn firmly secured by my mother. It would foster hopeless expectations if you, dear brother, resided here for a se'nnight."

Wickham swaggered toward me, ending within arm's reach. "You are bold, Elizabeth. A most attractive trait in a woman. But you have not considered your options." He smiled the same smile I once found charming. Now, it was a thin smirk. "A woman's right to property is, at best, that of a tenant. Your livelihood will be uncertain until a man holds Longbourn." He spread his arms in exaggerated self-presentation. "Who better than a loyal brother?"

The disturbing truth was that he was right. Some distant male cousin would hear of my father's death and announce a claim to Longbourn. With the prejudice against widows who held draca, I had no confidence the law would take our side. My mother was not Lady Catherine, whose personality and powerful connections could face down challengers.

But that was an unknown risk. The risk two feet in front of me was clear. "I prefer to wait for an even more loyal brother."

"Loyalty is earned," he said softly. "The sister with raven eyes and ivory spine is much more interesting than childish Lydia. You liked me once. Why not again? A man will take Longbourn. Better a man who appreciates you. I would give you a bedroom of your own. You could secure your place in a heartbeat."

He reached for my face.

"Do not touch me," I said. "This time, I will be less forgiving."

His hand hesitated an inch away.

I smiled, wide and cold. "Lest you wonder if my threats are idle…" I gestured lazily toward the windows.

Wickham's eyes followed and widened.

I did not need to look. I sensed our drake a dozen yards outside, watching us through the glass, his wings beating in the complex whorls he used to hang in midair.

Conversationally, I added, "I saw our drake put down a mad dog once. Right in front of me. I would not flinch to see it again."

On the other side of the room, the door burst open. "What is this?" cried Lydia.

Wickham backed away from me, hands raised in apology. More than apology; he was frightened.

"Your husband has chosen to stay in town," I said to Lydia. "Your ferretworm will stay with him. But you are welcome at Longbourn, if you wish."

Lydia stalked between us to face Wickham, her tall frame tight with fury. "You *fool*." She slapped him, a crack that startled me and made him wince. He fumbled the start of an explanation, but she cut him off. "Get out!"

Wickham scurried out of the room. He was cowering. I felt a surge of triumph.

Lydia's back was to me, her shoulders heaving with anger. Or tears.

"I am sorry," I said and reached for her shoulder.

She spun and shoved my hand away. "*Sorry?* You meddling, jealous thing!"

"What?" I said, taken aback.

"*I* am married. *I* am the foremost sister. Not sickly Jane. Not *you*. But can you imagine what Mamma has been whining at me?" She crumpled her face in cruel mimicry of our mother. "'*Mr. Bennet said Lizzy is mistress of Longbourn*.' Even dead, Papa is playing favorites. Longbourn should be mine!"

I was speechless with shock.

In the sudden silence, the flapping of our drake's wings was audible. He had drawn closer, looming and threatening. Dust and leaves lifted by his wings chittered against the glass.

"Go away," Lydia snapped irritably and flipped her hand at the window. The drake wheeled through the air and flew out of sight.

She thrust her other hand impatiently toward the doorway. Scrambling sounds approached, then her ferretworm scampered in, a quadruped with a narrow body like a ferret, although people argued which creature was named first. Lydia's had sleek black scales and heavy claws on his front paws for digging. She scooped up the creature and scowled at me.

I was still struggling to comprehend what I had seen. She had summoned their ferretworm with a thought. Banished our drake with a wave of her hand. No ordinary wyfe had those skills.

And I had not called our drake. Why had he come? Had Lydia sent him to spy on Wickham and me?

"Husbands are disappointing," Lydia said, in the petulant tone she would use to dismiss an ugly bonnet. "I do not much like marriage. Except there is no other way to be rich." She stabbed her finger at me. "Do not try to dash out and win a husband. I would be most vexed. Not that any man would want a shrewish, tiny thing like you."

"What has *happened* to you?" I said, not believing my ears.

"I have become important. I have a most famous admirer. And I have better toys than men." She grabbed her ferretworm's jaw, forcing him to look up at her, and crooned, "You know to behave, don't you?" She pinched the skin on the ferretworm's throat, and the creature squealed in pain.

In a reflex of revulsion, I closed my eyes and cast my awareness to her ferretworm. It was an impulse—to free the creature, or to humble and embarrass her.

My mind slogged to a stop, caught in a murky morass of darkness that was foul but powerful, like the suction of mud in a bog. I sensed the glimmer of the ferretworm's mind buried far beneath.

I pressed against the murk. Darkness surged, a flood of sticky filth that extinguished the glimmer. Effortlessly, I was driven out.

I opened my eyes and met Lydia's narrowed gaze.

"Imagine that," she said softly. "Precious Lizzy has tricks." She stalked to the doorway. "You would be wise to keep your tricks away from me, sister. I am the Child of the Lake."

41

The rattle of a coach faded. I stood in our sitting room, one hand pressing my temple, fingernails biting to anchor my spinning mind.

Mary came in. "Our sister is more foul than I thought. She was horrid to Mamma, who is hurt and miserable. I must go back—"

"Our drake!" I cried. If Lydia took him, we were lost.

I cast my mind outward and sensed the brilliant gleam of his awareness. I raced past Mary, through the hall, and out the front door.

Our firedrake was clumsy on his perch, wings tense and askew. He thrummed a whistling growl unlike any sound he had ever made.

I stopped in front of him, relieved to find him but disturbed by his behavior.

"Are you hurt?" I asked.

His burnished claws made a grinding sound on the iron perch. His black eyes met mine, wary and rebellious.

I stepped closer. "This is not a time for contests. We must be allies." Slowly, I reached out a finger and stroked his shoulder. The muscle under his bronze scales was vibrating. "What has she done to you?" I drew my finger up his neck, and he began to relax, curling around my touch. I ended with my fingertip under his narrow jaw and guided his gaze to mine.

Images filled my mind. Wickham and me behind window panes, the color of our warmth distorted by passage through glass. I saw anger in the set of my shoulders and felt it echo through the drake's feelings, anger and protectiveness both.

Savage darkness grabbed like an armored fist, freezing and violent.

The scene vanished as the drake hissed.

"Hush," I said. Whatever influence Lydia had exerted, our drake had not enjoyed it. My fear ratcheted down a notch.

Without thinking, I lifted him from his perch. That was a habit I formed with the Gardiners' tykeworm. Tykes are famously tolerant of being held.

Our drake, however, had never been held. He scrambled in my grip, wings flapping for balance. I got a stinging smack on my nose. Then he settled, folding his wings, and I cradled him in my arms.

He was much heavier than a tyke, more like a solid child of eight or nine months. And much longer. His neck swanned upward. His chisel head tipped one way and another, peering at my face, then drifted around the side of my head, examining my ear.

My gaze landed on the sharp gouges his claws had cut in the iron perch.

I froze. Cautiously, I felt for his feet.

The dull outside curves of his claws pressed my forearm, harder than steel but no more dangerous than the back of a spoon. He had clenched his toes, folding the razor edges against his scaled body. I let out a relieved breath.

"Are we friends now?" I asked. His head craned farther, inspecting the back of my head. I tried to remember how the maid had done my hair this morning.

This was becoming a heavy armful of draca, so I shifted him into the crook of my arm. Something rough scraped my skin. I moved my hand away from his body to see.

A few loose, bronze scales sparkled in my palm. "What is this?" Our drake had never shed scales before. Had Lydia struck him?

Now that I looked, there were scales on the slate roof under his perch. And scattered on the ground around us. Some were pressed into old footsteps in the soil.

Whatever caused this, it had begun before Lydia came.

"Let me see you," I said and lifted him to his perch. He grabbed on obediently.

There were tiny dull dots in his gleaming bronze where scales were lost. My gaze traveled downward.

A claw was missing from his left foot.

His right foot had the usual three in front, meshed with the long, wicked curve of his rear claw. But on the left, the third toe ended with an unhealthy-looking pit where the claw had been.

Dread burst into my mind, worse because it was so unexpected. Our drake had been unchanged my entire life. Never ill. Never hurt. Was he sick? I had been feeding him myself, and he ate normally.

I crouched so our eyes were close and opened my mind, projecting concern and imagining his lost claw and scales.

An image formed. Sparkling, cool water.

"Are you thirsty?" I asked, not really believing it. There was a birdbath only a dozen yards away. He sometimes sipped there, often with sparrows or thrushes splashing beside him. Little birds were strangely unafraid of our drake.

Whatever the cause, this was serious. We needed him to be healthy. But why an image of water?

I went inside and dug out one of the jars from Pemberley lake. They had revealed no benefit—or any effect at all—on Jane. But I had a case full of them, so I could try something new. Maybe the wyvern thought Jane had bound an ill draca.

I carried the sealed jar outside. The drake's head darted while I broke the wax seal. I pried out the cork and offered the brimming jar.

With a screech and frenzied flapping, he shot skyward. He landed on the tip of the manor's roof, squawking down at me like an annoyed jay.

I looked up in frustrated disbelief and jammed my palm against my forehead. I shouted up, "I do not require more mysteries!"

By wash day, our world was collapsing.

When I woke, Jane was hunched under the covers and breathing in shuddering gasps separated by long, frightening silences.

I ran to the kitchen in my nightgown, dodged a scullery maid done up far more elegantly than me, and snatched a chunk of old bread. Back in our room, I coaxed Jane's dose of medicine-soaked bread between her lips. Her breathing calmed, and my panic receded to simple fear.

I pushed tangled hair out of my eyes and tilted the brown-glass bottle given to me by Mr. Darcy. More than half was gone, but not yet two-thirds. Four weeks had passed, so it would last a little longer than he had predicted. Perhaps three more weeks.

Should I write to ask for more?

The question hung, roiled by a muddle of concerns. Fear of the emotions unlocked when I wrote his name. A morbid whisper—Jane was worse every day; would it even matter?

Of course, I would write. What would he think when he received a letter from me?

Perhaps Miss Bingley was visiting Pemberley. After all, Mr. Darcy required amusement while Mr. Bingley was exploring America. Miss Bingley could join Mr. Darcy for breakfast, her hair perfectly coifed, and snipe at me while he ignored my letter.

That was such an unpleasant mental image that I reveled in it while I dressed. Jealousy was wonderfully simple compared to dying sisters and ill firedrakes.

Pondering unpleasant women brought back my confrontation with Lydia. The good news was she had not returned. But her power over draca was frightening. And I was mystified by her claim to be the Child of the Lake. I did not know what she meant, or even how she knew the phrase. We had never discussed the Longbourn journal.

The burr of a familiar accent drifted up the stairwell. I abandoned pinning my hair to hurl downstairs, shouting, "Mrs. Bruichladdich," having learned something vaguely like the pronunciation of our Scottish laundress's name.

"I'd of come up, ma'am," she said as I landed in the hallway like a diving wyvern in long skirts.

"Please, I require your advice. For our drake. I fear he is ill." As we went outside, I explained about the missing scales and claw.

Our drake was curled atop his perch, looking very forlorn. There were now tiny patches without scales.

"What is wrong with him?" I asked.

"I never seen this, ma'am. Draca don't take ill, as a rule. When did it start?"

"I noticed a few days ago, but I believe it began more than a week ago. Perhaps more than two—"

I stopped as I realized the significance of that date.

"When Mr. Bennet passed," Mrs. Bruichladdich said quietly.

"That is likely." What could be more significant than the death of one of the married couple who bound him?

"Ma'am, with respect, could I speak honest to ye?"

"Of course. Please."

"I was not expecting Mrs. Bennet to hold your drake. Good wyfe as your mam is, them who hold draca as widows are… strong ladies, if you take my meaning." Her wizened voice was cautious. I nodded for her to continue. "In the north, there's a story of a lord who dinna wish to lose his draca when his wyfe passed. He had a lesser worm, not a powerful breed, so he caged it in heavy iron. Thought he could keep it by force, ye see."

She stopped, and I wondered how much she had guessed. "What happened?"

"The beast wasted away and died. The story is an old one, in verse. I recall because the cage was dusted with fallen scales, like stars. Sounded both pretty and sad."

I walked to our drake and ran a fingertip along his back. Our laundress breathed some unintelligible Scottish oath.

I said, "When a draca leaves his bound master and wyfe, where does he go?"

"Nobody knows, ma'am."

I remembered the image our drake had shown me, sparkling and cool. "Back to the water."

After my father's death, our firedrake was not held by the strength of my mother's bond. I had forced him to stay. Imprisoned him. And he had known I would. Those images he shared—inescapable traps, crushing boulders—were *me*, a woman with the power to seize him and the complacent selfishness to want him as a slave.

But my power was an illusion. I could release him, or he would die. One way or another, the keystone of our family's estate was lost.

Inside me, an artifice of ego shattered like hollow porcelain. I had been proud to conquer our prestigious firedrake. It was satisfying to crush his protests with a thought, then celebrate with an extra dollop of jam on my morning crumpet. A captive drake was such convenient proof I was special. That I deserved the trust my father had placed in me.

I leaned close, and he stared into my eyes. "My beloved father is gone," I whispered. "My dear sister drifts after him. Our home will be lost. But you have shown me a duty I can accomplish. You can be free."

I lifted the command, *Stay*, I had driven through him like a spike. He reared, startled.

I stepped back. His wings half-spread, fanning the air. My skirts danced against my shins.

Mrs. Bruichladdich plucked at my sleeve. "Ma'am." She had said that several times now. I ignored her.

"Go," I said to our drake. Would I have to order him to leave?

Instead, his head dropped, a furious rumble building. His shoulders stiffened below furled wings.

Mrs. Bruichladdich grabbed my arm, hard. "Ma'am, there's folks coming!"

"What?" I said as she tugged me toward the manor entrance. I heard shouts and pulled free.

A crowd was approaching, twenty men at least with Mr. Sallow in the lead. Beside him was a young man I did not know. He wore fine clergyman's dress of shining black silk, but his vest and collar were brilliant crimson, a style I had never seen.

And beside him, in a severe black gown, was Lydia.

The crowd closed to ten yards from our draca house, then our drake's shriek cut the air. His wings spread wide. His neck stretched, ebony teeth bared at Lydia.

The crowd stalled in a milling mass.

Mrs. Bruichladdich was calling for me to come inside. But whatever was happening, Lydia was the cause. I would not hide from my sister.

Across the dozen steps that separated us, I called, "Have you misplaced 'Wickie' this morning?"

"My husband is on an errand," Lydia replied. "A most important engagement. But I can deal with my selfish sister before I join him."

The young priest called out to the crowd. "*This* is the house of corruption! A den of sinful women in congress with Satan!" A few shouts rose.

That was too ridiculous. "I fear Longbourn will disappoint you. We are rather a dull lot. May I ask your name?"

Mr. Sallow answered for him. "This is Curate Mincekeep."

My bemused disbelief became apprehension. I knew that name.

Hertfordshire society, naturally, adhered to the uncontroversial and undemanding mainstream of the Church of England. The few exceptions were families that followed the evangelists, a movement I found unpleasantly strident although I admired their support for liberal causes. Several of their founders were women who advocated prison reform and the abolishment of slavery.

But England had other, more extreme, factions. Curate Mincekeep led a populist movement fighting liberalization of the Church. He was notorious for fomenting violent protests against shelters for fallen women. One of his mobs had torched a shelter in London, killing two women.

The men behind him looked rough and unpleasant. I had seen a few of their faces in town, but there was no one I knew, and no gentlemen other than Mr. Sallow.

Curate Mincekeep shouted, "Our mighty inquisition will purge this evil!" Scattered yells rose.

That chilled me. The terrors of the Catholic Inquisition, and the equally violent purges of the Protestant Reformation, had ended with the Enlightenment. But before that, thousands of women were tortured into false confessions of witchcraft and burned at the stake.

That horror had never infected England. Not until last year, when English extremists claimed "inquisition" as their rallying cry to raise the Church above the state.

I was alone, facing a mob.

The manor door opened, and Mary stepped out beside me. She wore Lydia's scarlet gown, now so ornamented with black ribbon that it was passable mourning dress. It might even be fashionable. Scarlet mantels for mourning were a fad in London.

"Curate Mincekeep," Mary called out. "You are far from your parish of All Hallows Barking."

"Show respect when addressing the Church, woman," he shouted back.

"My respect is for ecclesiastical law."

My eyebrows rose. I had seen Mary read church texts, but solely to practice her scorn. That seemed rather far from respect.

Mamma arrived on my other side, standing arm-in-arm with Mrs. Hill.

Mamma looked flustered but annoyed, like she had overheard an unflattering rumor in a shop. Kitty trailed her, looking nervous.

Four ladies of our household now stood opposite the crowd. Five, really. Mrs. Hill certainly counted. She was scowling with tremendous authority.

An unshaven man pointed a dirty finger at Mary. "Is she one of them ladies in congress with Satan?" He sounded more enthused than disapproving.

Mary ignored him and called out, "The Holy Inquisition is a Catholic barbarity rejected by the English Church. It is forbidden by English law."

The crowd quieted, and several men exchanged concerned glances. A few heads nodded, presumably approving of sensible English law over outlandish concepts like Catholics.

The curate eyed his new opponent. "I am an agent of *episcopal* inquisition."

I bit back a laugh. Only a stranger would argue semantics with Mary.

Mary cleared her throat, a bookish habit that signaled the beginning of serious debate. "Episcopal inquisition?" she said in a puzzled tone. "That requires an *episcopus*—a bishop. I am sure you are merely a curate, and one who was reprimanded by Archbishop Manners-Sutton for association with radical elements. Our own parson is superior to you in rank. Mr. Fernsby, Mr. Sweet,"—she nodded to two men in the group, neither of whom I could have named—"you attend his services. I suggest we send for him and hear his opinion of your 'inquisition.'" She pursed her lips, then added, "*Tantum religio potuit suadere malorum.*"

I did not know the Latin, but from Curate Mincekeep's flush, it was not flattering.

The crowd, however, was shuffling in a bored manner. This was much less exciting than women in congress with Satan.

Mr. Sallow apparently reached the same conclusion. He grabbed a fistful of the curate's robes and pointed to our firedrake. "There is the proof! A firedrake, improperly bound to an inferior estate. The animal is a menace, uncontrolled after its master's death!"

That made me angry, and I spoke before Mary could reply. "The Longbourn drake is bound to my mother, and has been for decades. Mrs. Bennet is no stranger to you. Longbourn is an old and honorable estate. Why is Mr. Sallow disturbing a household of ladies in mourning? I think it is self-interest and bitter envy."

There was a buzz from the crowd. Curate Mincekeep lifted his arms and silence fell. "The Lord will decide! His power shall deliver this fire-drake to the rightful owner."

Mr. Sallow looked dangerously satisfied. Some deal had been struck. I did not know how Lydia convinced him she could deliver our drake, but I knew the chosen owner would be Mr. Sallow. In exchange, doubtless he would support Lydia's claim for Longbourn.

I met Lydia's gaze and was struck by how unwell she looked. Her eyes were feverish, and the black of her pupils had swollen to swallow the blue. She had powdered her face even more than when I last saw her, but the cakey white did not hide a cobweb of discolored lines on her cheeks and forehead.

A mocking smile stretched her lips, and an oily sensation chilled the back of my neck. Our drake squealed in distress.

I closed my eyes and reached out with my mind.

The bright shine of our drake's mind was buried under pounding, writhing darkness. It was a terrifying assault—the same sticky blackness Lydia had thrown to drive me away from her ferretworm.

I pressed at the dark with my mind, and a filthy surge blew me back like a leaf. I threw myself harder and was tossed away. There was no contest. I was utterly overmatched.

But there was something I had not seen before. A hair-thin thread of silver extended out of the black storm. It reached almost to me, humming with tension as if tethered to something.

I tightened my grip on my mother's hand, and the thread shimmered brighter. It was the bond between my mother and the drake.

I cast my mind along it, following the thread as it shook under the force of Lydia's assault. The darkness closed around me, buffeting and tugging. I had to drag my awareness along the silver string, like a sailor clutching a lifeline in a night of raging storm.

A crystal wall stopped me, the defense our drake had built to repel me now deployed as a shield against Lydia. Fingers of filth clawed at it. Beyond, the brightness of our drake's awareness shone.

The crystal wall shuddered and fell inward, then caught and held again. Our drake's defense was being crushed.

Let me in, I thought. *Let me help you. Please.*

Like sprawling through an unexpectedly opened door, I fell into the drake's awareness. His brilliant senses flooded my mind.

I saw the crowd, fists raised and bodies twisting. Their motions were slowed and pitiably clumsy. My human mind recognized a fight: a thrown punch, a man falling.

But those glimpses were peripheral. The drake's attention was locked on one person. The enemy. The corrupted wyfe.

In the drake's senses, Lydia seethed with muddy, suffocating power. She was a vile goddess surrounded by insignificant rabble.

And, with a shock that stopped my breath, I recognized this tall woman shrouded in dark corruption. I had seen Lydia through draca eyes before—at Pemberley, when the tyke ran into the forest and saw a woman and man ride away with the stolen books.

Lydia and Wickham had been in Derbyshire. They had conspired with the thieves that killed Mr. Rabb.

My shock ignited into fury. I clenched my mother's hand, and her binding flared, a brilliant cord to channel my anger. I screamed, "You shall not have him!" even as I plunged deeper into the drake's awareness. I heard my words through his ears, distant and distorted.

The crystal wall exploded in radiance. Lydia's dark assault shredded and burned like a handful of peat tossed into a smith's furnace.

I sang in triumph, tones high and pure. Wings caught air. The world fell away as I soared upward.

A remote, human part of me thought: He is leaving.

Dizzyingly, flight arced and hung. Effortlessly, sky and earth spun. I stared down, a bird's view of our manor and grounds, and with inhuman ease, my vision locked on Lydia's figure in the crowd, dazed and falling to her knees.

Wings folded. Killing rear claws stretched. Flame swelled my chest. I plummeted, a bolt of fury that would slice and burn. Wind roared as screams rose in the crowd.

"No!" I shouted. With a jarring snap, my awareness yanked free.

Heat scalded my face. I struggled to see with weak and watering human eyes.

Lydia was on her knees. Unhurt. Glaring at me, disbelieving and furious.

A foot from her dress, the earth was burning, a yard-wide strip that ran the length of the garden between us. Dying embers of leaves and petals spun in the air, glowing crimson and gold.

At the last moment, our drake had heard me and turned his attack to flame the earth instead.

The crowd was wide-eyed and still. And it had grown. Mr. Hill and a half-dozen of our tenants had arrived while I fought Lydia. They were mixed with the strangers, caught in small, frozen scuffles. Their poses—mouths open to shout, fingers clenching clothing, fists cocked—looked almost comical.

With a flip of his wings, the drake landed on my shoulder. Landed with his claws open, as was painfully evident even through my thick dress. I gritted my teeth as he settled and found his balance.

"The Lord has delivered this drake to his rightful owner," Mary announced.

I had forgotten about that. Thank goodness for Mary. Although, it would be better if our drake chose Mamma. I considered asking him to move, but my mother would not enjoy having a heavy, razor-clawed animal drop onto her shoulder.

One man ran, then it was a scramble. In seconds, only the Longbourn tenants and Mr. Hill remained.

Mrs. Hill walked to her husband and hugged him—something I had not witnessed in my entire life—then scolded him for standing in the daisies.

"That Mr. Sallow is very rude," Mamma said. "I shall tell him my opinion when we meet in town."

"Thank you, Mamma," I said and kissed her cheek. She clucked. "And you, Mary. You were remarkable."

Mary was pensive. Finally, she said, "I will thank our tenants," and crossed the smoldering garden to mingle with our defenders.

I watched her methodically speak with each person—serious, as she usually was, but receiving warm replies. While I was north, Mary had assumed my estate duties with Papa. My sister was very changed in the last six months.

"Your shoulder is bleeding," Kitty said timidly.

The cuts beneath the drake's claws felt thin as hairs, but the cloth was wet. And this was my new bombazine twill. "At least it is a black dress."

42

In our room, I loosened my dress-tie, eased the dark cloth off my shoulder, and adjusted the looking glass.

My collarbone was decorated with shallow cuts from our drake's claws: three vertical slashes from his right foot, and two from his left with its injured toe. I dabbed at them with a handkerchief, then reached over my shoulder, feeling for the cuts from his rear claws.

Jane's fingers took the cloth. "You are always hurting yourself." The cloth wiped, gentle but shaking.

I was afraid to speak. Afraid my voice would break the spell of normalcy.

The cloth touched again.

"How do you feel?" I said.

"I had a bad dream. Lydia was drowning in darkness. Silver light burned the darkness away, but she was gone."

Strange. Was another Bennet sister imbued with unusual skills?

The bloodied handkerchief fell to the floor. "There. It is better." Her fingers, once so deft, fumbled trying to refasten the tie.

"I shall do it," I said. "Would you like to come down?" She nodded, and we went down together.

Our household was long past worrying about Jane appearing in her nightgown. Mamma settled her in a chair, fussing for tea to be made, while

Kitty's bright voice chattered of a new fashion they must try. I watched them pretend that all was fine and fought to keep my eyes from spilling.

The doorbell chimed. Our housemaid rose from fixing Jane's hair, but I said, "No, Sarah. I shall go." I doubted a mob of torch-wielding fanatics would ring, but if they did, I would rather they met me than a maid.

At the door, I swallowed my tears, settled myself to be presentable, and realized the shoulder of my dress was shredded. Oh, well. I opened the door.

Mr. Bingley, his curly hair handsomely messy from riding, looked at me in surprise. His blue eyes crinkled into a delighted smile.

"Miss Elizabeth Bennet! I did not expect you. What on earth has happened to your park?" A blue haze of smoke still hung in the air behind him.

Both my hands were over my open mouth.

His smile became charmingly self-conscious. "Is your sister Miss Bennet at home?"

Running feet passed me, and Jane's nightgown-robed figure thumped into Mr. Bingley. Her arms wrapped his neck. Her face burrowed into his shoulder. A single muffled word, "Charles," emerged over and over from somewhere in his jacket.

Hesitantly, protectively, he wrapped her stick-thin figure in his arms. His hand patted her shoulder. "I am back," he whispered.

"But you are in America!" I burst out.

We had moved to the parlor. Mr. Bingley was seated at one end of our settee. Jane, wrapped in a dressing gown, was… well, cuddled against him.

"I *was* in America," Mr. Bingley replied. "It is a grand story."

Mrs. Hill interrupted. "Miss Bennet. Would you not prefer a seat with more room?"

"But she is so wobbly," protested Mr. Bingley. "I am afraid she will…" I watched him struggle to invent a dire risk. "Tip over," he finished, a little unsatisfactorily.

"That is quite right," Mamma spoke up. "She could strike her head."

Mr. Bingley appeared distressed by that. His arm encircled Jane's shoulder.

"Why America?" Jane asked softly.

I was still surprised when Jane joined the conversation. She was as frail as ever, but her eyes were brighter than they had been in weeks. Months.

Mr. Bingley, of course, thought answering questions from Jane was normal. "I was an utter fool," he said bitterly. "Convinced I had deluded myself and—" He stopped, suddenly aware of his audience of intrigued ladies. "I have not the words to say everything I wish. But my return all came down to Darcy. He sent an extraordinary letter. That was during your visit to Pemberley, I believe, Miss Elizabeth."

"That cannot be more than five weeks ago," I said. "I thought the post to America was ten weeks. Each way!"

"By post, perhaps. But this was a ship that sailed from Liverpool with the sole purpose of finding me. An astounding new schooner of an innovative American design. They have not even settled on a name for the class of vessel. I gather it may be called a clipper."

I was still struggling to believe he was here. "But how did you return so quickly?"

"The same way. The ship was sent to scoop me up and bring me home. The crossing was astounding! If I had not been sick as a dog half the time, I would become a sailor this moment. We flew over the waves, full canvas rigged even in the highest winds."

"You cannot mean that Mr. Darcy hired a *ship?*" The cost of a crossing was immense.

Mr. Bingley laughed. "You are not thinking like a Darcy! He *purchased* a ship. The captain had never seen such a transaction. Three hours, done, and Darcy was turning for his carriage. But the captain insisted he rechristen the ship before he left. Some tradition, I gather. These seafarers are all superstition. And you should hear their language! It would make a Londoner blush. Before I knew it, I was shouting the occasional 'drat!' myself."

"Mr. Bingley!" My mother's brows furrowed. Apparently, a gentleman embracing Jane in our parlor was acceptable, but oaths were another matter.

"I assure you, drat is nothing by their standard." He gave me an amused smile. "The ship had your name, Miss Elizabeth."

I was sitting in stunned silence at the idea of Mr. Darcy purchasing a ship and returning to Pemberley, all in less than a day. I had thought he posted a letter.

Mr. Bingley's words sank in. "Named for a queen, I should think," I said primly. "Elizabeth is popular for ships."

"Ah. But the ship was named *Lizzy!*" My face exploded scarlet as he continued, "The crew enjoyed the name greatly! We were battling through a squall, and they were up in the rigging, shouting, 'Turn, Lizzy, you sea bit–'" His lips snapped closed mid-word.

In the pause, Mrs. Hill tried again. "Shall we lay out your clothes, Miss Bennet?"

Jane shook her head, but Mamma stood. "Come, Jane. You must be presentable." She drew Jane away. "I am sure you can wait, Mr. Bingley. We shall be down promptly."

"I am at your service," he said gallantly, and Mamma and Jane vanished toward the stairs.

I rose to follow, but Mr. Bingley said, "Miss Elizabeth. I wonder if we could have a word?"

His tone was serious, and I realized how critical this visit was. Here I was listening to stories and blushing like an idiot when all that mattered was Jane. Her life was at stake.

"Shall we step outside?" I said. That was proper for a private conversation.

We went out the front door. Mr. Bingley did a slow revolution, admiring the scorched earth and trampled flowers.

When he was done, I began. "For Jane's sake, we must be frank. Your return is remarkable and most welcome. But you did not say why you have come."

"Darcy wrote that Jane was dangerously unwell. And he expressed great remorse for… a disagreement he and I had before I left. It would embarrass him if I explained. But if it is important, I will do so."

That would be Mr. Darcy's false claim that Jane was not in love with Mr. Bingley. "He has told me already. Did he explain the nature of Jane's illness?"

"He said it was aggravated by my departure. And that I should speak to you and believe every word you said. I confess I have missed Jane desperately since I left. It was wonderful to hold her again. But she is wasted away to nothing."

They had embraced before, then. That, and the ease with which they called each other Jane and Charles, revealed that more had passed between them than I knew. But that was good.

"I will be extraordinarily blunt," I said. "If saying this offends you, all is lost in any case. Jane's health will deteriorate until she marries and binds. Time is short. It may be counted in days."

He gave a nervous laugh. "I admit I had a hint of what you might say." He fished in his pocket and drew out an official document. "When we landed, I was met by a message from Darcy. He included this. A special license for marriage."

Another miracle. English law required calling the banns for three Sundays before the wedding. But the Church could issue a special license to expedite a ceremony. The Bennets had neither the funds nor the influence to acquire one, but a Darcy was another matter.

Mr. Bingley bit his lip and furrowed his brow, becoming quite determined. "Your bluntness is welcome. I wonder if Miss Bennet has returned."

"Let us see," I said, and we went in.

We found Jane, prettily if hastily dressed, sitting with Mamma and Kitty in the parlor. We joined them.

Expectant silence fell. I tried to think of an excuse to leave Jane and Mr. Bingley alone. But I need not have bothered.

Mamma rose. "I must check if tea is prepared. Kitty, Lizzy, I require your assistance." Mamma and I tugged Kitty into the kitchen, ignoring her loud questions of why three ladies were required to check on tea.

In less than five minutes, there was a hesitant tap on the doorway. Mr. Bingley and Jane stood together with radiant, embarrassed grins.

Jane rushed in and hugged our mother. "Oh, Mamma. I am so happy!"

Mr. Bingley watched them embrace with a huge smile, then surprised me with a hug. "We are decided, Miss Elizabeth. I only regret that I left in the first place."

"I am very happy for both of you," I said. I was bursting with joy.

"I must speak to Mr. Bennet!" Mr. Bingley announced.

I had not known one could be brimming with grief and joy together. I took a long breath, searching for balance before I explained.

43

On the morning of the twenty-seventh of April 1812, two days after I stared through our doorway, astonished, at Mr. Bingley, Jane prepared to be wed.

Most of our family was squeezed into Jane's and my room. Kitty and Sarah were braiding daisies into Jane's hair and giggling like they were sisters rather than a lady and a maid. Mary flew in and out, asking if the lace on her dress was lying smooth. I, my mother, and Mrs. Hill were wedged on the window seat, having convinced our housekeeper to sit and sip her tea rather than battle the pleasant madness.

It was impossible not to be happy, but under that, I was rigid with nerves. I had spent my night listening to Jane's breathing grow hoarse and uneven. Hours too early, I lit a candle and prepared her medicine. Now, I feared she would collapse before the end of the day. I had bread and a tiny bottle of medicine in my reticule. If she weakened, I would risk giving her a second dose.

We had ended our formal mourning for Papa. That was sooner than was customary, but there was no true rule, and a mourning daughter could not marry. And my father would have scoffed at being held captive by vague social convention even without the urgency of Jane's health.

Jane was dressed in her favorite gown, a delicate forget-me-not blue trimmed with white lace. It had always been beautiful on her, but when she tried it on yesterday, it hung like a tent. After a moment of dismay, Mamma gave an annoyed *hmph* and sent for the dressmaker. Then we all helped, sewing like fiends to take it in while the daylight held.

Now, with a fluffy petticoat, the dress fit, and I had purchased Pear's White Imperial Powder to hide the bruised shadows under Jane's eyes—a much more delicate product than the talc Lydia had caked on her face. Although no one would mistake the gaunt woman at our dressing table for the healthy Jane of last year, her eyes were clear, and she shone with quiet joy amid the fuss.

I hopped off the window seat and bent my head beside hers. We smiled at each other in the looking glass, and I said, "You are beautiful, and I am so happy."

Then, it was off to the church in our carriage decorated with lilac and bluebells.

Our uncle would perform Papa's role in the wedding. As Jane's bridesmaid, I had another responsibility: to be *green wyfe* at the binding-of-gold, a small ceremony before the marriage that prepared gentry to bind draca.

The pastor greeted Jane and me in the little side chapel of the church. He stammered through my name, and I returned a curt nod. I had not forgiven him for sitting like a useless lump while I was accused of witchcraft. Or for his gossiping with Mr. Collins.

"Gentlemen," he called, and my selfless nerves for Jane's well-being turned to heart-thumping selfish nerves of my own.

Mr. Bingley came in, carrying a fist-sized cloth bag—his marriage gold, said to be one hundred guineas. Jane lifted her embroidered purse, which held two guineas, a token by comparison but proof of our standing.

The tiny chapel altar table was prepared for the binding-of-gold. In front of the chalice lay a thick branch of hoary oak decorated with scraps of mistletoe. The oak was hollowed to form a rough bowl the length of my forearm.

The parson poured in the gold, a symbolic joining of the wealth of two gentry families. The virgin-struck coins chimed and glittered, each an inch across and brilliant. The gleaming metal filled the bend of the branch, shining like the scales of our drake's neck. I was sure our parish bowl had never held so much.

Jane and Mr. Bingley knelt, and each placed their fingertips on the gold, careful not to touch each other as this was not yet the marriage. The parson draped his ceremonial preaching scarf, or *tippet*, across their two hands. Then he looked at me.

I took a deep breath and stuck out my hand by my side. I was too tense to look.

My fingers hung, untouched. Nothing happened other than the parson's eyebrows folding in crooked impatience.

I blew out my breath and looked.

Mr. Darcy—the best man, and green husband for this ceremony—was beside me, staring into the distance, his white-gloved hand outstretched as blindly as mine. We had missed each other by a foot.

I grabbed his hand. The parson began the binding ceremony.

I had never been a green wyfe before, so it was new to me. The parson recited excerpts from Church texts but also passages in a lilting language I did not know. Probably Gaelic.

Even gloved, my held hand was heating unnaturally fast. It was bizarre to stand like this with Mr. Darcy—as proxies for touch between the soon-to-be-married couple. We had not even greeted each other. Our last conversation ended when he told me never to return to Pemberley.

Well, today he was required to go to Longbourn. And I, for at least a little longer, was the mistress of Longbourn. It would not be so easy for him to flee.

"Mr. Darcy," I murmured.

"Miss Bennet," came back softly. His fingers moved a little. Had he squeezed my hand? The parson had not said anything about squeezing. Was I supposed to squeeze back?

I went back-and-forth on that, concentrating on keeping my fingers perfectly motionless until I decided. Before I did, the parson lifted his tippet and we were done.

Determined to face my fears, I snapped my lips into a smile and spun even as Mr. Darcy turned to me. We ended up face-to-face and rather close. He straightened in surprise, then stared over my head with desperate seriousness.

I had forgotten how sharp those cheekbones were.

"Do you admire my hat, Mr. Darcy?" That popped out before I could stop myself, the same words I said when we first met.

"Would it be impolitic to admire your thoughts?" he said—whispered. The skin over those cheekbones flushed. He backed a step, bowed, and left.

That left me flustered with my heart racing. If we proceeded like this, Jane might survive the day, but I would not.

The wedding ceremony was in the church proper. Miss Bingley, Mrs. Hurst, and her husband attended for Mr. Bingley's family. I received no greeting whatsoever from Miss Bingley, which was very rude, but I forgave her as her schemes had failed so outstandingly.

Mrs. Hurst greeted me graciously. Jane would have a friend there.

Mr. Darcy sat with Miss Darcy. Miss Darcy had worn her unusual red dress embroidered with gold renderings of Chinese dragon myths. As I passed, I pointed a fingertip to it and gave her an encouraging grin. I knew she was hesitant to wear it in public. She returned a self-conscious smile below her red-and-gold bonnet.

Lydia and Wickham were not invited, but I could not have contacted them even if I wished. They had left Hertfordshire after Lydia's failed attempt to control our drake, and I had no idea where they had gone.

The ceremony was beautiful, simple, and moving. My sister was married.

A LUNCHEON AT LONGBOURN FOLLOWED. This was the fashion in London, although rare in country weddings. But Lydia's rushed wedding had left Mamma deprived of maternal exhibition, so she was determined to make up for it.

That was good because I needed to speak with Mr. Bingley. I was already buttressing my bravery for that.

Unlike the wedding, the luncheon was a large event. The guests included local gentry, the Longbourn tenants all wearing their Sunday best, and those friends who could manage the trip on short notice. Colonel Forster was in Meryton arranging a new militia tour, so he attended with his wife. Charlotte could not attend so soon from Rosings, but the Lucases were here, Sir William pontificating about dukes while Lady Lucas inventoried our guests with an envious frown.

And of course, my aunt and uncle were here with their children. Their tykeworm bounded across the grass to greet me, only a faint crease in his side marking where he was shot. I scooped him up, ignoring the stunned stares.

This lured Miss Darcy to leave her brother, who was keeping a wide distance from me but was actually conversing with other guests.

Miss Darcy greeted me demurely, then tickled the tyke's nutmeg-brown muzzle above his amiably bared obsidian teeth. The staring eyes around us widened further.

"Is your pianoforte repaired?" I asked, mostly as a joke.

"Yes, but I am dissatisfied with the voicing of the hammers." She began an explanation peppered with technical German I could not begin to understand. I stopped her with a laugh, then had a thought and waved Mary over.

"Miss Darcy, may I introduce my sister Mary. She is our most accomplished musician, and a proponent of Beethoven."

"How wonderful," Miss Darcy said, and they began discussing his latest sonata.

Mary had reworked Lydia's scarlet gown yet again for the wedding, wrapping it throat-to-thigh in open black lace scavenged from old scarves. She wore an improvised hat of the same lace, and her brown hair was down and defiantly uncurled, the ends hanging past a choker of black ribbon. The effect was so confidently unfathomable that ladies were studying it, assuming it was a new fashion.

Mary and Miss Darcy made an interesting pair—young, slim ladies in unusual and striking dress. They had started a little shy but were now gesticulating over some detail. Miss Darcy began to smile. Mary's expression became manically intense, a promising sign as long as her partner was unintimidated.

I noticed gentlemen admiring them. Miss Darcy was a great curiosity, but eyes followed Mary as well, and I smiled to myself.

Deprived of his sister, Mr. Darcy's tall frame, clad in gray tails with a matching tall hat, began spiraling closer to me, although without obvious attention in my direction. I fixed my eyes on him. When he next stole a glance, our gazes met. I raised an eyebrow—an invitation to speak.

He arrived, stiffly proud to a casual eye, but I understood him better now. He was determined but profoundly uncomfortable.

We greeted each other, then he said, "I was deeply saddened when I heard of your father's death. I had only a few days to form our acquaintance. To *correct* our acquaintance, for I had formed an unjust first impression."

I thought of Mr. Darcy witnessing my father's mockery of Mary, so painful to a brother who had raised his young sister as his sole family.

"I would not accuse you of injustice," I said. "You did not first observe my father at his best. He would agree without reservation. We all do things we regret."

Mr. Darcy nodded, then inclined his head toward Mary and Miss Darcy, who were talking with great animation. "Your sister thrives."

"And yours." I took a breath. "Mr. Bingley explained your extraordinary efforts to help Jane."

"I was obligated to do everything in my power. I am happy to have accomplished some partial amends."

"My father described your rescue of Lydia as an unpayable debt. You have doubled that debt. More than doubled. I can never thank you enough."

"I thought only of you," he said, his voice low.

That wrenched like he had reached through my skin and grabbed my heart. But I hardened myself and said nothing. Because his selfless behavior was also the problem.

The silence stretched. His shoulders straightened, sensing a rebuke. "My intervention between your sister and Mr. Bingley was self-centered. Cruel and ungentlemanly."

"I thoroughly agree," I said.

His lips parted in surprise. In our social dance of apology, I had just stamped on his foot.

"So," I mused, "having learned that separating a couple is cruel and ungentlemanly, why do you persist?" He seemed frozen, so I proceeded, "I speak of us, Mr. Darcy, if you have not yet made that leap. Indeed, it is fortunate that I resisted the temptation to ban you from Longbourn. As you have forbidden me from Pemberley, I would have had to book the assembly hall for our luncheon, and it is not as nice as either of our gardens."

An uncertain smile grazed his lips. "You must be…" he began, then stopped, seeing my expression.

"If you are about to suggest I am joking, I advise you reconsider. Although I have never before had a gentleman flee from me, let alone ban me from his property, I am certain you omitted a required step."

"What step is that?" he asked quietly.

"An explanation."

"I sought to protect you."

"As you protected Mr. Bingley?"

"The situation is different. This is a burden *I* assume."

"That is conceit." My voice was becoming heated. "Can you imagine no other party you hurt?"

"You speak of yourself," he said. "Whatever hurt you feel is outweighed by the serious risk you would face."

"It is not your place to judge risks for me. Do you not see this is exactly your error with Mr. Bingley and Jane?"

"You do not understand the gravity of the situation. I could not bear to see you hurt."

"That is condescending. How can I understand when you do not explain? It is not endearing to have you protect me by stifling me. Would you choose a wyfe who hid you in the cellar to keep you safe?"

His eyes widened, and I realized what I had implied. I had to fight to keep my embarrassment from knocking me off course.

Truthfully, I had long since lost my direction. When I imagined this conversation, by this point Mr. Darcy had abjectly apologized and admitted some trifle of social etiquette to overcome.

I was staring into his dark eyes when he said, "You know the wyfe I would choose."

I swallowed against the sudden heat in my throat. "When I spoke of the darkness of Pemberley, you fled. *Why?*"

"I cannot answer," he burst out at the exact moment that Miss Darcy joined us, glowing with pleasure.

"Fitz?" she said, her smile collapsing to concern.

"You must excuse me." He strode through the crowd until he was on the other side of the garden.

Fingers encircled my hand and squeezed. "Elizabeth. Are you all right?" I tore my gaze from Mr. Darcy's back and met his sister's blue, worried eyes. "Did you quarrel?"

"No. Yes. I do not know."

"Here." She led me to a shaded table, sat me down, and put something in my hand. A crumpet. I took a bite. Strawberries. "Tell me what has happened."

I was being comforted by Mr. Darcy's sister. This was not a good solution. But to pretend all was well was too disingenuous. "Mr. Darcy and I have a disagreement. Over his protectiveness."

"I will certainly take your side. It is his most disagreeable trait." She spoke with such sisterly annoyance that a laugh broke through my lips. She leaned closer. "Since I was eleven, I have lived within my brother's protectiveness. Protection is well and good. But it can become foolish."

"Excessively foolish," I said tartly.

"Let us speak of something else. Fitz will return." A corner of her mouth twitched. "He cannot leave without me."

"True." I took another bite of crumpet, leaned back in my seat, and looked around the garden.

Jane, radiating joy with Mr. Bingley at her side, was speaking with the Lucases. Everywhere, there were smiles and happiness. My tense anticipation of speaking with Mr. Darcy had distracted me from what really mattered.

An unnamable dread fell away with a lurch. So much had gone wrong in the last few months that I had trouble accepting a happy ending. But here we sat, surrounded by a miracle for Jane.

"I greatly enjoyed meeting your sister Mary," Miss Darcy said. "I have even persuaded her to show me her compositions. I think she is shy about them."

That caught my attention. "Compositions? *Music* compositions?"

"Did you not know?"

"I had no idea. Do women compose music?"

"Your sister does," observed Miss Darcy, with the same self-assured manner I had seen in her music room. Her eyes were on Mary, who was speaking with Mrs. Trew, one of our tenants.

My eyes drifted to Miss Darcy's necklace with its single golden musical note, then the gold embroidery on her dress. The Chinese dragons were rendered in a strange style, stretched like snakes yet capturing the motion of draca. They had no wings, but they reminded me of our drake.

One shape was different, with wide, webbed feet and a thin tail like a fish. It was surrounded by a few simple lines that suggested reeds. "There is an aquatic dragon on your dress."

"The Chinese have their own myths. Dragons that change to carp, and back again." Miss Darcy's voice was distracted. She was now watching Jane and Mr. Bingley.

Softly, she said, "I shall never marry."

I almost scoffed. When I was a few years younger, I had imagined that myself in flashes of rebellion or frustration. But Miss Darcy seemed serious, so I answered seriously. "It will not be for a lack of opportunity. Already, gentlemen admire you."

"I do not desire their admiration." She was quiet for a minute. "Once, a man asked me to marry him. I knew he was dishonest, but I said yes. Just to… to be what is expected. Girls should dream of being married. I thought I could act the role dictated by the adamant expectations of society. But it would be a cruel jail."

Mr. Darcy had told me his sister's history with Mr. Wickham, although I would never admit that to her. But this was a different explanation than his—more complex than a young girl seduced into thinking she was in love then admitting the truth to her beloved brother.

There was a question I could ask without revealing my knowledge. "Mr. Darcy said you have renounced marriage gold."

"We chose that together. Fitz worries that my fortune makes me a target of unscrupulous men." She bit her lip. "I have not told him I do not plan to marry." I nodded to indicate I would keep it in confidence. "But I still have a fortune, with or without marriage gold. There is a more important reason. The more I learn of draca, the more uncomfortable binding leaves me. Fitz said my mother worried about this also, so together we decided we would not bind. Binding is… hard to understand. I fear draca have no choice in the matter. That they are slaves." Her laugh was bitter for such a young woman. "Forced into an unwanted marriage."

"I see why you enjoy Mary," I said. Miss Darcy gave me an extremely startled look. "Mary has decided that society is unfairly and selfishly controlled by men. She denounces England as a patriarchy and disapproves of society's expectation that ladies marry. You should share your thoughts on marriage with her."

Miss Darcy riveted her attention on the ground at her feet. A flush spread below her bonnet.

I was thinking about Miss Darcy's dress. "I must speak to Mary for a minute. Will you excuse me?" Miss Darcy nodded, and I found Mary with Kitty, Colonel Forster, and his wife, Harriet.

I drew Mary aside and asked, "Do you recall a drawing in our journal? A sketch at the top of a page?"

"Yes," she said. "A few lines. It is hard to make out." She waited, looking curious. Only Mary would be intrigued by being pulled away from a party to discuss a book. Well, I suppose I was doing the same thing.

"I think it is the shore of a lake, with reeds," I said. "Drawn very simply."

"It could be. The writing below is archaic and difficult to comprehend…" Mary closed her eyes. I had seen her recall passages this way before. "It means, 'The three sisters repel high creatures.' It made no sense to me. But 'high beasts' is written elsewhere and means draca."

I was excited now. "There are three sister lakes, of which Pemberley lake is one. For miles around, there are no draca. It is emptiness to my vision. *That* is what the journal describes. Mr. Darcy calls that the 'darkness of Pemberley,' but it exists at *three* lakes! And it has for hundreds of years." Triumphantly, I finished, "The darkness is not due to Pemberley, but the lakes!"

"Is that important?" Mary asked.

My triumphant smile became puzzled. "Perhaps not. But it might drag some answers from Mr. Darcy."

While I pondered my strategy, Mary noticed that Jane and Mr. Bingley were, for once, not mobbed by well-wishers. We headed over and exchanged our first embrace since the ceremony.

I held Jane longer to gauge her health. She was not trembling, her usual symptom of relapse. It was like the mere presence of Mr. Bingley was a tonic.

I let go and sketched an amusingly formal curtsy to her. "Mistress of Netherfield."

She smiled back. "You were mistress of an estate long before me."

"It is all one big family and one big estate!" cried Mr. Bingley with his usual disarming enthusiasm, although in this case he had more foreknowledge than he knew—if Jane's and my plan succeeded. To me, he added, "We are brother and sister now."

"Indeed, you are stuck with me. In fact, I wonder if I could briefly steal you from Jane?" He nodded, and we moved aside, leaving Jane and Mary to be besieged by a gaggle of older ladies.

"Is this where you warn me to treat your sister well?" he asked with mock concern.

"I already trust you will," I said. "I wish to speak of Jane's health."

He became serious. "We have the medicine you provided, and the instructions have been shared with our housekeeper. She is much more efficient than I."

I smiled at that. "I hope you will not need it." I summoned my courage and barreled forward. Jane's life was at stake. "You recall that both marriage and *binding* are crucial to Jane's recovery?"

He nodded. "You told me. You attended the binding ceremony yourself."

My last fear, driven by the experience of Mr. Collins and Charlotte, was that Jane would fail to bind. I could not imagine Mr. Bingley praying all night like Mr. Collins, but Jane could fall ill as the evening progressed, and then Mr. Bingley might be… too considerate. Too patient.

My face was heating. I turned a quarter turn, stared at a rose bush, and said in a rush, "Binding requires more than ceremony. I have it from good authority that success requires a passionate night. *This* night." I dug my nails into my palms. "To be safe, excessive passion might be advised."

When there was no answer, I stole a glance. Mr. Bingley was staring at the same bush and as scarlet as I.

"In fact," he said, in an artificially matter-of-fact tone, "Mr. Darcy provided a book from the Pemberley library on this subject."

"A *book?*" I was so surprised, I turned to Mr. Bingley. Alarmed, he spun completely away from me, so I addressed his back. "What *kind* of book?" He shook his head in desperate silence, and I realized I really did not want to hear him explain. "Well, references are helpful for…" For *what?* In growing panic, I cast about for a word and finally reeled in "novices."

The back of his head nodded up-and-down, and I fled.

Colonel Forster found me traumatized by a tray of mince tarts. He gave an understanding smile. "Weddings are emotional affairs. Harriet became quite misty at ours." He waved a glass of punch, which I took, gulped down, and handed back. He tilted the empty container, looking bereft. Was that *his* drink? My throat was burning. The fumes climbed into my nose, reeking of juniper and making my eyes water.

The colonel talked about his wedding while warmth spread from my belly.

"Miss Bennet," Mr. Darcy said as he joined us.

Oh, not now. I tried to remember where we had left our conversation, but all I could think of was books. "It is good I did not peruse the library."

Mr. Darcy looked puzzled, and I realized I had spoken aloud. What was in that punch?

Mary and Miss Darcy arrived, discussing the atrocious tuning of our pianoforte. They had been inside, testing it.

Mr. Darcy greeted Mary with a brief, crisp bow. I was beginning to enjoy his incessant bowing. It was so… male.

"Must we return to Pemberley today?" Miss Darcy asked her brother.

"I regret that I must return for an important business matter," he answered, looking at me for some reason.

Miss Darcy was dismayed. "When shall I hear Mary's compositions?"

"*You* could stay another day," Mary offered. "At Longbourn." Then her eyes went wide as if she had surprised herself.

"Oh! Could I, Fitz? Just for a day. Or two would be better. I could tune their pianoforte." She looked at me. "If it is convenient, of course. You must have been busy with the wedding."

"Why not?" I blurted cheerfully. Everyone stared, and I realized that was not the accepted response. Concentrating, I articulated, "You are very welcome, if your brother concurs." A tray of tea was nearby. I grabbed a cup and took a restorative sip.

Brother and sister negotiated. Really, Miss Darcy widened her eyes wistfully and her brother surrendered, rather like I had been able to do with Papa. Mr. Darcy would travel in a hired coach, leaving the Pemberley coach, driver, and a housemaid in Meryton to return later with Miss Darcy.

Mary and Miss Darcy drifted away. I drank tea, listened to Mr. Darcy and Colonel Forster discuss shooting, and concentrated on steadying my balance.

Mrs. Hill gestured to catch my eye. She was by the manor with a man in regimental uniform. I went over.

"A messenger, ma'am," she said. When the soldier explained the urgency, I asked him to accompany me, and we returned to interrupt Colonel Forster and Mr. Darcy's conversation.

The soldier saluted the colonel. "Sir, our militia is called up to Southend. French ships have fired on English vessels at anchor by Margate. Bonaparte means to raid up the Thames."

"Impossible!" The colonel had an amused smile. "The French will be thrashed if they approach our coast." The soldier handed the colonel an envelope, which the colonel opened and read, frowning.

A pool of quiet curiosity was spreading from our group. The two other militia officers at the luncheon threaded through the crowd to join us.

The colonel looked up from the message, his face grave. "Gentlemen, we are to Southend. Miss Bennet, my apologies for our premature departure." He bowed and swiftly said farewell to my mother, and to Jane and Mr. Bingley. The officers departed.

The party resumed, buzzing with speculation.

"I agree with the colonel," Mr. Darcy said. "It is foolhardy for Bonaparte to attack England. The French navy is outclassed. He may accomplish some brief damage through surprise, but he will take heavy losses."

"I am sure you are correct," I said, relieved that feeling had returned to my lips. "But even his enemies agree Napoleon is a great strategist. He must have a purpose. An objective that is worth the risk." I thought about the shape of the coast. It was rather fun to pretend to be an admiral. "Raiding up the Thames is ridiculous. They would be trapped."

"The thieves at Pemberley were French spies. They seem to grasp at the ridiculous."

Mr. Darcy did not know that Lydia and Wickham had conspired with those thieves.

Until now, the gravity of that discovery had escaped me, buried by my shock at Lydia's powers, the fight to prevent their stealing Longbourn, and the frenzied rush of the wedding. Had all that happened in two days?

The last traces of warmth from the colonel's drink were driven away by an icy realization. My sister and Wickham were accomplices to the murder of Mr. Rabb. Or worse than accomplices. Whoever shot Mr. Rabb had escaped.

If sentenced by English law, they would be hanged.

Was I sure?

The images I had seen through the tyke's vision were etched in my mind by pain. I saw the woman mount her horse. The set of her shoulders. How she adjusted her hat. It was Lydia.

But I could not call a constable and accuse my sister claiming I saw visions from draca. I would be laughed at. Or called a witch. If I was even willing to accuse my own sister.

However, Mr. Darcy would believe me. Wronged by Wickham once, then betrayed again, he would demand revenge for Mr. Rabb. He had the resources to find Wickham and Lydia. He would challenge Wickham, and they would duel. Wickham would choose pistols, and one would die. Or both.

"What is wrong?" Mr. Darcy said with quiet urgency. I realized the two of us were standing alone.

"I cannot answer," I said.

He winced as if slapped. Unintentionally, I had used the same words he cried out earlier.

"You do not know what you ask," he said. "You would have me reveal secrets I have told no one. Expose you to danger that has caused me great pain. But I cannot fault your honor. You unmask my own fault." He took my hand. "I will conquer this, whatever the cost. I swear it."

I hardly heard him. Our earlier conversation was an unfinished puzzle I had put aside, and now he had mixed it with this new conundrum, and the result was chaos.

He bowed low over my hand, never looking away from my eyes, then left. Lady Lucas replaced him, briefly noting how happy she was for Jane, then commenting at length on how our party was ruined by so many gentlemen departing early.

THAT NIGHT, alone in what I still thought of as Jane's and my room, I stared at the ceiling while my mind whirled. But I had barely slept the prior night. The whirl slowed to sleep.

I was thrown into wakefulness, my senses singing.

The room was black as pitch, but an afterimage blazed across my vision —a shimmering silver line, distant but bright. My ears echoed with the triumphant bells of a glorious cathedral.

I could not hear Jane's breathing. I sat up in panic, then remembered she was at Netherfield.

Whatever woke me left hints, like scents in the air. Celebration. Loyalty. Ancient remembrance.

My sister Jane was a bound wyfe.

44

I woke with the dawn, dressed, and went out to our front garden.

Our drake was on his perch. One foot now had no front claws; the other had one. I bent to examine them and felt his warm nose explore the back of my hair.

I spread his toes. The webbing between them was almost complete.

I straightened and looked into his gleaming black eyes. "You have been a loyal friend to remain so long. But you must begin your next life while you are strong." I wiped a wet eye and forced a smile. "I think we have learned a lot together. At least, I am less foolish than when we began. And you have new memories to carry. Will you become a drake again? Or a tyke? Or is the path always upward, and you are destined to be a wyvern? You are most worthy."

He fluttered his wings, birdlike, then pressed the crest of his head against my forehead, the tip of his narrow muzzle between my eyebrows. I closed my eyes. He stayed unmoving, the touch firm and warm, like a long kiss.

I heard his wings open. Wind rushed. And he was gone.

I TOLD BARBARA, our cook, to expect two more for breakfast.

Mamma came down in good spirits. "Lizzy, dear, have you fed the beast?"

"He is gone, Mamma. But we will be all right."

"I thought we must keep him. Are you sure?"

"Wait and see."

Miss Darcy came down next, hesitant in a strange home, and we welcomed her. Mamma, who would have preened and flattered around such an important guest a few months ago, was polite and gracious, if no less scattered than usual.

Kitty and Mary appeared next. Mary, freed of mourning, had dressed in featureless black neck-to-toe with her hair down in a braid. Miss Darcy was in a white muslin frock with her hair twisted up. They made an amusing pair as they chattered about music. Like two keys on a keyboard.

The doorbell chimed, and Sarah proudly announced Mr. and Mrs. Bingley. We all dashed to the door. Jane hugged everyone. She was still a skinny wraith, but her cheeks glowed with health.

"How do you feel?" I asked her.

"I feel awakened from a long fever. Everything sparkles like the world has been scrubbed. And I am starving for breakfast!"

I was grinning like a fool with relief. "We have a good breakfast ready."

Jane leaned close and whispered, "And we have the most incredible news…"

"I know," I whispered back.

Amid the babble, I slipped outside.

Jane and Charles's wyvern was beside our draca house, examining the abandoned perch with evident curiosity. She was a little larger than Lady Catherine's wyvern, at least the size of a heavy foxhound. But instead of bronze, she gleamed resplendent gold in the morning sun. I had never heard of a gold draca.

I closed my eyes. Her mind shone, wise and old. She was aware of me.

I opened my eyes. Her eyes flicked through shades of the rainbow as the sun touched them.

"Are you already our drake, transformed to a wyvern?" I wondered because she was interested in his perch.

child. he will swim for more than a lifetime of man

"'Child' again? Are you all so old?"

you are so young

"I am happy you have bound with my sister." Her wings rustled. Best to get to important questions. "I wish to ask, what is the darkness of Pemberley? Draca flee the three lakes. Another wyvern told me to go there to help Jane. But it did not help."

emptiness is not darkness. deference is not fear. jane is healed. the sisters of the child are revered

"That is a very vague answer, if it is an answer at all. If you are so old, you should have learned to be clear."

Her jaws opened in the panting laughter of her kind.

Behind me, the manor door burst open and Mamma ran out. She stopped beside me, her trembling fingers over her open mouth. The house emptied into our garden, forming a half-circle of awed faces. The wyvern looked back at her admirers with scintillating eyes and equal interest.

Jane and Charles were hand in hand. "Is she not beautiful?" said Jane to nobody in particular.

JANE and I explained our plan to Mamma and Charles after breakfast.

"Take Longbourn?" Charles was astonished. "We cannot! It is yours."

"It is very precariously ours," I answered. "And not for long. With our drake gone, Longbourn is sure to be claimed. But the entailment is clear. You are bound consort to an heiress. Reside here with your wyvern for seven nights, and you and Jane assume the title." He was shaking his head. "You must, or our home will be lost, and likely to someone unfriendly."

"Lizzy is quite right," Mamma said. "I have been recently disappointed with the quality of Hertfordshire gentlemen. Even members of the clergy. I am certain some horrible cousin from London would cast us out to starve."

"If we do this, it will be in name only," Charles said to her. "It will remain your home." He looked at me. "Your estate." He added, with a helpless laugh, "I am already quite overwhelmed sorting out Netherfield! Although now I have Jane to help." He smiled at Jane adoringly, and Jane melted a little with happiness.

I suppressed an eye roll. For all that I loved them both, my tolerance for adoration was being tested this morning. Jane passes the butter and is adored. Charles pours the tea and is adored.

I wandered the house, restless. For two long years as Papa's health worsened, I had been driven to protect my family. Then there was the desperate fight to save Jane. It was strange to have the two worries that consumed my life vanish overnight.

Mary and Miss Darcy were seated together at the keyboard of our small pianoforte, discussing chords and cadences. Pages of manuscript were laid out. I recognized Mary's distinctive hand even in notation.

I listened as Mary played fragments of music. It was unfamiliar and modern. This was her composition.

They stopped so Mary could write changes. She looked up at me, smiling. Another happy sister.

"I like it very much," I told her. She ducked her head to the music and thanked me, her smile pleased behind her swinging braid. "I should like to hear it all."

"May I play it?" asked Miss Darcy. After a stillness, Mary nodded, then came to stand with me. She was nervous. I watched her eyes on Miss Darcy. That was the audience that worried her, not me.

Miss Darcy began to play. It was not what I would have imagined Mary would write. It had her intensity, but it was incandescent with emotion. Romantic. Longing.

I became lost in the music, and in hearing Miss Darcy perform again. This was different from the roaring Beethoven she had played at Pemberley. This was lyric. Every note sang.

"It is wonderful," Miss Darcy said softly after the last tones faded.

Mary was staring in astonishment. Perhaps this was the first time Miss Darcy had played for her.

I walked over to look at the music. "There are words."

"It is an old Greek poem titled 'I have not had one word from her,'" Mary said. "By Sappho." The name meant nothing to me, but the admission left Mary flushed.

"Well, I have never been interested in those tiresome Greek men," I said. "You two shall have to explore Sappho on your own." Now they were both blushing furiously, so I left them to it and wandered on.

In front of the manor, the draca house was empty. I ran my fingers along the iron perch, trying not to feel sad. Our drake was free and starting a new life. Perhaps hundreds of years, cycling endlessly between water and land.

Jane and Charles's fabulous golden wyvern had also begun a new life, bound to them.

Would I want to bind draca when I married?

"No," I decided aloud. Even though draca did not chafe at being bound, it bothered me. Once bound, they were trapped. Like Miss Darcy, I felt it was too much like slavery. And for what purpose? Prestige? Our drake may have saved our lives, but most draca were idle fixtures for social display.

Far away, I saw Jane's wyvern soaring in the sky.

No, it was a different wyvern. The wings were shining bronze, not gold.

I shaded my eyes. An ostentatious iron-barred chaise and six was approaching. The horses were post, changed for speed, but the livery on the carriage was familiar. Lady Catherine de Bourgh, mistress of Rosings, was coming to Longbourn.

Doubtless I should dash inside to assume a ladylike pose, perhaps with embroidery.

Instead, I whacked some dust off my skirts and waited. I could not imagine why she would visit.

The carriage pulled up. The door was thrown open, and Lady Catherine descended with an air even more ungracious than usual.

"Good morning, Lady Catherine," I said.

She seemed disconcerted to meet me without the pomp of announcement. Her reply was a slight inclination of the head. Then she jabbed her scowling jowls toward the manor. "*That* would be Longbourn House, I suppose."

"Yes," I said, concisely as I did not like her tone.

"You have a decent looking doorknob." Her gaze followed the swath of ash burned through our front garden. "Your park is very odd."

"We enjoy it. I am afraid we have breakfasted already. May I offer you tea?"

"You have had a wedding," Lady Catherine said in an accusing tone.

I was becoming irritated. "We have had two weddings. My youngest sister, several weeks ago, and my eldest, yesterday."

"Your eldest sister made a very advantageous match." That was coarse, so I did not answer. Lady Catherine continued with a deeper scowl, "You can be at no loss, Miss Bennet, to understand the reason for my journey. Your own heart—your conscience—must tell you why I come."

"You are mistaken, madam," I said coolly. "I cannot account for the honor of your visit."

"I will not be trifled with," she snapped. "However insincere you may be, *my* character is celebrated for sincerity and frankness." She drew a commanding breath. "A report of a most alarming nature has reached me."

I folded my arms. "I am all attentiveness."

"I was told that my own nephew Mr. Darcy seeks to give up Pemberley."

"*What?*" Finally, she had shocked me with something other than rudeness.

"Do not pretend surprise. Is this not your doing?"

"*My* doing? How could I do this?"

"By industriously circulating rumors that you will soon be married to my nephew and that you will demand he surrender his ancestral home. Though I know it is a scandalous falsehood."

That was an astounding accusation in many ways. After a moment, I asked, "Which part?"

"I beg your pardon?"

"Which part do you know to be false? That I would marry your nephew, or that I would demand he give up Pemberley?"

"Disrespectful girl! They are both false."

"Well, I quite like Pemberley," I said. "So, that part is false."

"*Like* Pemberley! What temerity. Who are you to *like* Pemberley?"

"Her ladyship must choose what she wishes to be false. I either like Pemberley and covet it, or I dislike it and demand your nephew surrender it. It is not the sort of thing I would be undecided about."

Abruptly, I remembered Mr. Darcy's last words to me: "I will conquer this, whatever the cost. I swear it." Giving up Pemberley was exactly the kind of foolish plan he would invent over his fixation with the "darkness of Pemberley." A noble sacrifice for an imagined problem. He would reveal it after the damage was done, accompanied by many distractingly handsome bows.

Lady Catherine was staring in disbelief, apparently beyond words.

Another question occurred to me. "Is it only Pemberley that concerns you?" I was a little surprised by that.

"Certainly not! You cannot mean there is a foundation for this unthinkable rumor of marriage?"

"I do not pretend to possess equal frankness with your ladyship. You may ask questions which I shall not answer."

I heard steps. Mary and Miss Darcy had come out.

Miss Darcy was wide-eyed with surprise. "Hello, Aunt Catherine."

"Georgiana!" exclaimed Lady Catherine. "Heaven and earth! Why are *you* here?"

"I am visiting Miss Mary Bennet," she replied in a defiant tone.

Her ladyship appeared overwhelmed by irritating Bennets. She turned to me. "I wish to confirm, Miss Bennet, that you have acquired no brothers. I will be most disappointed if there are rumors about my niece as well."

"I remain without brothers," I said. "May I ask your purpose in visiting today?"

Lady Catherine eyed Mary and Miss Darcy, loath to continue with an audience. But they showed no signs of leaving. In fact, Miss Darcy took Mary's hand and set her feet, as if she feared her aunt would drag her into the carriage.

Lady Catherine answered with heavy emphasis, "I have come to insist you immediately and publicly contradict this impossible report, which I shall not name."

Just to irritate her, I asked in puzzlement, "You refer to the report of Mr. Darcy's and my impending marriage?" There were loud gasps behind me.

"Obstinate, headstrong girl!" shouted Lady Catherine. "There will be no marriage!"

I addressed Mary, who was flabbergasted. "Her ladyship has declared it impossible. Does that not mean contradictions are unnecessary?"

Miss Darcy asked breathlessly, "Are you engaged to my brother?" Her eyes were circles.

While irritating Lady Catherine for sport was amusing, it would be unfair to mislead Mr. Darcy's sister. "I am not."

Miss Darcy's face fell into huge disappointment.

Lady Catherine, however, was smiling. "As I thought! Now, will you promise me never to enter into such an engagement?"

"I will make no promise of the kind," I said. What nerve.

Lady Catherine stared in disbelief. Then her smile returned, but it was cruel. She pointed to our empty draca house. "What has happened to your firedrake?"

The memory tightened my throat. "Gone," I said softly. "After my dear father's death."

"Then your mother is weak. Miss Bennet, your status as gentry is lost. Know that I can find a respectable heir to Longbourn in days. I will send them to claim your home."

I had never liked Lady Catherine, and after I learned she owned slave plantations, that had deepened into active distaste. Even so, this surprised me.

"You hold Rosings as a woman alone," I replied. "You have faced prejudice. Would you strip away our estate because my father had no son?"

"Without a moment's hesitation. You have drawn this upon yourself with your pretensions. No Darcy would lower himself by marrying a common woman. Despite your arts and allurements, my nephew will marry whom I intend. My daughter."

I looked down at myself in a well-worn, plain white dress. Allurements?

"You do not know my brother!" shouted Miss Darcy. "You do not know *Darcys!*"

I held out a cautioning hand. There was no need for her to fracture her relationship with her aunt. Lady Catherine's threat was empty. Jane and Charles would arrive within an hour for their week stay at Longbourn, and their wyvern would fend off any challenger.

But now, I was angry.

I thought, *Will you come, please?*

Lady Catherine was gloating. "I expected to find a reasonable young woman. Instead, I find a selfish social climber in a fallen family. Do not deceive yourself that I will waver out of pity. I will use every tool I have to end this." Her smile widened. "I am no stranger to the particulars of your youngest sister's infamous elopement. I will share that information with my nephew. And with the papers. Darcy will be disgusted."

"I am rather disgusted by Lydia myself. But you will be disappointed by your nephew's reaction."

A shadow flashed, then Lady Catherine's wyvern winged to a neat landing at my feet, blowing leaves and twigs across the ground and flapping my skirts.

Lady Catherine retreated several steps.

I said musingly, "If the prestige of draca is so important to you, I should replace our drake. Perhaps I shall take your wyvern. That would be a pleasant elevation of our status."

I had no intention of stealing anyone's draca; I had called Lady Catherine's wyvern for show. But it was nice to meet her again. I reached out and rubbed her scaly head. She pressed her crest into my hand, then threw her head back in a silly pose so I could scratch under her chin. *Not now*, I thought.

"You are like her!" Lady Catherine had thrown out a hand to ward me off. "An unnatural woman! Have you come to boast like she did?"

"*You* came to *me*," I pointed out. "But what do you mean, I am like her?"

"My sister! Arriving when we had finally bound, after trying for weeks, then brazenly displaying her witch's skills. Stroking our wyvern. Speaking to the animal."

Trying for weeks? One did not try to bind for weeks.

I closed my eyes. My anger fell away—it was irritation, really. My breathing settled. The world of draca revealed itself.

The bronze wyvern shone. I could sense much more now than when we had last met. With my fingers on the wyvern's skin, I searched for the silver link of binding to Lady Catherine.

There was nothing.

Are you not bound? I asked in silent disbelief.

the great wyfe summoned me for her sister. the sisters of great wyves are revered, so i remain

I opened my eyes, astounded.

Lady Catherine de Bourgh—the sole widow to hold a wyvern—had never bound. It had been Mr. Darcy's mother, a great wyfe with extraordinary power, who summoned a wyvern. Who created a pretense of binding.

Lady Catherine's raised hand was trembling. Her dominating persona had shattered. The person exposed before me was cringing and insecure.

do you wish me to leave her? the wyvern asked.

I looked at this woman, whom at first I had respected for her independence, then came to dislike, then condemn. Her life was built on a fraud. No, fraud was the wrong word. Lady Catherine herself did not know. This was another Darcy intervention, unasked for and concealed. Lady Anne Darcy had acted in secret to save her sister's reputation.

Are you unhappy? I asked the wyvern.

i am content

It is your choice whether to stay or go, I replied.

Lady Catherine pulled her posture into a fragile semblance of her proud self. "You have ensorcelled my nephew, but I am unintimidated by your tricks. You are an upstart, inferior woman without honor, determined to ruin my nephew and make him the contempt of the world."

"You have now insulted me in every possible method," I said. "I must ask you to depart."

"I will go. But I take no leave of you, Miss Bennet. I send no compliments to your mother. All society will follow my example. You will be shunned and condemned." She drew a huge breath for her final riposte. "I am most *seriously* displeased."

Lady Catherine stomped off to her carriage. The driver snapped the whip. Loose bolts clattered.

The wyvern pushed at my hand until I scratched her thoroughly under her chin. Then she launched into the air, blowing the pins from my hair, and followed the carriage.

Miss Darcy and Mary came up, standing together beside me.

"She is a horrid aunt," Miss Darcy observed.

"Mary," I said, "can you manage the estate while entertaining Miss Darcy?"

"Of course." Her brown eyes assessed me. "Where are you going?"

"Pemberley," I answered, and Miss Darcy clapped her hands with excitement.

45

The hired coach arrived at Longbourn mid-afternoon, delayed by a surge of travel due to the rumored French invasion. The militia were leaving Hertfordshire to reinforce coastal towns in the southwest, while gentry on the coast were rediscovering their longing to visit inland relatives.

As my bags were loaded, Miss Darcy said, "Tell my brother I will be cross if he does not act sensibly."

"I will certainly end his ridiculous plan to sacrifice Pemberley," I said.

"I expect more than that. Do not let him just bow and mutter." I laughed at her description but flushed at her implication. Relations with gentlemen always seem simple to ladies offering advice.

Mary handed me the Longbourn journal—the Loch bairn journal. She had searched for passages relating to lakes and high beasts, and several black ribbons had sprouted, each marking a folded page of notes. I promised to read them on the road.

Jane's golden wyvern was crouched imperiously by our draca house. I had explained her responsibilities as best I could to a creature who neither counted days nor cared about entailments. I gave her a scratch, then whispered, "Will you be able to keep other draca away?" She panted her laughter, eyes shimmering.

Then we were on our way. I started out up top with the driver—the same driver I used for my trip from Rosings, so he grinned as I clambered up. I admired the Hertfordshire spring while the horses trotted, and he told me the latest news.

"Napoleon's bringing sixty thousand men," he explained. "All on one giant raft, big as a city. There's a dozen windmills that spin paddlewheels to make it go. And a hundred cannon. And a stone castle with turrets! I seen drawings in the paper, and they was marked 'Accurate Plan' in big letters."

"That sounds formidable," I said and kept my opinions on the accuracy to myself.

We stayed overnight at an inn in Bletchley I had visited with my aunt and uncle. Not long ago, I would have feared social condemnation for staying alone. Now, sneers and missed invitations seemed a trifling worry.

We set out in the morning at a relaxed pace, nothing like the sprint when I returned from Pemberley.

With a long day of solitary travel, I pondered Mary's notes. The passages she marked were near the beginning of the journal, in archaic English I thought indecipherable. Mary had translated them. The most interesting was this:

"La Tarasque was a high beast as long as a horse, but water-bound in the Rhône, with teeth like swords and a serpent's tail. It jetted flame and burned any who fought it, or slashed them with the claws of a bear. Saint Martha cast her holy splendor upon it, and it emerged from the river in foam and stood as quiet as a lamb, where she petted it and made it her servant."

Mary added this comment:

"If, as you propose, draca are aquatic before being bound, I believe this recounts a wyfe summoning and binding a wyvern, which would be 'as long as a horse' if one includes the tail, or exaggerates the retelling. This indicates that draca existed in ancient France, even though there are now none. Perhaps the French spies were searching the Pemberley library for clues to draca in modern France?

Lastly, I was sadly unsurprised to find our journal's story conflicts with the Church's account of Saint Martha in which villagers kill the beast. Doubtless, the Church's male establishment falsified their version to disempower a female saint."

With darkness falling, I leafed farther and found a note I missed. Mary had written no explanation—just copied the faded text into legible script. I read it, disturbed and unsure what conclusion she intended:

> *"Unholy is she who drinketh of crawler and wyrm, for she is the most foul wytch and a great clerk of necromancy. The clawes of devils stain her skin. Beware her mischiefe, for she is cruel and vile."*

Still twenty miles from Pemberley, we stopped at an inn outside Derby. The innkeeper and his wife kept a flock of long-haired Herdwick and were astounded to find a lady interested in their sheep, which were quite different from Longbourn's half-dozen Suffolk. We talked long after the candles were lit before I retired.

In the morning, I joined them for a simple breakfast of sheep's cheese, oat bread, and tea. But the table decorations were anything but simple: elaborate weavings of flowers and leafy branches, and hollowed eggs dyed red.

"Your decorations are beautiful," I said, touching a red egg.

"'Tis eve of Beltane," the wife explained. "The eggs are colored for the bonfires. Green for the summer god Bel, and red for *teine* which is fire. At least, that's what we say hereabouts." She gave me an appraising look. "Are you staying for the bonfire?"

"I am afraid not. I am bound for Pemberley."

"Pemberley? You'll see dances, then. The Peaks keep the old ways, and the hills of Pemberley more than most. You're a bonnie lassie, if you don't mind my saying. A lad might ask you to dance."

In a few hours, I would ring at Pemberley House. I had thought on what to say but not gotten much beyond imagining Mr. Darcy's surprise.

"The lad I am visiting does not care for dancing," I replied. "But if he asks, I will say yes."

We climbed into the Peaks, and I saw decorations beside the road: a wreath of yellow cowslip hung in a tree, then a figure of a man, woven from hawthorn branches with shining green leaves and blossoms that dripped white petals. We drove through the town of Lambton. A maypole ten feet high stood in the small square, surrounded by a few awestruck children.

I did not watch our approach to the house—I was nervous enough—but as we passed Pemberley lake, my eyes were drawn to the waters, as darkly burnished as draca claws under the overcast sky.

The coach climbed the other hill, then the driver knocked on the roof to announce arrival. I stepped out, and the massive visage of Pemberley House was before me.

There was a taint of acrid smoke in the air. Something unpleasant had burned. Wool, perhaps. In the distance, a horse whinnied and another answered.

"Please take my things to the stable," I told the driver. "I am sure someone will meet you there."

"Yes, ma'am," the driver said. He gawked at the manor's stone edifice before returning to the coach.

The huge windows reflected the cold steel of the afternoon sky. I caught a flicker of movement behind one, gone before I recognized a face. Dark and cold seemed to brush the nape of my neck, and I shivered.

"It is only a house," I said to myself, annoyed for being foolish. I marched up the steps and rang. The stone around my feet was muddy with boot prints as if a hunting party had tromped in and the staff had forgotten to clean.

The door opened.

I looked up into the unshaven face of Mr. Wickham, framed by the desultory collar of his scarlet uniform.

"Miss Elizabeth," he said with a broad smile.

He grabbed my arm and pulled me, stumbling and stunned, through room after room: past a handful of scruffy men in army uniforms lounging and smoking, their filthy boots resting on embroidered pillows; through an empty parlor, the floor sprayed with shards of a white porcelain vase that lay in pieces; down a grand hall where smoky remnants of broken picture frames and burned canvas overflowed a huge fireplace.

He threw open a door and pushed me into a luxurious chair in a well-furnished man's bedroom. Then he sat on the bed, watching me with predatory interest.

His hand traced an arc, showing the room. "My humble abode," he said. "I grew up here. Steward's quarters. Comfortable enough, if inferior to the family residences. They never let my father forget his place. Then Darcy ascended. He enjoyed depriving me of what I deserve."

Explanations were spinning through my mind. The best was that militia had been quartered at Pemberley and had grossly abused their status. The worst was robbery, a massive raid on the manor.

A sudden fear caught me. "Where is Mr. Darcy?"

"I wish I knew," Wickham said with soft menace. "Here is my question. Why are *you* here?"

Relief fanned my first spark of outrage. "Whatever you are doing, you cannot succeed. The townsfolk will notice. You will have constables at the door. Let me go. Or run and leave me here."

He walked to the window. "Come see." After a moment, I got up.

The window overlooked a yard behind the stables. Dozens of horses were tethered. Men were unpacking bags and carrying equipment. Some wore uniforms, others common clothes, but they all carried muskets or pistols. A few had swords as well.

"If constables come, we will take them also," he said. "I have fifty men. For this day, I am master of Pemberley."

"What has happened to my driver?" I saw no sign of our coach.

"Detained, and less gently than yourself. Although that may change. I have not decided what to do with you."

That chilled me. Stop asking every question that pops to mind. This man likely shot Mr. Rabb in cold blood.

I remembered that cold sensation on the nape of my neck. Pretending to be overcome, I closed my eyes and opened my mind. Everywhere around me was empty of draca, but toward the lake, darkness churned.

I opened my eyes. "Is Lydia here?"

"Of course." Wickham said it like a threat. "Now, answer me. Are you here for Darcy?"

Broken furniture. Burned portraits. Wickham's hatred for the Darcys was flaunted in every muddy boot print and broken dish.

"I am to meet Mr. Bingley and Jane," I invented. "Tomorrow. For a tour of the Peak District."

"And yet, your first question was for Darcy."

"It is his house."

Wickham laughed mockingly. "No longer."

"What do you want of me?" We were alone in his bedroom. My muscles tensed.

"That is the question, isn't it? Answer me this, Elizabeth. Lydia returned from her visit to Longbourn with her tail tucked firmly between her legs. She was furious with you. What happened?"

"Lydia's scheme to steal Longbourn failed."

"How? My wyfe's schemes are formidable. As are her talents. I expected your firedrake to grovel at her feet like that disgusting ferretworm."

His tone was distrustful and angry. But Wickham had aspired to be bound gentry his entire life and achieved his goal by marrying Lydia. Something had gone wrong.

"Your wyfe's talents are less impressive than you think," I said.

"That does not explain why she cursed *you*. Why she ranted about sister Lizzy's '*draca tricks*.'" He raked his fingers through his hair. "Listen, dear Elizabeth. You have stumbled into the war. Tomorrow, I am bound for France, so I do not care what you see or say. But there are men here who would cut your throat in a heartbeat, and others who would do worse. If you live out the day, it will be thanks to me. And I may require payment before the day is done."

"You disgust me," I said.

"You misunderstand my terms. I shall explain later. First, it is time to visit my wyfe."

He grabbed my arm and hauled me through the manor. On my first trip, I had been stunned and disbelieving. Now, I was terrified but angry and alert. I counted the men we passed in the house: nine. I listened. Those in uniforms gave nods to Wickham and spoke English, although of the lowest class. Those without uniforms stayed apart, ignored us, and I caught a few words of fluent French.

A barouche with the Darcy crest waited in front, incorrectly harnessed with a single pair of horses. The driver was an obese, grimy man bulging from an army uniform much too small. He eyed me. "Who's this crumpet, then?"

"Keep your bloody eyes to yourself," Wickham snapped. He pushed me into the back and sat beside me. The driver snapped the reins. We started down beside the coursing stream.

Maybe a naïve question would encourage explanations. "Are these your militia soldiers?"

Wickham's lip twisted. "The militia are gentry fools who pay for the privilege of bad food and parading in circles. I have my own force. Men with good reason to hate the army, nothing to lose, and much to gain. We are privateers, Elizabeth, but on land. Acting with an Emperor's letter of marque." He barked a laugh. "You should call me daring Captain Wickham."

I did not know how much I believed, but only one man was called emperor. Napoleon Bonaparte.

Ahead, activity had erupted on the lakeshore. At least two dozen armed men in laborer's clothes were milling around a large wagon. Some were erecting three modest-sized canvas tents, each about six feet square. Four others were lugging a small wooden chest to the edge of the water. The chest, not much bigger than a hatbox, was suspended on poles like a sedan chair, one straining man holding each corner.

Farther ahead, two carts filled with men dressed as English militia were climbing the road to town.

We stopped near the wagon. Wickham jumped down, then with exaggerated civility, offered his hand. I took it, hiding my distaste. If holding hands encouraged the pretense of gentlemanly behavior, I would let him touch my fingers.

A clean-shaven man with a commanding bearing strode over. He wore common worker's clothes, but his belt held a pistol and gilded sword. Two men attended him with military precision. This was a senior officer.

He greeted me with a European bow. "Mademoiselle Darcy." His French accent stressed the last syllable of Darcy.

"This is Miss Elizabeth Bennet," Wickham interposed in an annoyed tone.

The French officer's eyes narrowed. "*Bennet?*" He knew the name, but I could not imagine how. He glared at Wickham, who slouched in grudging deference. This Frenchman was in command.

"You have secured Monsieur Darcy?" he asked sharply. "And the household staff?"

"We are still searching for Darcy," Wickham said tightly.

There was an angry exclamation in French. "With fifty men, you lost a degenerate English noble?"

"His horse is stabled. We will have him soon."

The French officer shook his head in disgust and spoke a blur of French syllables. I caught only *Lambton*, the town near Pemberley. If I was to continue meeting spies, I should practice my languages.

Wickham's reply was as fast and indecipherable. It seemed everyone's French was better than mine.

The officer stalked to where the chest rested on the gravel shore. The four men were now laboring to bring a second chest.

A cart arrived, carrying three young women dressed in white linen gowns, their hair elaborately styled. Their slippers were fabulous ball attire, embroidered with golden thread and tassels. As they walked to the chests, each gown dragged an arm's length of elegant train across the rough stones and dirt.

The officer threw open the first chest. Even under the gray sky, it glittered. Gold coins. An unthinkable fortune.

Women in beautiful gowns. Gold. "They are attempting to bind draca," I said.

"They are," Wickham said. "And you must ensure they succeed."

"*What?*"

"Even my sweet Lydia was impressed by your draca tricks, and I can attest that Lydia is not easily impressed. I think there is more to Elizabeth Bennet than raven hair and striking eyes. And if you want to survive this day, you must use those tricks to ensure that one of these women binds."

"Even if I could, I would never assist a French woman in binding English draca."

"If you don't, Lydia achieves all she desires. That will go poorly for you. And for me as well." He stiffened, looking over my shoulder. Steps were approaching on the stones. "Say nothing of this!" he whispered.

"What a laugh," came Lydia's voice behind me.

I turned to my sister. Lydia wore black, but not mourning dress. Her gown was elaborate and expensive, ornamented with sewn pearls and ivory beadwork. It was a dark counterpoint to the white gowns of the French women, and even more extravagant.

She had caked her face with white paint so thick that it cracked around her eyes and lips. Her cheeks were rouged, her lips bloodred. The effect was grotesque, like a French aristocrat of the last century or a poor-quality porcelain doll. But even through those heavy cosmetics, her veins were dark as purple ink, spiderish around her eyes and crawling across her cheeks.

"Are you unwell, Lydia?" I said.

She gave an irritated smile. "I did not think to find you here. Are you chasing Mr. Darcy? Or… is it an *affaire*? Has perfect Lizzy at last loosened her skirts?"

Her coarseness silenced me. Finally, I said, "Why are you here?"

"*I* am preparing for my coronation." She made a moue of exaggerated pity at Wickham. "Do not be sad, Wickie. You can be captain of my guard and visit me every day. I am sure the Empress's guard has handsome uniforms." Her mocking smile turned cross. "But now I must talk to Lizzy alone."

Wickham gave a short, uncomfortable nod and walked off.

"He is jealous," Lydia said.

"Jealous of whom?" I asked.

"Emperor Napoleon." Lydia lifted her eyebrows flirtatiously, as though we were giggling about a handsome officer in the local regiment. Flecks of white paint fell from her forehead onto her black dress.

"That is insanity. You are married, and sixteen. And *English!* He is married, and the emperor of France. You have never even seen him."

"I will have you know that I have spent hours with him. In France, surrounded by handsome *aides-de-camp* and snobby French noblemen. He is very commanding and proud, but old and a little dumpy. More than forty, I think. Poor man. He is so unhappy in his new marriage. They say he was sad to divorce Joséphine. He did it because she could not give him an heir. I think it most romantic that he is sad."

"You find his love for his divorced wife *romantic?*"

She jabbed a finger at me. "You are being silly. It is not like I am in love with an old man. It is his rank, Lizzy. Think of it. Empress. And he is very rich. All that gold is nothing to him." She waved a finger at the three chests, each heaped with gold. "Imagine Mamma! She will fall over with shock. I shall not be able to breathe for laughing."

I had called this insanity because it was ridiculous. But I watched Lydia giggle, imagining surprising our mother as Empress of France, and I said, "You are mad," and I meant it.

"Clever Lizzy thinks I'm a foolish girl, but you are the simpleton. Use that wit Papa admired so much. If an Emperor will divorce the woman he loves to gain an heir, think what he will do for what I offer."

"What do you offer?" I asked slowly.

"What he desires most. Victory over England." Her grin was savage. "I proved my power in his court, while all his fancy guards and nobleman watched. I killed a man in front of them. Oh, you should have seen their faces, Lizzy, when he named me *l'enfant du lac*, the Child of the Lake. He sought me for a year. And when those stupid French women fail to bind, he will have no choice. He said he would give me anything I want. And I *want* to be Empress."

This had to be imagined. A fantasy.

The French officer approached and stopped several steps away.

"*Oui?*" inquired Lydia in her best French accent.

"Madame Wickham. We are ready." His eyes were lowered. His lips were tight. He was frightened of my sister.

"You may proceed," Lydia said grandly. He hurried off, and she raised her eyebrows at me. Little Lydia, wanting to impress her older sister.

I tried to make sense of this.

A French officer and at least fifty armed men had come to the middle of England, with what had to be a hundred thousand gold guineas. It must be marriage gold, so worth far more. Over two million pounds. An astronomical sum.

And that officer deferred to my youngest sister. That was why he recognized my name, Bennet. He must have met Lydia before she married.

Lydia was right. I should be impressed. Or terrified. What if all she said was true?

Three men joined the French women. The couples lined up, each by a chest of gold. Another man put on the trappings of a priest, although Catholic. He opened a bible and began reading in English with a heavy French accent.

Lydia watched the ceremony with contempt. Softly, she spoke to me. "Now, Lizzy, I must talk seriously. At Longbourn, you did… something nasty. It hurt my head, and it kept me from taking my drake. I want to know what you did."

"I do not know," I said. That was true. It had been instinct. Anger.

"If you cannot tell me, then *you* must do it. If one of those girls binds la Tarasque, Napoleon will choose her instead of me. He likes French girls."

"What do you mean, la Tarasque?" That was the beast from the story of Saint Martha, which was centuries ago.

"The dragon of the lake."

Before I could help myself, I laughed. "There are no dragons. La Tarasque was a wyvern. And there are no draca in Pemberley lake. Of any kind."

"I know there are no dragons. But Napoleon is obsessed with the legend. And a wyvern would impress him. Even a firedrake, which is why it is very unfair I did not get the Longbourn drake. I would have taken it from dull Mr. Sallow once we had the manor." Her light blue eyes, feverish and hot, met mine. "Why do you say there are no draca in the lake?"

Could Lydia not sense draca the way I did? I had no idea what she was capable of. She had incredible power, but it seemed different from mine.

Regardless, I had no intention of giving her lessons. "Draca in the lake would be obvious. We would see them swimming around like ducks."

"You are a bad liar," she said. "Here is the thing, Lizzy. If one of those women binds, I shall have to kill everyone, then invent some story to explain it. Napoleon will be suspicious. The whole thing will be most tiresome."

I could not have heard right. "That is a poor joke."

Lydia wore a small reticule at the waist of her dress. She opened it and drew out a writhing worm the length of her palm. A worm with many legs. A foul crawler.

I recoiled, but her other hand grabbed my shoulder. "Do not run. There are hundreds around us. Under rocks. In the woods. You would not get twenty feet. They all do what I want."

Gently—affectionately—she placed the crawler on the shoulder of her dress. It ran down her sleeve then along her bare forearm, rows of legs rising and falling. It stopped on the back of her hand, inches from my bare neck.

"I could make it sting you," she said.

The tail flipped up and over its head. Two sharp points thrust out like curved needles, and an oily drop formed on each point. My nostrils filled with a vile odor. Sour orange and bitter almond.

"Stung in your neck, you would die in minutes," she said. "Or in your breast, near your heart. That would be more painful, but still quick."

"We are sisters." I could not believe the monstrous things she was saying. I did not believe this was my sister.

She flipped her hand, catching the crawler so the tail and stingers protruded from her fingers. She thrust out her tongue and dragged the needle-like stingers across it, leaving twin oily trails that discolored to steaming black. Her tongue curled into her mouth, and her lips worked rapturously. Her eyelids fluttered closed. Her shoulders shuddered.

"I do not *wish* to do it," she whispered. Her eyes opened. The pupils swelled, swallowing blue into hollow black. "It is only if one of these women binds. So, sister, do your draca trick. Prevent them from binding. Because if one of those light-skirts binds a wyvern—or anything at all—I will take her draca, then kill her and everyone else."

46

What do you do when your sister is mad?

There had been an editorial in the *Times* on the treatment of mad people. They applauded the regular inspection of madhouses required by the Lunacy Act, but they criticized current medical treatment. Rest and care at home were preferred.

Perhaps we could fix up a room at Longbourn. Or wait until her coronation. Presumably, Napoleon had spare rooms.

My laugh cracked. Maybe I was mad, too.

"He is very bad at it," Lydia said, misunderstanding what amused me. She had returned her pet crawler to her reticule and was watching the French weddings. The priest was stumbling over the Gaelic text in the binding-of-gold.

The couples had no green wyves or husbands behind them. Did that matter? Maybe that was a Hertfordshire tradition. Otherwise, they seemed knowledgeable about the Church of England's ceremony. It was hardly a state secret.

I was supposed to be using my draca tricks to prevent them from binding. And to ensure they *did* bind. Lydia and Wickham had demanded opposite outcomes.

I laughed again. Could this be any more insane?

With everyone watching the weddings, I turned, examining the trees and the distant hills. I was certain Mr. Darcy was out there. Had he seen us? We were not subtle, with dozens of men, three gowned brides, and three chests of gold. Mr. Darcy would know the grounds of his estate from hunting. That was an advantage, even if he was pursued by soldiers.

It was strange they had not captured him when they arrived. Even if Wickham had knocked at the door with a dozen soldiers, I was sure Mr. Darcy would meet them. The assumption of gentlemanly behavior and rule-of-law was too natural. Rather like when I confronted the crowd outside Longbourn. In hindsight, that was rather foolish.

I eyed Lydia. Even sane, my youngest sister was notoriously bad at keeping secrets. "What happened to Mr. Darcy?"

"Wickie was angry over that." Lydia smiled, amused. "He sent Mr. Darcy to be locked in the wine cellar. The guards did not come back, so Wickie went to look and found them dead." Her smile widened. Impressed. "*Three* men, killed. All the servants were gone as well. They had been in the wine cellar."

I remembered Mr. Darcy taking a Frenchman's sword. When he killed that man, he had sworn never to freeze again. But overcoming three men seemed impossible.

More important was their escape. Pemberley House was lightly staffed, but a manor that size required at least a dozen servants. If they had all escaped knowing that Pemberley was overrun, it was a matter of time until word reached the authorities. My best strategy was to be patient and wait for rescue.

But I was not the only one who needed rescue.

"Wickham has done something to you," I said. "Infected you. Poisoned you."

Lydia's gaze did not leave the weddings. "Poor Lizzie misses her Wickham. Is he not more handsome now he is frightened? We pretend brave men are handsome, but I know better."

"It is not Wickham I care about. It is my sister."

Her head turned to me, listing at a disquieting angle. "He thought I was a little girl he could tempt with sweets and frighten with scary old books. But I always liked whispering to crawlers. The books just told why. Then Wickie brought a crawler to scare me, and I *tasted* it. Oh, Lizzie, how he shouted! I have such tricks."

Scattered cheers erupted, and she turned away, leaving me unsettled.

The weddings were done. All three women—wives, now—hugged their husbands. And *kissed* them, in full view of everyone. How shocking. Of course, they were French.

The new wives looked thrilled. These were willing partners, not victims of imperial decree. Two couples ran off, each ducking into one of the small canvas tents. The third stayed on the shore, still kissing.

"Now they race," Lydia said. "It is a competition. Whoever binds first keeps their chest of gold."

The French woman was wriggling while they embraced. Her gown fell to the ground. She wore nothing beneath.

I spun away desperately. The watching soldiers began to whoop and yell in approval.

Lydia watched with interest. "Well. He is… impressively eager." I heard water splashing. "Oh. They think doing it in the water will raise la Tarasque. They are brave. It must be cold." She looked at me, eyebrows narrowing. "Make sure you do your trick. They must not bind."

My disbelief—my denial—of this bizarre situation had vanished. Oddly, it was the finality of marriage that drove home the reality. However strange this was, a country at war with England had managed an elaborate sortie into the heart of Derbyshire. This was not a whim or folly. Captured French spies were executed, and Wickham's men, whoever they were—deserters?—would not fare better. These men faced death. The stakes could not be higher.

And the French commander was no incompetent. To accomplish this much was incredible. That frightened me for the escaped staff of Pemberley. And for Mr. Darcy. In truth, I was frightened for all of us. Including those poor French women being married in hostile England.

"Lydia," I said. "I have no trick to do. No way to stop a binding. And it does not matter. Do you not see this is doomed? We are a day's travel from the coast. You will all be caught. Tried as spies." She watched me, and I fought to reach her. "The guards trust you. We could escape together. Find somewhere to hide. Constables will come soon, then the army. Bring Wickham, if you must. Tomorrow, we can go back to our lives."

She cocked her shoulders the way she did while considering something. A hat in a window, or a gentleman at a ball. Behind me, I heard water splashing rhythmically amid enthusiastic shouts from the soldiers.

"I do not *want* my life," Lydia said. "I *want* to be Empress." She grabbed my wrist and pulled as she walked to Wickham. "Lizzy is useless. Can we not be rid of her?"

"*Are* you useless?" he asked me. His eyes held a silent question. Asking if I was fulfilling my part of our bargain.

"I can do nothing," I said. I was tired of pretending I had a role in their feud. Tired of guessing what magic words would save me.

"That is a shame," he said. He called out, "Put her with the others."

The obese man in a too-small uniform prodded me to a small cart pulled by a single horse and squeezed in beside me. We began plodding back up the hill toward the manor.

We rode in silence. I tried to ignore the rank odor of my companion, and his fleshy leg pressed against mine.

How long would it take authorities to arrive? Avoiding the road, Lambton would be six or eight miles on foot through woods. Two or three hours, if the ground was not too bad. My guess was Wickham had been here that long. Although the escape might be more recent. Rescue could be about to arrive, or hours away.

The sounds from the lake faded to nothing. We had climbed the hill but turned away from Pemberley House. The horse puffed as it pulled over the crest. The lake vanished behind.

"Where are we going?" I asked.

"With the others," the man said in a rough monotone.

We rolled along a narrow path. There was no sign of buildings or people. I did not like this.

Could I outrun this man? He did not look fast, but it was a cool morning, and I had two petticoats under my dress. Running would be a desperate thrash. And the man had a pistol on his belt. I would have to dodge a bullet.

Running was a last resort.

We clopped another two hundred yards, then he stopped the cart. There was nothing in sight but trees.

"Now what?" I asked quietly.

"A bit of a stop. A little fun. If you're good to me—"

I hit him in the face, feeling his greasy nose flatten under my palm like a piece of dough, then vaulted out and ran. On my fourth step, something snagged my dress, cloth tangled my legs, and I slammed face first onto hard roots and earth.

For a second, I was stunned, pain shooting from a knee and an elbow. A voice cursed a foul stream behind me. I shoved myself up, but my dress caught, holding me half bent over. I yanked with both hands. It tore free just as a boot slammed the small of my back, sending me flat on my face again.

I had to see. I rolled on my back.

The man stood over me, fingers pressed under his nose, blood dripping over his lips and down his chin. He snorted wetly. "You'll bloody pay for that, woman."

I closed my eyes and threw my mind outward like I had never tried before.

The emptiness of Pemberley opened around me. But I was away from the lake now. I stretched my mind the other direction, farther and farther. Farther than I had ever reached before. Too far. Nothing so distant could be here in time.

There was a glimmer, dust motes in the air. Something tiny.

Help me! I screamed in my mind.

A kick hit my ribs. I curled up, gasping. Damp loam ground the side of my face. I tasted dirt.

The man stomped into the brush beside me, still swearing. Meaty fingers grabbed my hair and yanked my head up. Our faces were a foot apart. His breath filled my nose, hot and fetid from decaying teeth.

A buzz whipped past, like a bee, but far faster.

The man started back, releasing my hair. "What the?" A two-inch red line had appeared on his forehead. He touched it, puzzled, smearing blood from his fingers. No, his forehead was cut. Drops began to run.

Another buzz whipped past, and another. Motion flicked in the air.

The man scrambled to his feet, waving like he was fending off a cloud of gnats. There was buzzing all around us. "Gotcha!" he exclaimed, raising a fist. I heard a crunch as he squeezed.

I sat up, and something stopped stock-still inches in front of my nose. It had the iridescent jade body of a dragonfly but was two-legged like a miniature firedrake. The wings were an invisible blur. An instant later it was gone.

Do not sit like an idiot. Run.

I leaped to my feet, turned, and found myself face-to-face with a gentleman I had never seen before. Taller than me, which was not saying much, but not as tall as Mr. Darcy. He had short dark hair with a slight wave, refined features that placed him in his forties, and dark eyes. Above his dress trousers, he wore a white shirt tied with a starched cravat, as if he had discarded a formal coat and waistcoat.

"Pardon me," he said. His hand pressed my shoulder. Like a dance, I stepped aside. His other arm raised a pistol where I had stood and fired.

The report was two feet from my head and incredibly loud, drowning my startled shriek. The echoes quieted, leaving soft buzzes, the tones differing just enough to clash like pianoforte strings slightly out of tune.

The man who had abducted me lay on the ground, half his head blown away. I looked away, fighting a wet heave in my stomach.

The gentleman's arm was still outstretched, a curl of smoke rising from the pistol. Tiny jade shapes surrounded him in the air, all pointed at his face in a threatening manner.

"What are these?" he asked conversationally.

"Some form of tiny draca," I said. I sensed them now, pinpricks of awareness. I swallowed, calming myself, then held out my hand. *I am safe now. Will you come to me?*

The little flock dispersed, but one landed on my hand. She had four rigid, insect-like wings. Her two legs were much sturdier than insect legs, more like a lizard, and had glistening red feet.

She advanced an inch across my palm, dragging the tip of her tail for balance. The feet tickled and left a trail of minuscule red dots.

Blood. From the man who was killed. My hand shuddered, and the creature took to the air. I wiped my palm on my dress. It was ruined anyway.

"Miss Elizabeth Bennet, I presume?" the gentleman said.

I blew out a frustrated breath. "*How* do you know that? People I have never met keep knowing who I am. It is very disconcerting."

"I sympathize. But you are a young lady with dark eyes and a strange affinity for draca who is visiting Pemberley. I would have had to ignore Darcy for months not to know you."

"You know Mr. Darcy?"

"I do."

The gentleman had not introduced himself. But he looked familiar.

"Are you sure we have not met?" I said.

"Pardon me. Arthur Wellesley, at your service. Recently raised to Earl of Wellington, if that helps."

His face was familiar from the papers. This was the acclaimed leader of England's armies in the Peninsular war against Napoleon.

47

Our horse plodded deeper into the woods. I was riding in the cart and driving it—something I had never done before, but it was simple enough with a single horse in harness. Mr. Wellesley walked alongside.

I should say, Lord Wellington. He was an earl now. At this pace, he would be the Duke of Wellington before long.

A complication occurred to me. "Will they not have heard your gunshot?"

"We were over the hill from their encampment. Without line of sight, a gunshot is a rambling echo. If they noticed at all, the direction will be unclear. But we are wise to move on."

"I neglected to thank you for my rescue."

"You are most welcome. You were doing quite well on your own. What do you call those little draca?"

"I have no idea. I did not know such things existed."

"Nor did I." There was a pause. "So, you summoned them, unaware of their existence, and they defended you?"

His tone was factual, but I hesitated, remembering the military's desire to use draca in war.

After the silence dragged, he added, "Of course, I shall respect your privacy in this matter."

"I am sorry to appear reluctant. I have been accused of witchcraft twice in the past week."

"Then, in your position, I would be reluctant myself." He spoke as if accusations of witchcraft were no more shocking than being criticized for an unfashionable hat.

"Have you seen Mr. Darcy?" I asked.

"Yes. He and I are partners in this adventure. He is unhurt. We should meet him at our destination."

"Thank goodness." A tension I had not recognized drained from my shoulder blades.

"You are not the only one to have an exciting day," Lord Wellington said cheerfully. "Men arrived at Pemberley and took Darcy at the door. I am embarrassed to say I was enjoying a soft-boiled egg at the time. Hearing the violent invasion of many armed men, I retreated to the cellars. I armed myself with a bung puller—rather like a large corkscrew. Then fate intervened, and Darcy arrived with proper weapons."

"Proper weapons held by his three guards?"

"*That* part was inconvenient. How do you know of the guards?"

"I spoke with… the men by the lake." I balked at naming my sister as a collaborator.

"Interesting. Did you learn anything more?"

"You will find it incredible. They are French soldiers, here on Napoleon's orders. They wish to bind draca to a French wyfe. They married three couples by the lake."

"I watched." His tone was bemused. I wondered if he observed the post-ceremony activity. "Who was the young lady in black?"

I licked my lips, stalling. "Which young lady?"

"The lady treated by the French *capitaine* as a superior, which is a peculiar military organization. The lady with whom you spoke for a considerable time."

His tone was not accusing, but it was exact. I was foolish to think I could conceal information from an officer who both employed and interrogated spies.

"She is my sister Lydia," I said.

"Why is your sister in a position of importance with invading French forces?"

"She has unusual abilities. Not unlike mine." I would not condemn her without defense. “Lydia is only sixteen, and recently married. Her husband is George Wickham, a rogue who has drawn her into some dishonest scheme. There are more than French soldiers here. Wickham has recruited English thieves or deserters to help him.”

Lord Wellington made a *hmm* sound. At least he found the situation complex.

I was feeling remarkably normal, all things considered. The horse was a smallish, gentle animal, well-groomed and content to pull a light cart for miles. Dappled forest light rolled across his back. Other than some scrapes and a sore side where I was kicked, I was hardly the worse for my adventure.

“Why were you visiting Mr. Darcy?” I asked.

“He desires to divest himself of Pemberley. He asked if I would acquire it. I was honored by the offer. Pemberley is an extraordinary estate.”

“I trust you told him that giving up Pemberley is an absurd idea.” That came out more sharply than I intended.

“Of course.”

Well, that was good.

“May we stop for a moment?” he said. I reined in. He studied a hazel bush twenty paces ahead, then called out, “Well met!”

Leaves rustled, and a grinning boy of fourteen or fifteen stepped out and walked to us. He was tanned, ropey and fit, and barefoot below rough-spun shirt and trousers.

There were regular streaks of blue on his cheeks and forehead. Dried mud, I thought, until he came closer and I saw it was a stain on his skin. He had dyed a pattern onto his face, neck, and arms with woad, a flowering weed used to dye cloth.

“Sir,” he said to Lord Wellington with a bobbing, inexpert bow.

“You make an excellent sentry. Has there been any action?”

“Not a peep. Haven’t even seen a man cross the hill from the house. They are a poor lot of hunters, is all I can say.” The boy looked at me shyly. “Ma’am.”

“Good day,” I said. It was late afternoon by now.

We set off again, the boy chattering inconsequential cottage news to Lord Wellington, who listened seriously.

The blue streaks on the boy’s face were pulling at a memory, but I could not place it. Something important. “May I ask why your face is decorated?”

"'Tis eve of Beltane. Afore them folk come to trouble Mr. Darcy, we was preparing for the Pemberley festival."

"Are we within the estate?" We had come several miles at least.

"'Course, ma'am. Pemberley is the biggest estate in the world."

I smiled at his enthusiasm, even though I knew there were larger. "Do you work the land?"

"Not like farmers. We're Britons. Hill folk." I cocked an eyebrow and he explained, "We live the old ways, and keep the true gods. Hunting. Fishing. Raising goats. Pulling up what grows natural." He added a wry grin. "Sometimes, we trade with the house. Get some bread and tea."

"Mr. Darcy lets you hunt his land?"

"He does. That's why we're on Pemberley. Most lords don't let nobody hunt. They want to ride about and shoot foxes. Pemberley's different. Honors the old ways. There's us!"

He ran ahead. We followed at the horse's plod and entered a village. There were a dozen small homes scattered, each with walls of wattle and daub, and thatched straw roofs dotted with green where stray seeds had sprouted.

In the center was a clearing, and within that rose an unusually thick maypole cut from a birch trunk. The top reached as high as the thatched roofs.

Lord Wellington went to speak with a pair of men, their faces also striped with blue woad. I clambered off the cart, shook out my stiff legs, and took a closer look at the maypole. The top foot of the birch was stripped of bark and beading with sap. At the height of my head, a wreath of flowering rowan and pale honeysuckle wrapped the pole in white froth.

I stuck my nose in and took a sniff. The scent of rowan was rich and musky. The sweetness of honeysuckle dripped beneath. I pulled my face out, feeling a little dizzy.

"You'll be asked to dance, you do that," a woman's voice said beside me. I turned to find a smiling, yellow-haired woman a few years older than me, wearing a simple linen dress. "I'm Agnes, but everyone calls me Aggy."

"I am Lizzy," I said, deciding that a French invasion justified informality, and curtsied. I felt foolish as Aggy bit her lip and returned an inexpert imitation. Obviously, curtsies were not done here. I gave her an apologetic shrug and grin, and she chuckled.

"Guess you ran from them soldiers," she said, looking me over. "You're a bit of a mess."

"Am I?" I looked down. My dress was smeared with dirt and clay, and dotted with burrs and dried leaves. A chunk of torn petticoat dangled.

"Only for a lady," she amended, even though she looked far better than I.

"I have rather abandoned being a lady."

"Lady is as lady does," she said in a singsong that made me think it was a local saying.

She clicked her tongue, and something small barreled towards us and jumped up. She caught it expertly and tucked it into the crook of her arm. A roseworm. The scales on his back shone forest-brown above the rich red of his belly.

"You are bound," I said, shocked.

"Four years," she said with a comical eye roll. She held up her left hand, showing a narrow wedding band of silver. "Got a daughter running about, too. She's three, and a right handful. Full of strong opinions, like her father."

"I should like to meet her," I said, but underneath, I was stunned. Only gentry bound draca. Only gentry were *able* to bind. Or so I had been taught.

She gestured to the woods. "Jacob—that's my man—he's off with Mr. Darcy checking the house." Her expression became worried. "They was to be back afore now."

"I am sure he is fine." In fact, fear had tightened my chest, but meaningless reassurance was a social habit—one I found irritating when done to me. However, Aggy smiled her thanks, then cocked her head, watching me.

"You know Mr. Darcy?" she asked.

My concern must have shown. "Yes." I waited for her to declare that I was the notorious Elizabeth Bennet, but she just nodded in sympathy.

"Would you like a cup of tea?" she offered.

"That would be wonderful," I said fervently.

Aggy's house was nicely kept and roomy enough to have a separate room for sleeping. It was less polished than the houses of the Longbourn tenants, but as comfortable. The kitchen had a table, a few chairs, and a tiny iron stove. The village must trade for more than bread and tea.

Together, we brushed the less ground-in debris from my clothes. I tore off the dangling strip of petticoat and borrowed Aggy's tin looking glass in a doomed attempt to discipline my hair, as several pins had been lost.

We sipped nettle tea and chatted about village life. Although her conversation was light, Aggy was worried about her husband's absence. When any voice called, she stopped mid-word to listen. Her nerves were contagious, and I became more worried for Mr. Darcy. When she straightened in her chair then dashed out the door, I dashed out myself.

Mr. Darcy was on the other side of the clearing, clasping arms with Lord Wellington.

I stopped. Seeing him was a tumult—a shock of relief, a pull like a magnet, then acute uncertainty for how I would be greeted. An unannounced visit was a far cry from our choreographed meetings at Jane's wedding. And he had forbidden me from Pemberley.

Behind Mr. Darcy stood my driver from Longbourn, his head hanging. He looked exhausted. Beside him, a fair-haired man in a cotton shirt was being hugged by Aggy.

Unlike Lord Wellington, Mr. Darcy still wore his coat, but he had discarded his waistcoat and neckcloth, leaving his collar open. A curved saber hung from his belt, and a pistol handle protruded from his coat pocket. His face was grave and determined. There was a cut and bruise high on his forehead, half-hidden by his mussed, hanging hair.

"—I must go back," he said. "They have Miss Bennet. I still do not know—" His eyes found mine, and he stopped.

Then I was crushed up against him, the side of my face pressed into his chest, his arms enclosing me. I slid my arms up behind his shoulder blades and held tight. After a breath, his arms loosened. "Do not let go," I whispered, and his grip tightened again.

Finally, the silence made me self-conscious. I heard only the forest—tweets and chitters, rustling leaves. I relaxed my fingers, and Mr. Darcy let go a moment later.

I stepped back, looking up into his eyes, brown with flecks of green like the woods around us.

"I was most worried for you," I said. He nodded. A barrier between us, something that had been tearing and reforming, seemed to fall at last.

Lord Wellington was winding his watch with many meticulous shakes and peering adjustments. My driver was staring at Mr. Darcy and me with wide eyes. But Aggy and her husband were oblivious, their arms around each other's waists, foreheads pressed together while they murmured inaudible secrets. I felt a surge of jealousy for their openness.

Lord Wellington looked up from his watch to Mr. Darcy. "Ah. I see you spotted Miss Bennet. Excellent. If you no longer need to run off and search for her, we should pool our information. I—and Miss Bennet, for that matter—have made discoveries."

"By all means," Mr. Darcy said. He gestured for me to precede him to one of several long tables at the edge of the clearing. We walked, and I imagined his eyes on my hanging hair and bedraggled dress. The sensation was oddly pleasant. His clothes were as bad as mine; when we embraced, my temple had pressed bare skin through his open collar. That thought heated the back of my neck, a heat that drifted down to stir unexpected warmth low in my belly.

While I bit my lip and stared at my toes to settle myself, Mr. Darcy recounted how he and Aggy's husband approached Pemberley House.

"We saw no guards, so moved closer. There was raucous noise inside the house. Yells and coarse songs. Many horses were tethered in the yard, with few men watching them. We swung by the stables and observed they had a new prisoner, which irritated me as we had so diligently relieved them of their last batch." He acknowledged Lord Wellington, who returned a polite nod of his own. "That, and the temptation to reclaim my horse, convinced me to confront the sole guard in the stable, a man of poor loyalty who was willing to be tied and gagged rather than run through. We untied their prisoner and discovered he had driven Miss Bennet here from Longbourn."

Mr. Darcy stopped then, his eyes distant.

"And you chose to investigate further," Lord Wellington said.

"We three chose that together. Even Miss Bennet's driver. He is a stout man and was determined to save his passenger. Together, we snuck into the house cellars."

"What?" I exclaimed. "You went *into* a house full of enemy soldiers?"

"It is my house," Mr. Darcy said as if that explained it.

Lord Wellington seemed unsurprised by this idiotic behavior. "What did you learn?"

"Nothing useful, other than confirming there were no prisoners in the cellars. There was some excitement, and we were forced to depart. But we escaped with my horse, and two others."

"Capital," Lord Wellington said with a grin, as if Mr. Darcy had described an afternoon of shooting quail.

I, however, was annoyed by this masculine bravado. "Wickham is defiling Pemberley House. Portraits were ripped down and burnt. Furniture and decorations smashed."

"It is only a house," Mr. Darcy said.

"It is a very *nice* house!" I exclaimed, then remembered that was not my point. "You must be cautious. Wickham's vendetta is personal. The French commander wished you captured, but if not for that, I distrust how Wickham would treat you. Your life would be at risk."

"Indeed, he made that threat," Mr. Darcy noted calmly.

I crossed my arms and gave Mr. Darcy a glare for his cavalier attitude. He had the decency to appear abashed.

Lord Wellington stepped into the breach. "I counted thirty men around the lake. An even larger force is at the house, and at least ten deployed toward Lambton. We may face a hundred men. Half are disciplined soldiers, French from their training although camouflaged in English civilian clothes. The other half are a decrepit bunch in cast-off English uniforms."

"The ones in uniforms are Englishmen, but of a most poor quality," I said. Mr. Darcy nodded his agreement.

"Even so, we are vastly outnumbered and out-armed," Lord Wellington continued. "Our strategy remains the same: scout, do not engage, and wait for reinforcements." To me, he added, "Darcy and I dispatched two Pemberley footmen by separate routes to raise the alarm. I sent written orders in my name with both. In Lambton, they will notify the constables to raise the army, then requisition horses to proceed to Sheffield. There, they can send notice to the navy by messenger pigeon. The navy will seal any chance of escape at the coast. I assume the French put their men ashore at Gibraltar Point—" He stopped, and his eyes widened. "The French attack at Margate was a feint. They drew our navy south so they could approach this coast."

Mr. Darcy said, "The claim that they would raid the Thames was always ridiculous."

I waited for him to mention that I pointed that out to him, but apparently he had forgotten.

"Are we safe here?" I asked.

"Very safe," Lord Wellington replied. "We have sentries posted, and we are four miles from Pemberley. A four-mile circle is fifty square miles of woods—far too much to search. If they are even searching. I have seen no sign of such an effort, and they cannot start so close to sunset."

"The army will arrive in the morning," Mr. Darcy said with some relish. "And the navy will prevent escape."

"The impossibility of escape seems very obvious," I said.

Lord Wellington looked at me thoughtfully. "Miss Bennet is correct. We have misunderstood something. Their plan is well-provisioned and executed. They would not ignore escape."

"Perhaps they are not searching for us because we do not endanger their plan," I said. "Even if we summon help."

"What is their plan?" Mr. Darcy asked.

I realized he had missed the events by the lake. "They seek to bind a French wyfe to draca. They married three French couples by Pemberley lake. With a stupendous cache of marriage gold."

"Then they may already have left."

"Not yet," I replied. "Wickham said, 'Tomorrow, I am bound for France.' Binding does not occur during the ceremony. The bond forms during the marriage night. It was close to dawn when my sister Jane bound."

"How do you know?" Lord Wellington asked.

"I sensed the creation of their bond."

Lord Wellington's brows rose.

"The strange thing is why they came to the center of England," I said. I looked at Mr. Darcy and braced to reveal a painful truth. "I regret that I believe Mr. Wickham and my sister were conspirators in the theft of books from your library."

Mr. Darcy's shoulders drew rigid. "That is how they knew the location of the library, and that it contained books on draca."

His tone was coldly furious. Wickham's actions were a betrayal. And I had not even shared my darkest suspicion that Wickham himself had shot Mr. Rabb.

"They came because Napoleon is obsessed with the legend of la Tarasque," I said. "He believes it is in Pemberley lake."

"The story of la Tarasque was more than a thousand years ago," Mr. Darcy said. "In France."

"What is la Tarasque?" asked Lord Wellington.

"A wyvern," I said even as Mr. Darcy answered, "A dragon." He clarified, "The French *call* it a dragon. The legends differ, but all describe a creature at least somewhat larger than a wyvern. If we are to name anything a dragon, why not that?"

Lord Wellington was musing. "That would answer another mystery: why attempt such an expensive and risky plot? One wyvern—or three—has no military significance. We proved draca will not fight in battle. And even if the French succeed where we failed, a wyvern would be a single weapon in a sprawling war. Formidable, but no worse than adding one more cannon."

"A wyvern would be worse than a cannon." I was remembering the destruction even our drake could deliver, and how men looked through draca eyes—clumsy, slow, and weak.

"Perhaps," Lord Wellington conceded. "But something uniquely superior, like a dragon, has more than military value. It would be symbolic. A man who calls himself Emperor cares about symbols."

Perhaps Napoleon actually would divorce his second, unloved wife to marry a wyfe who brought a dragon.

Lord Wellington spoke decisively. "None of this affects our military position. The sun is setting. We are secure until morning. Overwhelming reinforcements will arrive. As in many battles, victory is a matter of patience."

48

People were arriving in twos and threes and fours, mostly Britons with blue woad patterns stained on their faces and arms. They were greeted with happy cries and hugs—friends and family spread between villages. The rescued servants from Pemberley had sheltered at a neighboring village, and they arrived together. I received a warm smile from Mrs. Reynolds, and I interrupted little Lucy's curtsy with a tight embrace.

Mr. Darcy caught the eye of a gray-haired man with a spectacular flowing mustache. He joined us at the table, setting down a large canvas bag, and Mr. Darcy introduced him as Mr. Digweed, "headman of the Pemberley Briton clans, and a partner in management of the Pemberley estate."

"I go by Ed, for the most part," Mr. Digweed added as he shook hands with Lord Wellington, who introduced himself as Arthur.

"Miss Elizabeth Bennet," I said, feeling some formality was required when meeting a man, and extended my hand.

He took my fingers, studied me with eyes that reminded me of Papa's penetrating gaze, and executed a tasteful bow over my hand. "Miss Bennet. We are honored that you join our Beltane eve celebration. I know you did not intend your visit, but you are welcome." He nodded to the gentlemen. "As are you, Arthur. And you, Fitzwilliam. It has been some time."

"Three summers," answered Mr. Darcy. "I am pleased to return. It has been too long."

Mr. Digweed dug in a pocket and consulted a hefty gold watch. "If you will excuse me, my duties call." He rustled in his large bag and put on a leather headdress with a pair of spiraling ram's horns affixed to the sides, then withdrew a two-foot-long bronze trumpet which flared into a roaring wyvern head. He nodded to me, "Miss Bennet," the heavy horns flopping, then walked to the center of the clearing.

The sunset was lighting the edges of broken clouds with flaming orange, and the fire colors gleamed on bronze as Mr. Digweed lifted his trumpet. The instrument was shaped to rise vertically like a tall swan's neck, and the wyvern-mouth bell faced forward high above his head.

He blew a long, tenor note, strident and brassy, and a shout rose from the scattered crowd. He blew again, and silence fell, then a third time. With that, a cloud caught the reddening sun, and dusk spread over the sky. The glade dimmed as if the blast was a breath of night.

"*Druí wides!*" he called. "Oak friends! Gather, for it is the eve of summer! Eostre ripens in lazy splendor. Bel stokes the heat of sun and earth. Drown the hearths. Brighten the world afresh for swelling fruits and glorious bounty!"

Around us, torches and fires hissed and sputtered as they were quenched. The gloaming deepened, as if woad had infused the world.

"What need we now?" cried Mr. Digweed.

Fire! came the shout from all around. Beside me, Mr. Darcy called it out in his baritone, as loud as anyone else. His face shone with the same unashamed celebration as the others. I was the outsider, observing and ignorant.

He saw my gaze and leaned close to speak. "Every year, my parents brought me, and later Georgiana as well, to the Beltane festival. Since my mother's death, I have come less often, but it is a joy to return. The celebrations are ancient, older than England. They existed before the Romans came. Even before Christ." He gave a reassuring smile. "And the Britons are generous hosts. You have been welcomed, and nothing is expected. You give no offense if you simply watch."

"I am honored to attend," I said.

The boy who met Lord Wellington and me walked solemnly into the clearing. He knelt and began sawing a bow back and forth to spin a stick, the bottom end buried in wood shavings. When a thread of smoke rose, he set the bow aside to blow gently. Flame crackled to life, and a cry rose: *Teine eigin! Teine eigin!*

The strange trumpet blew again, and a flutter of wings rose from the forest—a flock of wrens. They swirled into the clearing, a darting cloud that circled three times then soared into the sky and scattered.

Mr. Digweed returned to our table. He removed his heavy horned headdress and thumped it onto the bench, saying wryly, "Gets hot, that." Lord Wellington asked him about the ritual, and they began conversing, for all the world like two gentlemen at a refined dinner. I overheard their pleasant surprise at discovering they both attended Eton. It seemed Mr. Darcy's father had sponsored Mr. Digweed's education.

"Would you care for mead, Lizzy?" Aggy was balancing a carved platter with a half-dozen wooden cups.

"Is it strong?" I asked doubtfully. I still remembered my headache after gulping Colonel Forster's drink at the wedding.

"A bit. I'll give you a lady's taste." She poured most of one cup into another then passed me the almost empty container. I sipped. Honey and spirits swirled on my tongue, but no more potent than port.

"Mr. Darcy?" Aggy offered him the platter, a little shy.

"Thank you, Aggy," he said and took a cup.

In the clearing, four enthusiastic boys had built the kindled flame into a roaring fire. They placed spits with trussed hares and joints of goat.

"Is that the end?" I asked Mr. Darcy.

"No, only the start. There are other ceremonies after the feast." The fire reflected in his eyes as his mood became grave and disciplined. "Miss Bennet, when the army has restored order, I must ask that you leave the Pemberley grounds."

"Because the 'darkness of Pemberley' is such a danger?" I asked lightly. He nodded. "I am afraid, Mr. Darcy, that you have not convinced me. 'Darkness' sounds frightening, but all I have observed is an area without draca. In fact, I have learned the emptiness is not due to Pemberley at all. It is an effect of the lake. All three sister lakes are surrounded by an area empty of draca."

He pushed his hands through his hair, his knuckles white. "You do not understand."

"Inform me, then. But do not decide for me. You have a habit of secretly solving problems—real or imagined—with excessively noble solutions. I prefer more communication and less self-sacrifice." His eyes had widened. Good. "I am aware you seek to divest yourself of Pemberley."

"How can you know that?" He seemed stunned.

"Your aunt visited with the sole purpose of castigating me." Mr. Darcy closed his eyes and groaned. "Also, Lord Wellington told me."

He took a deep breath. "Abandoning Pemberley would remove the risk. I am more than willing—"

"*Really*, Mr. Darcy," I exclaimed in my most affected imitation of Miss Bingley's coquettish tone. "You must pay attention. Men are convinced that grand self-sacrifice is romantic, but women are practical. I quite like Pemberley. I shall be vexed if you lose it."

I thought he would smile at that, but he became more serious.

"You are right," he said. "You deserve to understand. If my hesitation seems cowardly, it is because I am sharing a secret so dark that I have told no one. Not even my sister."

My teasing mood fell away. He wet his lips and began:

"The darkness of Pemberley stains the death of both my parents. My father was a vigorous man. His death was tragic but innocent, a fall from a spooked horse where he struck his head. The suddenness would shock any family, but to my mother it was… devastating. Her affinity with draca revolved around skills of healing. These were most remarkable when tending wyves and their draca, but she was a great healer for all, and it was rare when she could not save a life.

"When my father fell, she was miles away. She had ridden far to be outside the darkness of Pemberley, which she found oppressive. 'A lifeless void,' she called it. I had been hunting with my father, and I tended him while Mr. Rabb raced to find her. They returned at a gallop, but my mother was too late to save her husband.

"She blamed her absence for my father's death. Blame became obsession, and her obsession fixed on the darkness of Pemberley. She would sit for hours, eyes closed, immersed in it. She began to rave. She claimed it was aware. Lurking. She became convinced her wyvern was blocking her from seeing the truth of it. 'Too bright,' she cried when her wyvern was near. One day, a month after my father's death, she invoked incredible power. My sister, Georgiana, felt it. She screamed in her room. And I… I felt something also. I saw something. A flash in my mind. My mother had severed her binding to her wyvern."

He stopped speaking, his eyes narrow with remembered pain.

"A wyvern's awareness is a wonderful thing," I said softly. "Wise and old. But brilliant to behold." It was hard to imagine the pain that would drive a wyfe to such a choice.

Mr. Darcy continued as if he had not heard.

"My mother's sanity had held until then. She had been unbearably saddened by my father's death, crying for hours each day, but rational. But when her wyvern left—when she commanded him to leave, for he did not leave willingly—binding sickness attacked her mind. When a wyfe has bound before, it is fast, much faster than you saw with your sister. And before she married, my mother battled her own evils of the mind. Those returned to torment her.

"In days, she was retreating into fantasy. But I was certain she had the power to cure herself. When she was lucid, we discussed it. When she asked me to gather rowan flowers for the ritual, I rejoiced, thinking her senses intact. But when I returned, her face was sunk in her bath, weighted with a scarf tied around heavy ornaments. Her death was unnatural. Self-inflicted. If I had stayed, I could have saved her, but like her, I was away when I was needed by someone I loved.

"Facing that horror, I chose to conceal the manner of her death. I could have borne the stigma—I care nothing for condemnation by puritanical society or the hidebound Church—but I wished to shield Georgiana from learning her mother chose to abandon her. I am sure the closest of our staff guessed the truth, but Georgiana was only eleven." His shoulders rose and fell. "She has no idea."

He was staring into the fire, the planes of his face carved with pain. The night had deepened, and we were lit by the shifting warmth of the bonfire while surrounded by dark woods.

"I did not intend to force your revelation," I said. "But I am glad you have trusted me to understand." When he did not respond, I took his hand. "Look around us. What do you see?"

After a few breaths, he looked away from the fire. "Blackness."

"A mind, hurt and mourning, may fear the dark. But the darkness of Pemberley lake is no more evil than the dark wood around us. Does the dark of night plunge you into despair?"

"No. But the dark of night ends."

I closed my eyes and opened my mind. His fingers tensed as he recognized what I was doing. "The darkness of Pemberley ends. We are outside it here, a half mile or so past the edge. I can sense it. A circle of emptiness around the lake. But it is no more malevolent than a stretch of rock without grass or trees, or remote, unsettled countryside."

"You see the *entirety* of it?" He was surprised. "My mother could not. She had to ride miles to sense anything but emptiness."

I was surprised as well. When I summoned those tiny draca, I had strained to reach past the edge. Now, I sensed sparks of awareness beyond the lake, more than twice as far.

I opened my eyes and met his wondering gaze. "My abilities have been growing for some months." The suddenness of the change left me uneasy. I myself did not understand what was happening.

When I traveled here to confront Mr. Darcy's obsession with the darkness of Pemberley, I was emboldened by a slightly smug sense of superiority. After all, I was the one who experienced the sensation, not him.

His revelation had not changed my opinion. I had no fears for my sanity in the presence of Pemberley lake. But his pain was real, fueled by guilt and regret. Watching him remember that horrible day tore me as well. Things that seem simple in the complacency of self-satisfied confidence become intricate puzzles when you care enough to understand the layers and folds of another life.

I tightened my grip around his tense fingers. Under that symptom of his unease, his hand was strong, thick with muscle and solid with bone.

"I would not presume to advise on the intimacy of a brother and sister," I said. "But Georgiana is a woman now. A stronger woman than an older brother's memory of a child may recognize. There may be comfort in ending a secret you have held alone."

"I no longer hold it alone," he said, and the tension in his fingers relaxed. "But your advice is good."

"Then remember what I said about Pemberley lake. Before I left, I asked Jane's wyvern about the darkness of Pemberley. She answered, '*emptiness is not darkness. deference is not fear*.' I do not fear it."

He gave an amused chuckle. "I had not heard your sister bound a wyvern. Although I am unsurprised. She is your sister, after all. I believe that is only the sixth bound wyvern in England."

"She is a beautiful creature. Gold," I said absently, thinking of my own secret: Mr. Darcy's aunt, the formidable Lady Catherine, had never bound her wyvern. But that secret was no burden. It could stay hidden.

A memory that had been gnawingly vague snapped into focus.

"I have seen these people before," I exclaimed. "These Britons. At Rosings, Lady Catherine's wyvern showed me their image while telling me to seek Pemberley lake. They were decorated for Beltane…"

I closed my eyes. There were five bound draca in the crowd. I touched them and felt their attention shift to me. One was curious, and I let our awareness merge.

A draca's vision of the celebration entered my mind. The fire was a column of swirling heat high into the sky. Human and draca bodies were bright with the warmth of life. And the Britons' faces were like the images shown by the wyvern, the blue stripes of woad dye shining brilliant indigo on their faces.

The draca's view turned and loped past swinging skirts and men's legs. The view settled on me seated at one end of the table, with Mr. Darcy's straight-shouldered frame beside me. But to the draca's vision, I looked different from the other people. I was surrounded by a golden glow, and my eyes burned like sunlit diamonds.

The night had become eerily quiet. I heard only the crackle of the fire. I opened my eyes.

The five draca were seated in a perfect semi-circle, staring up at me.

Everyone was staring at me.

In the silence, Mr. Digweed stood and raised his wooden cup. "Elizabeth Bennet. Guest of the *druí wide*. Bel's high beasts honor the wyves who carry his most brilliant fire. Behold! A great wyfe graces Pemberley's hills. Our Beltane is blessed!" Cups were raised amid shouts of approval and thumping on tables.

Mr. Darcy lifted his cup with an amused smile. Lord Wellington raised his also and held it until our gazes met. His expression was serious and considering.

There was a rush of activity around the fire. Meats were pulled from spits and carved, heaping platters with chunks of rabbit and slices of goat. Bowls of roast tubers were passed—small potatoes, slices of cattail root, and little round roots called pignuts, which were a delicacy at Longbourn as they are tiresome to gather. I was handed a dish of white goat butter mashed with tiny garlic flowers to slather on top. I had never had goat butter before, and it was delicious—creamy with an aroma of spring grass. I would need to procure some at home.

A string of people introduced themselves, some shy, others boisterous. There were more names than I could remember, although I learned the names of the bound wyves. The curious draca whose vision I had shared was Aggy's roseworm. He was affectionate for his breed, almost like a tyke, although one that could throw fire. Mr. Digweed's wyfe had bound a breed of winged draca no larger than a swallow, and a newly bound wyfe of eighteen had a broccworm, a more robust cousin to Lydia's ferretworm and a prodigious tunneler.

The wyves seemed unconcerned that the outside world would consider their bindings remarkable. I was sure they knew their status was unusual; the villagers were not ignorant or isolated. Several husbands had studied at universities before returning to the hills, and many children attended the Lambton school.

Aggy and another young wyfe named Ellen squeezed into our increasingly crowded table. At the other end, their husbands laughed and traded stories with Mr. Darcy, Lord Wellington, and Mr. Digweed.

I asked Aggy if the bound wyves were married in the Lambton church.

"'Course not! I was married right here," she said. "Ed married us in the true way. None of those crosses and Christ. We do as nature and the Mother command."

I thought of the French couples plowing through an unfamiliar English ceremony. Perhaps the Catholic service would work as well. Or was the binding-of-gold the key?

Aggy was so happily unreserved that I asked a question that would be rude elsewhere. "Did you have marriage gold?"

Aggy petted her roseworm, curled in her lap. "The Darcys gift a gold guinea to any wyfe who wants to bind."

"Mind you," inserted Ellen, "not all the girls choose that as their wedding favor. Some ask for a stove, or good pots."

A guinea of marriage gold. That was an astonishingly generous wedding gift.

I heard a buzz, and a familiar tiny shape flashed past us in the air.

"A needledrac!" cried Ellen. She pulled a flower from her hair and dangled it over her head.

"She hopes it will land on her flower," Aggy explained through laughter. "'Tis good luck to have a visit."

"I have never seen that flower before," I said. Ellen was now waving it wildly. It was long and tubular, like an oversized honeysuckle blossom but blue and mauve.

"Draca breath," Aggy said. "They grow only by a needledrac hive, and the dracs gather only their nectar. So the dracs give you a prick if you come close. But we risk it for the essence."

"*What?*" I could not believe my ears.

"Draca essence," Aggy said, mystified at my reaction. "From stewing the flowers. We keep doses in case of crawler sting."

She spoke with such nonchalance that I felt foolish. But after both our Scottish laundress and our journal mentioned draca essence, I had inquired at every apothecary in Hertfordshire. No one had ever heard of it.

The celebration was becoming noisy as food was cleared and the mead jug was passed. I took a tiny splash and received some teasing for my restraint.

No teasing was required for the male half of our table. Lord Wellington and Mr. Digweed were trading rambunctious toasts, alternating between stout English officers and a pantheon of gods and goddesses. Mr. Darcy was good-naturedly keeping pace, although he sipped rather than swigged.

He saw me watching and raised his cup in a quiet salute, smiling in the firelight. I smiled back, and my stomach did an unexpected, trembling flip.

What would happen between us after this evening? My encounters with Mr. Darcy had become driven by my determination to… to speak the truth. To unravel the tangle of our complicated intersections. But our tangle had come free on its own. We had shared secrets and fears and wishes. I was more intimate with this man, whom I had thought so coldly proper, than anyone but Jane.

I remembered Papa's words before he died: "Mr. Darcy, to my surprise, is a man who draws confidences."

Papa's posy ring hung under my dress, suspended on a thin chain. I touched the cloth and felt it on my breast, close to my heart. The ring my father gave me to carry his blessing.

If there were no more painful truths to spill, what came next?

Two men began a lively tune on reed flutes, music in an unusual mode that made me think of Irish folk tunes. Couples began to dance. It was unlike any ball I had ever attended. A man and woman danced the entire song together without changing partners, spinning each other enthusiastically. When the music ended, they returned to their seats, laughing and holding hands, while the musicians raced into the next.

Aggy and Ellen's husbands arrived to claim them for a dance. Aggy parked her roseworm on the bench beside me where he curled up, peering at me.

Mr. Darcy and I were now an island of stillness in the rollicking crowd. Lord Wellington and Mr. Digweed were waving their arms in some clashing rendition of an Eton song.

"Miss Elizabeth Bennet," Mr. Darcy said with sudden decision. "If you are not already engaged, would you honor me with this dance?"

I was so surprised that I answered very ungracefully. "Are you serious?"

"I am."

"I do not know the steps."

"Nor do I." He stood and offered his hand. "Perhaps the cotillion?"

I took his hand and we walked among the dancers.

The cotillion is a dance for four couples in a square. One spends half the dance with other partners. It cannot be danced by two people alone. And yet, we began, crossing the imaginary square hand-in-hand to start the pattern. When I turned by habit to change partners, Mr. Darcy was there to take my hand and continue. Around us, couples inked in woad spun past, somehow never colliding as we traced our elegant shapes in the firelight. I began to smile, then I laughed at the ridiculousness of it.

We met in the center of our imaginary square and took each other's hands.

"Do you enjoy the cotillion?" I asked—the same words that broke the silence of our first dance—as we stepped to one side, then the other.

"With you, I do," he replied, and my heart skipped as we turned, then took each other's hands again.

The song ended at an awkward point of the pattern, standing side-by-side with my right hand in his left. We turned to each other, then let go. In a way, we had been doing this since that first assembly ball in Meryton—a step closer, and then a retreat. But closer each time, pressing toward some irrevocable threshold.

Happy shouts rose from the other side of the clearing. Mr. Digweed had donned his horned hat, and a couple was kneeling in front of him while children waved branches of yellow flowers and sang lilting words.

"What are they doing?" I asked.

"They are handfasting," Mr. Darcy answered. "A Beltane betrothal for a year and a day. At the end, the couple chooses to marry or to go their own way without recrimination. Most decide sooner, one way or the other."

The couple held out their clasped hands. Mr. Digweed began winding a red cord around their wrists in a complex knot.

"The statue of your mother has a red cord in her hand," I said.

"My mother and father were betrothed at Beltane."

"Oh." I swallowed. "That is romantic."

"My father asked my mother to dance. After they danced, he asked her to marry him." My heart took flight like a scared rabbit at that, and my pretended courage for speaking my mind vanished with it. I was staring at my feet when he continued, "You are too generous to trifle with me. If your feelings are still what they were at Rosings, tell me so. My affections and wishes are unchanged, but one word from you will silence me on this subject forever."

"My feelings are altered," I managed. That did not really make the point. I forced my gaze up to meet his, and it became easy to speak. "My feelings are profoundly changed and most favorable."

Wordlessly, he held out his hand. I took it, thrilling as our palms met again. We walked to where Mr. Digweed stood, chatting with his wyfe while the couple he had betrothed swirled into the dance. He turned to us with a wide grin, then became serious.

"Mr. Darcy," he said with a formal bow.

Mr. Darcy said in solemn recitation, "On this eve of Beltane, we would tie our hands." Mr. Digweed's wyfe drew a surprised breath, her eyes shining. Whispers and nudges spread through the crowd, turning heads and quieting the clearing.

Mr. Digweed's wise eyes were on me. "Miss Bennet. Honored guest and blessed of Bel. This man would be your betrothed. This is a solemn choice of great import. Knowing this, would you handfast with him?"

"I would," I said.

A murmur was growing in the crowd, but not due to my words. Brilliant pinpricks of light were streaking in swooping paths through the forest, mauve and violet and blue like cool sparks among the trees. These were not the dim flickers of glowworms on a summer evening. The branches and leaves were illuminated in moving patterns, as if by hundreds of bright candles.

Mr. Digweed raised a red cord in his hand. "Offer your hands, and I shall bind you." We held out our clasped hands, my right in Mr. Darcy's left, and Mr. Digweed began to wind the cord in an elaborate pattern that joined our wrists. He said:

"This knot is your solemn troth beneath star and sky, a promise to join your lives like two green shoots that are braided by their summer's growth. For a year and a day, flourish with one another. Then wed, and your joined love will ripen to eternal heartwood."

Our hands were now tied in an elaborate figure eight of doubled cord. Mr. Digweed lifted his hands to the sky. "Or, without remonstration or reproof, you may unfasten and let the winds lift you like seeds of maple, carrying you apart to land afresh and grow again. By undoing this cord, I declare you free to leave betrothal without harm or broken promise."

He reached for the knot, but with my free hand, I caught his fingers. "What if the cord is left?"

He cleared his throat. "If the sacred knot remains tied, by our ways, betrothal becomes marriage. Although English law would not—"

Our clasped hands had tightened around each other while he spoke. I was staring into Mr. Darcy's eyes. I did not care about English law.

I said, "I would keep this knot tied."

Mr. Darcy's free hand rose. His fingertips brushed my temple and cheek. "I do not require a year and a day to accept this most profound honor to myself and my family."

The pinpricks of light in the forest rushed skyward like shooting stars, then swooped and circled into the clearing—needledrac, the same tiny draca that had come to rescue me earlier, but in the thousands, their bodies shining in the night. They swirled around us, a cyclone of blurring color that lit us like lanterns, then rushed around the clearing, darting among the people as joyous cries rose.

Mr. Digweed's eyes were wide and joyful. "Bel has blessed you!" he cried. "Behold our May Queen and Oak King. This is the sacred wedding. The union of Earth and Sky!" A cheer rose.

In the noise, Mr. Digweed bent his head close and said, "It is customary, though not required, to exchange rings. Do you, by any chance…"

With my free hand, I drew the chain with my father's ring over my head. I let go of Mr. Darcy's fingers to open the chain and remove the ring.

I looked into Mr. Darcy's eyes. "When my father returned from your rescue of Lydia, he knew we were destined to marry. He gave me his ring as his blessing. He would wish you to wear it." Mr. Darcy, his eyes brightened, nodded. I placed the ring, still warm from my breast, on his finger.

Mr. Darcy withdrew his pocket watch and pressed a catch that opened the back, revealing a delicate ring of braided hair. "My sister wove this after our parents' death. It is her symbol of our continuing family. She would wish you to wear it, at least until I can provide something more permanent." He gave a wry smile. "I know this because she has expressed great frustration with what she calls my 'glacially slow courtship' of a woman she wishes were her sister." Even as the significance of his offer pulled my heart, I laughed, remembering her unsubtle hint to me.

I offered my left hand, and he slipped the ring on my finger. Emotion flooded me, cool and profound and purifying as ice-cold water.

Mr. Digweed lifted a wooden cup. "Repeat these words: The sweetness of honey for love. The sharpness of spirit for challenges to overcome. Under the night sky, I am wed." We said the words together. The cup touched my lips. I drank, mead sparkling on my tongue, then Mr. Darcy drank. My husband drank.

Then we were standing, facing each other, grinning like fools, our tied hands clasped again, and the crowd cheering while blue and violet streaks filled the sky with celebratory corkscrews and twists.

Hands pushed and tugged us across the clearing. Voices shouted "May Queen" and "Oak King." Branches of yellow blossoms were banged over our heads, raining golden petals.

In the frenzy, Aggy caught my arm, her grin touched with friendly concern, and asked if she should shoo people away.

"This is glorious," I answered. I had never been so happy.

White cloth was drawn aside. Eager hands pushed us through, and the cloth closed behind us.

We were alone in an improvised tent of linen draped over a frame of willow branches. Two small oil lamps lit the intimate space. Amber and gold blossoms were tied in graceful sprays and scattered over the ground, soaking the air with sweetness. Woolen blankets and cotton quilts lay thick atop a mattress of soft green branches. Our marriage bed.

Outside, the music resumed, and the sounds of revelry retreated.

My right wrist was still tied to Mr. Darcy's left, and our fingers were twined in their own knot. I took his other hand, looking up at him.

"This is the bed of the May Queen and Oak King." His tone was stilted, a return of the old, excessively formal Mr. Darcy. He drew a deep breath. "It is a custom of the Britons. I… I am excruciatingly happy. We will marry again, of course, under English law. Miss Bennet, with the suddenness of this, if you would prefer—"

"I am not Miss Bennet," I whispered.

His grip on my hands tightened. "Elizabeth."

"You are getting closer." The smile on my lips was trembling.

"Mrs. Darcy," he whispered. "Wyfe."

I stood on my toes and pressed my lips to his. Our tied hands were clenched tight, but I freed my other hand and buried my fingers in the tousled hair on the back of his neck. His arm caught my waist, pulling me into a kiss that was stunning, and ferocious, and hungry.

I JARRED AWAKE. My closed eyes held the shimmering afterimage of a distant silver line. My ears heard the echo of a joyful chord.

Hesitantly—remembering where I was—I opened my eyes. It was dark in our tent, the lamps extinguished. The sole radiance was moonlight illuminating the cloth roof. Outside, there was the creaking of crickets.

I lay curled against Mr. Darcy, our bare skin together, a quilt pulled crookedly over us. The chill of night cooled my exposed neck and shoulders.

The muscles of his shoulder and chest shifted under my cheek. "What was that?" he muttered, his voice blurred with sleep.

"A wyfe has bound," I said. "By the lake."

His breathing was already returning to the rhythms of sleep.

49

I woke to the singing of thrushes. The linen roof glowed honey-yellow under fingers of morning sun.

The village outside was still. It had been a late night for the revelers.

It was a late night for us as well. The red cord that had tied our wrists lay in a corner, tangled with our clothes. We had worn the cord a long time, dragging it around like a clothesline hung with his coat and shirt and my dress and petticoats. What *had* we been thinking?

"I am married," I said to myself wonderingly.

Mr. Darcy stirred. His hand slid over my shoulder blade and down my spine until it rested low on my waist. I felt myself warming below his fingers in a remarkable manner.

I nuzzled his shoulder. "What shall I call you? I can hardly refer to you as Mr. Darcy."

"I should like to call you Elizabeth."

I smiled. "Did you not name your ship 'Lizzy'?"

His shoulder shook with a chuckle. "That was in the heat of the moment."

"I approve of heated moments." I traced my fingers across his skin, hair tickling under my fingertips. I had never touched a man's bare chest before last night. His upper ribs were wrapped in thick muscle that rolled into impressive shoulders, a little more solid on his right side. All those fencing bouts.

"What are you pondering so seriously?" he asked.

Guiltily, I dragged my gaze up to his dark brown eyes. "I am meditating on the very great pleasure which a pair of fine shoulders can bestow." He chuckled again. But in fact, I was wondering about something. "Had you done that before? What we did last night?" I felt biting jealousy at the thought, but it was rumored that gentlemen had such experiences.

"No."

I pushed up on my elbows to see him better. "Then how did you have all those ideas?"

An endearing pink flush climbed his neck. "There are books in the Pemberley library. Documenting the duties of a husband to ensure that his wyfe binds."

"The famous books! Mr. Bingley said you gave him one."

"*Lent* him one, yes." His eyes crinkled as he smiled. "I kept the best ones."

"And what makes one better than the others?"

"Some have illustrations."

I laughed and curled against his side again. "Well, I can attest they are effective. Although we shall never really know."

Because we had not bound. The finality of that was a little strange. I had no regrets, but it would be challenging to explain to Mamma. Fortunately, Jane's wedding had been very traditional.

What *would* I call Mr. Darcy? I could not imagine Fitz. But Fitzwilliam was a huge mouthful. Rather like some of those ideas in the dark. I chuckled, shocked at how wicked I was being.

My unnamed husband sat up and began untangling our clothes.

"You cannot be thinking of leaving," I said in a warning tone.

"Only for a minute. I wish to confirm that sentries are set. We are in the middle of a war."

I caught his arm. "A minute is too long."

"Half a minute. Wait for me." He kissed me hard, a hand on each side of my face. I was rather gasping when he finished, and I watched him pull on trousers and a shirt in a dazed state. He kissed me again, then pushed out through the white cloth flaps of our door.

I curled under the quilt to find the warmth of his body, then buried my nose for a hint of musk and maleness.

I WOKE with a start in the cold bed. The sun had moved. At least an hour had passed. Outside, I heard the relaxed chatter of people at breakfast.

I dressed and pushed through the flaps of the tent. There were a dozen vaguely familiar faces around the clearing, but no one I knew. I went to Aggy's cottage. Her door stood open, so I poked my head in.

"Lizzy!" she exclaimed and came to take my hands. "You two surprised us last night! This will be a storied Beltane. I am so happy for you." Her smile became predatory. "And such a man! I would still be abed."

"Yes, I… have you seen Mr. Darcy this morning?" I was embarrassed by the question but too uneasy not to ask.

"No. Is he out and about, then? Here, let's find Ed."

She led me to where several men were talking, including Mr. Digweed and Lord Wellington, who rose as I approached.

"Good morning…" Lord Wellington's greeting trailed off. Probably he wondered if he had actually witnessed a wedding.

"Mrs. Darcy," I confirmed for him, and he nodded. "Have you seen Mr. Darcy this morning?"

"No," he said, becoming brisk and efficient. "He is not in the camp. When did you see him last?"

"An hour ago. Or more. He said he wished to check if sentries were placed. I expected him back long before now."

We walked to a group of boys talking in a mix of childish sopranos and freshly deepened men's tones.

"Has Mr. Darcy been to see you this morning?" asked Lord Wellington. There was a chorus of No's, but the boy who had met us in the woods pushed to his feet. With nervous eyes, he held out a folded paper.

"Here you go, ma'am," he said. "He made me swear to wait 'til you come out."

The paper was addressed with a single word in Mr. Darcy's hand: *Elizabeth*. A rush of foreboding made my fingers tremble as I unfolded it. Tucked inside was a folded envelope of different paper. I put that aside and read his note first:

"Dearest Elizabeth,

Forgive me for not seeking your permission. In this one thing, I have no choice. I will do all in my power to return to you.

Your loving husband, Fitzwilliam Darcy."

With a shaking hand, I pushed that into Lord Wellington's fingers, then picked up the other envelope. It was addressed in savage, large letters: *DARCY*. A two-inch vertical slash severed the R in Darcy.

The boy said, "I found that when I checked Pemberley House this morning. The house was empty, but that was on the door. Stabbed through by a big knife."

I pulled the envelope open and something sparkling fell into my palm. But my eyes were fixed on the text, which I recognized as Wickham's hand:

"Life has a funny way of balancing the scales. Come alone and unarmed. We will be at her favorite place. Hurry, or I shall grow bored and amuse myself. —GW"

In my palm was a few broken inches of fine gold chain and a golden musical note.

"Wickham has Miss Darcy." I said it even as terror froze my breath in my throat. She had planned to return to Pemberley a day after me. But if she traveled fast with few stops, she could have arrived last evening.

Men began running and calling. I was rooted by my frightened imagination. This would not be an honorable meeting. There would be no duel. Wickham would simply kill my husband.

Lord Wellington was beside me and repeating something. Finally, he said, "Miss Bennet!" I realized he had been addressing me as Mrs. Darcy. I must learn my new name.

He stood with another grim-faced man, both of them armed with musket and pistol. "Do you know where they are? Where Miss Darcy's favorite place is?"

"She enjoys her music room at Pemberley," I said. "But it cannot be that, if the house is abandoned."

"You have no other idea?"

I shook my head. The men turned away and began conversing at a furious pace.

"I can find them," I said. The ability to act altered my terror. Compressed it. Throttled it into a hard core of fury.

Lord Wellington turned, his cool eyes assessing me.

"I can find Lydia," I said. "She will be with Wickham. But you must take me with you."

"Impossible," Lord Wellington said.

"My sister can kill you with a thought from a hundred yards away. Only I can counter her."

I remembered Denny, killed by a massive foul crawler. There had been some break between him and Wickham, and he had argued with Lydia as well. Had he been targeted for death? His clothing had been smeared with foul crawler venom. Did that attract the monster, or had Lydia commanded it to murder her friend?

"It is too dangerous for you to accompany us," Lord Wellington was saying. "We have two saddled horses and no lady's tack. I cannot lose a man to—"

I was becoming impatient. "I am not one of your soldiers, Lord Wellington. You do not command me. If you wish my direction, you have no choice in this matter." He did not answer, so I continued, "Are the horses saddled? We must hurry."

His lips compressed, but he nodded.

Mr. Darcy, of course, had taken his own horse. Fortunately, one of the remaining horses was a modestly sized mare. She was saddled for a man, but that was almost a relief. I had not ridden much since I was a girl, still young enough to ride astride.

Lord Wellington gave me a leg up, his face averted. I hauled up my skirts and threw my leg over the saddle, then plucked at my bunched petticoats in a futile attempt at modesty. I managed to hide my knees.

"Where?" Lord Wellington asked after he mounted.

I closed my eyes. That core of fury refused to fade—it blazed like a red-hot coal in my chest—but this time, emotion did not block me. Instead, the world snapped crystal-clear in my mind. The void surrounding the lake. Sparks of awareness elsewhere.

And there, on a hill beyond the lake, was a seething, churning spot of black filth.

I opened my eyes, comparing the hills ahead with my mental impression. "This way." I tapped my heels and led off at a trot. For once, I regretted not being a better horsewoman—if I tried to gallop through these rough woods, I would be unseated in moments.

Mr. Darcy would have galloped. He handled his powerful stallion with perfect ease. He must be far ahead of us.

I tightened my legs, and my mare quickened her trot.

A mile was eaten up, then three. Twenty minutes. The astringent scent of horse sweat grew, my mount's chest heaving as we climbed another peak. The valley with Pemberley lake came into view.

"Wait," called Lord Wellington. I reined in, and he pulled up beside me. "Gunpowder. There has been a battle."

A hint of sulfurous smoke caught my nostrils.

Distantly, I made out scattered bodies on the lakeshore. Dozens. All still.

"Has the army come?" I asked.

Lord Wellington shaded his eyes to study the lake. "Not our army. Where do we go?"

I closed my eyes to check, then pointed. "Around the lake, and over that hill."

"Let us proceed cautiously."

We headed down, abreast at a slow trot. The carnage resolved into human detail—limbs trapped at angles disturbingly unlike the calm of sleep, and dirt-smeared faces with gaping mouths. Lord Wellington counted under his breath. "Five… Ten… Fifteen…" He reached thirty-five and fell silent.

Ten yards short of the nearest body, he said, "Stop. Wait here." He dismounted and walked between sprawled shapes until he reached a man I recognized as the French commander.

The smell of gunpowder was strong. And something beneath it. Sour orange and bitter almond.

I dismounted and walked to the nearest body, a man of twenty in nondescript worker's clothes. A pistol had fallen on the stony ground. The man lay on his side, arched backward as if bent on an invisible rack. An agonizing pose, even in death.

His face was swollen and discolored. His eyes bulged. A pair of savage punctures, one on his cheek, the other on his neck, had risen in hideous purple blisters. They were six inches apart. This was not the sting of a palm-sized crawler.

"All dead," Lord Wellington said beside me. I had not heard him approach. "All French. None are shot. They were killed by some foul method. Their weapons are discharged, but they did not reload. Their powder is hardly touched. A short and brutal battle."

"Lydia killed them. She summoned foul crawlers." The words left my mouth even as I wondered if I believed them. "She threatened this if a French woman bound." I looked over the strewn bodies, then began walking toward a different shape on the rocky shore. A woman.

It was one of the French wives. Her beautiful gown had been replaced by a coarse-woven brown dress. A disguise for escape. One finger bore a plain gold wedding ring. Her face was not discolored, but her neck and chest were soaked in sticky, drying blood. A tiny gold cross hung askew from a chain around her neck.

Lord Wellington knelt beside her. "She died differently. Her throat was cut—" He stopped when I held out a hand. I had heard something.

I whispered, "Someone is alive." I ran to another figure. Another woman.

A pair of gray eyes, crusted with dried tears and exhausted by pain, met mine.

"*Dieu merci. La sorcière l'a prise…*"

I knelt beside her. "*Je parle très mal le français.*" I speak very bad French.

Her hand caught mine and squeezed. "The witch. She took Alouette and her beautiful firedrake. *Il était si beau…*" Her voice became a ragged gasp. "*Où est mon mari?*" Her other hand fumbled until it found the hand of the dead man beside her. Her husband.

Lord Wellington knelt and lifted the torn side of her blood-soaked dress. He became still. Gently, he set the cloth back.

"*Le lac tremblait,*" she whispered. "The water moved."

The lake was dark glass. But a few feet above the water's edge, there was a line of damp flotsam.

"Did Alouette bind la Tarasque?" I asked. A worse thought occurred to me. "Did Lydia?"

Her head fell back. She whispered, "Stay away from the village."

"What?"

"Lambton. *Ses hommes le surveillent. C'est dangereux.*" Her words were fading.

I looked at Lord Wellington. He said, "They hold Lambton. She says it is dangerous."

The French woman rested, her eyes closed. Around me, the nightmare landscape seemed to flicker and jar.

My sister could not do this. This foreign woman was hiding the truth. She should not even be here. I pushed her shoulder. "Who killed the French soldiers?" She lay still. I shook her harder. "*Who did it?*"

Lord Wellington's hand caught my wrist, his fingers digging in hard. "She is gone."

I yanked my hand free and stood. Stones grated under my feet. I turned, looking for some way to understand what had happened. What was true.

"She had no reason to lie," Lord Wellington said behind me. "There is no sign of English troops. I must assume our messengers were intercepted in Lambton. Wickham's men could secure it by claiming to be English militia."

"She said a French woman, Alouette, bound a firedrake." My pulse was a hammer. It was hard to think. "Lydia wanted a drake, so she would take the woman with her. But she would not do… all this."

I remembered being woken in the night by a binding. I remembered Lydia's threat.

Lord Wellington was guiding me toward our horses. "We must go at once, and stealthily, to get word to the navy."

I dug my feet into the gravel. "We must find Mr. Darcy."

"Fifty armed men are unaccounted for. The third woman as well. While we speak, they may be escaping England with a French woman bound as a wyfe—and with one of the most lethal breeds of draca. They must not reach France."

His face was earnest. I had seen that expression a dozen times in newspapers, captioned as heroic. "You would *abandon* your friend?"

"Our enemy killed thirty soldiers in seconds. There is no chance that you and I can free Darcy, and an attempt would risk your life. Darcy must rely on the mercy of his captors. He would make the same choice if our positions were reversed. Miss Bennet, he is my dearest friend, but the security of England is at stake."

"I am Mrs. Darcy. And you are a coward." His face turned ashen. I walked to my horse and managed to drag myself into the saddle.

"Wait," he called beside my knee. "Let me ride to Lambton to confirm her story. I will return soon, then go with you. You can do nothing on your own."

I laughed at that, turned my mare, and galloped along the shore beside dark water.

After a hundred thumping yards, I reined in to a trot. I would not be much use if I flew out of the saddle and broke my neck. But the rhythm of a galloping horse continued, approaching behind me.

Lord Wellington slowed to match my pace. He bowed from his saddle. "Mrs. Darcy."

I nodded, and we continued.

50

The day had dawned with a few low, puffy clouds, but the puffs had grown until the sky was white with splashes of blue. As we entered the woods and climbed, the sun vanished and the air chilled.

"Mrs. Darcy," Lord Wellington said as the horses walked up the steep slope. "I understand your reticence, but for military purposes, I must understand the capabilities of your sister. And, for that matter, of yourself."

"I cannot precisely answer either question. Lydia has skills I do not. She can command foul crawlers. Are you aware that the French weapon used against our draca was crawler venom?"

"Yes. Mr. Darcy informed the English command some months ago."

"And you know that crawlers can be large?"

Conversation paused while we guided our horses over an uneven, rocky patch, then he replied, "I know that foul crawlers can reach five inches, at which size they are extremely dangerous."

"My sister commands crawlers twice the length of a horse. They run faster than a man, climb trees, and have heavy armor plates. Their heads have serrated pinchers, like a pair of swords, and there is a pair of stings at their rear, although they can curl their bodies to strike in front of their heads as well." What else did he need to know? "Their venom confuses and hurts draca, like the French weapon. And of course, it is lethal to humans. I believe the sting of a large crawler kills much more swiftly than the small variety. The French soldiers who died so horribly were stung by monstrous foul crawlers."

We rode in silence for a good minute before he replied dryly, "I see."

I was thinking of how to finish my answer. "I can summon draca, even unbound, and ask them to do things, although I do not like to command them. And I can look through their eyes."

"That is remarkable." He sounded more hopeful.

"Lydia can also command draca. When she tried to take the Longbourn firedrake, she was far more powerful than I."

"I see."

"When I became angry, I was able to stop her."

"Let us hope you become angry."

I was becoming irritated by his tone. "I am simply answering you. Lydia cannot sense the presence of draca like I do. And… and she is my sister. She will not hurt us."

Lord Wellington made no reply. Well, at least he did not turn around and head back.

We rode in silence for ten minutes, then I said, "We are close. She is over that rise ahead, perhaps three-quarters of a mile. They do not seem to be moving. At least, Lydia is not. I cannot sense anyone else."

We were following a narrow trail. Lord Wellington led us into heavier brush. He stopped when we were screened.

"You said you can look through draca eyes," he said. "Can you use draca to scout ahead?"

I was a little embarrassed that had not occurred to me. "I have done that when closer. Let me try."

I dismounted and knelt, dry leaves crackling under my dress. I rested my hands in my lap, seeking calm. This would be farther than I had ever thrown my awareness.

Lord Wellington dismounted and sat cross-legged a few steps from me, at ease in the rough. One would think he was on a social excursion, if not for his attention to the forest around us.

I closed my eyes. The oily, churning blackness that surrounded Lydia was obvious. There were sparks of draca near her, but they were hard to distinguish at this distance. I bit my lip, thinking how I had reached out to summon those tiny flying draca, then tried to push my awareness closer.

There was a sense of motion—like riffling the pages of a book—and I was there. Right there. In the midst of the blackness. A hundred oily, ice-cold rags dragged across my bare skin.

Hurriedly, I pulled back a dozen yards. My arms were rigid with goose flesh. My breath shook. I hugged myself, rubbing my forearms to warm up.

"Are you all right?" came Lord Wellington's concerned voice.

"Yes. I am near them now. My awareness is. I sense Lydia's ferretworm, and the firedrake." The burning presence approached a wyvern in brilliance. "Lydia has not bound the drake, but she is… caging her. The method is unpleasant." Sheets of oily black swirled around her.

"Can you see through the drake's eyes?"

"I dare not try. Lydia would sense me. But there is a feral draca nearby. Very dim, which happens when they are asleep."

I gave a prod. The awareness sparked into light, and a draca's exact senses filled my mind. But not vision. This was touch—cool earth, flecks of clay, edges of rock. An open tunnel that I sensed without sight, descending with twists to skirt large rocks. The scalding heat of day was screened by a few inches of insulating earth above my head.

I gave a breath of laugh as I realized. "A tunnelworm. Underground. But maybe he will take a look for me." Already, he was scrabbling upward with remarkable speed.

Light flooded. By reflex, I mimicked his blink against the brightness. My eyes had been closed, so that just added a confusing second image until I shut them again.

Lydia's corrupted silhouette was visible. The revulsion of the tunnelworm spilled into my own body, vile in my stomach. I guided his eyes in another direction and blew out a relieved breath as the sensation faded.

"There is a wagon… and many people—" I stopped as a hand brushed my side. My real side, not the tunnelworm's. I heard a crunch. "Was that you?"

"Pardon me." Lord Wellington's voice was strained. "How many people?"

"It is hard to judge… draca do not see like we do. More than twenty. Oh." My voice choked.

"What is it?"

"Mr. Darcy," I said in a small voice. "I see him. He is alive." My relief was so intense that it hurt, as if my heart had been so tightly bound that it lost feeling, and now each joyous beat drove out a stab of stale fear.

"I think you had best stop now." Lord Wellington sounded strange.

"I may be able to recognize Miss Darcy—"

"Stop. We have little time."

I pulled my awareness back, took a breath to settle myself, and opened my eyes.

Two feet in front of me, a gentleman's penknife stood vertically in the ground. It had skewered a foul crawler six inches long.

I remembered a hand brushing my side. "Was that *climbing* on me?"

"I am afraid so. I neglected the obvious risk that your sister would have a similar ability to use crawlers as sentries. We are discovered. You must take your horse and ride for the Briton village. I will stay to slow their pursuit."

I was having trouble dragging my eyes from the myriad, twitching legs. "Certainly not. It was inevitable that I confront Lydia. I will simply do so without surprise. Perhaps you should go—" I looked at him and stopped.

Lord Wellington's jaw was corded in pain. Beads of sweat dotted his forehead. On his shaking wrist, I saw the discoloring, twin punctures of a crawler sting.

"I am in no condition to ride," he said through clenched teeth. "I will be done for soon enough. You must run. They may yet free Darcy."

"No. The Britons can treat this! They have draca essence—"

A man in an ill-fitting English uniform stepped out of the brush, his musket leveled at me. Another emerged and pressed the barrel of his pistol against Lord Wellington's temple.

51

Why does a draca bind?

The men marched us uphill. When Lord Wellington's steps faltered, a man struck him with the butt of a musket, then half-dragged him.

We entered a meadow. A brook splashed through the tufted grass. At least forty armed men were scattered in disorderly clumps. Two wagons waited, the grass heavily rutted by their wheels.

I saw Pemberley House in the blueish distance, although the lake was hidden by the hills. Breaks in the clouds cast pillars of sun that lit patches of forest and field.

Mr. Darcy and Miss Darcy sat by the brook, guarded by four desultory men in ill-fitting uniforms, muskets at the ready.

Our escorts threw us to the ground. Mr. Darcy gave me one tortured look, then deliberately looked away. He did not wish to reveal our relationship. I trusted he had a reason and swallowed the words pressing my lips.

The French wyfe huddled on the grass a few steps from me, her arms hugging her knees. She was modestly pretty and about my age, tanned and fit. A farm girl. Her eyes were fixed on the dirt, her face streaked with dried tears and exhausted by grief.

She wore a wedding ring. There was no sign of her husband. He was likely dead by the lake. Had she witnessed that massacre?

Curled beside her was a lithe, bronze firedrake. Her scales were a shade more coppery than the Longbourn drake had been, and the delicate ribs in her wings curved into elegant, upswept tips.

So, French women could bind. Why could they not bind in France? There must be no draca.

I gave the drake a mental nudge. Her head turned to me, tilting inquisitively.

"Be careful," whispered Miss Darcy, on the ground to my right. "Mrs. Wickham is powerful."

"I know," I said softly. "I have felt her power before. And been overwhelmed."

Mr. Darcy heard. I saw his concerned glance. He sat on the far side of Miss Darcy.

To my left, Lord Wellington slumped, panting. His left hand fumbled at the cravat that held his collars. He pulled it free, then wrapped his right forearm above the discolored punctures from the crawler sting.

He slid his arm near me and whispered, "Tie it. As tight as you can."

Trying not to attract attention, I took an end in each hand and pulled hard. The cloth sank into his swollen flesh. It must have hurt, but he gave no sign. I knotted it, feeling the heat in his skin. His collar had fallen open, and yellow streaks crossed his right shoulder. Even if this slowed the remainder of the poison, he would die without the Britons' remedy.

Or we would be killed before that. But Wickham and his men had kept us alive so far. There was no reason for that other than mercy. Maybe they would tie us up and leave. That would be sensible.

Images of the massacre by the lake danced in my mind, mocking me.

Lydia and Wickham had been in conference with two men when we arrived. They finished, and men were sent to laboriously unload one chest of gold. They hauled it to the smaller cart and set off in the direction of Lambton.

Lydia and Wickham came to stand over us, their hands on their hips while they surveyed their prisoners. Lydia's ferretworm slunk on the grass behind her like a beaten dog.

Wickham's expression was an unreadable flicker—gloating, thoughtful, worried—as his attention shifted. Then his gaze settled on Mr. Darcy, and his emotion became clear. Hatred.

"How the manor-born have fallen," Wickham said.

"This is between you and me," Mr. Darcy said. "Free these others. They have done you no harm."

Lydia squatted before the French wyfe. "Not this one. I need her." She laughed. "You can all see my trick."

"*Our* trick," Wickham said, with an edge to his voice. "I discovered it. I waded through those tiresome, self-congratulatory histories of Pemberley. But I found it. The secret to break a draca's bond."

Wickham crouched in front of me, and his finger pulled my chin toward him. I stared back. I heard Mr. Darcy move and a guard threaten him, but I did not look away from Wickham's eyes.

"I hunted foul crawlers," Wickham said, his voice lower. "Lured them with rotting carcasses. Harvested their venom. Then I experimented. The odd draca here and there. But they all died. Even that pathetic tunnelworm of the Lucases, hiding in its bucket."

He leaned closer.

Lydia snapped, "Wickie!" For once, I sympathized with her. I would be annoyed if my husband stared at another woman.

Wickham ignored her. "But I was missing something. I needed a wyfe. A *strong* wyfe." His thumb caressed my chin, and his voice dropped to a whisper. "A Bennet. And I found one." He shoved my face hard with his palm, breaking our staring match.

He stood and stretched, oozing arrogant calm. From a pouch on his belt, he took a glass vial filled with a thick, oily substance.

"Not yet," Lydia said, squatting by the Frenchwoman. "I must be strong for this to work."

She opened her hand, and her ferretworm crawled into her grasp. She pinned him between her knees, then dug in her reticule and removed a short-bladed heavy knife, the kind used to shuck oysters. She grabbed her ferretworm's muzzle and bent his head back, exposing the underside of his neck.

The ferretworm's neck was injured, a handful of small, crusty cuts. Lydia pressed the point of the knife into one, twisting and prying. The ferretworm squealed. For the first time, the French wyfe looked up. My own fingers tautened until the bones grated. Beside me, Miss Darcy moaned in disgust.

The tip of the knife caught. Blood beaded. This was not the clear gold I had seen when I took a few drops for Jane. The swell was thick and reluctant, a murky, jaundiced yellow. I remembered the Scottish maid saying draca blood must be given willingly.

Lydia giggled in an obscene, wanton crescendo. She dropped the knife and wiped her fingertips through the blood then thrust them deep in her mouth like they held a delicious sweet. Her back arched. Her face, caked with cracking white paint, stretched in a rictus of gasping delight.

There were disgusted exclamations from her audience. Wickham made no sound, but his lips twisted in distaste. Miss Darcy was still moaning. Even her distress sounded melodious.

Lydia stood and spun, her arms outstretched. It was the pose of a little girl rejoicing on a spring day, but she looked strong and cruel. "Do it!" she shouted.

Even without opening my awareness, I felt power rolling off her, icy and foul on the back of my neck.

Wickham pulled the cork from the vial. The scent of sour orange and bitter almond burned the air. Both the ferretworm and the firedrake reared, hissing. Wickham waved the vial near the drake's nose. The drake fell on her side, convulsing and shaking.

The French wyfe screamed and reached for her drake, but Lydia cried, "Keep her back!" One of the guards dragged her away.

I had to stop this obscenity. I closed my eyes, and the power grinding at the back of my skull became visible, a black hurricane around the tenuous silver thread between the drake and the French wyfe. The drake's awareness was a dimmed, frantic spark, fluttering and shaking from the venom.

I pressed at the blackness and was thrown back. When I helped the Longbourn drake repel Lydia's attack, I had held Mamma's hand, and her bond had given me a path to channel power. Here, I was too far from the Frenchwoman to touch her.

But the storm was weakening. The atmosphere warmed. Vile blackness washed away like mud in a mountain stream. The drake's awareness settled, powerful and golden, even brighter than was usual.

Beside me, Miss Darcy's moan was a hum—a tune dancing through flickers of melody. The song filled my mind, each note a shimmering sheet of color that nurtured the drake, and me as well. The purity was glorious, art and mathematical precision merged. My thoughts became exact, a fugue where each note was the inevitable product of what has come before.

The bond between the drake and the Frenchwoman was singing like a plucked string, resonating with memories and emotions. And with crystal clarity, I saw something new. The bond reached from the drake to the wyfe. Its strength was from the drake. It was part of the drake.

And, I understood.

"It is not working!" Lydia shouted. Her tone was furious.

I was unnecessary—Miss Darcy was blocking Lydia without me—so I opened my eyes. The glow of Miss Darcy's power still filled me. I sensed Lydia's dark strength fluttering, trying to survive in the colorful radiance.

Lydia's jabbing finger accused the Frenchwoman. "I cannot break the bond. She is doing something. Make her stop!" The guard shook the Frenchwoman's shoulders. Her head snapped back and forth, and she began crying. Lydia screamed, "Wickie! I need this drake!"

Wickham swore. An atrophied, lady-ish part of me stiffened, preparing to admonish him for improper language, even as he drew his pistol and fired.

The blast blew a palm-sized hole in the cloth of the Frenchwoman's dress. I saw the curved inner sides of her small breasts, and a ragged red tunnel punched in her bare skin. Then it was blood.

The horror vanished as the silver crack of the broken bond overwhelmed my senses. Miss Darcy screamed, and her song stopped. Flaring silver fragmented into sparks that were swallowed by the blackness of Lydia's power.

Darkness swirled into a whip and struck like a serpent. The firedrake gave one abbreviated cry.

Lord Wellington and Mr. Darcy were shouting. My vision cleared. The guard holding the Frenchwoman pushed her lifeless body to the ground, then cursed and wiped at the blood spattered on his legs.

But Lydia was smiling. She crooked a finger at the drake. Whining piteously, the creature crawled toward her, pushing across the ground with the elbows of her wings.

I sensed what Lydia had done. The whip had become a writhing linkage between her and the drake. It radiated fear, like a chain fashioned of cruelty and threats.

"You are bound now," Lydia crooned. "My own firedrake."

"She is not yours," I said. The clarity from Miss Darcy's song still held. I judged the atrocity I had witnessed. Distilled it into precise fury.

Lydia spun to me. "What do you know!"

"She chose her binding. That is gone. Now, she is only captive." I was assembling the truth. "Have you never wondered why draca bind? Why such glorious creatures attach themselves to plodding humans for a lifetime? They treasure understanding. We are so strange to them that we make them curious. They collect memories of us across centuries. Across lives."

That was the meaning of the crest on our family's journal: the wyvern holding an empty chest. Marriage gold meant nothing. Bindings were not bartered, or purchased, or forced. Draca sought us out. But they were more considerate than humans would be. They chose only those who were willing.

"What a simpleton you are," Lydia said. "Draca are toys. Chattel."

I lost interest in her and turned my attention to Wickham. The pistol was smoking in his hand. His shoulders rose and fell while he stared at the dead woman.

"You are a murderer," I said. "You shot Mr. Rabb. You killed Denny. Did he discover you were spying for the French? That you were poisoning draca?"

"Denny would have betrayed me." Wickham's voice was shaking. He barked a false laugh. "He was a lickspittle for the colonel."

I was facing the rabid dog again. Except this time, I was not afraid.

I tested Lydia's black tether to the drake. It was repulsive, like sinking my fingers into a rope of offal, and strong, wound from many different filaments. Or it would have seemed strong not long ago. The music of Miss Darcy's power still sang inside me.

I snapped one filament to see what would happen. Lydia shouted, and filthy power exploded. It skittered off me like dry leaves off a stone wall. It changed course, reaching outward.

I broke the rest of the tether, and the drake's mind came free, brilliant and aware. I shielded her from the blackness around her, then opened my mind.

Our thoughts merged. She did not have language like a wyvern, but her feelings transcended words. Gratitude. Awe. Curiosity.

And an offer. Would I bind?

No, I thought. *You should go. But will you do one thing first?*

I could see Wickham with both our visions. I fixed him in my mind as he seemed to draca senses—the blustering posture that hid his fear, the bloom of heat that revealed his lies.

Kill him for me, I thought.

Her awareness pulled me inward. Human senses faded.

Instincts honed through centuries of hunt considered attacking with flame but rejected it. The man was too close to those I cared for.

Wings grasped air, and I soared upward. The clouds in the sky astonished my human mind—their shapes were exquisite, every wisp a story of wind and drafts.

The clouds vanished as I finished the third sweep of my wings and dived.

Wickham was turning to follow my flight, one arm sluggishly rising to point. I fell to kill him, claws outstretched.

A writhing shape reared into my path.

The collision was hard as rock, not soft like human flesh. A powerful coil trapped one of my wings. My bones snapped in a blaze of pain. Venom splashed my skin and burrowed into my mind.

The scene became a nightmare kaleidoscope. Spear-point legs struck at me. My scrabbling claw found a gap between armored segments and slashed.

Thunder. I screamed as the world vanished in white.

Vision returned in juddering stabs, tear-blurred through human eyes. Waves of pain reverberated between my temples. The gluey acid of vomit burned my tongue.

Lord Wellington's face, surrounded by cloudy sky, came into fuzzy focus. His hands pressed my shoulders. Held me down while I struggled.

"Mrs. Darcy!" he said. "Can you hear me?"

"What happened?" I croaked. I was so confused. Why was he in the sky? Oh. My head was in his lap.

"A monstrous crawler came. The drake fought it and is dead, shot by Mr. Wickham. You had a fit when it was shot."

A tremendous scuffle was nearby. I turned my head and saw Mr. Darcy struggling to reach me, pinned down by three men.

"I am all right," I said. He stopped his fight, panting.

I was not sure that was honest. My mind was shredded. I touched my face, and my fingers came away tipped with blood. My nose was bleeding. I fumbled for my handkerchief.

Lydia was screaming at Wickham about losing their drake. Wickham seemed not to hear. A smoking musket hung from one hand. The firedrake lay dead at his feet, her head blown away. Because I had asked her to fight for me. Regret and guilt surged.

Near him, a monstrous foul crawler twined, larger even than the one that had killed Denny. The broken ground revealed a dark tunnel. It had hidden until the drake's attack.

Lydia's shouting became frustrated silence. She came to me and crouched. I looked up at her from Lord Wellington's lap. Her makeup had smeared, revealing a frightening network of blackened veins.

She lifted my left hand, and her thumbnail dug into the ring of braided hair on my finger. "Clever Lizzy. You have been keeping secrets." She must have heard Lord Wellington call me Mrs. Darcy.

"Lydia," Wickham called. "This is over. We must go." He rested the musket against a rock, removed a pouch on his belt, then picked up his discarded pistol and began methodically reloading it.

Lydia shook her head. "No. I want my gift for Napoleon. I want to be Empress."

"*Stop!*" Wickham's voice was desperate. "This is madness. We have gold. We can hide—"

She jumped to her feet, shrieking, "I am not mad! I will be Empress, and you will be the handsome captain of my guard, and we will dance at all the balls!" She stalked to where the guards held Mr. Darcy. "Lift him." The men dragged Mr. Darcy to his knees.

"Darcy is mine," Wickham said. He rammed the charge into his pistol and screwed the ramrod under the barrel.

Lydia shook her head. "Not yet." She reached to stroke my husband's hair, but he strained back in disgust. She laughed. "I read the French legends of *l'enfant du lac*, the great wyfe who draws a dragon from the water. That is me! I am the Child of the Lake. And I *want* the wyvern that hides in the water."

Mr. Darcy's reply was coldly exact. "I told you before. I know nothing of this."

Lydia's lips spread in incongruous delight. Smudges in the crimson covering her lips revealed dark purple flesh like a spreading bruise. "Before I did not care much, so you thought it was safe to lie. Now, I *need* that wyvern." She stepped back, considering him. "Do you know my husband admires your sister?"

Behind her, Wickham had been listening with angry impatience. At her words, he stiffened. "That is not true." His voice was tense.

The man who had shot a woman in cold blood was afraid.

I would have laughed if his fear was for himself. But he had cast a worried glance at Miss Darcy. Could he be fond of her? Before his schemed elopement, they grew up together, almost as brother and sister. But it was hard to believe a murderer could care about anyone.

My head still spun from the shock of the drake's death. But under that, strength remained from Miss Darcy's song. My abilities hummed in resonance.

What if Lydia's claim about Pemberley lake was true?

I cast my mind toward the lake. I no longer needed to close my eyes. It was like part of me could fly, piercing the first hill that blocked my view, then the second. I fell into the water—clear, nurturing, and pure. But there was nothing. I sank ten feet. Twenty.

I was stopped as if I had struck impermeable ice. Hidden depths remained below.

Lydia raised her voice. "What did you tell me about his sister, Wickie? She plays harp… no. Pianoforte. Endlessly. I should find endless scales most dull. Shall we break her fingers?"

Miss Darcy had been huddled and pale since the Frenchwoman was shot. She scrambled to her feet in an attempt at flight, her thin limbs gawky as a frightened deer. One of the guards restrained her effortlessly.

Mr. Darcy also tried to rise. His guards beat him down, striking his legs with the butts of their muskets. He fell back, gasping.

Lydia's lips stretched in fascination. There was no concern. There was no feeling at all. Not even the empathy of cruelty.

I drove my mind against the impenetrable barrier deep in the lake. It was like pressing a finger against a mountain. But I was an idiot even to try. This was not about force.

I understand, I thought. *Everyone is wrong. They think we claim you. That marriage gold grants power to enslave. But it is just permission, like signing a contract to show we are willing. You are the ones who choose. You bind us for a lifetime to share our world. I will share my life with you. My soul. But I wish you would save these people I love.*

The guards had wrestled Mr. Darcy to a rigid, kneeling standstill. Lydia grabbed a handful of his hanging hair. "Or is a sister not enough? I do not like *my* sisters much." She lifted Mr. Darcy's left hand, her thumb pressing the ring on his finger. "What of a *wyfe?* What of Mrs. *Elizabeth* Darcy?"

Wickham spun. In two steps, he reached me and yanked me to my feet.

"Not *him!*" he cried. "He ruins me for sport! You will be nothing to him. A pawn to hurt me."

"I love him," I said.

Wickham slapped me, driving my face against my shoulder. My cheek burned under my tumbled hair.

But I had been hit harder than that.

I threw my hair aside. "The last man who struck me was dead within a minute."

Wickham shoved me, powerfully but without purpose, a bully pushing a smaller child. My heels caught on Lord Wellington's legs and I fell beside him.

Lydia shouted. Wickham shouted back, and they began a raging argument.

Beside me, Lord Wellington whispered, "There are men in the woods preparing to attack. When you hear gunshots, run."

I was not expecting that. "*What?*"

"The Britons from the village. Your sister is ignoring her foul sentries, and Wickham's rabble has set no guards. They will be surprised, but they are a large force. I do not know if the Britons can overcome them. The confusion is our best chance."

"I will not leave my husband."

I got to my feet as the argument reached a peak. Wickham pushed Lydia aside, and she fell to her knees. I recognized the outraged O of her mouth from our youth—little Lydia, furious at not getting her way. Soon, she would recall she was not little Lydia anymore. She controlled a monstrous crawler a dozen yards from us.

Shots rang out from the nearby trees. Wickham's men in their fake militia uniforms began shouting and running, firing their guns in every direction.

Wickham seemed not to notice. He raised his pistol, the steel muzzle a foot from Mr. Darcy's forehead. Wickham's face swiveled to me, his eyes crazed. "Tell him you do not love him!"

What an idiotic request. I could not renounce the purest feeling I had ever experienced.

The earth jerked under my feet. I stumbled. Wickham looked around wildly, his arms outspread for balance.

The ground shuddered like a wooden bridge crossed by an iron carriage. Confused cries of *Cannon!* rose from the men in the meadow. But I had heard no cannon.

Like ice and flame together, a silver dagger pierced my heart. My breath jammed in my throat. I folded at my waist, hands clutching my chest to hold the wound. But there was no blood. No pain. Slowly, I straightened, unseen silver radiance filling me.

A silver thread drew my eyes to the distant hills.

By Pemberley lake, a patch of sun streaming between the clouds flicked to shadow. An instant later, it was bright again.

"Say it!" screamed Wickham. Shots blasted to my right. A bullet whined past. But Wickham's eyes were fixed on me. The gaze of a man I hated.

The sunlight filling a nearer field turned dark, then relit.

"Kill me instead," I answered. "For I would sooner die."

CHILD.

The word sang in me, vibrating through the silver cord, shaking my bones like a colossal church organ.

CLOSE YOUR EYES.

The voice was ancient thunder in my mind. I closed my eyes.

My eyelids lit red, then blazed white. A tempest slammed me. My ears were overcome. I tumbled and landed on my hands and knees, my fingertips sunk into wild grass and clover.

I opened my eyes as the wind diminished. Wickham's militia rabble were sprawled across the meadow, arms thrown over their faces or fingers digging at their eyes.

I got to my feet. By habit, I smoothed my dress. My fingers came away wet and sticky. My dress was sprayed with blood.

Fear cut my heart. Wickham had shot my husband. The roar was the gun.

Terrified, I spun.

Mr. Darcy knelt alone, his eyes closed. He was untouched. He opened his eyes, and his astonished gaze met mine.

The guards that had held him were gone. Wickham was gone.

Where Wickham had stood, three parallel gouges were torn through the grass and earth. I recognized the pattern. Those same claw marks had decorated my collarbone after our drake landed on my shoulder. But this claw spanned the better part of two yards.

A matching set of three cuts tore the ground where the guards holding my husband had stood. A hat remained, and a broken belt with a sword, and a sleeve with a flesh-colored glove. No, it was a hand.

Wickham's boot lay on the ground at my feet. The heavy leather was sheared off ankle-high, as if by a huge razor. The boot was not empty.

Heat was scorching my forehead. I looked up.

The meadow beyond, which had held twenty armed men, was scoured to burning bedrock that glowed like coals. The brook had vanished. Water burbled over a rim of smoking turf then hissed into violent plumes of steam. Where the wagon had stood, a smoking puddle of golden liquid flowed lazily over slumping rock.

"What happened?" I asked.

Lydia pushed to her feet, not far from where Wickham had stood. Her ferretworm dangled from one hand like a child's toy, squealing in protest.

Lydia's face turned to the sky. "Oh. I feel him. He is beautiful."

The silver thread had drawn my eyes upward. The clouds were swirling —burning away like steam vanishing from a kettle. The blue sky opened.

Higher than clouds, scarlet wings soared in a slow curve. The silhouette was delicate and long winged, more like a drake than the muscular solidness of a wyvern. But so far above us. So large.

"A dragon," I said. The myths were true after all.

Child.

The voice was gentler now. The sense of wisdom and age was overwhelming, but it was not loud in the mundane, human sense of the word.

I choose you. Loch bairn. The Child of the Lake.

The cool silver of binding flooded my heart and filled the hollows of my chest. And it passed through me. The cord stretched from me to where my husband knelt.

Behind me, a flurry of gunshots rang out.

Some of Wickham's false militia were pointing at the sky. Others were shooting into the forest. From the foliage, the Britons' muskets spat puffs of sooty orange as they fired back.

The monster crawler was running on rippling legs toward the forest. Other large crawlers had emerged from rocky areas and were racing behind it. Sent by Lydia to attack the Britons.

A hand touched my shoulder. I turned to Lydia.

"Give him to me!" Her eyes were ecstatic, her mouth grinning. I had not seen her so happy since she was three years old and learned she could unwrap gifts by herself.

Below the joyful smile, the skin of her chin hung in sickly jowls. Her lips had cracked. Dark purple blood stained her teeth. Her gaze wandered across the features of my face, skittering past my eyes.

"He cannot be given," I said. "Or taken."

"*I* can take him!" She cried. "I can be stronger. I will be Empress!"

She raised her ferretworm high and stabbed her knife deep into his neck. She dragged the blade down, yanking inch by inch to cut the body open. The dying creature's curdling yellow blood soaked her hand. She lifted the twitching remains, steaming flesh dangling, and let the blood fall into her open mouth and over her chin.

"Lydia, stop." I forced the words through horror and revulsion. "It is over." Her power was growing, bloated with the false strength of hurt and death, astonishing and violent while it attacked the binding that pierced my chest. But it was a wisp against the strength of the being who bound me.

Lydia lifted her yellow-stained hands to the sky. "Come to me!"

Far above, the dragon had finished his turn and was gliding toward us. Around us, the earth broke as small foul crawlers wriggled out and crawled toward me.

"*I* am the strongest sister!" she cried. "*I* will be Empress*!* *I* will burn everyone! *I*—oh."

Her voice stopped with an arrested gasp. She turned to me, eyes wide.

"Lizzy," she whispered. Her hand caught mine. She sank to her knees, then fell on her side, her clenched grip pulling me to my knees beside her.

A sword protruded from her back. The hilt jammed against the dirt, propping her at an awkward, splayed angle.

Mr. Darcy was on his knees, bruised and bleeding. His hand was still outstretched.

"I swore I would not hesitate." His voice shook. "Not when those I love are threatened."

Lydia's fingers still held mine. Her grip relaxed.

A memory returned—the last time I sat with Papa in his library. While we talked, his finger had stroked the paper that entrusted Longbourn to me. As if it comforted him.

"I promised Papa," I said. "I promised to care for our family."

"She was calling the dragon!" Mr. Darcy's voice was strained. "You *said* she was stronger. I heard you."

"We are bound. She could never break that." But he would not know that.

The dragon's glide, so graceful in the distance, became a storm as scarlet wings a hundred feet wide screamed over our heads. Heat roared behind me, painful on my bare neck and lighting the meadow brighter than sun. Mr. Darcy threw an arm up to shield his eyes. Thunder shook my clothes and rumbled in the depths of my chest, then rolled back from the hills around us.

Mr. Darcy opened his eyes. "My God."

Still kneeling, I turned my head. A swath of meadow ten yards wide and fifty long had become a burning hell. The huge foul crawlers were writhing carcasses in the flames. Smaller ashen humps lay still. Men.

Please stop, I thought. *We are safe.*

"I failed you." Mr. Darcy's fingertips touched my wrist. They were trembling. "I have betrayed your promise."

Although my body was still, a hidden part of me was screaming. But I was a wyfe. I was stronger than this.

I forced my fingers open. Lydia's hand fell lifelessly. I fumbled for Mr. Darcy's hand, and our fingers knotted. I felt his warmth. His life pulsed in mine. My silent cries quieted to a shroud of grief.

"You betrayed nothing," I said. "My sister was already gone. She died long before this."

Miss Darcy was helping Lord Wellington, her arm around his waist while she explained the Britons' draca essence. Good. She would ensure he was dosed.

Lord Wellington turned as the dragon swept over a ridge. His eyes narrowed. Analyzing. Strategizing.

Gently—uncertainly—Mr. Darcy's arm circled my waist. He helped me to my feet. I pressed into his side, and his hesitancy ended. He pulled me close. Already, we fit together so well. Branches grown together.

"She would have killed us all," I whispered. Tears were wet on my cheeks. "She would have thrown down England." Lydia would have gifted an army of monstrous crawlers to Napoleon. If she survived the horrible sacrifice of her draca.

Air lifted my hair then whooshed down, billowing my skirts and blowing leaves and stones across the ground.

The dragon landed twenty paces from us, his wings hiding the sky before they closed. This close, his size was unimaginable. His body was twice the length of a carriage, his tail and neck long and sinuous. He balanced on two crouched legs, the muscles bunched like knotted oak. Fastidious, he adjusted his wings until they were neat, then he sat, raising his chest and shoulders high like a dog. His neck, glistening in a sheath of scarlet diamonds, twined until his head was a few yards from me. Inhuman eyes shifted through prisms of color. The border of my mind blurred as I stared into them.

Child of the Lake. I am called Yuánchi.

The reflex of introduction was automatic. "I am Mrs. Elizabeth Darcy."

"I hear him," my husband breathed. Miss Darcy and Lord Wellington had backed away. They looked at us in confusion. They had not heard.

You are the wyfe of war. The wyfe of war may not call me.

His claws, like edged ebony pickaxes, cut into the earth. The soles of my feet trembled as bedrock shattered.

I have slain your enemies. But you grieve. The wyfe of war does not grieve. Who are you?

"I grieve for my sister," I said. "I have killed her." My husband's arm stiffened around my waist.

The faceted eyes glittered. *Then you are ruthless. You are the wyfe of war.*

Pressure pried at my mind. A vibration grumbled in my skull, too deep to be heard. Fire building in a giant's forge.

"You killed no one," Mr. Darcy said, his voice by my ear. "I will not permit you to take blame for my actions."

"I killed Wickham." I remembered hating him as Yuánchi approached. Condemning him. "If I stopped him sooner, I could have saved Lydia." But I doubted my own words. I had seen Wickham's eyes when he watched Lydia. How afraid he was.

Mr. Darcy's fingers encircled my forearms. He cradled my elbows and drew me around, tearing my gaze away from Yuánchi. The pressure vanished.

I pressed my cheek to his shirt, dusty and damp with sweat. His voice resonated through his chest when he spoke.

"Now it is you who protects someone who did not ask for protection. I made my own choice. And Wickham doomed himself."

ANSWER. Are you the wyfe of war? Yuánchi's words were hammer blows.

But the blows skittered away. Unexpected as fury, iron certainty filled me. "No!" I said even as my husband said, "She is not!"

I raised my head. Each crystal facet of Yuánchi's eyes shone with an aspect of the world—the azure of blue sky, the emerald of a distant hill, the dirty carmine of dying fire.

"I will never be that," I said. "No archaic verse rules me. My destiny is my own. War is horrible. I will be no party to it."

Yuánchi's massive jaws opened, and he huffed with the laughter of his kind.

The Child of the Lake is old and wise.

The grumbling threat of violence faded.

Wickham's men had thrown down their weapons. The Britons were herding them together. But pairs of captor and prisoner kept stopping, gaping at the scarlet dragon.

I let go of Mr. Darcy but held his hand as I faced Yuánchi.

"What do you seek?" I asked.

My kind live in solitude. We seek what is alien. Love. Passion. But I, Yuánchi, want more. I seek what is shared. Moral right. Sacrifice. Loyalty.

Miss Darcy was helping Lord Wellington toward the Britons. But Lord Wellington stopped and called to me.

"Mrs. Darcy. We must speak about what has happened. It is a matter of urgency."

I did not answer. Miss Darcy helped him walk away.

Yuánchi stretched across the earth. His moving skin whispered like a bowl of jewels stirred with a finger. His chest and neck lowered to the ground, the scales glowing in the sunlight.

What do you seek, Child of the Lake?

I thought of Mr. Rabb's opinion of English ladies and their embroidery.

My husband opened schools. Mary wrote music that revealed her soul.

My father had written books. They were on a shelf in his library, covered with dust. Sometimes, while I had exercised my wit in scorn of foolish society, his gaze had drifted to them.

I had never read them.

I remembered Mary's summary of my life. Complacent.

"I would change the world," I said.

Hands clasped, Mr. Darcy and I walked forward together.

To Be Continued
in Book 2 of Jane Austen Fantasy

THANK YOU FOR READING! If you'd like the free ebook companion to *Miss Bennet's Dragon*, sign up for news at mverant.com/join. I've retold a chapter from Mr. Darcy's perspective, added an Epilogue and character guide, and included deleted scenes that I truly miss.

I'd be very appreciative if you take a moment to review *Miss Bennet's Dragon*. Reader reviews are crucial for a book's success, and they help other readers find stories they enjoy.

Find out more about me and my books at mverant.com or follow me on Twitter @M_Verant

May you be bound with love.

M Verant

ACKNOWLEDGMENTS

I started writing *Miss Bennet's Dragon* when California locked down for COVID-19. I began on an escapist whim, but my love for Austen was deep-rooted. I was a teenager when I found my mother's battered edition of *Jane Austen's Collected Works*. Then I bonded to the 1980 BBC miniseries (the most canon-accurate Mr. Darcy; there, I said it!) and I've reveled in adaptations, retellings, and rereadings since.

I drafted the first chapter (in rather more Austenesque prose than I eventually settled on) and immediately imagined the ending. But it was the relevance to modern themes that lured me. So off we went.

Fortunately, my family are also Austen fans. My wife read draft after draft, watched endless Regency-ish shows (*Victorian Farm*, anyone?), and cheered me on when I had doubts. My critique groups were inspiring and unsparing—shout-out to EBSFFW, CWC, and the Misfit Squad! My wonderful beta readers are too numerous to name, but I love you all. This book is vastly improved by your suggestions. I could not have done it without you.

ALSO BY M VERANT

Power in the Age of Lies